MALEDICTIONS

WARHAMMER™
HORROR

• THE VAMPIRE GENEVIEVE •
by Kim Newman

DRACHENFELS
GENEVIEVE UNDEAD (May 2019)
BEASTS IN VELVET (July 2019)
SILVER NAILS (July 2019)

THE WICKED AND THE DAMNED
A portmanteau novel by Josh Reynolds,
Phil Kelly and David Annandale

MALEDICTIONS
An anthology by various authors

PERDITION'S FLAME
An audio drama by Alec Worley

WARHAMMER™
HORROR

MALEDICTIONS

Cassandra Khaw, Richard Strachan, Graham McNeill,
Lora Gray, C L Werner, Peter McLean,
David Annandale, Paul Kane, Josh Reynolds,
J C Stearns and Alec Worley

WARHAMMER HORROR
A BLACK LIBRARY PUBLICATION IMPRINT

First published in Great Britain in 2019 by
Black Library,
Games Workshop Ltd.,
Willow Road,
Nottingham, NG7 2WS, UK.

10 9 8 7 6 5 4 3 2 1

Produced by Games Workshop in Nottingham.

A CIP record for this book is available from the British Library.

ISBN 13: 978-1-78496-881-6

See Warhammer Horror on the internet at

blacklibrary.com

Find out more about Games Workshop
and the worlds of Warhammer at

games-workshop.com

Printed and bound by CPI Group (UK) Ltd, Croydon, CR0 4YY

WARHAMMER™
HORROR

A dark bell tolls in the abyss.

It echoes across cold and unforgiving worlds, mourning
the fate of humanity. Terror has been unleashed, and
every foul creature of the night haunts the shadows.
There is naught but evil here. Alien monstrosities drift
in tomblike vessels. Watching. Waiting. Ravenous.
Baleful magicks whisper in gloom-shrouded forests,
spectres scuttle across disquiet minds. From the depths
of the void to the blood-soaked earth, diabolic horrors
stalk the endless night to feast upon unworthy souls.

Abandon hope. Do not trust to faith. Sacrifices burn
on pyres of madness, rotting corpses stir in unquiet
graves. Daemonic abominations leer with rictus
grins and stare into the eyes of the accursed. And the
Ruinous Gods, with indifference, look on.

This is a time of reckoning, where every mortal soul
is at the mercy of the things that lurk in the dark.
This is the night eternal, the province of monsters
and daemons. This is Warhammer Horror. None shall
escape damnation.

And so, the bell tolls on.

CONTENTS

CASSANDRA KHAW

NEPENTHE

In the warp, only the dead may dream.

'Not your best work.' Marcus glances at his brother, gaze lidded, tertiary optics cataracted with new overlays. They still give him a headache, this honeycombed perception of the universe, high-resolution imagery parallaxed with an eternity of mathematics scrolling into storage.

Data. Always more data. Always, always. To be passed onto the next generation and the generation after that, preserved in alphanumeric hieroglyphs and computational hymns. But their receptacles? Their shepherds? Nothing but interchangeable circuitry, anonymised and anonymous, no more important than their functions they fulfil. And oh, how Marcus despises the fact.

'The knife fits the ritual,' comes Cornelius' warbling tenor, a boy's voice, snapping Marcus from his melancholy.

Marcus shrugs, watches as his brother pares the skin from his face, documenting the neatness of it all. Of the two of them, Cornelius has always had the defter touch, the steadier hands.

'I don't understand why this is even necessary.' Marcus exhales. 'Skin's porous. Microfilament technology exists. I – it's just so *inefficient*, Cornelius.'

'Ritual, Marcus.' The Omnissiah would break before his brother's composure. 'It's about the ritual.'

'A waste of time. We should be preparing for the *Nepenthe*...' He shivers as the name unknots along his tongue. The things they'd said of the ship, of what had transpired in its gut, what they'd done inside it, what they'd done *to* it. '... the *Nepenthe*'s arrival. We should be researching. We should be doing something *useful.*'

'We've done everything we need to do. We are here, are we not? If we had failed, Veles wouldn't have permitted us this indulgence. We'd still be in the bowels of the ship, slaving over pointless minutiae.'

That hasn't yet changed, Marcus thinks sourly. They're still rotting in the belly of their vessel, still consigned to the smallest laboratory, still forgotten. He flexes his hands, takes note of the fluids clotting in his wrists and, not for the first time, Marcus feels like the old man he's become.

They'd lied. They said there was forever to be found in the machine but there was nothing, nothing but rust and rot and ruin. But the *Nepenthe* could change all of that.

'I wonder if she's as beautiful in real life.' Cornelius sighs, cheeks ruddy from the heat. The laboratory is kept repugnantly humid for the benefit of his studies, his speciality being the study of microfauna, complementing Marcus' own area of expertise, his fascination with the monolithic.

'If she was truly created in the Dark Age of Technology, I doubt it. Mankind was still so new to the idea of everything. They wouldn't have had time to make her beautiful.' Marcus rises, suddenly belligerent. Something about his brother's romanticism chafes. He rolls his shoulders, one at a time, then flexes the matrix of prosthetics cresting his lumbar region. A threat display, he supposes. 'And you presume too much of what is likely a dead abomination.'

'You've no poetry in your heart.' A long-practised sigh, pitched to irritate.

'I have several hearts,' Marcus retorts. 'I'm sure there's poetry in some.'

His brother doesn't reply, only cocks a grin before he fits a rebreather over his denuded skull.

'You are aware that if the Magos finds out, we'll be branded as traitors, hereteks. There's no coming back from this,' Cornelius whispers, voice slurred. Under the mask, Marcus imagines that a metamorphosis is beginning: larynx and somatic nerves, sinuses and visual system, auditory function, every one of them examined and edited in turn, unstitched and revised where required, a library of heuristic algorithms optimising future output to the brain.

'We are just fulfilling our duties. We've identified a possible threat. We're moving to dispose of it.' A familiar minuet: argument and counterpoint, reiterated so many times that ritual has become reflex. 'That we wanted to wait until we were sure of the legitimacy of our claim, I'm certain no one can fault us for.'

His brother says nothing.

'And if we are right, would you leave her alone in the darkness for another thousand years? She called to us. She begged for us. After all this time, after we've gotten so close, you'd turn tail and abandon her?' Six long strides take him across the laboratory to his brother Cornelius, younger and much taller, marionette limbs and a thorax conjoining steepled torsos, one organic, one entirely synthetic. He claps a hand around his brother's shoulder.

'We might find nothing. It's true.' Marcus' voice quiets to a whisper. 'But it is also possible that we might find her alive in that ship, waiting, our very own madonna of meat and machinery. And can you imagine, brother, the secrets we could gouge out of her bones?'

* * *

Magos Veles Corvinus' immense shadow drags behind him like the hems of his claret cape. His subordinates watch, their machinery in symphony, an arrhythmic *clack-clack-clack* of moving parts, telemetric devices logging the Magos' moods. Over the years, they've learned to be cautious of his emotional states.

'There's nothing here.' His voice is a hiss, refracted by his respirator into something monstrous, pupils aperturing as his attention fixes itself onto Cornelius' face.

Or so Cornelius' picters report, at least. He isn't certain. This new reality, while transcendental, is dizzying, limbic system still unconvinced of the profit of his recent mutilation. His neural circuitry mutinies against this darkness, the negative space where chemoreceptors once held court in the antechamber of the neocortex, describing the world in electrical staccato. Now, they've been bought out, made redundant by technology, and the brain, for all that it might be folds of shrivelled tissue, is unhappy.

'These are our best estimates. Temporal continuity is hardly a rule in the immaterium. Furthermore, the ship–'

'Enough.'

Cornelius lapses into silence.

'Accounting for errors, what is your current prediction?'

'The *Nepenthe*, according to records, has been in transit.' Cornelius pulls up his records, visions saturated with data tables. Mathematical theorems pirouette through possibilities, while Cornelius consults star-maps, black box transcripts in sodium hieroglyphs. Behind all of it, diffused, her song calling him. 'Since the Dark Age of Technology.'

'Might it not be a wiser idea to call the Adeptus Astartes' attention to this? An Ultramarine company is on a hive world only a solar system away. It wouldn't take them long.' A voice interjects, low and deferential, but only an idiot like Veles might mistake its sycophantic cadences as sincerity.

That damned enginseer again, Cornelius thinks, jolting from his calculations. They'd missed their last window of opportunity because of him. And the one before that. Ten years, and Lupus Agelastus fought them at every juncture, weaponising protocol and legislation; the common sense of the coward. If it weren't for Veles' own greed, this mission would have been butchered at its inception.

Even so...

'We don't have the time.' Cornelius modulates his response, runs a macro to regulate cortisol production. He isn't angry, *yet*, but precautions are necessary. The lizard brain is faithless, accountable only to its own agenda and it wouldn't take much, not after all these years, for it to snap. Such a slip-up would be more damaging to the brothers' machinations than anything that Lupus could author. So, Cornelius breathes in. Breathes out. Saves the interval to a loop that he then tethers respiratory function to. 'According to the Lexmechanics, we have sixteen hours, if that. Less, if we factor in the intrinsic instability of the warp. Magos, I beg you. Consider the logic. Ignore Agelastus' interjection. If we wait for the Adeptus Astartes, we risk losing the ship–'

'Space hulk. Genetor, I wish you'd cease ignoring the fact that this is a derelict husk that has been floating in the warp for centuries. There is a term for it. It is called a *space hulk* and precedent shows that–'

'The vessel is completely functional.'

'As are many space hulks, judging from reports.'

'And what would you have us do, Agelastus?' Cornelius turns on his adversary, teeth clenched. The best laid plans of men, indeed. Meat always finds its way. 'We won't have this opportunity again. The parabola of the *Nepenthe*'s trajectory makes it clear. If we do not take our chance now, we will not see the vessel in our lifetimes. It will be another millennia before it enters realspace again and by that time, we'll be nothing but scrap.'

The enginseer's regard is placid. 'You will be, at least.'

How Cornelius loathes him. Squat, perpetually swaddled in red robes too long for his frame, his mechadendrites sloppily architectured, devoid of any sense of aesthetics. No ambition. Nothing but the bare formalities of biological function. Lupus is a waste of resources, unfulfilled potential. A mere cog. But a blood clot can asphyxiate the most brilliant mind. And here, here was a nodule of useless mass, waiting to be a cause of death.

'Magos, this is entirely up to you.' Cornelius cocks his head towards Veles. 'If you insist that we stand down–'

'No.'

'You can't be serious,' Lupus snarls. 'Be reasonable, Magos. I understand that you wish for our Explorator fleet to be recognised. But surely, you understand the absurdity of the situation. What Cornelius is suggesting – you cannot seriously be considering this debacle.'

'Your objections will be taken into consideration, Enginseer Agelastus. If you'd like to place a formal complaint, I invite you to follow the appropriate procedure.' The timbre of Veles' voice disguises nothing of its disdain, and it is all Cornelius can do to not laugh. 'This is not your jurisdiction, *enginseer*. If you wish to circumvent the possible consequences of your doomsaying, perhaps you should take the next few hours to evaluate the condition of our equipment.'

'Magos–'

Cornelius' fingers bifurcate, steeple, a prism of wires and attenuated silicone.

'Magos,' he echoes, tone adjusted for a luxuriant pitch. Conciliatory, even compassionate towards his nemesis. Survival, he'd learned, necessitates a mastery of politics, however distasteful its flavour. 'I believe–'

He is not permitted to finish.

'Both of you. Quiet.' Veles traps the bridge of his nose between gloved fingers.

'Magos,' Cornelius hisses.

'Magos,' Lupus echoes.

Veles evidences no immediate awareness of their acknow-ledgement. Along the edge of Cornelius' perception, he sees the bridge being evacuated. No one wants to be collateral damage. It is only when the space is bereft of conversation, no sound save for the hum of navigational cogitators, that Veles straight-ens, hand collapsing to his side. 'The purpose of the Explorators has always been to make sense of the unknown. Where others falter, we strive forward. We cannot surrender this opportunity. It is antithetical to who we are.'

'Magos, I understand that. But it would not take long for the Ultramarines–'

'They'd raze it to the ground,' Cornelius cuts in, unable to help himself, his horror raw. 'It wouldn't matter if the vessel was free of hostiles, or even if it contained a – a crew of living tech-priests, preserved by the hand of the Omnissiah. They'd destroy it.'

And her, he thinks, for a sliver of a moment.

'A regrettable possibility,' Lupus ripostes, stepping forward. 'But the reverse will put this entire ship at risk.'

'And isn't that the damned point?' Cornelius barks in counter-point. 'The entire purpose of the Cult Mechanicus? To recover and preserve knowledge? Here, we have the opportunity to exam-ine something – something no one has touched in hundreds of years. We cannot be afraid. The flesh is merely vehicular. If we must die for the cause, so be it.'

'Your passions…' Veles steers his bulk to an adjacent panel, fingers deft despite their size. Monitors come alive in a cosmos of computations and Cornelius' voice hitches at the vision, pleas-ure serrating his thoughts. He recognises them, the visualisations fractalising across the screens. Veles had been listening. More vitally still, they had him. '…Have always caused you and your brother trouble, haven't they?'

'It was necessary, Magos.' A subtle tilt of his head. 'We were raised on a forge world. Our parents were worthless but we always knew we were meant to be more than cattle in the abattoir. We worked tirelessly to be recognised and the Adeptus Mechanicus rewarded our diligence with its attention.'

Not entirely true. Not entirely inaccurate either.

Cornelius recites the story with the practice of a pastor, muscle memory flattening the tale into a perfect truth. Lupus exhales, mid-way, a loud noise, intended to bring pause.

'We've heard this all before. No need to get into this again. Is there a *point* to this, Magos? Or do you intend that we listen to this blowhard repeat his history all over again?'

Veles dismisses the complaint with a motion. 'I hadn't asked for an interruption. And you, Cornelius. He's right, you know? There is no point to your rhetorics. Not everything is an excuse to expound on your history. A shorter answer would have sufficed. Whatever the case, I've made a decision. A boarding party will be dispatched to the *Nepenthe* when it reenters real-space. You, Agelastus, and your brother shall lead it.'

Cornelius tilts a look at Lupus, picters keyed to the microcosm of his expressions. But if the proclamation angers the enginseer, if it upsets him in any way, his face admits to none of it.

'Whatever pleases you, Magos,' Agelastus declares.

'Good.' Veles cuts at nothing with the flat of his hand. 'I imagine you'll need four maniples of combat servitors, at least. Take whatever you need.'

Klaxon notifications, repeated in a claret glow. Against expectations, the *Nepenthe* arrives early, spilling into the world like a portent, a warning of what is to come.

'If it isn't a space hulk,' Cornelius confides to his brother, 'it might as well be.'

Marcus says nothing, unnerved by the unease frissoning down

his spine. The dimensions of the vessel exceeded their initial estimates, nearer in proportions to a battle barge than a mere cruiser. He'd thought they'd mapped the ship completely, but there is so much space unaccounted for, bulwarks and bays that had resisted imaging. How could they have been so mistaken?

What if it wasn't their fault? What if something, something alive and sapient, had occluded their investigations? Edited the structural report? For one moment, the tech-priest is seized by the impulse to terminate the mission, reveal that the operation has been compromised, but there is no question. It'd mean lobotomy, indentured servitude until their muscles gave out from rot.

He glances over at the servitors they'd been assigned, their bodies inert, slack in the harnesses descending from the ceiling of the shuttle. *Like so much meat,* Marcus thinks. Carcasses rocking from a butcher's hooks.

'Have you…' Marcus begins, each word slow and thick, 'ever considered what it might be like to be one of them?'

'The leucotomisation process is painless these days. In the past, physicians would drive an orbitoclast through the bone at the summit of the eye socket and cut.' Cornelius taps his mask, where the alloyed carapace contorts into a subtly anguished brow. 'Now, it is a strategic overstimulation of the interface-meshing, at least in the case of the Adeptus Mechanicus. Very humane.'

'That hardly answers my question.'

Cornelius sags. 'No. But the theory fascinates. In all honesty, I think it might feel like a bit of a respite. Consciousness is terror, after all. With self-awareness comes the knowledge of one's eventual demise, the understanding that cessation is inevitable. Our entire biology is servant to that existential dread. Everything we do, everything that we are, revolves around the impulse to arrest that eventuality. It is really quite inefficient. Look at the genus Tyranidae. They've committed the burden of autonomy to their Hive Minds. Look at what they've accomplished.'

'The extinction of countless solar systems. Entire galaxies, eaten down to their heart.' Marcus palms his face, looking out again through the porthole. Outside, in the cthonic abyss, the *Nepenthe* floats, defiant of classification. Matte panelling and no viewports, no turrets, nothing that approaches the familiar accoutrements of a ship, a rectangular cuboid like someone had carved the ship wholesale from the void itself.

'Yes, but it isn't personal.' Cornelius rises, restless, moves to examine the servitors, while Marcus watches the *Nepenthe* expand from improbability to irrefutable fact. Probes orbit its obsidian mass, magnesium scintilla that somehow cast no reflection on the oil-deep surfaces. He charts their transmissions; still no indication of where a docking area might reside. If this keeps up, they'd have to gouge a route of their own. 'Tyranids do not have agendas. Their motivations are pure. It's simple hunger, bestial and uncomplicated.'

'Careful, brother. What you suggest is heresy.' A door opens. Hypaspists file into the room in lock-step and flank the brothers; silent, watchful.

'As is everything we believe in.' Under the mask, Marcus is certain that his brother smiled. 'You're not getting cold feet now, are you?'

There is no opportunity to reply. Another door apertures and the brothers turn to see Lupus corralling a phalanx of battle-automata into the room, Scyllax Guardians to the last unit. In spite of himself, Marcus is impressed. Who would have thought their expedition would warrant such vaunted protection? At his attention, the machines halt, half-skulls swinging to triangulate on his position, his reflection repeated in the multitude of their glass-green eyes.

'The Magos insisted,' Lupus explains, glaring. 'He thinks this is a good idea.'

An accusation implied in the inflection of the words, but

Marcus circumvents an answer with a half-smile. He pushes onto his feet and pads towards the enginseer. 'And I imagine it will be. The space hulk–'

It wriggles across his tongue, the phrase. *Space hulk*. Marcus had been so insistent on censoring its use, but the words slip now from his lungs, independent of conscious decision, effortless in their articulation. But Lupus doesn't comment on them, preoccupied first with his automata and then the sight unfolding outside of the window.

Slowly, the *Nepenthe* becomes reticulated with incandescent razorwire, the lines so narrow that Marcus might have missed them if it wasn't for the intensity of their fluorescence. As he watches, the ship dismembers itself, separating along axial points intelligible only to its private algorithms. Doors are configured, hinges; biometrics familiar to naval morphologies. A mouth opens in the anterior of the ship, beckoning, its throat studded with orange guard lights.

The entry point is the exact size of their shuttle.

'Report.'

Veles' voice is static-warped, higher than in actuality. The Scyllax, cervical vertebrae annexed by the Magos, jabbers in irritation, its resident machine-spirit clearly displeased by the parasitism. Marcus endures its regard without complaint, while the enginseer endeavours to soothe the automaton. Around them, silence save for the biometrics of their footsteps, broadcasting aggregate weight, positioning, number. Cornelius looms ahead of the vanguard, wax-white in the dim.

'Nothing so far.'

Marcus would have appreciated a psyker or two in their convoy, someone that might be able to predict an ambush, or at least emptiness. It must exist, after all. The brothers had communed with her for years.

'As far as we can tell, this entire docking facility is… *new*.' So fresh from parturition, in fact, that the scaffolding is warm beneath Marcus' grip.

The tunnel is concentric rings, bordered with ganglia of exposed circuitry, contact with their topology prevented by thick glass. One method of ingress, one option for exit. *A killing ground*, Marcus thought, and shudders at his own description.

'It feels like it was custom-built specifically for our landing or, at least, modified based on their morphometrics.' The climate is equatorial. Humid enough for condensation to bead and roll off the automata, and drip from the servitors as they lumber ahead of their operators. The air breathable, if faintly pungent with exhaust. 'The infrastructure is astounding. Entirely modular, as far as I can see. I don't recognise the polymers used here. We'll need to take samples. I wish you could see this, Magos.'

'Trust me, Genetor, I am perfectly happy experiencing this by surrogate.'

The passage dilates into open space, unexpectedly commercial in its make-up. The servitors illuminate an out-of-commission fountain, the centrepiece of what Marcus presumes was a stage, its rococo anatomy choked by pathways. Mechanical stairs abseil diagonally from higher levels, six flights in total, the space ascending into a domed firmament. Refracted by the displays is the halcyon vision of a terrestrial night sky, fast-forwarding through cosmic phenomena. Everything is clean, scrupulously maintained.

Except it shouldn't be.

The impractical design of the ship, its apparent devotion to leisure; all tenets of a time when interstellar travel was something to venerate. The air should be clogged with dust, the hallways stinking of effluvium, rusty water and decomposing protein. It shouldn't be so clean. Marcus runs his eyes along the landing again, searching, uncertain.

Despite everything, despite fact, despite logic, it feels as though they've breached a moment locked in freeze-frame and, any moment now, animation will return, bodies will shuffle into visual range, music will play...

'You should have started running.'

Marcus jolts at the voice, which, he realises too late, is being transmitted stereoscopically, ricocheting from old-fashioned transducers, syllables sawed-off in places, the upper registers completely missing. Not that it damages the message. A hololithic projection grafts itself together in the corner: a man, wire-slim, sitting astride the lip of the fountain, knee pulled to his chest.

Whoever the manifestation had been modelled upon, Marcus realises with a thrill of excitement, that person must have predated the Imperium. Nothing in his features is familiar.

Even as Marcus gawks, the figure articulates a smile, combing fingers through hair pomaded perfectly in place. To the tech-priest's surprise, the keratin fibres respond, tussling in obedience to physics, and the figure sighs.

'Really. You should have started running.'

'*Defensive positions!*' Cornelius, bellowing already, more cautious, more grounded in the practical. Hypaspists swarm forward, the servitors moving in parallel. But it is too late.

Around them, the ship awakens.

Once, when he'd been too young to imagine being old, Cornelius had pressed his nose against a pane of smudged glass and watched as a cephalopod crawled along the bottom of a tank. At first, it had been the same muddied colours of the sediment but as it scrabbled forward, its rubbery flesh had blued, had brightened; by the time it'd lunged for its prey, a dying fish, seeping gases and lacings of waste, the creature burned like plasma.

Metachrosis. He'd learn the word much later, and only remember it again in the black of the *Nepenthe*. Lights nictitate in undulating spirals, threading the outlines of bodies he should have seen, should have noticed long ago. Cornelius levels his gun, fires, fires again, even as screams burst around him. Their camouflage must involve some variety of neurotoxin, a specialised pheromone intended to impede memory encoding. Something, anything. How else could he have missed them?

Something massive shrieks at Cornelius through the bichromatic chiaroscuro, darkness and the red glare of energy weapons. He turns. He estimates it to be about two metres, maybe less, maybe more. Accurate telemetrics require a mind not at war with itself.

What successfully registers: tentacles slopping from a gaping jaw, each pseudopod teethed and stippled with hooks. Bipedal physiognomy, slightly hunched. A carapace that might have been skin once, but is now a scabrous leather. What he fails to process: a name.

Cornelius knows he recognises the aberration howling closer by the heartbeat, that some distant vector of consciousness has a name for this nightmare. But he cannot call it to his tongue, not even as the thing's arms petal into hooks. Six limbs now, seven, the last no doubt meant to spear him like a fish.

Even as the amygdala barks its denial, even as Cornelius' cognition shrinks into itself, something more ancient, a basal instinct scrimshawed into the bones, raises his gun again and shoots until the clip exhausts itself.

His artillery does nothing.

Cornelius' arm drops to his side, slack, gun clattering to the floor. He stares. The thing snaps its head back, cephalopodic mouth exposed under a ring of straining tentacles, and at the sight of it, a word unwraps from Cornelius' lungs.

'Genestealer.'

One of the hypaspists intercepts the creature's trajectory, knocking the genestealer aside and down, the two tumbling.

The world renders in hyper-vivid strokes, sensory oversaturation bracketed by screams and the screech of metal torn apart. Before Cornelius can recover equilibrium, the genestealer digs talons into the tech-guard's chest and *pulls*.

Ribs crack. Viscera – barely recognisable as liver and intestine, glands and other sweetbreads, genetic optimisation and augmetics having made for more streamlined offal – disgorge from the gash. The warrior does not cry out, only convulses as it begins haemorrhaging oil and blood, body sagging. The genestealer raises its prize upwards, tentacles burrowing through the mangled flesh.

'Genestealers,' Cornelius repeats, tongue heavy in his mouth. *No*, he thinks. *That's not right. No, not quite. Almost.*

Finally: 'Ymgarl strain. Omnissiah take them, I thought these were extinct.'

Pain cannot bypass programming. Even halfway to dying, the hypaspist will serve. It kicks against the genestealer, lasgun pushing into position, while the creature envelopes its face with its tendrils. Now, the warrior screams, a thin and animal noise. Its fingers clench and it pumps las-fire into the underside of its captor's mandibles. Over and over, until the feeding genestealer's skull splits from the assault.

Pale curds of brain, crisped by ballistics, splatter across the tech-priest's robes. All at once, Cornelius is no longer paralysed, animal brain supplanting terror, pushing him up, forward, away from what had transpired.

For the first time, Cornelius really takes a look at the tableau.

It cannot have been more than twenty minutes since their arrival. But the walls are soaked, the floor mosaiced with so much meat that Cornelius can no longer remember if the landing had a colour. Over and again, Cornelius finds himself being surprised by how much of it there is, every glob of debased muscle run-through with wires and broken tubing, like so many parasitic worms evicted from a home.

The servitors keep dying in clumps: thick-witted, slaved to targeting subroutines that are simply too slow to be effective against the xenos. But at least they serve a purpose, distracting the genestealers from more competent prey; the hypaspists and the Scyllax, closing ranks behind their monotasked peers. Unfortunately, there are only so many bodies to go around.

'Genetor. You are in danger. We should move.' Stilted delivery in a chrome-plated voice, full of squeals and pops as the larynx fizzles to uselessness. Cornelius shifts his attention to the hypaspist to his right, the cyborg drenched in gore. 'Genetor, you are without weaponry. You should correct the situation.'

No secret that the troops of the Adeptus Mechanicus undergo emotion-suppression surgery, but Cornelius can't help but wonder, as he falls into lock-step, just how much is flensed from the parietal lobe. What does it take to allow an animal to shamble through the act of dying without so much as a whimper? The hypaspist bleeds in ropes of grey offal, lasgun braced against the hollow of an exposed abdominal cavity, but it evidences no discomfort, nothing but a slurred vigil.

'Genetor, you are without weaponry–'

'We need to find my brother.' *We need to find her.* Almost simultaneous, that other statement, articulated with more fervour than any requests to seek out Cornelius' absent sibling. Since their approach, he's not been able to hear her, not even a chord to allay his fears, his grief at being so unfathomably alone; a self-aware cyst of neural tissue piloting a rotting corpse.

The hypaspist scissors straight with a crunch of bone, head cocked at a twenty-seven degree angle. 'Genetor Marcus is–'

Before it can finish, Cornelius hears his brother scream, a killing sound whetted by the raw crackle of electric. He pivots to find Marcus and Lupus, flanked by automata, retreating from a corridor he'd not noticed before. Above them, clinging to the balustrades, bodies coiled like upside-down raindrops, a writhing mass of genestealers prepares for the drop.

The *Nepenthe... blinks.*

A voice floods the capillaries of the ship: female, faintly adenoidal.

'You are in a protected void sphere,' she intones without inflection. Magnesium-white pinholes of light flare along the surface of the *Nepenthe*, even as the strange voice pours from every speaker, every stretch of space along the Explorator vessel. 'You are in a protected void sphere. Move, or we will register your inaction as a declaration of aggression.'

'Move.' Something cracks the monotone. 'Or there will be nothing of you to move.'

'Marcus!' Cornelius bellows in time for his brother to jump sideways, but Lupus moves a half-second late.

The genestealers descend as the hydra of Lupus' mechadendrites rise, servo-arms razor-ridged, snapping at the air with moray eel mouths. But the enginseer's enhancements are *industrial*, intended for fine work, not martial use. They break on hide intended to withstand worse. Two of the genestealers clasp Lupus by the shoulders, tug like dogs in competition for a wishbone, and as the enginseer wails, a third leans over the man, tentacles swaddling his gaunt face.

Something breaks.

Snaps.

Cornelius wastes no time on empathy, on fear, not even when Lupus' throat distends and tears, as one of the genestealer's smaller feelers breaks through the skin, a red-glazed jut of keratin. He knows what comes next. The Scyllax scream in one voice, inlays short-circuited by Lupus' misfiring synapses; there is no syntax for his agony, no way to translate that pain into coherent actionables, no option but to shriek in symphony, their machine-spirits algospasmic.

They continue to scream as Marcus butterflies a genestealer's arm, the parabola of his whip precise enough to flay even that tensile flesh, as Marcus bolts for his brother, as Cornelius splices noospherically into his escort's interfaces, both half-blind, but in the kingdom of the condemned, every little bit counts.

'Run,' Marcus pants, bleeding from a hundred places, his face ribbons.

'Genetors, stay behind me,' Cornelius' hypaspist intones, shambling between the brothers and the genestealers, the latter already on the prowl again, Lupus' dismembered corpse strewn between them, a boneless slaughterhouse of parts. And still nothing, nothing of the voice from the ship, nothing but this cosmology of death, Cornelius adapting macros to steady the hypaspist's aim, optimise its reflexes, anything to buy them time. Nothing, nothing, nothing at all. 'Genetor Cornelius, I advise that you acquire a weapon.'

The brothers don't argue.

'Where is Veles? Where is our support? He was supposed to be in charge of the servitors, but we're *alone* here!' Marcus demands, dragging his brother past a tableau of the dead. 'We have two options: we return to the ship or we find the control hub of this place. There must be a way. It can't end like this.'

'Something's cut off communications. I don't know when it happened, but the entire ship has become a null-zone. No signals in or out. She mustn't want us to leave.' Cornelius exhales and for a heartbeat, he is frightened to the bone of its implications. Perhaps, there is a reason as to why some things are branded tech-heresy.

'If you are looking for CAT, you should probably move quickly.' The hololith again, that anachronistic projection, materialising between the tech-priests as they race through the carnage, his feet skating across the air like it is a lamina of oil. 'They're almost done with the rest of your friends.'

Ambient electromagnetics cooking the air into patterns; pareidolia giving shape to the distortions. Under any other circumstances, Cornelius would have loved to dissect the technologies behind the manifestation. 'Establish identity protocols. Report.'

'I am MAUS. I am the CAT's plaything. I am her assistant. I am her arms and legs. I am her keeper. I am her opposite. I am what she is not.' Even wind velocity is replicated, the hologram's hair moving with the momentum, a whip-snap of fluorescent strands. 'She is not here, but I am.'

'Genetors.' A single salutation, bifurcated into two voices. The last of the hypaspists shamble into view, flamethrowers drooling combustibles. 'There is an exit.'

One points behind them through the holocaust of bodies and quieting screams, even the Scyllax cracked open, husked of whatever meat is wired inside their bodies, their engines cooling and already leaking radiation.

Their escape option is a gash in the wall, too small to have admitted whatever crowds might have once milled through the *Nepenthe*. A service entrance, perhaps, restricted to sanitorial personnel. No reason to think that it might lead them to freedom. Or her. Longing curves its hook around Cornelius' gut, tugs, and he opens his mouth to object when all of them, genestealer and tech-priest, the slurried neural tissue laced through the hypaspists' skulls, hear her sing.

'Identify yourself,' Veles barks.

'Move, or there will be nothing left of you to move.' The voice – it was coming from everywhere, every speaker, every channel – clarifies with every threat, acquiring inflection, unsubtle emotion. First: a modicum of pity, which diversifies shortly after to amusement, disdain. A strain of brittle loathing, something that has had years to mature.

'Move, or I–' *Finally*, Veles thinks, an iota of identity spun into the endless warnings. He almost welcomes the aggression. Better this than the silence, the insensate dark. '–will make sure there's nothing of you to move.'

'We repeat. Identify yourself.' Still nothing from his subordinates, no clue as to who might be issuing those statements, no way of verifying if it is a rogue machine-spirit or even, as some have theorised, a psyker who'd surmounted the trick of dying. But whispers of *heresy* have begun to seep through the listless ranks. Veles finds he can't argue.

'*Nepenthe*,' she whispers, when the ship is lit up like a supernova. 'I am that which interrupts grief, devours sorrow, an opiate.'

'What *are* you?'

'Yes.' The voice surprises Veles with its despair. 'That is the question, isn't it?'

'Marcus, she's calling us.' He feels fingers lace around his sleeve.

Though Cornelius' face now sits fermenting in a tide of bacteria, Marcus can still picture his sibling's expression, an urgent wonder. 'She's here. She's awake. She's *real.*'

He does not answer. Not at first. Too enraptured by the glissando of her voice, its notes decanted straight into his nervous system, Marcus can only exist, transfixed by the reality of her. They'd waited for so long. Yet, some treacherous nodule of his mind disdains from submitting to the ecstasy, instead persisting in pointing out that this isn't so much blasphemy as it is mutinying against self-preservation.

But they've come this far.

And what else do they have?

'Marcus.'

'I hear her, I hear her.' He untethers his brother's grip from his robes, every cell subsumed by the rapture of her acknowledgement. *Drunk*, Marcus thinks. He is drunk on the harmonics of her, somehow, that dose of oxytocin quickly metastasising into a full-on addiction. Anything so long as she doesn't go silent again. There is just enough of Marcus to understand he should run. But he can't, won't.

'Let's go.' They move, their escape obfuscated by the final coda of the Scyllax, the muzzle-flash accompaniment.

To Marcus' distant astonishment, the genestealers do not follow. *But why would they need to?* hisses a voice in his head. The brothers were herding themselves to the pantry.

A killing ground.

Marcus pushes the thought down.

The corridor narrows until they can only pass one at a time, the hypaspists taking point. Cornelius crab-walks behind them, the bizarre mathematics of his physique ill-suited for the restrictive space. Marcus comes last. No light whatsoever save for the radiation from their tacticals, the pallid glow from behind the hypaspists' visors. Briefly, as he anchors the flail at his waist, Marcus considers jury-rigging some method of producing actual luminance, but the thought is superseded by childish superstition: *if he can't see them, maybe, they won't be able to see him.*

'I wonder where she's taking us.' Cornelius breaks the quiet, voice muddied by pleasure, embarrassing almost in its intensity, like a lover's appetite wantonly advertised. His fingers click across the walls, an irregular heartbeat. 'I wish – I wish I understood what she was saying. But there is so much interference. I wish... I wish...'

Marcus says nothing. It occurs to him how empty of words he is. Especially now, with nothing but precedent fish-hooked through his breastbone, not even the euphonics of her voice to compel him, its notes dialled to faint static. White noise. Faith and white noise and the knowledge there's no way to go but forward. A hiss-click of vox frequencies, remarkable only in its stark duality: it means nothing to Marcus, everything to Cornelius.

In that moment, Marcus learns to hate his brother.

'What is she saying to you?' Try as he might, he can't scrub his voice of its envy.

Cornelius halts. 'Nothing. Nothing precise. But she has to know we're here. She has to be calling to us. Why else would she be... singing?'

Again, language fails him as his body has failed him, is failing him. Marcus digs the heel of his palm into his brother's shoulder, pushes him forward. They don't speak at all. Occasionally, Cornelius moans into the dark – *closer, closer, Marcus, oh, can't you hear her, she's telling us to come closer* – like some prophet wasting to bone in the desert, but neither Marcus nor the hypaspists reply, and there is no other sound save for the drip of condensation, their footsteps in lock-step.

A trapezoid of light razors through the gloom, dust-moted. Through the cavity in the wall, Marcus can hear machinery in respiration, meat in preparation. He breathes in, holds his breath pinned against the roof of his mouth as one of the escorts crooks their gloved hand, beckoning them onward.

'Here,' murmurs his brother, dazed-sounding, all eloquence drained to effortful slurring. 'She's here. She's here. She's waiting for us. Can't you hear her, Marcus? Can't you hear her call?'

'Yes,' he lies softly in return. 'Yes, I can.'

Inside they discover what might have once been a medbay, save it'd been repurposed for a specific purpose. There are vats everywhere, machines by the dozen, each devoted to a separate horror. Here, there is a system cultivating and curating bacteria cultures. Here, a sterilisation vat. Here, a miracle of engineering pulping the fungi, decocting them into food.

Here–

Marcus stares at the yellowed skeleton suspended at the heart of the facility, at the glistening sheets of grey tissue draped across its stretched arms. *She was female*, Marcus thinks, cataloguing the curve of the cadaver's pelvis bones, the swoop of its bowed spine.

Mite-like drones crawl across the stretched flesh, pruning it of necrotising cells, harvesting the healthy. Others build circuitry of what they'd collected, tenants them in glass, stacks them in silos twice as high as the gawking tech-priests, every last shelf an oozing constellation of blinking lights and stinking, green-yellow lymph.

The air convulses and suddenly *she* is standing before them. Like MAUS, her phenotype markers are distinctive, orbital sockets and jawline bare of ethnic cross-pollination. Unlike MAUS, her appearance demonstrates evidence of corruption: patches of sloughed skin, revealing ongoing computations beneath, arabesques of virtualised protein radiating from her skull in a mist. An aberration, an *abomination*. Yet for all the grotesquerie on display, she is everything they'd dreamed.

Marcus slows, arm flung out to stop Cornelius' motion.

'What are you?' Such a trite question. The momentousness of the occasion demands profundity, but all Marcus can supply is platitudes, pre-processed wonder as described in societal subconscious.

'It's her,' Cornelius whispers to no one at all.

'I was–' She saccades in place, a zoetrope in slow-motion, while the darkness twitches. Gleaming eyes flood the penumbra. *There*, Marcus thinks, surprised by his own resignation. *This is where we die.* He knows that. But he does not mind. All he wants is to talk to her a little longer. Just a bit more. '–was-was a psyker, I think. I think that was the word. Pssssskyer. Yes. Once, I'd been meat and hope and dreams everlasting.'

The air boils from Marcus' lungs.

MAUS renders on an adjacent wall. 'He means, "What are you *now*?"'

'I am the *Nepenthe*.' Her eyes empty of cornea and sclera, become engulfed instead in light so incandescent it is all after-image, an impression of glare.

This is why the past is heresy, Marcus thinks hazily, speared by her gaze.

'I am her protector, her-her mother, her guardian. I am the one who keeps her crew safe.'

Cornelius interjects, some ghost of him restored. 'Everyone's dead. There are nothing but genestealers on board this ship, and–'

'There are sixteen hundred and forty-five living beings on the ship,' she continues, unperturbed, and all Marcus can think of is how much he wishes he knew her name. Her name and not the ship's, the name of the girl who'd animated the bones standing centrepiece in the room, who was still alive now. 'I have monitored their biotelemetrics. I have adjusted the climate of the ship in accordance to their requirements. I have ensured optimal conditions for their survival within the limits of available resources.'

'Those aren't your crew.' Marcus staggers forward while tentacles bloom in the half-light steeping around the mainframe, an irridescing biome of creeping purples and then eyes, flat and animal. How many of them? How many of them are there? He cannot conjecture a number, refuses to even consider the exercise. The same way he cannot envision what it must be like to be here, alone in the nothing, surrounded by the dead and the hungry, trapped. 'They're all dead. Or… or changed. These things aren't human. Your–'

'Do not touch her,' MAUS snarls, suddenly in high-definition, three dimensional and already peeling from the wall. 'Do not touch her. If you touch her, I'll make sure that you will never stop dying. Do not touch her. Why are you even here, anyway?'

'She called us,' Cornelius whispers as their escorts finally sag onto the ground, offal puddling from their open wounds, slopping outwards in moist clusters. 'She called us here. Lady, we've come so far for you. Through the void and the silence, through the endlessness. Through the hungry dark.'

'There is no way,' CAT whispers.

Sccrrrrcccch. Something is pulling the bodies away, dragging them into the blackness.

'We have records.' Marcus can hear slithering, peristalsis: larynx and trachea violated, a cartilaginous tearing, *slurping*, and a sigh almost sweet in its pained relief. He doesn't turn. He can't. 'Decades of records. We documented the communication. We *spoke* with her. We tracked her.'

'Oh.' MAUS laughs aloud, bitterness in the twist of that sound. Elsewhere, *she* has begun humming again, a lullaby for monsters. 'Oh. No. No, that's not what happened at all. She doesn't want you here. No one wants you here.'

Marcus snarls. 'Then why did she call–'

'Psychic residue. They wanted something that'd keep the crew calm, something more tactile than a cool voice through the intercoms. So they vivisected a psyker, came up with a way to clone her tissues, over and again, bind that power to their machinery.' Here, MAUS releases his rictus. 'It hurts her. Every time.'

Outside, the universe trembles. Ballistics and a ballet of propulsion, moving parts thrumming through the bulkhead. Marcus ignores them all. 'So you–'

'You were never wanted here.' A clarity seeps into her voice, even as her image blinks into focus, the aberration – *I never asked for her name*, Marcus thinks again, strangely agonised over the fact – pivoting to face the two, hands joined, head cocked. 'You were *never* wanted here. You are not part of my crew. You do not belong on the *Nepenthe*. Why have you come here?'

Like them, Marcus is broken, unable to do more than reiterate patterns, his hands hanging nerveless at his side. All these years for nothing. *A killing ground*, repeats that ghost of his voice. What's worse is that the *Nepenthe* hadn't even been in active pursuit. He and Cornelius, they'd walked themselves there, down into the slaughterhouse, so they could lay their heads on the butcher's block. 'You called us.'

'No.' There is no sympathy in her eyes, blinding still in their fluorescence. If anything, it is disdain he sees there, scaffolded in the bend of her mouth. 'No, you were never wanted here.'

Hands circle Marcus' throat, fingers tenderly cupping the jut of his chin. This close, Cornelius smells of oil and charred metal, flesh weeping plasma beneath the metal. Sweat and desperation. Marcus exhales and relaxes into his brother's constricting grip, reality abstracted into a vague sense of self-loathing. Yes, this was always how it was meant to end, wasn't it? With them forgotten, buried in the belly of the ship.

'Lady, I'll do anything you need, as long as you let me stay. Let me stay in your song. Let me love you.'

The manifestations exchange looks, vibrantly alive.

'Why not?'

Snap.

The lights of the *Nepenthe* turn black. Veles jolts his head up from his screen and its rotation of panels, predictions conceptualised as shifting graphs, endless calculations.

'What is happening?' Veles growls.

Every screen is commandeered by a video feed. In it, Cornelius and Marcus, haloed by pinpoint glows, their faces bloodied but whole. Behind them, Veles can see chrome balustrades and unfamiliar architecture, screens and cogitator racks, acres of bizarre machinery.

And a body, a corpse, a skeleton suspended above pinpoints of lights, like a saint of strange places.

Veles feels the questions die in his throat, one after another, swallowed by wonder, by fear, by scholastic lust. The brothers had been right. And now the *Nepenthe* was waiting to be cracked open, suckled of its secrets, its heart interrogated. He would be remembered forever. They would be remembered forever. Their names would be scorched into the annals of history and even the Omnissiah would marvel at what they had found.

'Reconnaissance completed,' Cornelius states. 'There was a small brood of genestealers that had to be eliminated. The others are ensuring the rest of the ship is secure.'

Marcus dips his head. 'Whenever you're ready, Magos. Come aboard. There's so much waiting for you to see.'

RICHARD STRACHAN

THE WIDOW
TIDE

How did he die, she wondered? How frightened was he when he realised it was over?

She dwelled nightly on his pain, tormenting herself with his imagined agony. Smothered by the waves, perhaps, shouldered from his boat into the boiling waters; she saw him kicking against the current, the weight of his clothes dragging him down, choking and screaming for help though help was miles away. He would have watched with dread as his boat drifted off into the drizzling light, and then he was under, swallowed by the hungry dark, thrashing and scrabbling for air...

But perhaps it had been even worse. Maybe he had met his end in the jaws of some lurking horror of the Hopetide seas – a flensfin scavenging the catch, leaping from the sea as he hauled in his net. She saw its teeth rip the flesh from his neck, the spurt of blood in the water as he plunged his fingers into the gaping wound. The maddened frenzy of feeding things, tearing his body to pieces...

Why not? she thought. The worst was always the most likely.

She thought of this every night. Every night he died in a hundred different ways. Here on a narrow spur of land amongst the gravestones of the village cemetery, she looked down on the roiling water that surged and swayed and kept its secrets close. He was in there still, locked in the chains of the waves.

These were the widow tides, the fishermen said. A man left his boat at harbour in such weather and tried to ignore the old wives' tales of the daemons in the deep. Out there, all the cold acres of the ocean groaned and muttered for their prey.

'Katalina!'

In the sallow twilight, a figure moved up the slope from the beach. She huddled into her black sealskin, felt the wind pluck and harry at her.

'Katalina,' he shouted again as he came near, 'I thought it was you.'

'Radomir,' she said, and at the same time thought, *how does someone get so fat on a diet of fish?*

He leaned against a gravestone to gather his breath. Framed against the dying day, broad and unshaven, he looked solid and unflappable. For a moment she felt ashamed of her grief.

'For Sigmar's sake, Kat, can't you see...' He held his hands out to her.

'See what?'

'That this isn't good for you,' he said. 'Haunting the graves like this, spending so much time amongst the dead...' He touched the fishbone charm around his neck. 'He's not coming back, you know that. Borys is dead.'

'You can't be sure.'

'I loved him as much as anyone, really I did. His father was my oldest friend, the boy was like a son to me. But in the end you have to face the truth, no matter how painful it is. Hopetide's an unforgiving coast.'

She gazed down into the churning sea, picturing her husband, his thick yellow hair, the wicked glint in his eyes. The black waters of Shyish did no favours to anyone. She was under no illusions; her man was surely dead.

'I know,' she admitted. 'But how can his soul find the peace it needs if we don't have a body to bury?'

'Kat, it's–'

'He should be waiting for me on the Placid Shore, not lost out there afraid and alone. Don't *you* see? He'll come back to me, one way or another. The sea will give him up. And when it does, I'll be waiting right here for him.'

Radomir gave an exasperated sigh. He turned to the path again.

'You're too sensitive for this place. Always dreaming… I remember when we cut your first sealskin, you cried like a baby! I thought Borys would keep your feet on the ground, but the two of you were more wrapped up in each other than anyone I've ever met.' He smiled sadly. 'I'm headman of the village, Kat, I've got to make the effort. People are getting restless. Sympathy's a shallow well, and I think you've drawn as much of it as you're going to get.'

'I don't care about their sympathy. They can think what they like.'

He dismissed her with a wave, but before he disappeared back down the slope he turned and said in a low, uncertain voice: 'This isn't the kind of night to be out, Katalina, take it from an old man like me. Don't stay out much longer, please. It isn't safe…'

Before she left, she paused to read the names on the gravestones, as she did every night. Aleksander Cuffe, Eryk Olsein, Selton Harred. Some of the names were too worn to read, no more than dimpled suggestions in the stone. She ran her fingers over them, wondering if those names now lived upon the Placid Shore, far across the ocean, where the sea was always gentle and kind. Perhaps the very motion of her fingertips over the forgotten letters brought back a spark of memory inside a distant soul?

When the wind died down she headed back to the village. The low dwellings clustered like barnacles against the shore. The guarding totems on the beach gave a last sad clatter, their

poles decorated with bloodshark skulls and carved ivory; apo-
tropaic scrimshaw to keep the daemons at bay. The water shushed
and rattled across the stones. She paused awhile amongst the
dunes to listen to it, this endless music that underlay all life in the
village. Some nights she had lain out here with Borys, serenaded
by that sound. Now there was only a long and empty evening
ahead of her; the meagre fire in the grate, the pile of stinking
nets she still had to repair – for even widows have to earn their
keep. Home, she thought. It was a bitter image.

She heard it then: a noise in the dark.

She clutched a fold of her sealskin. Silence, nothing but the sea.

Her fingers fluttered to the bone charm around her wrist. After
a sour moment it came again – low and strangled, burbling across
the night. Her stomach was a shard of ice.

'Who's there?'

A skittering against the stones.

Crabs, she thought, picking through the surf. A seal, maybe,
wounded and waiting to die. *Something* was out there...

A sudden, twisted scream lanced out of the dark, and before
Katalina could think what she was doing she had flung herself
onto the ground, the breath ragged in her chest. The scream came
again, agonised, fainter. It clawed against her skin.

She peered through the dry grass. The sound came now as
an awful, huffing wail, like a tortured animal, and it was this
thought that finally put steel into her nerves. It took all of her
courage, courage she thought she had lost the day they came to
tell her Borys' boat was gone, but slowly she stood and stepped
onto the shore. If something was hurt out there, then surely it
didn't deserve to die alone.

The beach lay before her like an empty stage, tenebrous and
ill-lit. The totems were columns of shadow, and every now
and then she caught a glimpse of light from a breaking wave – and
there was something else there too; a pale, blue glow that pulsed

and shivered and fell. She stared at its afterglow, almost willing it to return, and when it did – still in that same weak pattern of pulse and fade – she moved cautiously across the beach towards it; towards the low slumped shape that floundered in the tide, white-skinned and wounded, gasping for breath and croaking out a single word:

'Help.'

'Eat,' she said. 'You must eat.'

She tipped the spoon against its blackened lips. The stew dribbled down its chin. Katalina had to still the fear that the thing was going to bite her when she reached to wipe it away.

It coughed. Spit flicked from its mouth onto the blanket.

She tried to make it drink, holding out a cup of water and supporting its head, her fingers splayed against its clammy, hairless skin. The rank feel of it tightened every muscle in her body.

'Drink,' she said. 'You must drink.' The thing snarled into the brimming cup.

Sometimes when it looked at her its gaze was delirious and vague. Bubbles formed on its lips, and it emitted a moan that reminded her of the deep-whales' mournful midnight call when they surfaced out at sea. But then the eyes would snap to her like steel traps, pale blue with bitter black pupils.

'I want to help you,' she said. 'You're hurt. I've done the best I can, but… I've never seen anything like you before.'

It groaned and rolled away. Eventually, by the laboured rise and fall of its chest, she thought it must have fallen asleep. In the shivering firelight it looked for a moment like a wizened old man, but when the flames leapt higher it felt instead like an image drawn from an old dream she could barely remember.

Her first thought had been of her husband – 'Borys!' she'd gasped – but then the tide had turned it over and she saw the pale, inhuman face, the sunken eyes and pointed ears, that narrow, tapering chin. It was wrapped in nothing but rags and broken scraps of what could have been armour, weird, conch-like whorls of metal that were tarnished with salt. On its chest were savage puncture marks. It had gurgled and retched, reaching for a caged shard of glass submerged in the surf. A jewel of some kind, she thought, the source of that dull blue glow she had seen from the dunes. She plucked it from the water and slipped it into her pocket, and despite the low, disturbing scent that clung to its skin, a smell like burning weeds or rotting fish, Katalina had managed to haul the creature from the water. It took her half an hour to drag it up the beach. *A mariner caught in the storm*, she thought. *Flung by the currents towards our lonely shore.* The realms were wider and stranger than anyone could understand, but even as she struggled into the dunes she knew this was no lost mariner. It wasn't a trader from Aqshy blown off course, or a Ghurish merchant sunk with his cargo. This was something else.

Once inside she had stripped off the rags and armour and cleaned its wounds. The creature's eyes had flickered as she lowered it to the bed.

She crept from its side now and settled herself into Borys' old chair by the fire, a blanket drawn across her shoulders. A cold wind threaded through the cottage. She tried to rest, tried to ignore the gagging smell exuded by the thing that was sleeping in her bed. It was a scent, she felt, of brackish tides and dead weeds, of shorelines long abandoned.

'Kattie! Are you up?'

The widow Agata's grating tones, the older woman screeching her name from the path.

The melancholic light fell clear through a gap in the curtain. Katalina saw the shape in her bed, heard the moist clicking of its breath. She cast off her blanket and stood for a moment gazing down at the smooth and savage blade of the creature's face, the frown of pain or sorrow that briefly marred it.

There was a brisk knock at the door. 'Still abed, girl?' Agata muttered. 'Up, up. Shift yourself, the day will near be done at this rate!' Then, with the widow's maddening familiarity, a second after that the door began to open. Quickly Katalina drew the hanging around the bed.

Agata was stooped and wrinkled like the strings of bladder-wrack the villagers hung above their doors for luck, but she wore her widowhood like a well-tailored frock.

'What is it?' Katalina protested. 'You can't just burst in like this, it isn't right!'

'And what do you think I'm like to see, hmm? With your Borys gone I'm sure there's nothing to offend my eyes. And right or not,' the widow said, 'there's work to be done.'

'I'll have the nets ready by tomorrow.'

'More than nets,' Agata grumbled. 'There's crab pots that need fixing too. The day's catch needs sorted for market. Think you're too good for that?'

'I'll help, I promise.'

The old woman trundled about the cottage, picking at the mess on the table, peering into the dirty pot on the hearth.

'I know your man's gone,' she said, not unkindly, 'but so's mine, a long time past. We all die, Kattie – Shyishans know this more than most. The village continues. So should you.'

She was about to leave when she noticed the rags bundled on the floor. Quickly, before Katalina could stop her, the widow hooked them up.

'What's this? Been out beachcombing have you?'

She held up the strange metal plates to the light, curved and barbed like seashells. There was something in her eyes then, Katalina felt; a lost memory resurfacing from deep places, an old fear finally confirmed. Like a change in the weather, the expression passed away. Agata cast the pieces down with a shudder.

'Huh. They'll make good flower baskets for your eaves come spring,' she said. She squinted at the younger woman. For a moment her face looked drawn and harried. 'Don't suppose you saw much else out there?'

'Like what?'

'Tracks on the beach, the young lads say. Something dragged itself from the sea last night, maybe. Or dragged itself back.'

Katalina said nothing. The older woman stared at her, but under that piercing gaze she made her face blank. Only the thin material of the hanging separated the old widow from the truth of the rumour.

'Well,' she said at last. 'Open a window, Kat. Get some air in. It reeks in here.'

When the door banged behind the old woman, Katalina fell into her chair. She wiped the sweat from her face and stilled her breathing, and when she could hear Agata back at her drying green she drew the hanging. The thing was staring up at her, its eyes a richer blue, the dark lips parted to show a sliver of silver teeth.

'You're safe,' she said. 'I won't let anybody hurt you. I promise.'

She took the dull blue jewel from her pocket and placed it on the pillow by the creature's head. It said nothing, moved not a muscle, but somehow Katalina was sure it was saying thank you.

Later in the day, she entered into the life of the village again, as she hadn't done for months. Warily, the villagers watched her. Men and women she had known all her life crossed the square to avoid her, and at the sorting baskets the fishwives shunned her attempts to talk. Some whispered as she passed. It was like her grief was contagious, a sickness no one wanted to catch.

'Pay no mind to them, Kat,' Radomir said later that afternoon, taking her aside and sharing his bread with her. 'Half of them think you've a lover in your bed, and the other half are jealous!'

Her face flushed red. 'I've no lover!' she said in a hoarse whisper. 'And Borys not a year gone!' *Agata*, she thought.

Radomir laughed and wolfed down his food. 'No matter to me if you did, girl! Village gossip, you know what it's like. Now come on,' he said as the horns blew from the harbour. 'That's the dusk catch back, we've work to do.'

The day's work laced her muscles with pain, but Katalina felt almost pleasurably tired when she headed home. She would sleep well tonight, she thought, and if she dreamed, she knew she would dream of Borys. He was close now, surely. All lost things will come home on the tide, in the end.

Radomir walked her back as evening fell.

'What will you do tonight then?' he asked her. Did he fear she would haunt the graveyard again, a lonely gheist maddened by her grief? Or did he half-believe in that village gossip?

'I've those nets to darn,' she said. 'And the cottage to tidy. Maybe it has been too long, Radomir... Today was a good day.'

'I'm glad to hear it, you need to move on with your life. Perhaps we could set up a memorial to Borys in the cemetery?'

'Even without his body?'

'Why not?' Radomir offered. 'I'm no philosopher, but do we really know that's how it works? None of us have ever actually gone to the Placid Shore, have we? But he'll be there regardless, I'd swear it.'

They reached the turn-off for the path that led to Katalina's cottage. The wind danced between them, kicking at the sand. From over the fretful dunes came the boom and mutter of the surf.

'Agata said they'd found tracks on the beach last night,' Katalina said. 'Something came ashore.'

Radomir did a good job of looking indifferent. 'Oh, nothing

to worry about!' he said, airily. 'Honestly, it'll turn out to be nothing in the end.'

'A ripperjaw, maybe?' she asked. 'One of them's beached in these parts before.'

'Nothing so dramatic! Just... just some things that were found on the beach. But they could have washed up from anywhere – it's no real worry. There'll be men out patrolling, just in case.'

They went their separate ways, but when she headed down the path to her home Katalina knew something was wrong at once. The door of her cottage was ajar, and even in the gathering night she could see flecks of what might be blood against the doorstep. She moved cautiously into the gloom.

'Are you there?'

The bed was empty. She could see the impression its body had made on the mattress. She stood and listened, but all she could hear was Agata's grumbling from the garden next door, the muted thunder of the surf.

The music of the sea...

She found it slumped amongst the dunes, not thirty yards from the cottage. If Agata had but raised her head when she was outside she would have seen it. The wounds had opened, and the bandages were wet. In the dusk's flat light its pale skin almost seemed to glow, and the eyes it turned on her as it panted for breath were pained.

'What are you doing?' she scolded. 'By the hammer and the throne, anyone could have seen you!'

She wrapped an arm around its shoulders and gathered it up. It felt light, diminished. There was something desiccated about it now, like a stick of wind-dried kelp. It scrabbled at her with its fingers, moaning, clawing her skin.

'I know, but you're not strong enough yet,' she said. 'A few more nights, please. Let me care for you a little longer.'

She heard the clank of metal, the tread of footsteps across the beach. Quietly she hunkered in the sand, drawing the creature down. Through the marram grass she could see one of the patrols Radomir had mentioned – two old salts and a boy, with gutting knives and a grimy lamp. The lad danced and slashed the air.

'One quick cut with this beauty and I'll be feeding it to the sharks!' he shouted. The old salts mocked him, passing a leather flask between them.

'Let me tell you now, boy, you wouldn't last a breath against half the things in those waters!'

The patrol ambled on, the old salts still laughing. When it had passed, Katalina breathed again. She was holding its hand, the clammy cold fingers in her own. The creature gulped for air and said only its second word to her:

'Why?'

She thought of Borys, flailing in the current. Alone.

'Because who else is going to help you?' she said.

Every night, as it rested, Katalina would darn and weave the fishing nets, practised fingers moving quickly over the twine. In the mornings, she would slip out and throw herself into the day's work, flashing her blade on the skinning bench or racking up the catch for the market wagons, ignoring the suspicious glances from the other villagers, the whispered conversations. Back home she would feed it fish stew, her every muscle tense as she heard the clatter of the beach patrols passing by her house. And in her bed, over the days, the thing grew stronger.

'This reminds me of evenings I spent with Borys. My husband,' she said softly one night. 'Just whiling away the hours, content in our company.'

The village was quiet. When she had checked the curtains earlier that evening she was sure she had seen a figure silhouetted on the headland, but when she looked again it had gone. There was no sound from Agata's cottage next door, no sound of the beach patrols. Perhaps they had given up? Maybe it was safe to move it back to the sea, although when she thought of being on her own again Katalina felt the silence like a weight on her very soul.

The creature breathed raspingly through its mouth.

'He died?' it gurgled.

'Yes. For a long while I didn't believe it. I wouldn't accept it, but these waters are dangerous. Our people don't always come back.'

'Where do they go...' it said. 'Your people... when they don't come back?'

'We go to the Placid Shore,' she told it. 'On the other side of Shyish, far, far across the ocean. When we die, we wake on those golden sands, where it's always warm and bright and the sea is always bountiful. It's a wonderful place.' She smiled. 'I will see him there, one day, but...'

'What?'

She dropped the net in her lap. 'Some say that... if there's no body to bury, then the soul must wander above the waves forever...'

She wiped the tear from her eye. She smiled again, a brief, brave flash of certainty.

'But who can really say they know anything about the soul.'

She took up the net again, her fingers flicking over the rends. The creature stared. Was it smiling at her?

'When we were married,' Katalina went on, nodding at the window, 'we were handfasted on that beach. Our hands tied together by the weeds of the sea, and a prayer to the God-King to keep us safe. He was so handsome... I *will* see him again,' she said, suddenly fierce. She felt it burning in her. Let all the gods and monsters of the realms try to stop her, but she would see her love again, on this shore or the next.

She looked at the bed but the creature was sleeping now. The fire was low, a scattering of embers. Katalina placed the nets aside, took up her blanket and closed her eyes.

You really want to know...

That strange, squelched voice. The hiss of strangled air.

She snapped awake at once.

It was cold. The fire was dead in the grate. Darkness, a thin spear of light falling from the curtains across the floor. She felt her heart shudder in her chest. A smell in the air of deep oceans, blackness. Death.

There was a crash against the door – harsh shouts, the sound of breaking glass. Katalina lurched from the chair. The creature was awake. Had it been watching her? It dropped now from the bed, and from the counter snatched up her skinning knife. It hissed, the blade held back.

'What–' The room swam into focus. Something groaned and settled in her chest. She had been crying.

Another crash at the door. Behind it there were voices she recognised. She could smell smoke.

'Kat! Let us in, Kat, or we'll burn you out – you and that monstrosity you're hiding!'

Old Kenning, she thought? Oleg, and Rafal? These men knew her, why would they treat her like this?

'I've done nothing,' she screamed. She cast about the room, looking for a way out. As the first panel burst from her door, and as the blades and cudgels were thrust through, she screamed again. 'Leave me be!'

'You've been seen, Kat! Consorting with that thing!'

The creature stood there, drawing bright patterns in the air with the tip of the blade. There seemed such fury in it then, and even this wounded and weak she feared it could kill half the men out there in a heartbeat. Any cornered animal would do the same.

Flames licked up the window, staining the glass.

'This way, please!' She took its arm and its skin was like ice. 'Please – don't hurt them.'

The door burst from its frame. At the back of the house there was a cupboard where she kept her buckets and brooms, and she ran there through the cloying smoke. High in the wall was a single-paned window just wide enough to climb through, but as Katalina fumbled for the latch she felt rough hands against her shoulders, smelled the stink of rum. Oleg – she had heard him singing in the temple on Sigmar's Day, watched him help the fishwives haul their baskets, always smiling and laughing. And now here he was with hate in his eyes, grabbing at her hair and trying to pull her back into the smoking hall.

'Oleg! Please…'

'Where is it?' he barked at her. 'Tell me!'

'Why are you doing this?'

The point of a blade flashed then like a silver tongue from his open mouth. She watched the slow horror on his face as the life slipped from him in a gout of blood. The creature drew the knife from the back of Oleg's head and threw his body down.

'Where?' it said.

Her fingers moved in a dream, reaching for the latch and popping the window open. Her face was wet with tears, and the sea air was a cold kiss against her skin. From somewhere in the blazing night she thought she could hear Agata's delighted cackle.

Katalina dropped from the window and sprawled into the muck. The creature leapt and landed beside her. Smoke was rising now from the cottage behind them, smoke and flames. The whole building was ablaze.

Gone, she thought. *All of it, my life. Gone. Oleg, I'm so sorry – it thought it was helping me, I swear…*

'Sigmar's Light! Katalina, step aside from that thing!'

Radomir stood there on the path to the dunes, a stave in his hands. Despite his bulk, his presence in the world, he had never seemed more fragile to her then. Appalled, he looked from Katalina to the creature who held her.

'I'm sorry, Kat. I tried to stop them, but Agata saw it and – it's right there!' he shouted. 'The creature, it's–'

The words were only a moment from his mouth before the blade flashed once, quicksilver in the firelight.

Salt, metal, the last trickling murmur of his breath. A great fan of blood unfurled from Radomir's throat, cutting a crimson line across her face.

'Go!' the creature wheezed at her. 'Now. Run.'

It took the dune paths, sure-footed, clutching its wounded chest. Katalina stumbled after in a haze. The smoke curled around their feet. She thought of Radomir – saw, as if scoured into her mind, the sight of his head falling back, the gaping wound in his throat vomiting blood.

'What have you done?' she whispered. 'What have I done?'

The path rose ahead of her, and in the wavering dark, half-lit from the fire of the burning cottage, Katalina stumbled along it. Her eyes were stinging from the smoke and there was the taste of blood in her mouth. She dragged herself on, and when she reached the cemetery she fell amongst the graves, weeping. The creature was hunkered there behind a headstone, looking back on the village and her burning home. The cottage streamed flames into the night. Katalina could see the villagers milling there with their boathooks and clubs, shouting, some of them even laughing.

She fell back into the grass, utterly spent. The sea was a blurred presence beyond the headland, the vast waters in constant motion, heaving against the brittle shore. To range yourself against such a thing... what bravery it took, as brave as any soldier. And far on the other side, past all the reckoning of men, lay the Placid Shore where in time all souls will meet. Oleg and Radomir, and Borys...

I'm coming, Borys. I am done with this place.

The creature was looming above her, moving like a cold current in warm waters. It held the caged light in its hand, and that strange, submerged glow began to pulse. It compelled her, lured out the essence that was seeded into every cell of her body and every contour of her mind. As she felt herself pulled along into black oblivion she saw the light from the fire smear out into incandescence, the totems shiver on the beach – and then it was cold, so cold she couldn't bear it. She heard dark laughter in the distance, and some dim and smothered part of her reached out for the Placid Shore, those gentle waters and perfect sands, but then she was gone, and every motion of her body was fluttering away into nothing, like spindrift, like the cresting foam untethered from the waves when the wind begins to blow, just a scrap of foam adrift and floating on a violent tide.

They found her body amongst the graves. Most thought she was dead. Some swore they felt the flutter of a pulse, but others were convinced that she would never wake. 'The sea sickness', they called it. There was no cure; everyone knew that. They placed her with Radomir's and Oleg's bodies in a back room of the mead hall. The next morning there would be a meeting to discuss what had happened – early, because a mist was rising across the water, ill-omens from the deep. The widow tides were up.

GRAHAM MCNEILL

NO GOOD DEED

They found the burned man on the frothed shores of a sump pool at the edge-drifts of the wastes. The last shift klaxon echoed from the ashward manufactories, and it was long past time for them to get back within the walls of the schola progenium. But the opportunity of a maybe-dead body was too enticing to let slip away.

Strang was looking to rob him; Pasco thought it'd be funny to push him further into the toxic sludge to see if he floated. Zara wanted them to drag him from the muck, but she was always the one with the biggest heart. Probably why Cor was a little in love with her, even if he could never bring himself to say that out loud.

'Go on,' said Strang, elbowing Pasco in the ribs. 'Check him. Big fella like him's bound to have a few credit chits on him.'

Pasco shook his head. 'I ain't touching him,' he said.

'You scared?' said Strang, bending to pick up a length of corroded rebar. He gave the body an experimental prod. 'Think he's some ash-scavvy, gonna get up'n bite ya?'

'Ain't clever to touch dead meat,' said Pasco. 'Sister Caitriona says corpses down here get all yukked up inside. Says spine-worms nest up in 'em. That's bad goo, Strang!'

'Yeah,' said Cor, bending down to get a closer look at the dead man. He was big; bigger than anyone Cor had ever seen, but his flesh was pale and wasted, like he'd been powerful once, but somehow the bulk had been sucked out of him.

His skin was punctured across his chest and arms, with what looked like plastek rings around the holes.

'What d'you reckon they are?' asked Cor.

'Look like medicae shunts,' said Zara.

'See!' said Pasco. 'Told ya. Sick, he is. Looks like he got ash-blight or summat.'

'Nah, they don't put medicae shunts like that in folks who're gonna die,' said Strang. 'Sister Caitriona's got a couple in her back.'

Cor nodded, though he wondered how Strang knew that.

The man had taken a bad blow to the head, and one of his legs was bent at an angle that made Cor wince. He looked into the haze overhead, past the dripping pipes and hissing vents worked into the stained rock of the cliffs to the soaring silhouette of the hive spires in the sulphurous yellow clouds.

Had the man fallen from somewhere there?

'Who'd y'reckon he is?' said Pasco. 'A heretic that got left behind when the Fists kicked the rest of 'em back to the Eye?'

'I don't think so,' said Cor, kneeling and pointing to the remains of an eagle tattoo, partially obscured by a nasty burn on the dead man's shoulder. 'Don't know of any heretics wear the Aquila, do you?'

Pasco shrugged and said, 'This guy got smacked up hard. Looks like a Dreadnought beat on him.'

The dead man groaned and rolled onto his back.

Cor yelled and fell back on his haunches. The others laughed as he scrambled to his feet. Zara helped him up and he wiped the grime from his patched and worn out breeches.

'This son of a grot-rat's still alive!' said Cor.

'Not for long, he ain't,' said Strang, and Cor saw him toying with the idea of sending the man to meet the Emperor with the sharpened bolt-shiv he kept in his pocket.

The older boy claimed to have bled three people, once boasting he'd even killed a slumming uphiver who wouldn't take no for an answer. Cor didn't know if that was true, but Strang had a quick temper and wasn't above using his fists on the smaller kids of the schola progenium.

'Don't,' said Cor, placing his hand on Strang's arm.

Strang threw off his hand and pushed him away. 'Don't you touch me! I'll bleed you deep and good!'

Cor backed away, his hands raised. Strang's normally sallow complexion was ruddy and his bloodshot eyes were wide with fury.

'Easy, Strang,' said Cor.

The boy coughed and spat a wad of dark phlegm into the pool.

'Help... me,' said the wounded man, holding a wasted and burned arm out towards them. His hairless scalp was coated in vivid red blood, and fragments of broken glass were embedded in his skin. 'Now...'

Zara stepped between Cor and Strang.

'Enough, you two,' she said, pushing them apart with a confidence Cor wished he possessed. 'We have to help this man.'

'Why?' said Strang. 'Don't look like he's gonna live, even if'n we *could* drag him out. You seen the size of him?'

'That's not the point,' said Zara, fixing Strang with a stare that had seen kids much older do what she wanted. 'That eagle tattoo tells me he's a fella as needs our helping. And anyhow, where'd you be if Sister Caitriona hadn't taken you in, Orson Strang? You'd be dead or worse in the forge-mines of the Mechanicus, that's where. So I'll hear no more from you on this. We're helping this poor man and that's that. Am I clear?'

'As up-spire air,' replied Strang.

Cor hid his grin as Strang nodded like a broken servitor and moved his hand away from the bolt-shiv.

The man was heavier than he looked, and it took their combined efforts to lift him from the pool. They hoisted him between their shoulders, groaning under his weight.

The man winced as his leg banged into a jutting piece of exposed pipework, and he turned pain-filled eyes on Cor.

Dark and depthless like a pool of clean oil, they were set in an impossibly wrinkled skull, rheumy with age and gunky cataracts. His breath reeked and his skin smelled like the vents around the crematoria.

Strang was right; this fella likely wasn't long for this world.

'Hey, what do they call you, old man?' he asked.

The man slumped between them, blinking in confusion, as if trying to dredge a memory up from an impossibly dark abyss.

'I don't... I don't remember,' he said.

When the Departmento Munitorum first built the Saint Karesine schola progenium in the lower reaches of Agri-Hive Osleon, they envisioned an institution dedicated to crafting new generations of officers for the Astra Militarum. Filled with orphans made in the First Equatorial Rebellion, it had been a magisterial edifice of ironwork columns, mosaic-frescoes depicting the heroes of the early Imperial crusades, and wide steps leading to its grand portico.

More than two hundred orphans of that war had been raised within its walls, many of whom had gone on to lead traitor regiments in the *Second* Equatorial Rebellion, forever poisoning its reputation and tainting the heroism of its later progena.

In the three centuries since then, the institution's fortunes had further waned as sector-adjacent crusades shifted vectors and that ill reputation had settled upon its walls like a curse. Uphive nobility and the commissars of the Officio Prefectus eventually decided they'd wasted enough time and effort on its upkeep, and that the sons and daughters of the Astra Militarum would be better served in other Imperial institutions.

As the hive grew and the influx of orphans dwindled, the Saint Karesine schola progenium became something of a joke among Osleon's sump-dwellers and juve-gangs. Its once-mighty roof leaked, the basement dormitories were partially flooded with noxious runoff, and the pipes supposed to pump warm air around its many rooms now spread fumes that smelled like an ogryn's crotch.

At last headcount, a mere thirty-three progena slept with any regularity at Saint Karesine's.

Cor and the others barged through Saint Karesine's front door, scattering a bunch of the younger kids prying nails out of the warped floorboards. The old man hadn't said much that made sense since they'd struggled to drag him from the pool, just some gibberish about someone named Nesh. Cor didn't know the name.

Maybe it was whoever had jumped him.

'Sister Caitriona!' shouted Zara. 'We need your help!'

The door to the prayer rooms swung open on rusty hinges and the mistress of Saint Karesine's emerged, wiping one hand on her grimy robes. The other hand gripped the leather-wound hilt of a long-bladed chainsword that hadn't housed a powercell in decades.

'What's all the noise?' she demanded. 'I'll have no shouting here!'

Sister Caitriona towered over the children in her care. Dressed in the flowing robes of the Orders Hospitaller, she was a dark-skinned woman with an augmetic arm she alternately claimed was the result of an ork cleaver or a tyrannic monster.

Her hair was shorn close to her scalp, and despite her severe appearance, Cor thought she was the most beautiful woman he'd ever seen. Apart from Zara, of course.

Sister Caitriona had stayed on even when the coffers ran dry and every other member of staff had left in search of more fulfilling roles. She took one look at the injured man and said, 'Strang and Pasco, you boys take him to the back dormitory.'

Cor shucked the old man from his shoulder, relieved to be rid of his weight and his smell. He went to follow after the others, but Sister Caitriona stopped him with a gentle hand on his shoulder.

'Corvus,' she said. 'Wait here, there's something I need to tell you.'

She knelt beside him with a wince and creak of popping joints.

'It's about your brother,' said Sister Caitriona, and Cor felt a cold hand make a fist over his heart.

'Nicodemus? He...'

'I'm sorry, Cor, but the blight–'

'Stop,' said Cor. 'Your voice only goes like that when someone dies.'

The back dormitory was quiet, its occupants mostly asleep.

Ever since the roof of the actual infirmary had collapsed, Sister Caitriona used this long, high-ceilinged room as an ad-hoc infirmary, and a dozen beds were occupied by children with rasping coughs or any number of the sicknesses that stalked the lower reaches of the hive.

Cor sat on a stool next to Nicodemus' bed with his head hung low over his chest. Tears and snot coated his lips in a greasy film, and he wiped them away with his sleeve. Cor held his older brother's hand, still finding it impossible to imagine he was gone.

Nicodemus had been three years older than Cor, built like one of the Adeptus Astartes and twice as mean. He'd looked out for Cor ever since their parents, a captain and a strategos savant, had been killed when their Aquila crashed over the ash wastes.

His older brother had put out three of Big Augie's teeth when he kept stealing Cor's water ration, and had gone in search of two uphive nobles who'd thought it was funny to throw rocks at Cor and his friends when they'd been walking by one of the exterior lifters.

And now he was gone. The ash-blight had gotten into Nicodemus' lungs and he'd deteriorated fast, his skin losing what little colour it had and his eyes filling with black fluid. A hacking cough had bent him double until he was retching blood onto the sheets every day. Counterseptics didn't help, nor did any of the medicines Sister Caitriona was able to obtain from her Order.

Nicodemus had rallied over the last few days and had been able to keep down some moist bread and soup. Cor had heard of folk who'd recovered from the blight and his heart had soared at the prospect of his brother beating this sickness like he'd beaten everything else in life.

Now he was dead and Cor was truly alone.

He rummaged in his pocket and pulled out a tiny mechanical toy he'd been given by a pretty girl on the day his parents had died. A tiny clockwork dancer, he'd treasured it all through the years, but now he just wanted to smash it to pieces. Tears spilled down his cheeks, but instead of breaking the dancer, he placed it in Nicodemus' palm and closed his cold fingers over the warm metal.

'You take her. I hope she dances for you at the Emperor's side.'

'He was your brother?'

Cor pulled the filthy sheets up over the dancer and turned on his stool. The old man they'd brought in was awake. He'd drifted into unconsciousness almost as soon as Strang and Pasco laid him down, and Sister Caitriona had warned them he might not wake up. Zara had cleaned the blood from his head wound and Sister Caitriona stitched it closed before wrapping the man's hairless head in clean bandages.

'Yeah, he was.'

'The… What was it you called it? The blight?'

Cor nodded and the old man let out a wheezing sigh. 'You have my sympathies. I have seen many people succumb to all manner of sicknesses over the years. It is never easy.'

Cor wanted to tell the old man to shut up, to stop talking, but Sister Caitriona had taught him better than that. The man was a guest in their house, and guests were always to be treated with courtesy.

'I wish he hadn't died,' said Cor, hating the childishness of his words as the tears flowed all over again. 'I wish I had him back again. I miss him.'

The old man swung his legs out from his bed, and Cor was struck by how wiry and muscular they were. The one that had been bent strangely was swollen and purple at the joint, but didn't seem to be giving the old man too much pain. The man reached over and handed him a square of soft cloth.

'To wipe your eyes,' he explained. Cor dried his tears and handed the cloth back to the old man, who neatly folded it and placed it under his threadbare pillow.

'What's your name, boy?' asked the old man.

'Cor. It's Cor.'

'Is that short for something?'

'Corvus. Sister said he was some important man from history.'

The old man nodded. 'He was one of the Emperor's Primarchs. A hero, they say. Didn't your parents teach you any history?'

Cor shrugged. 'I don't remember. They died when I was little.'

'Ah, well, one should always pay attention to history. Those who don't will only repeat the mistakes of the past,' said the old man, reaching up to touch the wound on his scalp.

His fingers came away tipped with blood.

'Does that hurt?' asked Cor.

'No,' said the old man. 'I imagine it should, but I do not feel anything. Is that a good or a bad sign, do you suppose?'

'I don't know.'

'Bad, I should think,' said the old man. 'Pain should be

embraced, it keeps us alive and teaches us valuable lessons. It tells us not to be so stupid the next time we think of trying something reckless.'

The old man twisted around to take in his surroundings.

'Tell me, boy, where am I? I don't recognise this place.'

'Saint Karesine's,' said Cor, wiping his eyes dry again.

'A schola progenium?'

Cor nodded.

'How did I get here?'

'Me and the others found you in a sump pool at the edge-drifts. Looked like you'd been attacked or you'd fallen from higher up the spire.'

'Like I'd fallen?'

'Yeah, maybe from one of the commercia levels.'

'How curious,' said the old man.

'Hey, do you remember your name yet?'

The old man looked thoughtful for a moment, his brow furrowing as he chewed his bottom lip.

He shook his head. 'I'm afraid not, but I expect it will come in time.'

'So what we ought to call you 'til then?'

'I'll tell you what, boy, why don't you pick a name until I can remember my real one?'

Cor sniffed and wiped his face with his other sleeve. He smiled and said, 'How about Oskyr?'

'Oskyr?'

'Was the name of a cliff-hawk I had when I was real young. It was my friend until it bit me then flew away.'

The old man laughed, the sound thin and reedy, but full of genuine amusement. He nodded and said, 'Oskyr. Yes, that will do.'

The old man stood, testing his bruised and swollen leg. It held his weight and seemed to satisfy him. Drawing himself up to his full height, Cor was struck by how tall he was.

The old man smoothed his long shirt down and cleared his throat.

'The children in this room? They are all suffering from blight?'

'Most of them, yeah.'

'Then we must get to work,' said Oskyr. 'Tell me, Cor, do you have any medicae supplies in the building?'

Cor shrugged. 'I dunno. Maybe Sister Caitriona has some. Won't be much, though.'

'Then you must ask, boy! We will need supplies if we are going to heal these souls!' cried Oskyr, with a sudden burst of energy. 'I'll not have such kindness as you and your Sister Caitriona have shown me go unrewarded.'

'Are you a medicae?' asked Cor. 'Can you heal them?'

Oskyr grinned and gave a curt bow.

'I believe I may have some skill in such matters,' he said.

Cor and Oskyr set to work immediately.

Sister Caitriona had been sceptical at first, but when the old man outlined his plan for the care of the sick children, she reluctantly allowed Oskyr to stay.

There had never been credits enough to keep a proper medicae on staff, so the prospect of Oskyr's help was too good to forego. The children set to work sweeping the back dormitory and warming it with fires banked in the grates. Blankets were washed in boiling water and Oskyr prepared a list of supplies he required.

Sister Caitriona excused herself from the room whenever supply runs were discussed, claiming she couldn't know the details of how they planned to obtain what was needed.

As the days and weeks passed, Oskyr's health improved markedly, though his memory remained clouded and no hints of how he had come to be lying bloody returned to him.

Cor and Zara went out together, hitching lifts up into the upper reaches of the hive on the exterior risers, and swinging from the bridge chains to reach the glassed-in commercia. The victory celebrations following the Archenemy's defeat on Gandor's Providence were winding down, and Agri-Hive Osleon was suffering a collective hangover.

The storekeepers were tired and less vigilant, but pilfering their goods was dangerous work and the hive wardens were still out in force. Everyone in the up-spire districts knew to look out for guttersnipes from below, and the shopkeepers were wary as soon as a sun-starved face showed itself. The children worked in pairs, one distracting the shopkeeper while the other darted in to steal what they needed.

Strang and Pasco hit the Mechanicus yards in the forge levels, making off with rubber tubing, glass beakers and flasks, crucibles, mortar and pestles, as well as a host of items whose purpose was a mystery. Other children procured ingredients from a variety of other sources, many of which seemed strangely at odds with the notion of healing. Over the course of five days, the progena of Saint Karesine's stole a small fortune in equipment and ingredients.

Then the real work began.

Saint Karesine's became a hive of activity, with a fully stocked infirmary of sorts set up in a section of the basement that wasn't completely flooded. Fluid from bubbling vats was drawn through yards of pipes and filters, dripped into spherical beakers and boiled before being mixed with powders, tinctures and acrid chemicals. The schola progenium was filled with sweet vapours that cleared throats and kept the occasional algal-blooms at bay where it vented into the outside world.

Cor acted as Oskyr's assistant, mixing vials of strangely coloured liquid and grinding powders with the mortar and pestle. He laboured night and day, and often the old man would carry Cor to his bed in the upper dormitory with paternal affection and lay him to rest.

Oskyr himself was no less tireless in his researches, working long hours to find the perfect balance of medications. By this time, Oskyr – or Papa Oskyr as he was now known – was as much part of Saint Karesine's as Sister Caitriona.

Progress was slow, but over the course of only a few weeks, the children in the back dormitory began to respond to Papa Oskyr's treatments. First in ones and twos, then in ever greater numbers they began to recover until, at month's end, the last child was given a clean bill of health.

Finally, the schola progenium didn't feel like a sick joke.

Cor woke one morning to the weak glow of light reflecting on the underside of pipework outside the cracked glass of his window. His head was pounding with a splitting headache and he groaned as he sat up in bed. The dormitory was deserted, every bed except his and Zara's empty and with the sheets pulled back. Zara sat on the bed across from him, pinching the bridge of her nose between her thumb and forefinger.

'Morning,' Cor said, his tongue struggling to form the words, and his thoughts moving sluggishly, as if through a thick fog.

'It's morning?' she said, blinking and rubbing her eyes with the heels of her palms. 'I hadn't noticed.'

'I think I see light,' said Cor, wiping a clear patch in the window's grime and peering out.

She nodded and said, 'Damn, it's hot in here.'

Cor leaned down and put a hand out towards the wire-mesh grille on the wall next to his bed. Warm air blew softly from the vent, sickly sweet and curiously fragrant. Cor coughed and spat a mouthful of thick, gummy saliva into the chamber pot beside his bed.

'Feels like I spent too long in a chem-fug last night,' he said.

'Me too,' said Zara, wiping sweat from her brow.

'Did we?'

'No. At least I don't think so.'

'Would we remember if we did?'

Zara shrugged and yawned. 'You know where Pasco is?'

Cor shook his head and looked out through the window. The high clouds parted for a second and he thought he caught a glimpse of sky through the murk. He smiled to see light reaching this far down into the depths.

'I ain't seen him,' he said. 'Figured he went out late with Strang and Hetta. Maybe Oskyr sent them for some more compounds.'

'I thought I heard him come back.'

Zara rose from the bed, steadying herself on its iron frame. Cor offered her his arm and the two of them walked towards the doorway. Cor felt weirdly light-headed, exhausted from the late nights and all-day supply runs up-hive.

When this was all finished, he'd sleep forever.

They reached the top of the stairs and gingerly made their way to the lower hallway. Halfway down, something struck Cor as out of place.

'Can you hear anything?' he asked.

'No.'

'You ever know this place to be quiet?' asked Cor.

Zara screwed up her face, as if he were asking her to describe the inner workings of a warp-engine. She gave up and simply shrugged, using the wall to support herself as she took the last few steps down to the ground floor. She made a half-turn and screamed at something beyond Cor's line of sight.

He ran down after her and it took him far longer than it should have to process the scene before him. A low-lying vapour drifted through the hallway, a noxious yellow green, and Cor covered his mouth at its reeking stench. He saw Sister Caitriona on her knees, her head resting on the floor in a pool of blood. Zara sank to the floor, staring in horror at the grisly sight.

'Sister!' cried Cor, and the fog wreathing his thoughts blew away like morning mist. He ran over to Sister Caitriona and lifted her shoulders, trying to shake her awake. 'What happened? Where is everyone?'

Sister Caitriona's forehead was bloody where it had been bashed on the floor, and her eyes were rolled back in their sockets. Thin ropes of greenish saliva drooled from her slack mouth. He saw the timber floorboards were splintered where her head had been lying. Cor tried to make sense of what he was seeing, but the only conclusion he reached was insane.

'Looks like she did this herself,' he said.

'What?' said Zara, pressing her hands over her mouth. 'Why would she do that? It don't make no sense.'

'None of this does,' said Cor, cradling Sister Caitriona's body in his arms and feeling his world come crashing down around him again.

He looked up as he heard a scrape of metal.

'Look out!' screamed Zara.

Cor threw himself to the side as a hulking form emerged from the door to the basement. He felt searing fire burn his shoulder, swiftly followed by warm wetness spilling down over his chest. He rolled to his feet in time to see Strang coming at him with his sharpened bolt-shiv. Its entire length was wet with blood.

'Strang? What are you doing?' yelled Cor.

'I'll kill you!' yelled the older boy. His eyes were wide and bulging, and yellow green saliva coated his lips.

'No, wait!' cried Cor, but Strang wasn't listening.

He charged Cor, swinging his bolt-shiv wildly. Cor ducked and threw a punch with his good arm. More by luck than judgement, it connected with Strang's chin and sent him sprawling. Pain shot up his arm from what was likely a bunch of broken fingers. Strang had a jaw like iron.

'I have to kill you!' yelled Strang, pressing his fists to his temples and drawing blood where the bolt-shiv sliced his skin. 'The worms in my head! It's the only way to get them out! Gnawing, gnawing me. They want your eyes, Cor! They're so pretty and wet!'

'Strang, please! What are you talking about?'

The older boy threw himself at Cor again, and this time there was no evading him. Strang's speed and strength was too great, and Cor was barrelled to the ground. The bolt-shiv stabbed down into his wounded shoulder again and he screamed in agony. He tried to throw a punch, to get his attacker off him, but Strang pinned his arm to his side.

'The worms, Cor! They wanna eat your eyes!'

Strang lifted his bolt-shiv high, ready to plunge it down into Cor's chest. He heard a screeching roar somewhere nearby. Cor screamed, but the blade never fell.

He looked up to see Strang staring in disbelief at the juddering teeth of a chainsword jutting from his chest. Blood dripped from its rusted edge. The blade tore clear and Strang toppled sideways, crashing to the floor with a bubbling sigh.

'But the worms are hungry...' said Strang, before the life fled his eyes.

Cor saw Zara standing over Strang with Sister Caitriona's chainsword held tightly in both hands. She was breathing heavily, looking down at the weapon she held. Whatever charge was left in the weapon died, and Zara let it fall from her fingers with a cry of horror. The ancient blade clattered to the floorboards.

'I killed him,' she sobbed. 'I killed him...'

Cor struggled to push himself upright, but only succeeded in propping himself up on one elbow. Thick mist was drifting from the basement, and Cor coughed, wincing as the wound in his shoulder sent a jolt of pain down his spine.

'You had to,' he said through gritted teeth. 'He was gonna kill us.'

She shook her head. 'No. No. No... this can't be happening. What's going on here, Cor?'

Before he could answer a blurred shape loomed out of the mist behind Zara. Cor shouted a warning, but it was too late. Tall and powerful, yet slender and wiry, the figure wrapped one arm over Zara's chest and planted another over her face. The bronzed mouthpiece of a rebreather covered the girl's mouth and nose, thick with wadded gauze that dripped chemicals from its outflow nozzle.

She struggled briefly, but whatever concoction was in the mask swiftly overcame her strength to resist. She slumped against the figure, who dropped her limp body to the floor.

'It never ceases to amaze me, all the different reactions to the chemicals,' said Papa Oskyr, looking down at Strang and Sister Caitriona. 'Of course, there will always be some individuals more resistant to the soporifics, and, given your natural immunity to the blight, I really should have suspected you might not have succumbed. Sloppy of me. I blame the blow to the head.'

Oskyr reached down and Cor flinched as a needle punctured the meat of his upper arm. He cried out as Papa Oskyr lifted him from the ground and slung him over his shoulder. Even bloodily wounded and groggy, Cor was stunned at the old man's strength.

'Who...?' managed Cor. 'Who are you?'

'I'm Papa Oskyr,' said the old man brightly as he bent to drag Zara by her hair. He bore them both into the back dormitory, propping Cor up against a bed and lying Zara on the floor next to him. Cor tried to get up, but whatever Papa Oskyr had injected into him rendered his limbs leaden.

It was all he could do to turn his head.

Every bed in the back dormitory was occupied, each figure's cheeks sunken and drained, their eyes fixed open and empty of life. A looping mass of rubber tubing ran from every bed to a pair of heavy tanks like a custom chem-lung rebreather rig. Viscous green fluid swirled in the tanks and brass-rimmed gauges were maxed out in the red.

'Why are you doing this?' said Cor. 'You *healed* them all…'

'Well, of course I healed them,' said Papa Oskyr. 'What good are *sick* people to me? Only fit and healthy specimens could provide what I needed to restore my physiology and memory.'

Papa Oskyr marched towards the rebreather tanks and checked the gauges. Satisfied by what he saw, he unhooked the pipes and slung the tanks onto his back. He fitted a fabric rebreather mask to the pipes and slipped it over the lower half of his face, leaving only his eyes exposed. Eyes Cor now saw were cold as napped flint.

'It has been quite diverting spending time here, and you have my thanks for giving me a place to hide from Imperial sweep teams while I healed, but, alas, all good things must come to an end, and I have much to do.'

'But… you wear the eagle…' said Cor, raising a trembling, palsied hand to point at Papa Oskyr's shoulder.

The old man glanced down at the pink flesh of his shoulder and the two-headed eagle tattoo there.

'Ah, yes,' he said. 'Didn't I tell you that history was important? You see, this eagle is special, Cor. This is the *Palatine* Aquila. My Legion was granted the honour of bearing this icon after we saved the life of the Emperor Himself during the Proximan Betrayal. In hindsight a foolish act, but we weren't to know that at the time.'

Papa Oskyr marched back down the chamber towards Cor, and squatted next to him. He reached inside the pocket of a wet coat that looked like three coats sewn together, and withdrew a small mechanical dancer, the one Cor had placed in the cold hand of his brother. The old man closed Cor's numb fingers over the toy and placed his other hand over his heart. His head cocked to the side as he listened.

'Your heart flutters like a little bird, boy, it's just aching to be free,' said Papa Oskyr, reaching into another of his coat's pockets. Cor tried to speak, but nothing came out.

Something sharp and metallic glinted at the corner of his eye.

'This may hurt,' warned Papa Oskyr.

Saint Karesine's schola progenium burned with bright, promethium-rich flames as Papa Oskyr strode down the steps of its grand portico with the spry vigour of a young man.

Not only was his physique restored, but his memory also.

His name was not Oskyr, it was Scaeva, and he was of the lineage of Primarch Fulgrim, Lord of the Emperor's Children. Long ago, he had served as an Apothecary, and – in a sense – he still did, albeit for a pallid master who scoured the depths of sensations possible in post-human flesh.

Scaeva paused at the bottom of the steps and watched as a crowd of sump-dwellers gathered to watch the growing inferno.

Imperial citizens liked novelty, and even the most macabre sights would draw a crowd. But he couldn't linger, not when there was work to be done.

Fighting alongside Hellbreed's Hounds of Abaddon on their failed invasion had been a terrible misstep, and he'd lingered too long in search of interesting flesh for his master's surgeries. He'd been cornered by a squad of loyalist Adeptus Astartes, trapped and wounded, before being hurled from the highest levels of the hive by a vengeful Imperial Fist.

He'd fallen over a kilometre, careening from stanchion to rooftop to pipe. Such a fall would have killed almost anyone else, but his master had elevated his flesh and bone beyond mortality, to something akin to godhood. A mere fall was not enough to end him.

How long had he lain in that pool?

Months, most likely, his life sustained only by his inhuman physiology entering a low-level dormancy and cannibalising its own mass to stay alive.

Judging by the state of his skeletal frame and memory loss when the progena had found him, it had been a close run thing. But he was alive, and he had to contact his fellow legionaries.

And secure fresh test subjects.

His master's great work must continue.

Scaeva adjusted the tanks on his back and took a deep breath of the sump level's distinctive atmosphere. This was air with *character*, air that had been around the hive's lungs more than a few times to acquire a texture all of its own.

He'd missed such flavours.

Only the toxin-laden air of Chemos, rich with the aroma of dying souls, possessed the same tang.

Yes, decided Scaeva, this tasted of *home*.

Lora Gray

Crimson Snow

The battle began with snow, heavy and rushing from a late winter sky. It drifted high in the ancient ash groves where the soulpods grew. It shoved past evergreens and into the sylvaneth forest. It pummelled the vast field beyond, where the armies of Chaos and the Wargrove of Winterleaf collided.

Night fell.

Snow deepened.

Young dryads, too small to join the Wargrove, huddled at the edge of the forest, their arms and branches twined together for warmth. The Song of War pounded through them, but the rumble of charging soldiers, the sharp clamour of claw on metal, the screams and dying sounds, had faded into the distance. They could see and hear practically nothing, and Kalyth was impatient.

She untangled herself from her sisters and, hands on her hips, marched to the edge of the tree line. The wind stung her cheeks. Snow bit her eyes.

They had been ordered to wait in the forest, to tend their wounded brothers and sisters when the battle ended. They were the last line of defence against the servants of Chaos, should the Wargrove fail. But it had been an hour now since sunset and they knew nothing of what was going on, out there in the dark.

Kalyth needed to do *something*.

Jaws clenched, she pulled herself into the low boughs of an evergreen. The tree was massive, large enough to hold a young dryad if she was careful. If she could climb high enough to see above the constant swirl of snow, maybe she could get a better sense of the battle. Bracing herself against the evergreen's trunk, Kalyth stretched, pulling herself up.

Her foot slipped.

A broad, clawed hand steadied her from below. Kalyth looked down and saw Idrelle, her face pinched against the snow, her branches whipping in the wind.

She helped heft Kalyth up and onto the branch. 'Can you see anything?' she asked.

Kalyth ascended two more branches before inching gingerly forward. Even in the daylight, there hadn't been much to see. The Wargrove's front line had dissipated hours ago, spreading wide as the dryads and branchwraiths, noble spirits and outcasts drove the servants of the Dark Gods from the forest, away from the soulpod grove. Now, in the dark...

Kalyth shook her head. 'I can't see much at all.'

But deep inside, she could feel the Song of War beginning to slow. Maybe the battle was finally dying?

A pair of warriors burst through the driving snow to the left of the evergreens, locked together and heaving, startling Kalyth so badly that she almost fell. Idrelle flattened herself against the tree's trunk with a yelp.

The warriors tumbled closer, a tangle of thick limbs and armour and claws; struggling, grappling until one of them broke away. His mask was half-shattered and askew, the long mouthpiece bent nearly in half. Kalyth glimpsed blood beneath the broken patchwork of metal, a human face, shredded nose to jaw and panting. The cultist took a halting step towards his opponent, the wind snagging his ragged cloak away from his body as he raised a jagged axe. The cultist stumbled. Grunted. And then, as if surprised by the blood spreading from the hole in his belly, he collapsed into the snow.

For a moment, Kalyth thought the cultist's opponent was one of their own enclave, perhaps one of their older sisters, but as the warrior rose and turned, Kalyth saw blue skin, a wide and dripping mouth, eyes flashing and wild. She had never seen an outcast so close before. He reared back, long claws splayed, and screeched. The sound shook the branch beneath her and she clung tight as the outcast pounced on the cultist's body, yanking armour and flesh away in grisly chunks. He ripped meat from the cultist's throat with his teeth, wrenched the axe from his dead hand and split his skull with it. He tore the cultist's arm from its socket with one savage pull and flung it across the field.

The arm arced high into the air, buffeted by the wind. It tumbled end over end and landed with a soft thump at the edge of the tree line.

The outcast's eyes shifted from the arm's trajectory to the trees. His gaze slid over Idrelle and then, slowly, climbed the evergreen and landed on Kalyth.

Below her, Idrelle whispered, 'No, no, no.'

The wind howled. Snow whipped between them. The outcast panted. Snorted. Stared.

Kalyth tried to tell herself the outcast wouldn't hurt them. He fought alongside their Wargrove, after all, even though he called Drycha Hamadreth queen and not Alarielle. He was more like them than not, wasn't he? Even with that scar puckering one side of his face like a long, sideways grin. Even though he trembled with bloodlust. Even though he was utterly, utterly mad.

Gristle dripping from his chin, the outcast cocked his head. His lips crawled away from his teeth. A smile? A snarl? He took one lurching step towards them. And then, with a roar, he turned and dashed away across the field.

As soon as it was clear the outcast wasn't turning back, Idrelle whispered, 'Cover your mouth.' Her voice quavered.

Kalyth could see the outcast still, a dark, loping figure in the gusting snow. 'Cover my mouth?'

'You don't want to catch the outcasts' madness, do you?' Idrelle gave the tree a shake. 'Cover your mouth!'

'He saved us,' Kalyth murmured.

'That doesn't make him any less mad!'

'Do you suppose he was a spite once? Or was it tainted soil that turned him? I heard there was a soulpod grove south of here that was cursed when–'

'Kalyth!'

Kalyth finally looked down at her sister. Idrelle's hand was plastered over her own mouth, her face bright with fear. Sighing, Kalyth descended. 'You worry too much,' she said. 'Outcasts aren't creatures from some sapling bedtime story. Besides, how can madness be contagious? It isn't wood blight.'

'You don't know that! Nobody knows how the madness spreads!'

'Idrelle, he *saved* us. Did you see how he swung that axe?'

'Kalyth, please.' Idrelle was on the verge of tears.

Kalyth wanted to tell Idrelle she was being ridiculous. The stories they'd been told, about the outcasts' contagious madness, were just that, stories. But Idrelle was trembling when Kalyth dropped to the ground beside her.

Guilt sank into her and Kalyth moved to wrap her arms around her, to apologise, when the Song of War shifted. Wavered. Stopped. The Spirit Song returned, flowing softly through the sylvaneth.

The battle was over.

In unison, the young dryads at the edge of the forest lifted their heads. They emerged together, filing across the stormy field towards the remains of the Wargrove, to tend their wounded brothers and sisters and, in the deep night, mourn their dead.

* * *

It wasn't long before the young dryads separated to cover more ground. The field was almost as long as it was wide and between the distance and the snow, Kalyth soon lost sight of Idrelle and the others.

She was alone when she first saw one of her sisters, dead.

Her body lay like a fallen willow tree, torso curved and slumped, her branches spiralling away from her in the snow. Kalyth waded as quickly as she could through the deep drifts, calling out to her as she knelt, but as she rolled the older dryad onto her back, her head swivelled at an unnatural angle. Her broken neck was crooked so far to one side, Kalyth could see heartwood punching through her skin. Her lower jaw had been ripped away. Snow, black with blood and riddled with bark, slushed out.

Kalyth pulled her hands back as if she'd been burned. Grief soured her gut. She realised now, as she looked around her, just how dire the situation was. There, what she thought were uneven drifts were half-buried bodies. There, a broken branch resolved itself into an arm, frozen stiff and jutting skyward through the snow. That small rise was nothing but a smothered jumble of bodies, a dozen of them, broken, puzzled together and still. Dead faces emerged from the shadows, depressions became open mouths. Every icy glimmer was an open, sightless eye.

Kalyth wanted so badly to help. To do something. To be useful. But what could she do when so many were already dead?

Shivering, she pressed her hand reverently to her sister's forehead and stood, marking the spot for the branchwyches to find so they could harvest her lamentiri and take her soul back to the sylvaneth grove.

Kalyth had taken no more than a few steps when, out of the corner of her eye, she saw breath rising in short, cloudy bursts from the side of a snow bank.

Kalyth ran towards it.

As she dug the snow away from the trapped and dying warrior, she realised it was the outcast.

His body was crumpled. A trio of spears pinned him to the earth. His right leg was severed, his hip a pulpy stump leaking blood, sluggish and dark, into the snow. His branches were torn away. His left foot was mangled. His right arm was crushed. His remaining eye swivelled towards her.

The outcast opened his ruined, bloody mouth and laughed.

Every story the branchwyches had told her, every warning that seemed so silly at the time, snapped through Kalyth. *Don't breathe their breath. Don't look them in the eye. Never touch them. Nobody knows how the madness spreads. Cover your mouth. Don't breathe. You'll catch it.*

You'll catch it.

But this outcast had saved them, after all, whether or not that was his intention. Didn't he deserve some sort of comfort? How could she leave him there? How could she not help him?

Kalyth hesitated and then touched an uncertain hand to the outcast's heaving side. His head whipped back and he snapped his jaws, enraged, gurgling and growling.

Kalyth forced herself not to pull away. 'I'm trying to help,' she said and wished she could blame the way her hands trembled on the cold.

The outcast bit at her again, so hard this time that his bark cracked. The stump of his leg churned against the wet snow. Still pinned against her, he jerked, desperate and violent, and Kalyth realised, as his jaws snapped together again and again, faster, faster, that he would bite her hand off if he could.

Kill her, maybe, if he could.

Did he even understand she wasn't the enemy? That she was sylvaneth? Or had the madness robbed him of that too?

'I won't hurt you,' Kalyth said. Her eyes stung. Her throat tightened. 'I'm sylvaneth. Like you.' She wanted, so badly, for him to understand, to see some spark of recognition. Instead, the outcast keened, the sound needling through her ears and into her skull.

'Oh, please, don't do that.' Kalyth pressed both palms to his chest. 'I want to help. Please let me help.' Kalyth was so close she could see the ridges in his bark, all the gashes and scars, every blow, every cut and scrape and wound. His face twisted. His body arched as far as the spears pinning him allowed and then, with a whimper, he slumped back towards the ground again. The outcast's voice crumpled into silence. Kalyth felt a tremor race through him and his eyes widened. For a moment, his gaze was so clear, so intense, so frightened, that Kalyth could imagine the sylvaneth he had been before the madness took him.

Carefully, Kalyth stroked his shoulder.

He didn't try to bite her.

He drew a breath instead, deep and ragged. He looked up at her and exhaled, his feverish breath washing over her, tasting like lost summers and blood and dying things.

He convulsed one last time.

Kalyth held him until his body grew cold in her arms. As the silence stretched around her, she thought she heard a whisper. It didn't sound like the Spirit Song. It was infinitely softer. Infinitely more mournful and deep.

Kalyth looked up. The snow was still falling but, for a moment, it wasn't white.

For a moment, it was crimson.

In the centre of the sylvaneth grove, where the evergreens gave way to ash trees, a thicket grew. The soulpods nestled there, spherical and shielded from the snow by a knot of low branches and thorns. They pulsed softly in the morning light. It wouldn't be long before new dryads emerged from them.

Kalyth wondered if the snow would still be there when they did. Would there even be enough sylvaneth to tend them?

There were so few of them left.

It wasn't until morning that the full impact of the battle became evident. The servants of Chaos had been driven back, but not before they devastated the Wargrove. They had lost nearly two-thirds of their army and the forest felt empty. There should have been branchwraiths with grave faces planning the next battle. There should have been dozens of dryads gathered beneath the evergreens, trading war stories, tending each other's wounds, grumbling or laughing in the cold morning light. There should have been noble spirits quietly listening to the Spirit Song, drifting between the trees, murmuring about the 'pettiness' of dryads, about how emotional and unstable and *loud* they were.

Only the branchwyches' numbers seemed untouched. They gathered in solemn circles, their broad backs hunched as they planted lamentiri after lamentiri, burying the souls they had harvested the night before in the cold soil.

The young dryads were silent, their heads bowed as they passed. Every one of those lamentiri was a sister or a brother, a friend, a face, a voice, a life. Even though the lamentiri would grow into new soulpods eventually, the memories and experiences that made each individual unique would never really return.

They had lost so many.

Kalyth felt physically sick with grief. It gnawed at her. It made her itch. She felt it like a living thing crawling through her in fits and spurts, as if the sorrow had grown legs and scuttled through her, racing through her and filling all the empty pockets inside.

Idrelle had been casting worried glances at her all morning and, as they reached the forest's edge with the other young dryads, she looped her arm through Kalyth's and pressed close. The snowstorm had stopped before daybreak and the field stretched before them, a pale sky against pale ground, smooth and rolling and still.

Kalyth tried not to think about what lay under the blanket of snow as the other dryads set out across it.

'You'll be careful, won't you?' Idrelle's voice was hushed, her body tense against Kalyth's side.

Kalyth squeezed Idrelle's hand, took a deep breath and tried to ignore the itching, the feeling of sickness. 'The rotbringers won't be that hard to find,' she said. 'Besides, scouting is a lot less dangerous than fighting. We'll all be back before nightfall.'

'But you'll be careful?'

Kalyth forced a laugh she didn't feel. 'I'm not planning on attacking them single-handedly, if that's what you're asking.'

Idrelle shifted, darted a look back at the forest. 'You shouldn't even be doing this. You're too young.'

'And you're not? Besides, who else is there?' Kalyth tried not to sound bitter. Idrelle wrapped her arms around herself, long claws ticking against her bark. 'It's just that we lost so many.' She sighed. 'I don't want to lose you, too.'

Idrelle always fretted, always worked herself into knots, even when there wasn't immediate danger. Now that there was, Kalyth didn't want to make it worse for her. Hands on her sister's shoulders, Kalyth rested her forehead against Idrelle's and met her gaze. 'I'll be careful. I promise.'

Idrelle nodded, her branches tickling Kalyth's. When she finally pulled away, she trailed her finger over Kalyth's cheek. 'You look unwell,' she said.

Kalyth felt unwell. She needed to put some distance between herself and the yawning emptiness of the forest. The memory of the field. The outcast dying in her arms. She could almost feel the heat of his last breath ghosting over her still.

'I'm fine,' Kalyth said.

'Are you certain? Maybe you should...'

'I'm *fine*.' Kalyth gave Idrelle's arm a squeeze. 'Let's go. The day isn't getting any longer.'

* * *

It wasn't until the sun was directly overhead, watery and pale, that Kalyth realised she had wandered west. She was far from where the armies of Chaos should have been. Boulders littered the landscape, rising up all around her like angry fists. In the distance, a blue-grey ridge arced skyward like a spine. The trees were sparse and small. The wind moaned, long and low.

According to the branchwraiths, the enemy would never camp here where there was so little cover.

Only the outcasts favoured this terrain.

But why had she come here? Why had she not realised where she was walking? It was as if her body had shrugged her mind away and drifted to this place of its own volition. She didn't remember the journey at all and it was unsettling, as if slowly surfacing from a dream.

Disoriented and dizzy, Kalyth leaned against a boulder and took in a lungful of sour, sulphuric air. She had the inexplicable urge to keep going, to let her legs carry her up and over that ridge. She envisioned summiting the blue-grey rock, looking down at an encampment full of outcasts, dangerous as a cluster of thunderclouds waiting to storm.

Kalyth shook herself and pushed away from the boulder. She needed to finish her mission, to scout the ground she'd been assigned, or she'd never make it back to the grove before dark.

Kalyth started back the way she came, but that itching, that horrible sense of something *wrong*, blossomed through her again. It was stronger than it had been in the forest. It was swelling. Spreading. It felt as if a thousand thousand *somethings* simmered in her legs and arms, and Kalyth knew it wasn't grief over her fallen brothers and sisters that she felt.

Something was inside her.

Cover your mouth, Idrelle had said. *Nobody knows how the madness spreads!* Kalyth's heart lurched. Had she been infected by Chaos after all? No. There had to be a simpler explanation.

Parasites perhaps? Kalyth's body was as much a part of the natural world as the trees themselves and sometimes other creatures made her their home. Perhaps the morning sun nudged a colony of insects from their winter sleep and they had burrowed into her for warmth?

As Kalyth walked, she tried to disregard it, but the itch intensified. Every step she took seemed to drive it deeper. She felt it in her hands, the crook of her elbow, the socket of her hip, places so deep she couldn't begin to scratch them.

Last summer, a colony of beetles had burrowed into her left calf, just beneath the thick bark of her skin. Kalyth remembered the scrape of their mandibles, the horrible tickle of their legs, wriggling, squirming. It wasn't until the first frost that she had been able to finally pluck their still bodies out. The carapaces had fallen onto the frozen ground at her feet, small and upturned, their wings half folded, their legs crooked and bent. She remembered her surprise at how small they seemed. Crawling through her, they had been impossible to ignore.

But this was different.

This itch became a throb. The further Kalyth went, the worse it became until she wanted to scream in frustration, rip her bark away in long strips. A shudder wracked her, as if her body was trying to shake the bugs loose.

Kalyth moved faster. She felt feverish. She needed to scout the land quickly and return to the grove and huddle beside Idrelle, warm and safe in the familiar forest, feel her brothers and sisters all around her, close her eyes and let the Spirit Song of Alarielle comfort her. She tried to connect to it now, but the buzzing inside her made that almost impossible.

For one terrifying moment, she couldn't hear the Spirit Song at all.

Kalyth ran. She bounded through the snow in great, loping strides, the wind bitterly cold against her skin.

A deep gelatinous heave knocked her off her feet.

Kalyth fell headlong into a snow bank. Something in the centre of her chest pulsed, round and moving and very much alive. It shouldered its way deep inside. Kalyth tried to tell herself she was imagining it. Parasites didn't do that. Her body would push anything that dangerous out of her before it bored that deep, wouldn't it? But she could feel it pounding; a second pulse. If she closed her eyes, she could almost see it there, coiled against her heart, bigger and brighter than all the other little things skittering through her.

Kalyth curled around herself.

She felt the Bright One shake himself in her chest. She felt his mouth shift, the hard press of his teeth from the inside as he smiled.

And then he spoke.

By the time Kalyth returned to the grove, the sun was setting. Sweat rolled down the crags of her bark. It took every ounce of effort not to dig at her own body. She was fevered, full of those thousand thousand horrible little things, the Bright One whispering over and over to her.

Don't you want us here? We just want to be warm. You're so warm. It's so cold out there. It's so cold. Please. Pleasepleaseplease.

Kalyth had spent nearly an hour on the ridge trying to ignore his voice, trying to dislodge the little ones that had somehow spread through her until it felt as if every inch of her was crawling with them. She beat her arms, pounded her palms flat against the boulders, plunged her feet and hands into snowbanks, hoping the cold would drive them out of her.

Nothing worked.

The little ones wormed into her ear canals. They squirmed around her jaw and into the roots of her teeth. And the harder she tried to get rid of them, the faster they moved. The Bright One chuckled softly, the sound vibrating against her ribs.

And as many times as she told herself what was happening was impossible, she could still hear him murmuring, whispering, sighing into her ear.

Now, Kalyth hurried across the snowy field. She needed to be home so very badly. She needed somewhere safe. Somewhere that made sense.

Idrelle waited for her in the copse of evergreens at the edge of the forest. The setting sun tossed shadows onto her face, violet and deep; so dark her eyes seemed as though they'd been spooned from her skull.

The Bright One hammered in Kalyth's chest and, for a moment, her vision hazed red. She didn't see Idrelle as she stood now, her mouth pinched with worry, one hand outstretched and wanting Kalyth to hold it. Instead, for an instant, Kalyth had a vision of Idrelle with her body broken and slumped against the evergreens. There were bloody holes where her eyes should have been and when Kalyth looked down, she saw those eyes, wet and round, in the snow beside Idrelle's upturned hand, bloody fibres trailing away like tails. It would be so easy to make that vision real. To reach up. To pluck those eyes out of Idrelle's skull. The Bright One wrapped his fingers gingerly around one of Kalyth's ribs. It would be so very easy. It would feel so good. All that blood. All that warmth.

'Kalyth, are you all right?' Idrelle's hand was cool when she touched Kalyth's face. 'You look even worse than you did before. Oh, I knew it. You *are* sick. You should have stayed here.'

The worry in Idrelle's voice sank through her. Kalyth shoved her panic aside and strained to clear her thoughts. She could control this. They were only parasites. Just a few bugs. There were bigger problems, an army swelling in the dark and waiting to attack and Kalyth wouldn't do anybody any good if she unravelled now. She needed to be strong.

For Idrelle, she needed to be strong.

'I'm just a little tired,' Kalyth said. Did she sound as breathless as she felt? Did she sound normal? 'I didn't find any enemy camps. Did you?'

Idrelle frowned, studying Kalyth carefully. The corners of her mouth were tight with concern, but she finally said, 'No. Berlyth did. Just south of the glassy lake. She said there were two hundred of the rotbringers there. The Wargrove is mustering at daybreak.'

'We're going to fight?'

'*We're* not. We've been ordered to hold the line at the edge of the grove. Oh Kalyth, don't look at me like that. Somebody needs to stay here. Besides, you don't look well. Are you sure you're not sick?'

The little ones scratched over Kalyth's shoulders, bubbled beneath the bark of her back. 'I just need some rest,' she said, and hoped against hope Idrelle believed her. When it was all over, she would tell Idrelle all about it. She would let Idrelle baby her and nurse her back to health. But for now, she needed to keep the truth of it to herself, for Idrelle's sake. For everyone's sake.

There were so few of them left.

As night settled over the forest and Idrelle nestled beside her in the grove, Kalyth told herself it was all for the best. Some secrets needed to be kept.

But she could still hear the Bright One whispering as she fell asleep.

Let us stay with you. You're so warm. And we're so cold. So hungry. We're starving. We're dying. We need you. We want you. Help us.

Please, help us.

In the dream, Kalyth stood in a pale field.

Tall grass rippled around her. Shadows hovered at the edges of her vision, though the sky was cloudless and lit by an indistinct sun. The air was hazy and thick. And everything, *everything*, was white.

Kalyth inhaled. The thick air slid into her nose and mouth like oil. It slicked the back of her tongue, rolled into her belly. Kalyth's chest tightened and she retched, but every time she opened her mouth, the liquid air poured in until everything inside of her sloshed.

But she could breathe. Her body pulled oxygen from the syrupy air like a fish inhaling water. Shuddering, Kalyth stilled herself and tried to concentrate on that. She wasn't dying. There was life flowing through her.

She reached for the Spirit Song, but it was slippery and she couldn't grasp it.

And then she realised she wasn't alone.

The parasites inside of her, those thousands of tiny squirming somethings, were all around her now, a slowly churning carpet where the grass had been moments before. Their bodies were bloated and gelatinous. Branches sprouted from their sides, tender new shoots above their stunted arms. Their heads wobbled on thin necks, their faces were wide-eyed and gaunt. They gazed up at her as they caressed her feet and ankles. They crawled up her legs and curled their tiny hands against her bark. They pleaded with her silently, vibrating with hunger and need, shaking desperation into her arms and chest.

They were so cold.

They were so hungry.

They needed blood.

They were dying.

They needed blood.

HelpusHelpusHelpus.

They needed blood.

The sea of tiny, bloated bodies quivered, and in the distance a mound rose from the earth beneath them. It ploughed languidly towards her, a giant rolling wave in an ocean of squirming bodies. It slowed to a stop in front of her and the Bright One emerged from beneath the blanket of his tiny siblings, letting them fall away from him as he stood, eye to eye with her. His skin glistened, his branches, so familiar, so much like a sylvaneth's, shimmered. His eyes shone.

A scar puckered the side of his face like a long, sideways grin.

We've been waiting for you, the Bright One said. The words coiled through Kalyth's mind, slow and steady. His lips didn't move. He laid his hand over his chest, fingers ticking over his colourless skin as if searching for something. He paused, grinned, and sank his fingers into himself, hand disappearing into a gummy wound. The Bright One's eyes fluttered, his grin widened, and when he slinked his hand back out again, he held an axe.

The axe was dripping when he handed it to Kalyth. A gory umbilical tethered its haft to the hole in his chest. The axe throbbed, that same slow thrum Kalyth had felt when the Bright One was inside her; a distant rhythm, a second heartbeat.

The little ones began keening. Wailing. Crying. They were so hungry. They needed her help. They *wanted* her help.

The shadows at the edges of the landscape detached and elongated, twisting and turning and growing, until they became bodies, faces, the servants of the Dark Gods rising from the pale earth.

Kalyth gripped the axe more tightly. How many of her brothers and sisters had these monsters killed? How many forests had they burned?

The Bright One stroked a smooth hand over her shoulder. *You know what you have to do,* he said.

Kalyth raised the axe.

The little ones clamoured up her legs, onto her arms, clung to her, dug their fingers into her. Thousands of needling hands, thousands of hungry, open mouths.

Kalyth rushed towards the nearest enemy, the Bright One beside her. There was no resistance when she swung, the blade cutting through armour and flesh as if through water. The dream world shuddered. Kalyth drew the blade out again. Blood fountained from the wound. The little ones scrambled off her, gleeful and diving into the river of blood, burrowing and sucking with their tiny, starving mouths.

The Bright One pressed against Kalyth. The axe, still tethered to his open chest, burned in her hands.

Again, he said.

Kalyth charged and swung. The world gushed red.

Again.

Blood rushed over her, hotter and faster, frenzied and full of jubilant need. Again she attacked, laughing, screeching, howling. It felt good; it felt so good, to finally do something. To attack, to let her rage bubble up and over like a spring. A geyser. A volcano.

When Kalyth finally stopped, gasping, blood raining from her branches, the ground roiled with parasites, their bellies pulsing red with gore. They cooed and purred, wriggling happily over her feet.

The axe hummed in her hand and Kalyth closed her eyes to let the rhythm of it settle into her, steady and powerful.

The Bright One nuzzled her ear and, even though there was nobody left to kill in the dream world, he breathed, softly, sweetly, *Again.*

Kalyth woke in the grove, the moon bright and full. The ground beneath her wasn't soaked with blood. Not yet. But she could smell it all around her, salty and sweet. Beside the frantic beating of her heart, Kalyth could still hear the Bright One whispering *Again.* Kalyth's hands clutched for an axe that wasn't there. Trembling, she sat up.

Idrelle lay beside her, her face soft, one hand looped around her own branches for comfort, the other outstretched where her arms had been wrapped around Kalyth. She didn't stir. Was she sleeping still? Kalyth wanted her to be. Because if Idrelle saw her now, feverish and full of bloodlust, she wouldn't be able to hide any of it from her.

And what if she did know? the Bright One whispered.

Kalyth couldn't seem to silence him now no matter how hard she tried, but the presence of him behind her thoughts was beautiful in its own way. Would sharing that beauty with Idrelle be so terrible?

Kalyth pictured holding Idrelle in her arms, her head against her breast. Maybe she'd be able to hear him, too. Maybe all the little ones would wrap their tiny hands around Idrelle's fingers. Maybe the Bright One would flow into her.

All she had to do was open Idrelle up.

It wouldn't be so hard.

She didn't need an axe. Her claws were her weapons. One slice, one carefully placed swing, would do it. She could hack into all the fleshy, woody parts of Idrelle and the Bright One and all his brothers and sisters could rush into her. And if Idrelle didn't want it, if she resisted, well then, her blood-sap would feed the little ones.

They were so very hungry.

Kalyth felt them jitter eagerly at the idea and the Bright One nudged Kalyth with a gentle hand. She leaned over Idrelle, one arm raised. Her claws glinted in the moonlight.

Idrelle stirred, frowning and fitful as she rolled onto her back, as if she could sense something was wrong. Idrelle was always so sensitive. How many times had she known something was wrong before Kalyth mentioned it? Idrelle cared for her, loved her.

She loved her so much.

The Bright One whispered how lovely it would feel, how warm. Idrelle's blood would be like velvet running over her skin. All

Kalyth had to do was drive her claws into the back of Idrelle's head, crush her body between her fingers, pop legs from hips, arms from shoulders, tear into flesh with her teeth and–

Breath hitching, Kalyth jerked upright. She staggered away from Idrelle, horrified. She lost her footing. Tripped. Turned. Ran. She crashed through the forest, past the ash trees and the soul-pods, through the copse of evergreens and into the field. Frost crackled beneath her feet as she sprinted across the snow and the little ones scampered into the warmer parts of her, coiled around her insides, fingers tugging, faces upturned and begging for heat and blood, blood and heat.

It wasn't until Kalyth reached the western ridge, towering blue-grey and cold, that dead landscape leading to the outcasts' camp, that she stopped. She collapsed against one of the boulders, her claws scraping against it, clenching and unclenching as she tried to gather herself together again, but she couldn't feel where the parasites ended and she began anymore. Everything was shifting, squirming, *moving*.

She looked up.

The Bright One stood beside her.

'You aren't real,' Kalyth whispered. She tried to believe it was true.

The Bright One chuckled. The little ones clustered around his feet, mewling as they wound between his legs. The Bright One reached out a hand. He stroked Kalyth's face tenderly. *What makes you say that?*

Shivering, Kalyth reached, one last time, for the Spirit Song, but there was nothing left to bind her to Alarielle or her brothers and sisters. There was nothing but an emptiness that seemed to stretch on forever.

Kalyth sank into the snow. The Bright One sank with her. Her hands trembled. Her insides quivered.

You know what you have to do, he said.

Kalyth clenched her teeth. 'You aren't real.'

The little ones crawled over her legs, inched onto her arms, around her hands, up and down the length of her claws.

'This isn't real.'

Cut. Kill. Break. Kill. Kill.

Kill.

'You aren't real!'

Kalyth's scream pierced the stillness. Claws whistling through the frozen air, shining, sharp, desperate, she raised her arm and swung. She struck her own body, pain razoring through her, searing, blinding, as she slashed at her branches, hacked into herself. The impacts shuddered through her and branch after branch fell into the snow at her feet. Cold snapped into the wounds. Sap and blood poured down her side and she swung again. Because the Bright One, the little ones, these *things*, whatever they were, weren't really beside her. They were in her body, in her head. And she would bleed them out, cut them out, if it killed her.

Kalyth swung again, woody pulp and bone splitting. She braced her left arm against a boulder. Locked her elbow. Swung. Her claw sliced through skin, bark, bone. Agony flared, a deep heave of pain. She swung again, awkward for the angle. She needed to get him out. All of them out. She swung. Again and again and again.

Her arm snapped in two with a wet crack. Shock. Pain. She looked down at the severed limb in the snow, her hand, palm up, clenching and unclenching still. Blood gushed from the stump of her arm.

With a sudden flare of light, the Bright One and all the little ones disappeared from her field of vision.

For a moment, Kalyth thought it had worked, that she was finally rid of them, but something jolted deep in her chest. Her heart tripped over itself. The Bright One squeezed, dug his teeth into a thick artery. He swelled, pushed himself against her organs, thrust hate and rage outward as if he could stopper the wounds with it.

Kalyth felt life rushing away from her and still, the Bright One shouted for her to kill. *Killkillkill!*

'Kalyth!'

Idrelle's voice snapped through waves of pain and Kalyth turned, severed branches littering the snow around her, what was left of her arm swinging, sopping and limp, against her side.

Idrelle bolted up the hillside, her hands outstretched as if she wanted to embrace her.

The Bright One roared.

The Bright One surged.

The Bright One shoved Kalyth away from herself, sliced her from her own body as surely as she'd sliced her own arm away and Kalyth watched helplessly as her body charged, her legs pumping against her will. Kalyth screamed, tried to warn Idrelle, but the Bright One's voice overtook her own. He flung her working arm back and leaped towards Idrelle. For a moment, Kalyth felt herself suspended, her body launched high into the air, and there was Idrelle below her, confused and terrified, as the Bright One sneered and swung Kalyth's claw at Idrelle's head.

Idrelle scrambled, skidding and sliding on the icy ground, narrowly avoiding the blow as Kalyth's body crashed to the earth. The impact shoved blood from Kalyth's mouth and nose. The claws of her hand lodged deep into the ground, wedged into ice and frozen soil. Kalyth bore down, trying to force her body to remain there, pinned to the earth so the Bright One couldn't attack again. But he took hold of her arm, his grip like a vice and he yanked at her buried claws with all his strength, trying to pull free, trying to kill Idrelle.

Kalyth screamed again as Idrelle moved into view and the Bright One kicked at her from the inside.

'Kalyth!' Idrelle's voice broke, her hands raised and defensive, her own claws ready. 'What are you doing?' Idrelle stepped closer and the Bright One snarled and heaved. 'You're hurt! Stop it! Stop!'

Kalyth gasped as the Bright One flared, thundering into every vein, every muscle, every pore. He wrenched her arm so hard Kalyth's claws shattered. Her fingers dislocated. The Bright One heaved Kalyth's body upright and rushed towards Idrelle, mouth slung wide, teeth like daggers, hand a cluster of broken, splintered spears.

Idrelle fell back, but she was prepared this time and her arm slammed into Kalyth's body as the Bright One attacked, knocking her away so sharply that Kalyth's body flew into the air. For one suspended moment, Kalyth saw the moonlit sky above her, and felt the wind, cold and terrible, whip into every open wound.

Kalyth slammed into the boulder spine first. A rib shattered. Her belly bulged where a jagged wedge of stone pierced her. Viscera drooled out of her back and onto the ground. She tried to inhale and couldn't. She couldn't move her arms. She couldn't move her legs. Her eyes were open, but blood was closing over everything. And there was Idrelle, kneeling over her and weeping.

Kalyth's breath bloomed over Idrelle's face, feverish and tasting like lost summers and blood and dying things. Idrelle watched as Kalyth's eyes unfocused. She watched her best friend die.

Idrelle pressed herself against Kalyth's ruined body and tried to beg the life back into her. She clutched Kalyth to her breast, the stump of her severed arm swinging against her side as she rocked her back and forth, back and forth.

She didn't understand why this had happened.

She didn't understand why.

Grief surged through her like a rainstorm, like a river. Every inch of her filled with it. She felt it like a thing alive. Like a thousand thousand somethings racing through her and wanting to fill her up. She felt it settle deep in her chest. She felt it grip her heart.

Idrelle wailed, low and long.

She held Kalyth until her body grew cold in her arms. As the silence stretched around her, Idrelle thought she heard a whisper. It didn't sound like the Spirit Song. It was infinitely softer. Infinitely more mournful and deep.

Slowly, Idrelle stood. Cradling Kalyth's body, she walked through the frozen landscape. But she didn't walk towards the sylvaneth grove. Instead, she moved without thinking towards the blue-grey ridge, travelling west towards the outcasts' camp where the land was rocky and still.

Just before dawn, it began to snow.

And the snow wasn't white.

It was crimson.

C L WERNER

LAST OF
THE BLOOD

Toshimichi felt a chill crawl through the hair on his arms as he stared up at the castle of Baron Eiji Nagashiro. The caprices of wind and sun had worn down the ancient walls, gnawing away at them like vultures picking at carrion. The outer battlements had crumbled away, lying in broken heaps around the foundations. Exterior towers were hollow shells, blank windows staring out across the desert, roofs reduced to skeletal beams and ragged patches of tile. The central courtyard was heaped with sand, great mounds that had drifted up against the inner walls. Only the central keep had managed to resist the elements, rearing up from the desolation in a series of tiered platforms with sharply angled overhangs and flared roofs. A narrow spire rose from its highest point and from its balcony a light shone, gibbous and forlorn.

The scholar clutched his robes more tightly, drawing them close about his body. The driving heat of the desert, intense even in twilight, could not offset the cold that gripped Toshimichi. His agitation was sensed by the demigryph that bore him across the sands. The half-bird clacked its tongue against the inside of its beak and stamped its feet in a display of uneasiness.

'There is no harm for you there,' Toshimichi told the animal.

He stroked its feathered neck and tried to calm its anxiety. The demigryphs of Arlk were renowned for their endurance, but also for their obedience. The most prized had an almost empathetic bond with their masters, sensing the intent of their riders without the need for command. Toshimichi's steed had picked up on his own reluctance to proceed. The animal, however, could not understand that sometimes a man must go where he did not want to go.

Sho Castle. Toshimichi had read much about this place... even before the deaths began. None of what he had read was to its favour. This, after all, was where the curse had started so long ago. His mother had had dreams of this place before she died. His brother had spoken of it that last night before he too...

Toshimichi focused on the beckoning light. He prodded the demigryph with his spurs and urged it onwards despite the feeling of dread that gripped him. 'I am expected,' he said. 'Baron Eiji has sent for me. It is unseemly to keep a baron waiting.'

The demigryph slowly advanced towards the ruined castle. Each step made Toshimichi's pulse quicken. The atmosphere of danger was palpable, but there was something else as well. The promise that had accompanied Baron Eiji's summons.

The promise of answers.

The promise that the curse could be undone.

Few improvements had been made to Sho Castle since Baron Eiji had reclaimed the fortress. The keep was largely barren, entire sections closed off and unused. The great hall in which Toshimichi was conducted by the baron's taciturn retainers seemed even more gigantic by dint of its scant furnishings. The long table that stretched across the middle of the room was its dominating feature, an opulent piece with ornate carvings of writhing dragons and fiery phoenixes adorning every inch of its surface. The chairs arrayed around it were similarly adorned, though their condition varied wildly from one to the next. Some gleamed with the lustre of care and polish while others were faded and scarred, pitted by worm-holes and worn down by neglect.

Though there were many niches in the walls for statues and trophies, only that directly behind the head of the table was filled. A suit of armour bearing the symbol of the Nagashiro clan squatted on a teakwood platform while a pair of crossed swords rested in the rack behind it. Toshimichi gave them only a brief glance. He knew what these pieces were meant to represent. He also knew that the real ones had been destroyed centuries ago.

That fact was clearly not lost upon the others who were gathered around the table. A hefty, sallow-faced man dressed in the extravagance of a cosmopolitan shook his head as he squinted at the armour and swords. 'I know artisans who could make more convincing copies in their sleep,' he chuckled. 'Eiji should have spoken to me if he wanted some fakes.'

'Perhaps the baron wished to have a less garrulous man handle so delicate a matter,' opined a white-haired man seated near the end of the table. Pale and thin, dressed in the robes of a priest, he was almost the antithesis of the rich merchant. 'You are quite boastful, cousin Masanori. Sometimes discretion is preferable to ostentation.'

'He'll fool nobody with those fakes,' Masanori scoffed. 'Even shut away in that temple of yours, Gunichi, you could tell they aren't real.'

The dark-haired woman seated across from Masanori gestured to the armour with a delicate wave of her powdered hand. 'Perhaps the only person Eiji is trying to fool is himself,' she suggested.

Toshimichi nodded in agreement. 'An interesting supposition,' he said. He gave the woman an apologetic smile. 'Do you know the baron well?'

The woman fingered the tassels on her silken tunic. 'No,' she confessed. 'I have never met him. I only know what his brother told me of his eccentricities.'

'That would make you Otami, Mikawa's wife.' The statement came from the head of the table. Seated in a high-backed seat was an elderly woman in white robes. Her silver hair was pulled back tight, held in place by a pearl-tipped pin. Her fingers were heavy with jewelled rings, the nails of her small fingers grown out to a length of several inches and sheathed in gold. About her neck she wore a simple chain from which depended an ivory carving of the Nagashiro clan symbol.

'You are Mikawa's mother,' Otami said, a note of uncertainty in her voice.

'I am the Dowager Nagashiro,' the elder replied, pressing a finger to the ivory talisman she wore. 'Mikawa was my youngest. He did not have a chance to introduce you to any of us before he was... taken.' The last word fell from the matriarch's lips as little more than a whisper. A haunted look entered her eyes and she looked anxiously at the shadowy niches all around them.

Toshimichi interposed himself into the awkward silence. 'If you have never met the baron then I doubt you have met any of us. I am Toshimichi, a student of the sage Baram in the lamasery of Khult. The sombre fellow at the end of the table is Gunichi, a lay priest in the temple of Dracothion.' One after the other, Toshimichi introduced the people gathered at the table. Masanori the wheat-trader. Hirao the demigryph breeder. Chihaya the brewer. Emiko the courtesan. Komatsu the swordsman.

'Except for the baron himself, we who are gathered about this table are all that remains of the Nagashiro clan,' Toshimichi announced when he was finished.

Komatsu stood up with such alarm that his chair went skidding across the bare floor. 'What do you mean? What is this?'

The man's hand closed around the grip of his sword as he glared at Toshimichi.

'Anger will not change truth,' the Dowager stated. She motioned for Komatsu to sit down, then turned her attention on Toshimichi. 'You are certain of this? We have not yet seen Sugihara or his daughter.'

'They are dead,' Toshimichi said. 'Sugihara took his own life after... after the curse took his daughter.'

Gunichi crossed his hands in front of him in the sign of the celestial dragon while Masanori drew a small bottle from his belt and took a swig of its contents. Komatsu was more voluble in his reaction.

'Curse? What curse?' the swordsman demanded.

'The curse that haunts all the Nagashiro clan,' the Dowager explained. 'The curse that rises once a century to visit death upon this family.'

Komatsu shook his head in denial. 'I am not of your blood! I married Masanori's daughter!' He looked at Otami. 'We are not of the Nagashiro. We have nothing to do with this!'

'But you do.' The words echoed through the desolate hall. The speaker came striding out from the doorway just beside the niche with the imposter armour and swords. He was a middle-aged man, his hair still a lustrous black, although traces of silver infiltrated his beard. The tunic he wore was a deep scarlet with the emblem of the Nagashiro clan embroidered in green thread. From the centre finger of his left hand, a huge ivory ring repeated that emblem and pronounced his rank and title. Baron Eiji Nagashiro.

The baron strode into the great hall, his sharp features drawn back in a reproving expression. Two burly retainers dressed in Eiji's livery flanked him as he approached the table. 'When you married into this family, you merged your blood with ours. The prosperity of Nagashiro, which you coveted, is yours. And so too is our curse.'

'I want no part of any curse,' Komatsu stated. He turned from the baron and gave Masanori a withering look. 'You said nothing about any curse when I courted your daughter.'

'It is a burden all the Nagashiro clan shares,' the Dowager said. 'For centuries its shadow has hung over us.' She wagged a bony finger at Masanori. 'You should have warned Komatsu. When he hears what is in store for him, he may decide to take your head before Yorozuya comes for it.'

Komatsu drew his sword, the sharp blade shining in the hall's dim light. 'Let this Yorozuya try to take my head! I am the best blade in all the Khanate! I have fought forty-seven duels and never suffered a scratch! Just let this Yorozuya dare show his face.'

The swordsman's boasts brought grisly laughter from many at the table. Toshimichi did not share in the morbid humour. He turned towards Komatsu. 'I have delved deeply into the history of our family and the curse that haunts us. Perhaps there was a time when you could have crossed swords with Yorozuya and emerged the victor, but that day is long past. Yorozuya died almost four hundred years ago.'

'You see, Komatsu,' Gunichi proclaimed, 'it is no mortal foe that threatens you, but a vengeful wraith from the underworld.'

The swordsman sat back down, his face almost ashen in colour. He laid his weapon across the table but kept a ready hand upon its grip. 'A ghost,' he muttered. 'A murdering ghost.'

'A ghost that seeks to murder us all,' Toshimichi said. He gave Otami a grave smile. 'When you married into this clan, you became part of our blood as far as Yorozuya is concerned. He will seek your heads as viciously as ours.'

Otami could not control the tremble in her voice. 'But why? Who is... or was... this Yorozuya?'

Baron Eiji took it upon himself to answer that question. 'Yorozuya was the Lord Executioner of King Ashikaga Hidenaga at the time of the Five Princes. One by one, King Ashikaga brought battle to each of the princes and one by one their castles fell.' He paused and gestured at the room in which they sat. 'This was one of those castles, and Jubei Nagashiro was one of those princes. The king was determined to solidify his rule and leave no spark of dissent to trouble his legacy. So when he defeated a prince and captured a castle, he called upon Yorozuya to execute the entire family. Down to the least trace of noble blood.'

Toshimichi pointed to the ring the baron wore and the pendant around his mother's neck. 'One of the Nagashiro escaped the massacre. Now, once a century, Yorozuya's spirit returns to try to complete his duty to King Ashikaga. When he begins to kill, he continues, relentlessly. Once a month, he seeks out a victim. For years he hunts us down, until whatever infernal force drives him is spent. At least for another century.'

Baron Eiji stepped away from the table and slowly paced the hall. 'When the wraith is loosed from the underworld, the descendants of Jubei die. It does not matter how far they run, or where they hide, Yorozuya finds them. He raises his great two-handed sword, the executioner's blade he wielded in life, and with a single stroke he removes...'

'Did you summon us here simply to remind us of the horror that hangs over us?' Masanori demanded.

Baron Eiji smiled at the merchant's outburst. 'No. I called you all here because this is where it all started.' He let his words linger in the air, watching his audience as they waited for him to continue.

'This is where the curse started,' Baron Eiji declared. 'And this is also where it can be brought to an end.'

Gunichi gave a sour look at the markings which Baron Eiji's retainers had scrawled across the floor. The priest of Dracothion did not care for this occult display and made that disdain obvious to the others. 'No good can come from dabbling in the profane arts,' he warned. 'This smacks of necromancy, the dark magic of Nagash.'

'If you are so opposed, you do not have to join the circle,' Baron Eiji told him. 'Of course, being outside the circle would mean forsaking its protection. Are you so certain your god values you enough to safeguard you against the wraith we would conjure?'

Toshimichi could see the doubt in Gunichi's eyes. A moment more and he walked forwards and took his place within the strange design that stretched across the floor. The flickering light from the seventeen black candles arrayed about the circle did strange things to the dragon embroidered on the priest's robes, making it seem as though the wyrm were writhing in protest and trying to pull Gunichi away.

Toshimichi fought to suppress his own misgivings. He wondered if the priest truly knew how deeply Baron Eiji had delved into the black arts to perform this séance. The scholar's own studies had touched upon these occult practices. The seventeen candles, for instance, had to be rendered from the fat of murdered men in order to evoke their arcane potency. The chalk that marked the floor drew its ghostly colour from the crushed bones mixed in with the powder. At the four cardinal directions, a tiny brazier smouldered and filled the hall with a sweet incense – an odour derived from the slivers of coffins exhumed under the full moon. All these things, and many other macabre preparations, were designed to draw into the room the magic of Shyish and the grisly energies of the dead.

With Gunichi's entry into the circle, the balance was complete. The priest took his place in the triangle where the stars of the celestial dragon had been drawn. Each member of the family stood within a geometric shape that contained a constellation peculiar to their nature. Masanori was in a rhombus with the stars of the weasel while Otami reposed in a hexagon with the lights of the dove. Toshimichi noted that his own place was a pentagram with the owl. Baron Eiji, at the centre of the complex intricacies of the circle, was bound by a chalk octagon and the constellation of the wolf.

The dour retainers were quick to act once Gunichi was inside the circle. Keeping outside the shape, they moved to cast down powder and seal the design, creating an unbroken perimeter around the Nagashiro survivors. Their task completed, the men bowed towards Baron Eiji. A gesture from their master sent the men scurrying away. Toshimichi could hear their hasty footfalls as they withdrew through the castle's desolate halls.

'Each of you has, in a way, attempted to defy the curse of Nagashiro,' Baron Eiji stated. 'Be it stealing away to the protection of a temple or trying to trick a renowned swordsman into serving as your champion. All of you have tried some way to escape the revenge of Yorozuya.'

'And you have promised a better way,' Masanori growled. 'A way that is certain to work.'

Baron Eiji nodded. 'It was not pride that caused me to restore this keep or fabricate the lost relics of our clan.' He turned and looked to the Dowager. 'You made a study of the arcane sciences in an effort to break the curse.'

The Dowager grasped the ivory pendant with a bony hand. 'It was my dream that I should be able to protect my children. I have failed in that ambition and now I find my last son to be rushing headlong into calamity.'

'There is an old adage, mother, that the man who would escape danger must first embrace it,' Baron Eiji stated.

Toshimichi felt a chill rush through his body. 'You mean to call up the spirit of Yorozuya,' he said. There was no question in the scholar's mind. He could read the intention in the baron's eyes.

Baron Eiji made a placating motion with his hand. 'Do not be afraid. What is there to fear except the thing that already menaces each of us? Would you go back, run away to wait and tremble until the Lord Executioner finds you? Or will you stand here and help me to break this curse?'

'Yorozuya will kill us all!' objected Masanori and his argument was taken up by many of the others.

'Not if you stand with me,' Baron Eiji said. 'The courage of a moment and you will save your lives.'

'What is it you intend with this rite?' Toshimichi asked. 'What do you hope to accomplish when you call Yorozuya?'

'I intend to deceive the ghost,' Baron Eiji stated. 'That is why it was necessary for all of you to come here, for all of you to enter the circle. Every living drop of Nagashiro blood is within this circle. When Yorozuya is called, he will seek a head to claim, but he will not be able to take any who stand in the circle. We will be invisible to him.'

'And when he finds none to slay, he will believe his task accomplished,' Toshimichi mused. 'At least until the next cycle begins.'

'That would be a century from now,' Otami said. 'There will be no menace over any of us.'

'A century from now, our descendants can simply repeat the ritual,' Masanori suggested. 'That will put them outside the wraith's reach.' He grinned at Baron Eiji. 'It is a brilliant design. You will save all of us.'

'I will confound the curse,' Baron Eiji declared. He looked over to the Dowager. 'The last of our blood will endure,' he told his mother. The Dowager said nothing, but simply removed the pendant from around her neck and handed it to her son.

The gesture brought dampness to Baron Eiji's eyes. He gripped the ivory tight in his hand and nodded to the others. 'The hour draws late and I must begin the ritual. Whatever may happen, keep silent and do not leave the circle. The least disruption of my magic could bring disaster to us all.'

LAST OF THE BLOOD

The baron pointed to each of the candles. As he did so, their flames billowed higher even as the light they gave off became subdued. Toshimichi felt a biting cold fill the room, his breath turning to mist as he exhaled. The smell of the incense became heavier, the sweetness fading into a rank, earthy smell. The reek of graveyard dirt and despoiled tombs.

Baron Eiji's voice rose in the sharp intonations of his ritual. The language was unknown to Toshimichi, but there was a sinister, inhuman cadence to it, evoking images of giant serpents hissing and the scratching of claws against stone. Through it all, there was one name that was distinct in the baron's invocation. That of the Great Necromancer. The name of Nagash.

Toshimichi felt his pulse quickening as the uncanny atmosphere within the circle intensified. A damp clamminess wrapped itself around him, making it difficult to breathe.

Then, with shocking abruptness, the great hall returned to normal. The glow of the candles was again restored, the eerie chill vanished from the air. Toshimichi had heard a cry, a voice raised in terror. He knew it was not Baron Eiji who had shouted, for his invocation could still be heard.

Who it was that had cried out, Toshimichi never knew. The question itself was forgotten when he looked towards Baron Eiji. A black mass, thicker than the shadows that filled the great hall, was rapidly gathering around the nobleman. There was just the suggestion of a head and shoulders, the dark outline of a raised sword...

Before anyone could move, the baron's invocation was silenced. Eiji's head leaped from his shoulders in a welter of gore, spraying blood as it rolled across the arcane circle.

'He's called Yorozuya!' Gunichi shrieked. 'But the Lord Executioner is inside with us!'

The séance exploded into a chorus of screams and shouts. Toshimichi fled with the others as they rushed from the circle and out across the gloomy great hall. For the rest of them, he supposed they had no more thought than escape, but Toshimichi cast a parting look at Baron Eiji's decapitated head, smiling up at him from a pool of Nagashiro blood.

Toshimichi ran down the stairs that stretched down to the keep's main gates. Far from the most robust of physiques, the scholar was well behind the press of panicked humanity that rushed ahead of him. He saw the terrified Masanori and Komatsu push past Otami, flinging the widow aside with callous disregard. He helped her back to her feet. She started to say something, whether of gratitude or protest he never knew, for in that moment her eyes widened with horror.

Otami was gazing at something on the stairway above them, something back in the direction of the great hall. Toshimichi risked a backwards glance and was at once riveted by an awful fascination. The Dowager was descending the steps, not quickly but with the indifference she might have exhibited at a public function. She had a sombre look on her face, almost wistful in its way.

Following after her was a dark mass, but far more distinct in its appearance than the shadow that had fallen upon Baron Eiji. It was the shrouded semblance of a man, its head wrapped in the leather folds of a headsman's hood. Its dimensions were incomplete, fading away into the tatters of its shroud. It did not stride upon legs, but instead drifted in a vaporous state. As it moved, a litter of grubs and worms fell from its body, squirming away into the dark.

'Run!' Toshimichi shouted, but the Dowager only smiled sadly at him. She did not quicken her pace or even turn around. She seemed to know what it was that stalked after her and had resigned herself to her fate.

Toshimichi did not wait to see the wraith make use of the gigantic sword clenched in its skeletal talons. Gripping Otami's arm, he took his own advice and fled down the stairs, hurrying after the others towards the main gate.

'It was Yorozuya!' Otami cried, over and again. 'He has come for us!'

'First he has to catch us,' Toshimichi told her, hating how empty the words sounded even to himself. Perhaps a great wizard could do something to defy the wraith, but the few spells and cantrips he knew would merely be an annoyance to such a monster. No, they couldn't fight it. Their only hope was to get beyond the Lord Executioner's reach. If such a thing was even possible.

Toshimichi could see the hulking main gates at the bottom of the steps as he led Otami down the final length of the stairway. The others were there already, but curiously none had made a move to open them or even approach too closely. He soon found the reason why. The brewer Chihaya lay sprawled on the floor, pierced through the breast by an arrow.

'Baron Eiji's servants,' Masanori cursed. 'They've barred the gates and will shoot anyone who tries to get past!'

The restoration of the keep had been haphazard and there were many gaps in the dilapidated gates. Holes through which a person, or an arrow, might pass. Toshimichi looked over at the torches that lined the stairway. The backlight they provided would expose anyone who tried to squirm through the broken panels. They were caught, trapped between the guarded gate and the ghost.

'We have to get through!' Otami shouted. 'Yorozuya is coming! We saw him murder the Dowager!'

Komatsu rushed towards the gate, hurling abuse at the men outside. 'You hear that, you curs! Let us out!' His only reply was the arrow that hissed past his head, nearly taking off his ear. The swordsman hurriedly drew back.

'They are afraid they will let the wraith out,' Gunichi said. 'You cannot reason with frightened men.'

Toshimichi glowered at the sealed portals and at the unseen archers beyond. He wondered if it was merely fear. 'Maybe the baron ordered them to keep us inside,' he suggested.

'Why?' Masanori demanded. 'To what purpose? Besides, he is dead.' The merchant turned towards the gate and shouted to the retainers outside. 'Do you hear? Your master is dead!'

Masanori's entreaties only brought more arrows hissing through the gaps in the gate. 'I can pay you,' he shouted, his hands fumbling to free the purse strapped to his belt.

Toshimichi felt the intense cold that suddenly swept through the air, a chill of soul rather than flesh. He turned and lifted his eyes to the top of the stairway. A dark apparition took shape there, manifesting as a rapidly forming shadow. The hooded Lord Executioner hefted its massive sword. The blaze of its eyes could be seen glowing behind its black mask as it stared down at the Nagashiro.

'It is too late,' Toshimichi said and pointed up at the wraith.

Masanori intensified his efforts at bribery while the others looked on. Toshimichi knew they were debating which death to prefer – Yorozuya's sword or the arrows. It was the same hideous decision he was trying to decide.

Gunichi chose to confront the wraith. Turning from the gate, he ascended the stairs, his steps slow and measured. A religious mantra droned from his lips as he moved upwards and his hands were folded across his chest in the symbol of Dracothion. Toshimichi did not know the priestly language, but he recognised some of the gestures Gunichi used. He was trying to invoke divine protection against evil forces.

Yorozuya remained at the top of the stairs, seemingly paralysed by Gunichi's prayers. That was, at least, until the priest was midway between the gate and the wraith. 'Stop!' Toshimichi called. 'Go no farther!' In his occult studies, his efforts to understand and break the curse on the Nagashiro, he had learned something of the black arts. Among the arcane principles that empowered profane magics was that of the crossroads, the midpoint between one thing and another. Dusk and dawn, the moments between day and night. Doorways and gates, neither within nor without. There was peril here as Gunichi closed the distance and put himself both equally near and far from the Lord Executioner.

The priest either did not hear or did not heed Toshimichi's warning. He took that final step, resting himself on the stair that was exactly between the gate and Yorozuya. Whatever power his prayers had to hold back the wraith was undone. In a flash of shifting darkness the ghost vanished from the top of the stair and reappeared before Gunichi. The shadowy form was enveloped in a fiery light, whatever sacred energy was yet gathered around the priest. By that light, the dark shroud was burned away, exposing a ragged skeleton, its bones pitted with the bore-holes of worms and beetles.

A moment only, Yorozuya stood thus exposed. Then the spectral shroud and hood flowed back into being, cloaking it in darkness once again. Silently, the apparition raised its executioner's blade. Gunichi's mantra faltered. He raised his voice in a scream of protest and threw up his hands to defend against the downward sweep of the razor-edged blade.

Toshimichi heard Otami scream and felt her clutch his arm in a terrified grip. They saw Yorozuya's sword shear through Gunichi's arms, sending them tumbling down the steps. With the same stroke, the priest's head was severed at the neck. In uncanny silence, his body slopped to the floor and rolled downwards until it crashed against the wall.

'No!' The cry rose from Komatsu. 'I am not a Nagashiro!' The swordsman spun around and seized Masanori. Before the merchant could react, Komatsu's blade stabbed into his side. The wounded man collapsed to his knees, his face gripped by shock. 'Listen to me, ghost! I will help you! I will give you the head of Masanori!'

Toshimichi recoiled away from the crazed swordsman, dragging Otami with him. They looked on as Komatsu hacked away at Masanori's neck. Blood spurted from the merchant's veins, spattering the walls and the onlookers as the blade slashed into him again and again. It took four blows before Komatsu decapitated his victim. Stooping, he snatched up the head by its hair and held it aloft.

'My gift to you!' Komatsu shrieked at Yorozuya. 'The head of a Nagashiro!'

While Komatsu murdered his father-in-law, the wraith had been slowly descending the stairs. Now it came hurtling downwards in a blur of darkness. In a heartbeat, Yorozuya hovered before the red-handed swordsman. He cringed back and waved the head back and forth, as though the ghost had simply failed to see what he had done.

The wraith merely raised its executioner's blade. Komatsu had time enough to react. He threw the severed head at the apparition. It passed harmlessly through the spirit and landed at the foot of the stairs. Yorozuya brought its heavy blade sweeping down. Komatsu met it with his own blood-drenched weapon. There was a crash of steel as the two blades met.

Toshimichi had to regard Komatsu with respect. Had his foe been mortal, the swordsman would surely have beaten him. The two weapons parried one another in a fierce display. The stairway echoed with the ring of battle. Twice, Komatsu slipped past Yorozuya's guard and slashed at the wraith's shadowy essence. A living man would have died from either of those blows, but instead all Komatsu accomplished was to send a few shadowy grubs and maggots spilling from the ghost's shrouded bones.

Panic seized Komatsu, and in that panic his skill faltered. His parries became sloppy and now it was Yorozuya's blade that prevailed. At first, there were only glancing cuts that nicked shoulder or arm, but then there came the grisly moment that had become inevitable. Weakened by fear and injury, Komatsu failed to block the killing stroke. Yorozuya's murderous sword came whipping around at him, hewing through his throat in a mighty stroke that cut clear through the spine.

During the fray, Emiko and Hirao rushed the gate. No arrows greeted the pair. Hearing the conflict within, aware of the monster which was coming for the Nagashiro, the retainers had fled. Now it was the courtesan and demigryph breeder who sought to escape. Squirming through the holes, the two deserted Sho Castle.

Otami would have run after them, but Toshimichi held her back. He was looking at Komatsu's body and at the gory mess of Masanori. 'Wait,' he urged her. 'There is something wrong here!' Even if his observation meant nothing, there was no salvation by simply running. As it rose from the swordsman, Yorozuya turned to the gate. The wraith's spectral essence needed no hole to squeeze through as it pursued Emiko and Hirao, it simply passed through the barrier as though it did not exist.

'We can escape now!' Otami pleaded, but Toshimichi would not let her go.

'Yorozuya would find us,' he said. 'Wherever we went, he would find us.' He shook his head. 'Baron Eiji had a purpose in bringing us all here. I think this is all by design, exactly as he wanted it to be.' He pointed to the bodies of Masanori and Komatsu. 'Look at them,' he ordered when Otami would have turned from the grisly sight. 'When Masanori was decapitated there was blood everywhere, but Komatsu's wound did not bleed.' He glanced up the steps at Gunichi. 'We saw no blood when the priest died.'

Otami shuddered at the ghastly realisation. 'But there was blood when Baron Eiji was killed.'

Toshimichi led her up the stairway. 'Was he killed? We have

to go back and see. We have to make sure.' He glanced back at
the gate. 'Hurry! There is not much time. When Yorozuya is finished with them, he will come back for us!'

The great hall in which the séance had been conducted was still
veiled in darkness when Toshimichi and Otami stepped inside.
The crawling cold that had impressed the scholar before was
absent, so too was that musky stench of the grave. Yet there was
still a sense of hideous evil here. Human evil.

'Be ready,' Toshimichi warned Otami. 'He may not wait for
Yorozuya to kill us.'

Otami shook her head. 'His own mother...'

'The Dowager must have realised what he was doing,' Toshimichi
said. 'That is why she gave him the pendant. It was her way of
telling him she accepted her fate.' He remembered the corpse of
the old woman and how different her visage looked from those
of Gunichi, Masanori and Komatsu. There had been a composure there, almost as though the Dowager were pleased to die.

Toshimichi's fingers tightened around Otami's arm. He stared
into the darkness where the arcane circle had been. 'The baron
is here,' he stated. He gestured with his hand, calling upon one
of the cantrips he had learned in his studies. The candles, extinguished earlier in the séance, flared back into life. Brighter than
before, their light dispelled the darkness.

Baron Eiji sat within the circle, a cold smile on his face as he
stared at Toshimichi and Otami. The scholar noted that the nobleman had kept within the octagon shape he had drawn earlier.

'That is the only real protective barrier, isn't it?' Toshimichi
challenged him.

Eiji nodded, his head quite secure upon his neck. 'The rest of
the circle is an illusion. A bit more tangible than the vision of
my murder, perhaps, but no less of a trick.' His smile broadened.

'The séance wasn't, though. You really did help me summon Yorozuya to this castle. He could not resist such a concentration of Nagashiro blood.'

'Why?' Toshimichi demanded. 'Why help the curse along? Why bring us here to simply kill us?'

'Your own mother!' Otami snapped at the smirking baron. 'You did not spare even her.'

Baron Eiji's visage flushed with colour, his eyes smouldering with fury. 'I could not spare anyone! I even brought you here because I could not risk that my brother might have consummated your marriage despite himself! If even one drop of Nagashiro blood was not here, I could never be sure...'

'Sure of what?' Toshimichi asked. If he knew why Eiji had done all of this, he might figure out a way to stop him.

Eiji laughed at the question. 'Of them all, Toshimichi, I was the most worried that you would have learned the truth as I did. Let me tell you, then.' He leaned forwards, to the very edge of the octagon that defended him. 'There is no curse on the Nagashiro family.'

The statement struck Toshimichi almost like a physical blow. 'But, the murders! The near extermination of our family...'

'Yet always the Nagashiro endure,' Eiji pointed out. 'That is because the curse is not upon us. It is Yorozuya that is cursed. Condemned to spend eternity striving towards an unreachable goal!

'I will tell you how it happened,' the baron continued. 'When King Ashikaga ordered Yorozuya to massacre our ancestors, the Lord Executioner betrayed his master. The captured Jubei had hidden away enough wealth to buy the life of his youngest son from Yorozuya. In exchange for the money, Yorozuya let the child escape. His treachery was discovered, however.'

Baron Eiji laughed, a grisly chuckle that echoed through the hall. 'Oh yes, the king's anger was great. No honourable death for Yorozuya! The executioner was bound in his own coffin and coated in honey to draw insects to his trapped flesh. Spells sustained his life while the worms and beetles fed off him. Even when there was no flesh left and even his bones were eaten away, his spirit endured.'

'Condemned to haunt the Nagashiro,' Otami said.

Eiji corrected her. 'Condemned to complete his task. Condemned to never rest until our family is wiped out. But he can never complete his mission. Always the last member of the clan is safe from him, just as Jubei's son was safe from him long ago. Yorozuya can never escape the taint of his treachery, so he can never strike down the last of our blood.'

Toshimichi felt sick as he appreciated Eiji's plan. 'That is why you did this. Why even the Dowager had to die. You can only be sure of escaping Yorozuya if you are the last Nagashiro.'

'Too late, you understand,' Eiji said. 'Tell me, if you knew what I know, how could you do anything else? It is the only way.'

Toshimichi glared at the nobleman. 'You forget one thing. Now that I know, I can do the same thing. I can wipe out that circle which hides you from Yorozuya. You can take the same chance the rest of us have.' He reached into the sleeve of his robe and drew out a long knife. 'Or I can mimic Komatsu and offer your head to the wraith.'

'You could,' Eiji conceded. 'If you had the time.'

Otami screamed. Toshimichi spun around, his gaze locked upon the dark shadow that loomed in the entryway. Baron Eiji had been so forthcoming with the details of his scheme because he had been playing for time. Waiting for Yorozuya to come.

Toshimichi shoved Otami aside. It was an even chance whether the wraith would go after her or him. Though he felt it would be a futile gesture, he tried to draw the ghost's attention. He let the knife fall from his hand and instead produced a bag of coins.

'Yorozuya!' Toshimichi shouted at the wraith. 'Once you sold your honour for gold! Once you cast aside your duty for a bribe! Here, murdering wretch! Here is your chance to do so again!'

The Lord Executioner swept towards him, its eyes leaping with angry flickers of ghostly light. The immense sword was raised, ready to deliver the killing blow to this mortal who dared to mock its curse.

Before the wraith could strike, an anguished shriek filled the hall. Toshimichi looked aside, following the source of the sound. He saw Otami standing over Baron Eiji, one of the heavy braziers clenched in her hands. Blood dripped from the implement, the same sanguinary fluid that now leaked in earnest from the nobleman's body. Eiji crawled across the circle, gasping for mercy.

Otami brought the brazier down again, smashing Eiji's skull.

An enraged roar rippled from Yorozuya. The grubs and maggots dripping from the wraith became a cascade, swiftly diminishing its shadowy essence. The Lord Executioner brought its sword flashing down. Toshimichi felt an icy cold sear through his body, slicing through him from neck to shoulder. But the cut was only a shadow itself, unable to truly harm his flesh. Unable to take his head.

Yorozuya raised the blade for another blow. The angry glow had fled from its eyes and now there was something akin to despair in the wraith's gaze. Toshimichi felt the same cold pass through him as the sword came slashing down, incapable now of harming him.

The worm-eaten bones were visible now, so much of the wraith's shroud and mask had evaporated with the crawling vermin. Toshimichi stared back at the leering skull as the last of the gravelight faded from its sockets. A moment more, and then the bones crashed to the floor in a confused jumble. Soon even this residue was gone, vanishing in a greasy fume.

Otami dropped the gory brazier. 'Is it over?' she asked.

Toshimichi looked over at her. 'For now,' he said. 'Until another hundred years has passed and Yorozuya rises again from his grave.' He glanced at Baron Eiji's body. 'He was right, Yorozuya couldn't hurt the last Nagashiro.' Toshimichi returned his gaze to Otami. 'But I don't understand. You should have been the last of our blood.'

Otami shook her head. 'No, you were the last,' she said. 'You see, Baron Eiji was right about something else.'

'I don't think his brother really cared for women,' she said, a sad look in her gaze.

Toshimichi thought of all the dead littered throughout the castle. 'That is for the best. Any family you had would have simply perpetuated the curse.' He stared at the spot where the wraith's essence had disintegrated. 'I am now the last. The Nagashiro line will end with me.'

'Then Yorozuya will have no reason to again rise from the underworld.'

PETER MCLEAN

PREDATION
OF THE EAGLE

Vardan IV, Astra Militarum Advance Firebase Theta 82
Three months ago

Sergeant Rachain read the names of the Missing in Action to the platoon every morning.

Every morning, the list was longer than it had been the day before.

'Emperor's grace,' Corporal Cully muttered to himself as the reeking, poisonous rain beat down hot around him, pounding on the canvas covering of the muster tent overhead. 'There won't be any of us left before we get out of here at this rate.'

'What say, corporal?'

That was Moonface, from Three Section. Cully looked at the boy's fat, sweating face, and he could see the fear written there in the premature lines around his young eyes.

'Nothing, trooper,' he said. 'Old Cully's just muttering to himself, don't you worry your pretty little head about it.'

Cully had no idea what Moonface's real name was, but it didn't really matter. On Vardan IV it didn't really matter what *anyone's* name was, at least not until they had survived their first firefight. Most of them didn't, after all.

The steaming jungles were infested with orks, and the Reslian

45th were chewing through new recruits as fast as the troop ships could deliver them. Cully, though, he'd been deployed there for the last two years. So had Rachain, of course.

They were tight, the pair of them, and Sergeant Drachan and Corporal Gesht and the others from Two Section. They were the old guard, the backbone of Alpha Platoon, D Company. The hardened veterans.

The survivors.

Corporal Rikkards and his mob were all right too, he supposed, especially that huge lad who Cully called Ogryn, but never where he might hear him. Lopata, he thought the man's name was. Still, they were in Beta Platoon and tended to keep themselves to themselves and didn't mingle much with the others, so to the warp with them.

No, it was the old guard who mattered. Rachain and Cully, Drachan and Gesht. Veteran sergeants and their top corporals, that was what made a platoon. Rachain was lead sergeant of Alpha Platoon. He was top canid in D Company, and Cully was his right hand man and his best friend.

That was how you ran an army, Cully thought. Lieutenants were only there to do paperwork and take the blame if the wheels fell off an operation, and who even knew what captains did. Anyone higher up than that might as well not exist, in Cully's opinion. It was boots in the mud that won wars, not generals polishing chairs with their arses.

'It's a lot of names, corporal,' Moonface said.

Cully had forgotten the boy was there. He blinked and looked at him.

'This is war, Moonface,' he said. 'People go missing, in the jungle. People die. That's what we're here for, in case it had escaped the memory capacity of the tiny brain that hides behind that enormous face of yours. We're the Imperial Guard. Dying is what we're *for*.'

'Yes, corporal,' Moonface said, and that really was the only right answer he could have given.

Cully headed up One Section, Alpha Platoon, and that made him *Rachain's* top canid. No recruit boot from a lower section was going to answer *him* back, not if they knew what was good for them.

'Corporal,' a voice rasped behind him, sounding like it was coming straight out of an open grave.

That was Steeleye, Cully knew. He turned and looked at the veteran sniper. Steeleye had been in One Section since even before Cully's time, and ever since she got her naming wound she had refused to answer to her real name anymore. Cully respected her capability enormously, but that didn't make her any easier to look at.

'What is it?' he asked, feigning nonchalance as his eyes took in the ruin of the woman's face.

Steeleye had met an ork up close, once. Very close indeed.

It had bitten her face off.

Her left eye socket had been crushed too badly for the medicae to be able to do anything except seal over the collapsed mess of broken skull with hideously shiny synthetic skin, giving her whole head a disturbingly lopsided appearance. Her right eye had been replaced with the bulbous metallic augmetic from which she took her name. She had no nose, just a ragged open snout from which thick green snot ran almost constantly, and the bone was exposed along the length of the left side of her jaw where the synth-skin had refused to take.

She carried a specially customised long-las over her shoulder, topped with a scope that interfaced so perfectly with her augmetic eye that the entire weapon became part of her body. She had recorded eight hundred and thirty seven confirmed kills on Vardan IV.

'Stop winding the poor brat up,' Steeleye said, nodding sideways at Moonface. 'You ain't been listening to the list.'

Cully shrugged. He hadn't been listening to the morning list for the last eighteen months.

'So?'

'Drachan made it.'

Cully blinked. Sergeant Drachan had been the platoon's top scout.

Making the list, that was what they called it when you went out into the green and didn't come back. Sometimes a trooper might be confirmed Killed in Action, if they were shot down right in front of their comrades and someone managed to bring their ident-tags back for the Munitorum to log the death and send The Letter to their next of kin, but it was rare. In the impenetrable, greenskin-infested jungles of Vardan IV, ninety per cent of casualties were officially listed as MIA for the simple reason that no one could find what was left of them after an engagement.

'You sure?'

Steeleye nodded, and paused to wipe her oozing snout with the back of her already crusty uniform sleeve.

'Emperor's word,' she said. 'He went out with Two Section yesterday, didn't come back. Gesht's in pieces.'

Cully nodded slowly. He knew Drachan and his corporal had been close. Maybe too close, if you cared what the regulations said.

Cully didn't care one little bit.

'I've got some sacra in my tent,' he said. 'I'll go see her. Thanks, Steeleye.'

The old veteran nodded her ruined head at the corporal, and no more words needed to be said between them. Moonface just looked on in simple, naive bewilderment as the day to day business of the Astra Militarum went on around him.

Death, loss, grief.

It was just another day in the glorious Imperial Guard.

* * *

Vardan IV
Now

Cully squeezed down on the trigger of his lasgun and blew the ork apart with a sustained burst of full auto.

'Emperor's teeth, but there's a lot of them,' Gesht's voice growled in his vox-bead.

The other corporal was five, maybe six hundred yards to Cully's left, away through the curtain of suffocating rain with her own section spread out around her.

Alpha Platoon were deep into greenskin country, on an advance recon mission.

'I hear you,' Cully replied. 'Concentrate on the big ones, they're the bosses.'

'You think I'm some new boot?' Gesht snapped. 'I know that, Cully.'

Cully shrugged, for all that he knew the woman couldn't see him.

'Sure, Gesht,' he said. 'Just watch your arse, and watch your section's arses even harder.'

'Teach me to suck a bleedin' egg,' Gesht started, then her inevitable obscenities were cut short by a crackling barrage of automatic lasgun fire through Cully's vox-bead.

'Say again?'

'Nothing,' she said. 'Sorry, I was just doing my job. What are *you* doing?'

Cully bit back a reply and pulled himself forward on his elbows and knees through the stinking mud and rotting vegetation. The light was greenish yellow in the rain, filtered through the high jungle canopy above them. Everything in Cully's world was made of sweat and mud and filth.

His webbing chafed at his shoulders through his flak armour, rubbing his sodden undershirt against the constant friction sores that were a simple part of life on Vardan IV. Enormous insects swarmed around him, biting at his exposed skin, and more than once he'd had to stop and brush hideous, translucent arachnids off his sleeve.

'Status report,' he said, after a moment.

'About five hundred on your nine,' Gesht said. 'No more contacts. Closing on the boss.'

'Acknowledged,' Cully said. His section were finally out of orks to kill, too.

They were both closing on Rachain, bringing their sections forward to the sergeant's position. He was in the command squad, of course, with Lieutenant Makkron who was at least nominally in charge of Alpha Platoon's deep recon patrol.

If Makkron had even half a brain, Cully thought, he would be doing what Rachain told him. The officer was fresh out of the cadet scholam back on Reslia itself. They still did things the old-fashioned way on Reslia; sent anyone with good breeding straight to officer school. That meant anyone with money, obviously. He was maybe twenty Terran-standard years old at the most. Rachain was almost twice his age, and had spent all those extra years in the Guard. He knew what he was doing.

A newly commissioned lieutenant outranked a platoon sergeant, of course, but he would have to be a special kind of stupid to try to enforce it. Cully really didn't want to have anyone that stupid in command of him and his men.

'Hey, Gesht,' Cully said, flicking his vox-bead over to their private channel. 'What do you make of the lieutenant?'

Gesht snorted in his ear. 'Wetter behind the ears than the last one was,' she said. 'The next one will still be in nappies, at this rate.'

'I hear you,' Cully said. 'You reckon he's listening to Rachain?'

'He'd better be, or he might get shot in the back by an ork,' Gesht said.

'Like the last one did, you mean?'

Their last lieutenant had been the special kind of stupid that had almost got thirty of them killed when she marched them straight into an ork ambush despite Sergeant Drachan's insistence that it was a trap. It had only been the honed reactions of the veterans, and Steeleye's stone cold sniping, that had got them out of it alive. The lieutenant had been gunned down from behind by a lone ork on their way back to the base. No one ever found that ork, and platoon lore had it that perhaps its name had been Gesht, but of course no one could prove anything and in honesty no one much cared. As far as Cully was concerned that was all well and good.

The jungle did strange things to a man's sense of right and wrong, and he had long since come to accept that.

'Don't know what you mean,' Gesht said, and her voice was flat and emotionless.

Cully could have kicked himself for a fool for bringing it up. That had been *before*.

Before Drachan made the list.

Before Gesht lost her mind to grief.

'Don't mean anything,' he assured her. 'We're good.'

'We're good,' Gesht agreed, and the moment passed.

Cully remembered the day Steeleye had come and told him Drachan had made the list. He remembered going to Gesht's tent with his illicit flask of sacra, to see how she was.

Deranged, that was how she had been. He had found her field-stripping her lasgun and anointing its few moving parts with her own blood as she recited the Emperor's Litany of Vengeance over and over again. She'd had plenty of blood to work with, what with the mess she had made of her left arm.

The scars were still plain to see even now, hard ridges of white tissue against her tanned skin where she had half-flensed her own forearm with her combat knife in a furious outpouring of grief and rage. Cully had had to restrain her, he remembered, pin her down before she bled to death, and call in a very private favour from their squad medic to keep it quiet. He had drunk the sacra himself, afterwards.

He had kept her secrets, for all that he should have made a report, and he honestly thought that was the only thing that had stopped her from killing him in his sleep when she was nominally recovered. He had seen her in her weakness, in her shame and her torment, and he knew that didn't sit easy with her.

She had never been quite right in the head since, all the same.

He keyed the vox to the platoon channel.

'Cully to Rachain,' he said. 'One Section, coming up on your eight.'

'Two Section,' Gesht said. 'Five hundred to the nine, closing.'

'Three Section,' Corporal Dannecker chimed in. 'Closing on the four, eight hundred.'

'Acknowledged,' Rachain said. 'Form up on the command squad.'

The patrol fan began to close in on the command position, the veterans moving silent as ghosts through the crushing humidity of the jungle. The fresh recruits in each unit, the raw boots who had yet to earn their names, made enough noise for everyone.

Cully winced as he heard Webfoot from his own section trip over an exposed root and land in a stinking pool with a splash. He turned with an angry gesture, but Steeleye already had the stupid boot back up on his feet with her iron-hard arm around his throat. She jabbed him hard in the ribs, doubling him over, and met the corporal's eyes over the boy's back. There was no emotion on her ruined face, but Cully caught her meaning all the same.

Emperor's sake! that look said, and Cully had to agree with her.

Webfoot eventually stopped gagging, and they moved on.

He didn't trip again.

The whole patrol platoon made camp together that night, on a relatively dry knoll that rose above the endless mud and filth of the jungle floor. Rachain had ordered a double watch, and Cully supposed that was sensible even if it meant no one got anywhere near enough sleep that night.

Double watch or not, though, come the dawn Webfoot was dead all the same.

Cully was roused from his bedroll by Hangnail screaming.

She was a boot from Two Section, one of Gesht's, and she was the one who found him.

You poor bitch, Cully thought. *Welcome to the sodding Guard.*

Cully himself was a hardened veteran and he had seen worse, but not by much. Hangnail wasn't, and she hadn't, and she was on her knees puking even as the platoon came to full alert all around her.

Webfoot had been disembowelled.

He was hanging from a great tree, maybe a hundred yards from the camp, with his intestines dangling from his open belly in great stinking purple ropes. His hands had been bound in front of his chest with the stiffening fingers spread in an awful travesty of the sign of the Aquila.

They had set a double guard, and still no one had heard a *thing*.

'Orks ain't quiet like that,' Corporal Dannecker said softly to Cully, when there was no one else close enough to hear. 'No ork did that.'

Cully just nodded slowly. He had been thinking much the same thing, and he would have bet a month's pay that Rachain was thinking it too.

'Don't be saying things like that in front of the boots,' he cautioned the junior corporal. 'They're spooked enough as it is. The first person I hear so much as whisper *eldar* is getting my bayonet up his arse, you understand me?'

'So what are we saying it was, then?' Rachain asked from behind them.

Cully managed not to jump. Dannecker didn't.

Rachain could move quiet as the night, when he wanted to.

'Don't know, sergeant,' Dannecker said, too quickly.

Cully winced. That wasn't the right answer.

Rachain belted Dannecker in the guts almost too fast to see, knocking the younger man to his knees in the mud.

'Orks, you bloody idiot,' he said. 'What else could it be? It was orks. We're here fighting orks, scouting orks, so it was *orks*. Is that abundantly clear, you stupid bastard?'

'Yes, sergeant,' Dannecker wheezed, trying to get his breath back.

Cully nodded. 'Orks,' he said. 'Course it was. *Really* quiet ones.'

He exchanged a long look with Rachain, and the sergeant nodded.

'I'll explain it to the lieutenant,' he said. 'You go and take a proper look.'

'Sir,' Cully said.

He gave Dannecker a pitying look, down in the mud and the filth, and made himself go and inspect the corpse.

Webfoot had been hanged with a rope made of twisted jungle creepers, plaited thick and strong. Someone had taken their time to make that rope properly, Cully thought. The man's hands had been bound with a finer version of the same stuff, and thin cords of it had been used to pull his fingers out into the distinctive spread and to hold his thumbs twisted together like the double heads of the sacred eagle.

Someone, Cully thought, had gone to a lot of trouble with that. *Someone* was making a point, and they had made it far too bloody quietly for his liking.

Cully sighed and took his helmet off for a moment, pushed a hand back through his sweat-sodden hair. He bowed his head and spoke the Emperor's Benediction over Webfoot, then turned away. There was nothing there to tell him anything. The man had been murdered, silently and expertly, and then someone had strung him up and bound his hands in that symbolic way. Cully was about to return and report to the sergeant when he paused for a moment.

He never did know what made him do it – perhaps it was just instinct, or perhaps the Emperor responded to his prayer. Whatever it was, he paused and walked around the hanging body to look at it from the rear.

What he saw there made him vomit violently on the ground in front of him.

The back of Webfoot's combat trousers were drenched with blood. Both of his buttocks had been hacked off with some sort of heavy blade, the sort that the orks carried. Whatever had killed him, they had cut themselves a couple of good steaks afterwards.

'No,' Rachain said, when Cully told him. 'No way is *that* going in the official report.'

'But sergeant,' Lieutenant Makkron said, in the sweaty darkness of the command tent, 'surely we have a duty to–'

'No!' Rachain snapped. 'Sir.'

'I know, I know,' Cully said. 'The Officio Prefectus…'

'Yes, exactly,' Rachain said.

The lieutenant looked from one man to the other in obvious confusion. Cully idly wondered whether the boy had actually started shaving yet.

'Will one of you please explain what you're talking about?' Makkron said.

He was trying to sound commanding, Cully realised, but all that he could hear was a plaintive, childish whine.

Rachain sighed.

'Sir,' he said, 'do you have any idea how many men the Astra

Militarum have lost on this miserable bloody planet in the last two years?'

'No,' Makkron confessed.

Two years ago your balls hadn't even dropped yet, Cully thought. *You wouldn't have so much as* heard *of Vardan IV.*

He envied the lad that, if little enough else.

Rachain fixed the lieutenant with one of his famous glares, and dropped his voice to a flat tone that even the junior officer could tell meant he was in no mood to be messed with.

'Almost two million,' he said.

Makkron swallowed, and he paled under his new boot's sunburn.

'How... *how* many?'

'Two. Bloody. Million,' Rachain said. 'Give or take. No one *knows,* don't you understand that? That's the whole problem, *sir.* People go out into the green, and they just... don't come back. Over and over and *over* again. And now it's us. Now it's *us* sent out of our nice strong firebase and into this *hell!*'

'But I still don't see...'

Rachain slammed a hand down on the camp table in the command tent and got to his feet.

'I can't,' he said. 'I can't do this anymore. I'm in no mood for this level of stupid. It's your turn to babysit, Cully. I'm going to walk the line, talk to the troops. Do my sodding *job.*'

He stormed out and let the tent flap fall closed behind him, leaving Cully alone with the lieutenant.

'The sergeant... well, he cares about the troops, sir,' Cully said awkwardly. 'He's under a lot of pressure just at the moment.'

'I understand, corporal,' Makkron said. 'I'm not as naive as Rachain thinks I am. Well, perhaps I am about this particular theatre of war, but I do understand all the same. Morale, and all that.'

This particular theatre of war, Cully thought with disgust. *Like you've ever seen any other* theatre of war, *you utter oilrag.*

'The point is, sir,' Cully said, 'that this war is utter and total grinding hell and it has been for *years*. The orks are bloody unstoppable. There are millions of them, and this is their terrain, not ours. And we're not winning. You do grasp that, right, sir? We are *not* winning this war, not even a little bit. But now? Now there's something *else* out there! You saw Webfoot, right?'

'I saw what?'

'Webfoot,' Cully said. 'The body?'

Dear Emperor, how slow is he?

'Ah, you mean Trooper Verlhan? Yes, yes I... I saw the body.'

Verlhan, was that his name? Cully supposed it must have been, not that it mattered any more.

'Yes,' he said. 'Yes, him. Well, listen, sir. He was killed in the middle of the night, when we had a double watch set. Not everyone in this platoon is a recruit boot, you know. Emperor's sake, *Steeleye* had watch last night, and still no one heard a thing, not even her. Orks are about as stealthy as a grenade in a promethium plant. It wasn't an ork who did Webfoot, and it wasn't an ork who cut his arse off for its dinner, either. There's something else out there. Something even sodding worse than orks, as if this war wasn't going badly enough as it is. Something that looks an awful lot like a drukhari. Do you *really* think the Officio Prefectus want to hear that? Even more, do you think they want anyone *else* to hear that? You put that in the official report and there will be a commissar's bolter up your arsehole before you can say Ave Imperator, do you understand me, *sir*?'

Makkron just sat and stared at Cully, blinking like a newly landed fish as sweat rolled down his smooth face in thick rivers.

'I...' he started, and fell silent.

The Officer Cadet Scholam probably didn't prepare Command Lieutenants for being soundly and loudly sworn at by corporals, Cully realised, for all that it really should do.

Lieutenant Makkron looked down at the reeking black mud that encrusted his new Munitorum-issue boots for a long moment, then back up at Cully.

'Drukhari? Do you really think so?'

Cully nodded slowly. That was what it was, he was sure of it. It *had* to be.

He refused to think about the alternative.

They buried Webfoot that day, and broke camp the next morning. When Rachain called the roll there was a name missing.

'Where the hell is Hangnail?' he demanded.

Cully led the search of the camp and the surrounding jungle, but in his heart he already knew what he would find. No one would desert in the deep jungle, after all.

He was right.

Hangnail had gone the way of Webfoot. They found her dangling from a tree five hundred yards from camp with her guts hanging in tangled loops around her feet. There were rough tracks where she had been dragged, alive or dead, from her sentry position to the place she had been hanged. Again, her hands were bound in front of her in the sign of the Aquila.

'*Imperator nos defendat*,' Cully whispered, one of the few phrases of High Gothic he knew.

Emperor protect us.

Cully was a man of devout faith, but as he looked at Hangnail's corpse swinging from the tree he wondered if perhaps the Emperor's gaze had turned away from Vardan IV. Hangnail's left arm had been taken off at the elbow, the gristle of the joint neatly butchered and showing white against the ragged red of the surrounding meat. There was no sign of the missing limb.

Someone's taken themselves a shank, he thought, and swallowed bile.

'Oi,' he said quietly to Rachain, when he could be absolutely sure there was no one else around who could hear them. 'We need to talk.'

'No, we don't,' Rachain said. 'It's the drukhari. I know that, you know that. What's to talk about, other than how to kill it?'

'What if it isn't?'

'It is.'

'Are you *sure* about that, Rachain?' Cully asked, putting a hand on his old friend's arm to stay him as he tried to turn away. 'Because what if it *isn't?*'

Rachain turned and looked at his corporal.

'I know what you're trying to say, Cully,' he said, 'and I'd like it a lot more if you stopped right now. It's *drukhari*, you hear me?'

That sounded to Cully a lot like the way Rachain had told Dannecker that it was an ork, even though they all knew it wasn't. He swallowed. Him and Rachain had been friends for years, and not too many Guardsmen lived long enough to get to say that. He trusted the older man, and could only pray to the Emperor that he was right.

But he didn't believe it.

'So let's talk about how to kill it,' he said.

Whatever it is, he thought. *Because it's* not *a drukhari, Rachain, and you know it isn't every bit as well as I do.*

Cully thought that, but he didn't say it. Rachain was his friend and his boss, and, if Cully was utterly and totally honest with himself about it, he had always been a little bit afraid of the veteran sergeant.

'Anything that lives can die,' Rachain growled. 'We find it, corner it, kill it. We've got *Steeleye* in our platoon, for the Emperor's sake. There's nothing alive within half a mile she can't drop with a clean headshot. We just need to give her that shot.'

Cully nodded. At least Rachain was prepared to do what

needed to be done, that was the main thing. They could argue about how to cover it up later.

They lost Booger Boy and Twitchy and Pretty Girl the next night.

All three of them were found hanged, the same as Webfoot and Hangnail had been. All three of them disembowelled. Booger Boy's left leg had been taken off at the hip, neat as neat.

There was a lot of meat on Booger Boy, Cully couldn't help but think. How the lad had ever passed basic training carrying that much weight was a mystery, but one that he supposed was largely irrelevant now.

He was dead, after all.

So was Twitchy, who had been Steeleye's spotter and the platoon's up and coming apprentice sniper. So was Pretty Girl, who had been one of the best scouts they'd had.

It took Pretty Girl, Cully thought, and his blood ran cold. She was young but her scout skills were extraordinary. *Had been* extraordinary, he corrected himself as he dragged his eyes away from the gaping wound in her abdomen. Something had crept up on Pretty Girl. Something even quieter and scarier than she had been.

Cully swallowed.

He was right, he *knew* he was. Whether Rachain wanted to hear it or not.

Of course he didn't want to hear it. Cully didn't want to hear it himself, and it was him thinking it.

I'm wrong, he told himself. *I must be.*

But he knew he wasn't.

They were deep in the jungle now, perhaps a hundred miles from where they had started at Advance Firebase Theta 82. They fought orks on a daily basis as their recon patrol cut deep into enemy territory, but to Cully that was almost secondary now. He had been fighting orks in the steaming jungles of Vardan IV for two years and more. He understood orks, he respected orks, but he no longer truly feared them.

Cully feared the other thing.

Voxjockey was gone now, and Wanna-be-a-pilot, and Lickspittle.

Voxjockey had died in combat like a normal person, shredded by an ork's heavy stubber, and Cully had managed to gather the boy's ident-tags as they fled the ambush zone. His family at least would get The Letter. Well, they would if Cully made it back himself, he supposed. If not, what the hell did he care?

Wanna-be-a-pilot, though, and Lickspittle, they had gone the way of Webfoot and the others. Hanged from the trees in the dead of night, disembowelled and their hands bound in the pious sign of the aquila. Lickspittle had been cut for steaks too, where Wanna-be-a-pilot had been left alone. There was no meat on her skinny body anyway, Cully thought, and he had to rest his forehead against a tree until the nausea receded.

It's a drukhari, he told himself. *The sergeant said so. It's a filthy bloody drukhari.*

It wasn't a drukhari, and he knew it and Rachain knew it and he was starting to suspect that Steeleye did as well. He wondered whether Gesht did, too.

No, no, no. Oh Holy God-Emperor of Terra, don't do this to her. Please.

Please don't.

On the twelfth day of their recon patrol they found an ork encampment. Steeleye had the point, and she voxed her position back on the command channel. She was the only non-command trooper to warrant a personal vox-bead, but she was a near-legendary sniper so Rachain hadn't had any trouble getting it for her. Even the chair-polishers at the Munitorum had heard of Steeleye, and to be honest no one wanted to piss her off. If she wanted a vox-bead, she got one.

'Understood,' Rachain said, and voxed through to Cully. 'One Section, move up to support.'

Cully tapped his vox-bead in acknowledgement and waved his squad forward.

They crept through the perpetual gloom of the green, lasguns at their shoulders as they closed on Steeleye's position through the constant pissing rain. Rachain himself was bringing Two and Three Sections up on the far flank, Cully knew, the sergeant not entirely trusting Gesht or Dannecker to hold the command all by themselves.

I'm top canid, Cully told himself as he swiped a fang-leach off his shoulder before it could get a hold through his sweat-soaked combat uniform. *He trusts me.*

Did he, though? Did he really? According to Rachain they were still hunting a renegade drukhari, but Cully knew that was just so much groxshit. He knew *exactly* what it was. Every night in his tent, twisting in his own rancid sweat in fever dreams of horror, Cully saw the face of their murderous foe.

That was the nights, though, when the humidity was trying to drown him alive in his tent. This was now. A Guardsman has to live in the now, or he'll sure as hell die in it. There was no time for distractions.

The ork settlement was rough and crude, as everything the orks built was.

Cully and One Section bellied down in the swampy filth between the trees, their lasguns held tight to their shoulders and the rain beating down on them, and waited for the signal. He had absolutely no idea where Steeleye was. She was like a ghost, in the green. Silent, invisible. Like all the veterans were.

Shut up, Cully, he told himself. *Don't think about that. Just don't.*

He sighted along his rifle, picking targets, for all that they had been ordered was to wait until the master sniper gave her word that it was time. There were orks out there – cleaning weapons, mending the crude thatch of their huts, cooking meat over open fires that sizzled and smoked in the rain.

Cooking meat.

Could I be wrong? Cully wondered.

So much simpler, this way. Forget about drukhari, and perish the other thought; maybe it *was* orks. Very, very quiet orks. Orks who knew what the sign of the Aquila was, and what it meant.

Don't be bloody stupid, he told himself.

Obviously, he *wanted* it to be orks. He *understood* orks. He hated them, of course he did. They were filthy xenos, the enemies of the blessed holy God-Emperor, but after two years deployed on Vardan IV he understood them all the same.

No.

No, that just wasn't going to work, was it?

It wasn't orks, however much he wanted it to be.

Cully snugged his lasgun to his shoulder and sighted on a big greenskin who was threading an ammunition belt into a heavy stubber with its left hand and vigorously picking its nose with the forefinger of its right.

Still Steeleye waited.

It's not an ork.

Cully really, *really* needed to kill something, anything, to take his mind off the alternative, even if only for a little while.

The jungle did strange things to a man's sense of right and wrong, he thought again. The jungle did strange things to a man's mind in general. What could it do to a man like that?

Shut up, Cully. Shut up, shut up, shut up.

One of the hut doors was flung open, and a huge ork came stomping down the crude wooden steps in front of it, a big rusty cleaver in its hand. It wore a spiked leather vest and a pair of heavy, ugly boots, and nothing else. It was enormous, even by ork standards, and quite clearly the boss of the whole encampment.

Steeleye put a hotshot through its left eyeball at three hundred yards, blowing its brains out of the vaporised remains of the back of its skull.

The vox crackled into life in Cully's ear.

'Go,' she said.

Cully put a three-round burst into the nose-picker without hesitation, blowing the hideous xenos off its arse and onto its back beside the camp fire. Its legs flailed up into the air, and Cully put another deliberately targeted shot into its crotch simply because he could.

Kill!

The horrible thing flailed and howled on its back, and then Strongarm landed a krak grenade right next to it and that was the end of that.

Strongarm was Cully's top boy in his section, a born thrower who carried most of the squad's grenades strung from a heavy bandolier that crossed his shoulder and made him walk with a perpetual lean to the left. A sniper like Steeleye was all well and good, Cully reasoned, each shot a personally addressed missive of death, but grenades were addressed to everyone in the vicinity at the time. When you were fighting orks, there was a lot to be said for that.

'Advance!' he shouted, rising up from cover and spraying a burst of full auto into the camp as he went.

There was nothing moving there anymore, and it would suit Cully just fine if it stayed that way.

Of course, it didn't work out like that.

Orks came boiling up out of the huts, out of the trees, out of holes in the ground. They always did.

Heavy calibre rounds flew around Cully as he charged them with his squad behind him, his lasgun barking in his hand. Orks were terrible shots but they all had heavy stubbers; big, ugly home-made things daubed with red paint that showered sparks when they were fired but spat out huge explosive rounds at a terrifying rate. Cully ducked behind the massive trunk of an ancient tree and took aim. He chopped one ork in half at the waistline with a scything blast of las-fire. Another's head exploded as Steeleye dialled in on it and unleashed the killing power of her long-las from wherever the hell she was concealed.

'One Section, kill!' Cully bellowed, and his squad ran forward again to do their jobs.

Killing and dying, that's what the Imperial Guard are *for*.

The air sizzled with las-fire.

'Kill, kill, kill!' Cully roared.

This was what *he* was for.

Death and death and death.

The unofficial mantra of the Astra Militarum.

Kill. Kill. Kill.

Afterwards, Cully found he had no real memory of the battle. Steeleye had been up a tree, he discovered later, and she had taken out fifteen orks in that battle alone. The battle that had lasted perhaps ten minutes at the most.

It had felt like an eternity of flying red-hot lead and las-shots and shouting and adrenaline and terror, and yet it had been over in a handful of minutes. Cully slumped against a tree trunk and watched as Steeleye clambered down from her perch in the canopy, her long-las over her shoulder.

She looked at him for a long moment, her single augmetic eye clicking as the bezel adjusted from targeting mode to more rare human interaction.

'You know it's not an ork, right?' she said quietly.

Cully sighed and nodded.

'I know,' he said.

'It's not drukhari either, is it? They're no friends of the orks, so why the bleedin' hell would it be?'

'No,' Cully admitted. 'It's not a drukhari. The sergeant... he said that, but he knows it's not really.'

Steeleye looked at him for a long moment, green snot welling up in the open hole in the middle of her face.

'Didn't think so,' she said at last.

Cully swallowed, then spat on the ground between them.

'I don't want to...' he said.

Steeleye shrugged. 'No one does,' she said. 'No one wants to bloody well admit it, do they? I don't care, Cully. Why the sodding hell should I? So what, a commissar comes after me? So what? I'll say it like it is, if no one else will.'

'Emperor's sake, Steeleye, he's one of us.'

'*Was* one of us,' she corrected him. 'He's officially MIA anyway, no one will know. He made the list, remember?'

Sergeant Drachan wiped the grease off his fingers and kicked dirt over his camp fire. The last one had been *delicious.*

Emperor but they were hopeless soldiers, in the main, good for nothing but corpses and meat.

Rachain knew the work, and Cully too when he had his mind on the job and not on the card table. Steeleye was an avatar of Imperial Justice, her long-las like lightning from the heavens. He might let her live. This new lieutenant was a child, though. The bloom of Imperial youth, perhaps, but in no way hardened enough for the realities of Vardan IV. He supposed he would have to kill him too.

That would be a shame, Drachan had to allow, but the thing had to be done. The platoon had to be strengthened if they were ever going to defeat the enemy. Tempered in the fire like a fine blade. In *his* fire.

And then there was Gesht.

Gesht had slept with her sergeant, there was no getting away from that. Gesht had loved him. That was disgraceful.

That was weakness, right there in itself.

Gesht was part of the problem with Alpha Platoon.

* * *

'You honestly believe that?' Cully asked.

Steeleye nodded.

'I really do,' she said. 'It's Drachan. You know it. Rachain knows it, and so does Gesht. I'm sorry, I wish she didn't every bit as much as you do and I know *damn* well she won't admit it, but she does, and there we are.'

'What... what do you think she's going to do?'

Steeleye shrugged and looked at Cully.

'What would *you* do?'

What do Guardsmen do?

Kill, and kill, and kill.

'How do we do it?'

Steeleye wiped the hole in her face again.

'I wish I knew,' she said.

The fools had a triple guard set that night, more of them awake than asleep. Boots, most of them, barely trained and scared out of their minds, utterly and totally useless in the face of the true reality of war. Drachan had been two years on Vardan IV. He knew the jungle. He lived it, every foetid breath of rotting humidity giving him life.

He loved it, loved it in a way that he had never been able to love the artificial environments of barracks and troop-ships and firebases.

Stinking and rotting as it was, the jungle was *real.*

This is my home, now, he thought as he hung upside down from the tree, his knees locked over the branch that held him. Invisible, his face and the ragged remains of his flak armour smeared black with the charcoal and burned human fat from his camp fires. The noose of tightly woven vines hung from his left fist. The knife, clamped tightly in his right.

Death, and judgement, and natural selection.

The Emperor's Will.

I'm top sergeant, he thought. *Not Rachain, me! You think he could survive what I've been through? Two months an ork prisoner, before I fought my way out with my teeth and fingernails?*

No.

No, Rachain couldn't have done that. I'm *top canid in Alpha Platoon.*

He was top canid, and they would all come to see that.

In time, they would. The survivors, anyway. The few who he would allow to live.

The worthy ones.

Navylover from Three Section died that night, the boy who had been oh-so fond of the female Valkyrie pilots stationed at Advance Firebase Theta 82.

Triple guard, and still no one had heard anything.

'It's like a ghost,' Rachain said, when they found the young trooper hanging from a tree with his entrails dangling in great, reeking purple ropes. 'Nothing's that quiet.'

'Someone is,' Cully said, and he exchanged a long look with Steeleye as he said it. 'Someone we know.'

Rachain turned on Cully with his fist raised in preparation for a punch that would have floored him, but Cully met his old friend's eye and faced him down.

'Come on, Rachain,' Steeleye said, and spat snot onto the ground out of the hole in the middle of her ruined face. 'Who was your top scout? Who did you send out into the green when you needed ork advance parties murdered nice and quiet in the dark? It was Drachan, every time.'

'Be quiet!' Rachain growled. 'It's not...'

'Isn't it?' Cully snapped. 'Isn't it, Rachain? Who else? It's no ork, and we all know there aren't any drukhari on this planet. Who the *hell* else could it be? Who else is this good?'

'No one,' Rachain admitted with a sigh. 'You're right. Oh

Emperor's love, you're right. It's him, I know it is. I've known for days. I just... I didn't want to be right, you know what I mean?'

Cully turned and looked at his friend, recoiled from the expression in his eyes.

Betrayal, and murder, and despair.

'Yeah,' he said at last.

Rachain's jaw set in a hard line.

'Then we end this,' he said. 'We end this now.'

They were busy for the rest of the day. There were pits to be dug, deadfall traps to be rigged and wooden stakes to be cut and sharpened and set. The jungle steamed around them, making combat uniforms and flak armour stick to them disgustingly even as hideous insects crawled through their hair.

Vardan IV was hell.

The Emperor created Vardan IV to train the faithful, Cully thought to himself; the old joke, bitter with irony. No, no He did not.

Vardan IV was created by monsters. Vardan IV was, in Cully's experience, the very worst place in a galaxy pretty much *made* of bad places. And now they faced one of the very worst monsters it had to offer.

One of their own.

The jungle did strange things to a man's mind.

Drachan had lost his mind altogether. Cully had no idea where he'd been in the three months since he made the list, and Emperor's truth be told, he didn't want to find out. The thought of being an ork POW... no.

No, that didn't bear thinking about. How he had escaped was anyone's guess, but even if he'd got his body out he had quite clearly left his sanity behind.

Cully wiped the back of his hand across his sweat-slicked forehead and remembered an ork camp they had liberated a year ago, him and Rachain and Drachan and Steeleye and the other old guard of Alpha Platoon. The prisoners had been kept in tiny bamboo cages, with the new shoots growing up around them like spears. Their bodies contorted into hideous shapes, unable to move, twisted to avoid the plants that would have impaled them as they grew, inches per day.

The others, the unlucky ones, had been shut in metal boxes. In the jungle heat of Vardan IV.

It was a point of discussion, among the veterans, over sacra and dice, whether or not the heat exhaustion and dehydration killed a man before the meat cooked on his bones. Whether, starved to the point of madness, he was tempted to eat his own limbs before the heat overcame him. Whatever the questions, they had found no one left alive in the metal boxes to tell them the answers. Some of them, yes, had shown the signs of having tried to eat themselves.

Cully shuddered and looked down into the pit. It was twelve feet deep now, with sharpened stakes lining the bottom. Nothing that fell in there was getting out alive. They had dug eighteen of them around the camp.

He could only pray it would be enough.

It wasn't enough.

Drachan walked through their traps like they weren't there.

He laughed as he killed, laughed his special silent laugh into the jungle night. The laugh the orks had taught him.

Somewhere deep down in himself, he knew he had changed. Knew he was no longer the man he had been. He had *evolved*. The orks had done that, taught him new things. New ways of being. New priorities.

Amongst the orks, the biggest and strongest was always in charge.

And why not?

It made perfect sense, when you thought about it. Might made right, everyone knew that. The whole Imperium pretty much *ran* on that principle, so how was this any different? The jungle made things clearer in a man's mind.

Everything was very clear, now, to Drachan. What he was.

What he had to do.

He laughed as he hauled Sharpknife up a tree, his noose tight around her throat as he hung upside down over her from his knees and drove the point of his combat knife into her sternum, dragged it down hard to spill her guts out over her boots.

He hadn't had a firearm since before he was captured, but he found he didn't miss them anymore. The Guard-issue knife, to kill with. The stolen ork cleaver, to cut his meat with. So simple. So clean.

Might and steel.

That was all he needed.

Drachan walked the jungle like a spirit unavenged, looking for the lieutenant. Blood and blood and death, drummed into him over and over again in basic. Reinforced in the fires of war on twenty planets. The unofficial mantra of the Imperial Guard.

Death and death and death.

Kill. Kill. Kill.

That was what the Imperial Guard were *for.*

'Emperor's *teeth*!' Rachain swore, the next morning.

Triple guard, and *still* they had lost two. Lieutenant Makkron had been almost inevitable, but they had lost Sharpknife, too. She had been a real soldier, not just some recruit boot. Rachain wanted to beat his head against a tree in frustration. Rachain very, very badly wanted to kill someone.

Anyone, anyone at all.

'Cully!' he roared, when he was shown the hanged corpses. 'Get here!'

Cully got there, fast as fast. Rachain was his friend, yes, but sometimes you just didn't mess with a veteran sergeant.

'I... I don't know what to say,' Cully said, as he stared at Sharpknife and Makkron's disembowelled bodies.

The lieutenant was a kid and an idiot, but Sharpknife had been one of the tough ones, one of the veterans. There had been nothing not to like about Sharpknife, except...

'She liked to play Crowns,' Cully said, the words vomiting out of his mouth before he had time to think about them.

You didn't tell tales to the boss, not about a comrade, you never, never did, but when she was found hanged from a tree and you could smell the shit running out of her ruptured guts maybe you did after all, just that once.

'Oh holy God-Emperor, Rachain, don't you see it? He hated gambling. He hated wet-behind-the-ears officers and he hated weakness, too, in every form he saw it. Webfoot fell over in the swamp and gave our position away, and Hangnail threw up when she saw Webfoot's corpse, and the lieutenant...'

'Shut. Up,' Rachain said, and the tone in his voice made Cully take a long, hard look at him.

'You know I'm right,' Cully said. 'He's purging us. Getting rid of what he sees as the weak links in Alpha Platoon.'

'What about Gesht?' Rachain said.

Cully gave him a level look.

'Gesht's next,' he said.

Gesht wouldn't hear it, of course.

There was no way, according to her, just no bloody way. Her Drachan was dead, everyone knew that. Of course he was. He'd gone down fighting orks like an Imperial Hero. He *was* an Imperial Hero.

He hadn't survived, of course he hadn't. Heroes never did.

He wasn't the man who was hunting them. Killing them.

Eating them.

Except of course he was.

Cully and Rachain and Steeleye knew damn well he was. Deep, deep, *deep* down, Gesht had to admit she knew it too.

She remembered how Drachan had walked her back from the mission where they had used heavy flamers on an unmapped rural settlement, how he had kept her together afterwards. The settlement hadn't been on the Munitorum survey.

Afterwards, no one could put their hand on their heart and swear that the settlement hadn't been Imperial after all.

Drachan had just shrugged. 'They might have been orks,' he had said to her.

Yeah, they might have been orks, Gesht told herself, for the hundredth time since that dark, burning day.

'Better safe than sorry,' Drachan had told her.

Always.

Always better safe than sorry, she knew that now. That was what you learned, on Vardan IV. It was always better to be safe than sorry, however sorry that made *you*.

So you creep into a settlement, rotting prefabs standing in a jungle clearing. What's on the other side of that wall?

An ork warband?

A scholam?

A hospital?

A nest of anti-aircraft guns?

Who knows.

Darn it, throw a grenade over. Better safe than sorry.

Bodies are bodies, meat is just meat.

Burning.

The roar of the flamers.

Bodies, burning in the jungle.

At least it's them not me.

Burn it all, he had said. Better safe than sorry. Burn it all, and tell no one.

I know, Gesht thought, all at once. *I know it's you, you mother lover.*

She straightened up all at once, checked her webbing and her reloads. Looked across their camp fire, saw the slick gleam of the snot that oozed forever out of Steeleye's face. Met the other woman's eyes.

'I'm doing this,' Gesht said. 'Tonight. Come, or don't.'

'I'm coming,' Steeleye said.

She stood up, and she shouldered her long-las, and followed Gesht.

Cully looked at Rachain, and the veteran sergeant looked back at him.

'Yes,' Rachain said.

Together, their few surviving men behind them, they set off to hunt a ghost.

Sergeant Drachan wiped the grease off his fingers.

It was time to go again.

They were coming for him, he could smell them.

Time to kill, and kill, and kill again.

He was Guard.

This was what he was *for*.

Cully led his squad through the drenched, reeking green. They were doubled up with Three Section, following Gesht and those of Two Section who had gone with her.

Drachan was a master scout, silent as a ghost and deadly as a shark. No one else in Alpha Platoon could hope to match him for stealth.

So they didn't even try.

Every sound, every flicker of movement, earned a burst of full auto.

Overkill. *Any*kill.

Kill, kill, kill.

Moonface kicked the body of the indigenous simian he had just blown apart, and cursed.

'I don't get it, corporal,' he said. 'Shooting at everything like this. He'll *hear* us.'

'He can hear us *breathing*, you stupid sodding boot,' Cully snapped at the boy. 'Drachan was – *is* – the most dangerous man in Alpha Platoon. There's no sneaking up on him, my lad. We've just got to–'

'Blood and fire!' Rachain roared, blasting away into the trees on a furious rampage of full auto until he drained his lasgun's power-pack to empty.

His finger stayed clamped down on the trigger even then, the weapon clicking empty in his hands in impotent desperation.

Cully raced towards the sergeant's position, stopped short when he saw what had provoked Rachain's outburst.

Dannecker was down, his throat hacked out by a heavy knife.

'He was right behind me,' Rachain cursed, 'and I never heard anything!'

Strongarm hurled a grenade into the trees, throwing up a great fireball of shattered branches and pulped vegetation. Somewhere in the green, someone laughed.

Cully's blood ran cold.

There was nothing sane in that laugh, nothing human any more.

'Drachan,' he whispered.

Rachain nodded.

'That way,' he said.

Steeleye heard the laugh.

That was Drachan's mistake. His one and only and final mistake.

Drachan is the most dangerous man in Alpha Platoon, Cully

had told Moonface. Steeleye hadn't heard that conversation of course, didn't hear about it until much later, but she wouldn't have cared anyway even if she had. He was probably right, looking back on it, but Steeleye wasn't a man and she knew *exactly* what she could do.

She was already up a tree, the custom long-las held tight to her shoulder and her bulbous, augmetic eye snugly interfaced with the scope. It clicked as the bezel rotated in her face, dialling from night vision to the heat spectrum.

The steaming jungle showed as a livid background of green and red. The simians that swarmed in the canopy were flashes of yellow as they moved.

There.

The bright white patch of human heat, moving oh so quietly through cover, deep in the undergrowth a hundred yards off Two Section's position.

Drachan.

Steeleye took a breath, lined up on the shot, ignored the hot rain that fell relentlessly across her back and shoulders. Data scrolled across the scope and into her eye.

Range, obstructions, refraction index, diffusion potential.

This would probably be her one and only opportunity, she knew.

Better safe than sorry.

She pushed her hotshot charge up to absolute maximum, a whole power-pack discharged in a single furious shot. Released half her held breath. The crosshairs flashed red in the scope as the heavily customised rifle made guaranteed target lock.

She *squeezed*.

'Holy Emperor!' Cully shouted as the hotshot bellowed across the jungle night, a single, searing flash of power like lightning and the very wrath of the Emperor Himself. 'Tell me that was Steeleye?'

Rachain tapped his vox-bead.

'Alpha sergeant to Steeleye,' he said. 'You read?'

'Five by five,' the woman's voice came back to him. 'Give me ten, I've just got to see to something.'

Gesht was there before her, as she had expected, standing over the body of her lover.

Sergeant Drachan lay sprawled against the trunk of a massive tree, a smoking hole in the middle of his chest. He had a Guard-issue combat knife clamped in one hand, a heavy ork cleaver in the other. Long ropes of twisted vines wound around his waist.

'I thought headshots were your signature,' Gesht said, not looking up as the other woman approached her.

Steeleye shrugged in the darkness.

'Tricky shot through the undergrowth,' she said. 'Had to go for the centre of mass.'

Gesht nodded, and still she wouldn't look away.

'Better safe than sorry,' she said, her voice sounding bitter and far away.

She unslung her lasgun, flicked it over to full auto, and opened up at Drachan from point blank range.

'Better safe than sorry, mother lover!' she bellowed.

That was how Cully and Rachain found her, still shooting, and Drachan was nothing but chunks of burning blackened meat in the undergrowth, and Steeleye watching and saying nothing.

'Enough, Gesht,' Rachain said at last. 'It's enough, now.'

Gesht lowered her weapon and looked at the sergeant.

'It's never enough,' she said. 'Kill and kill and kill, remember?'

All Rachain could do was nod.

They returned to Advance Firebase Theta 82 eight days later, those of them who had survived. Rachain had salvaged the ident-tags from those Drachan had killed, so at least their families could receive The Letter and take what closure from that they could.

He had sworn every survivor of Alpha Platoon to secrecy, Cully and Gesht and Steeleye and Strongarm and Moonface and the others. They had run into a lot of orks, and that was all it was.

That was nothing new, on Vardan IV.

Drachan's name was never mentioned again.

Three weeks later Gesht went into her tent alone, and shot herself.

Death, and death, and death.

It was just another day in the glorious Imperial Guard.

David Annandale

The Last
Ascension
of Dominic
Seroff

The debris dropped from orbit and fell beyond the horizon. The explosion of its impact lit up the night, the flash reflected by the toxic clouds of Eremus. Dominic Seroff lifted his goblet of amasec. 'To your health, inquisitor,' he said to Ingrid Schenk.

She raised her drink in return. 'And to yours, lord commissar.'

The amasec was a poor vintage. It made Seroff's tongue curl against its sweetness, and it tasted of machine oil. It was the best he and Schenk could manage. There was no good amasec to be found anywhere on Eremus. This poor synthetic was the least offensive that could be had. It had the benefit of being potent, at least. It warmed Seroff's chest as it went down.

Commissar and inquisitor were seated on the balcony of Seroff's quarters at the top of a thin tower of blackened rock-crete and iron. It overlooked the endless vista of wreckage and decay that covered the entire surface of Eremus. If the planet had once had individual hives, they had long since blended together, their names lost to history. Eremus did not even have the filthy grandeur of Armageddon's towering hives. The mounds of this human anthill were low. The higher structures that had existed had been scavenged for parts over the course of the last few thousand years. On Eremus, everything and everyone had been brought low.

The planet was dying. Its population had been in decline for centuries. There were fewer than five billion citizens struggling in the wastes now, a tenth of what there had been five hundred years ago. There were no more resources, no more ore, and very little coin for the few imports that still arrived. Eremus' civilisation had become cannibalistic, everything used and used again, until it broke down into nothing.

The world was moving towards extinction, but the process still took time. Seroff did not expect the end to come in what remained of his life span, and he did not care what happened after that. There wasn't very much he did care about. There hadn't been since Armageddon, and that was a very long time ago now.

Seroff leaned back in his chair. The leather cracked. The rusted iron framework squealed. He took a healthy swallow of the amasec. 'Do you know,' he said to Schenk, 'I can no longer remember if we use each other's titles out of respect or as an insult.'

Schenk nodded. She brushed a strand of lank, grey hair out of her eyes. Her face was gnarled with age, clenched and hard as a mummified fist. 'I think it was about ten years ago,' she said, 'that I last asked myself that question. I couldn't remember then, either.'

Seroff shrugged. 'It doesn't matter, does it?'

'Does anything?' Schenk asked.

They toasted each other again.

Debris streaked the clouds again, but it burned up before reaching the surface. The wastes of the land were mirrored by the graveyard of Eremus' orbit. The planet moved through an endless cloud of broken ships, military and civilian, of satellites, and of dead defence platforms. Eremus' Mandeville point was little better than a cosmic sewage outflow. Seroff sometimes felt that the wreck of every ship caught in the warp found its way out of the immaterium and into this system, and then to Eremus. The derelicts fed the scavenger economy, and were, for Seroff, yet another symbol of the world's identity. Eremus was decay. It was a refuse dump for the galaxy, and Seroff and Schenk were just as much refuse as the debris burning up in the atmosphere.

A large chunk came down midway between the tower and the horizon. The blast was huge. The fireball filled the night for a satisfying length of time. Seroff listened carefully. Faintly, over the night wind, came the screams of the wounded and dying. There would be many casualties from that blow, though the deaths would barely be noticed outside the zone of destruction. Life on Eremus meant accepting the fact that death could come at any moment. Seroff was at ease with the knowledge that every day he was granted was the result of blind chance. He nodded at the expanding fire. 'What about that one?' he said. 'Shall we say he was on that one.'

'Yes,' said Schenk. 'That would be a true, fiery end.'

They raised their goblets.

'Sebastian Yarrick,' said Seroff.

'The Emperor grant you were on that,' said Schenk.

This was part of their nightly ritual. They watched for the best debris impacts, and then drank a toast, hoping for the death of the man they blamed for their fates.

Seroff acknowledged the mistakes he had made. Allying himself with Herman von Strab on Armageddon had been foremost among them. It was the error that had, for all intents and purposes, ended his career. He had, at least, cut ties with von Strab early enough in the Second War of Armageddon to have avoided the appearance of treason. Seroff had simply been part of the political establishment of Armageddon, though it was an establishment that had failed in every way that mattered. He had remained loyal to von Strab longer than he might have otherwise because of his opposition to Yarrick. Seroff had let decades of hatred for Yarrick blind him to his own self-interest, and to what was right for Armageddon.

Seroff and Yarrick had been friends once. They had come up through the schola progenium together, they had become commissars together, and they had served together under Lord Commissar Rasp. When Rasp had proven weak, Yarrick had shown how little personal loyalty mattered to him, and had put a bolt shell through Rasp's skull. Seroff had never forgiven him for that, and when Seroff had ascended the ranks, becoming one of the youngest lord commissars on record, he had made it his mission to ensure Yarrick never received the same title. He had been successful in this. He only wished that Yarrick had cared.

It was hard for Seroff to believe that his career had once risen so far, so fast, and blazed like a comet. That was someone else's life. His punishment after Armageddon had been this posting to Eremus. Here, he oversaw the conscription of troops to be sent off to fight for the Emperor. What Eremus could offer was very poor. Its soldiers were the weakest sort of cannon fodder, fit for nothing except to absorb enemy fire for a time while the Catachans or the Death Korps took the fight to the enemy.

Schenk had just as much reason to hate Yarrick as Seroff. Her encounter with him was also well over a century ago, when she too had been young. Schenk was a Revivificator. Her faction of the Inquisition dreamed of finding the way to restore the Emperor to true life. A worthy goal, Seroff thought, one that justified many extreme means. On the planet Molossus, Schenk and her fellow inquisitors had been experimenting with the Plague of Unbelief. In order to control it, they needed to understand it. In order to understand it, they needed to see it in action. They had unleashed it in an underhive. Yarrick had brought ruin to the experiment, to the plans and to the careers of the inquisitors involved.

Schenk still performed tests on the population of Eremus. Her means were limited, the material for her work barely acceptable as specimens. As far as Seroff could tell, she had succeeded in giving her subjects new and unpleasant ways to die, but had nothing to show for that work. He suspected that, for a long time now, she had really just been going through the motions. She had no real expectation that the torture she engaged in would lead anywhere.

It was all the same to Seroff. He was going through the motions too. Each found in the other someone who understood and shared their bitterness, and who was capable of intelligent conversation. They had both fallen from great heights into the most profound abyss of humiliation, and they had discovered that there was no comfort, but much resentment, in knowing that things could not get worse.

There was another sudden streak of light in the sky. The debris came straight down, striking the ground with purpose, only a few miles away to the south and east. The object was small, and the blast affected a much lesser area than the last impact. The tremors from the explosion barely shook the tower. But Seroff took notice.

'That looked different,' said Schenk.

'Yes.' Seroff stood and moved to the pitted, rockcrete parapet. 'That hit like a torpedo,' he said.

'Are there any ships in the area?'

'I have not been told of any.' Seroff had given standing orders to the spaceport personnel to let him know of any traffic in the system that was not just more wreckage. Ships coming to Eremus were increasingly rare. Those who came were almost exclusively the freighters of low-end trading companies bringing meagre and substandard supplies, or troop ships arriving to take Seroff's charges to a distant battlefield slaughterhouse.

Schenk joined him at the parapet. They watched the glow

fade from the initial blast. The object had hit in a region that was, by the standards of Eremus, still quite densely populated. The secondary fires spread outward from the impact site, looking like angry candlelight in the darkness. They multiplied quickly.

Seroff frowned. 'Do you see a glow over that sector?'

Schenk hesitated. 'I can't decide,' she said. 'Perhaps. The area seems brighter than it should be.'

A faint orange nimbus, tinged with green, hovered over the city.

Seroff put down his goblet. 'Then we will have to have a closer look at this. I don't know whether to feel interested or inconvenienced.'

'I think both,' said Schenk.

But there was still duty. There was always duty. Neither of them had ever turned from it. *Nor will we*, Seroff thought, even though every act in the performance of duty was another blow to injured pride. There would never be any reward for the loyalty of their service.

There were very few real streets now on Eremus. There were only their remnants, blocked every few hundred yards by the fallen shells of buildings. Seroff and Schenk wound their way through the wastelands, past jagged, rusted slabs of iron reaching fifty feet or more into the air. They took detours around hills of jumbled, indistinguishable refuse. Here and there, flames guttered, feeding on gas leaking from ruptured, mostly empty reservoirs. Rivulets of filthy, black, grease-thickened water ran down slopes and across fractured thoroughfares. The last maglev transports had ceased to run the year before Seroff had begun his exile. There was no way to get around the city except on foot.

Navigating at ground-level on Eremus meant weaving through the canyons of a planet-wide scrapyard. Seroff's tower was one of the few landmarks in the region, and it was easy to lose sight of it behind the cliffs of wreckage. A newcomer to Eremus would be lost within moments, but there were no newcomers on the planet. There had been none for a very long time. Seroff had lost his bearings the first time he had strayed from the memorised route that took him from his quarters to the barracks. Now he barely needed a torch at all to find his way to the impact site.

Seroff wore the greatcoat of his rank, and Schenk had donned a dark cloak, her Inquisitorial rosette pinning it closed at her throat. Their clothes had seen better days, and soon were covered with dust and ash as Seroff and Schenk drew closer to the impact site. Seroff knew that he and the inquisitor had become shabby caricatures. But on this world, that still gave them god-like authority. They were escorted by twenty troopers of the Eremus Bayonets. They were the elite of Seroff's current batch of recruits, in that they were at least competent. He had made them his detail until they were called off-planet.

They heard the sounds of unrest and violence. Screams echoed from the refuse gorges. There were other sounds that Seroff could not identify. They reminded him of the snap and crackle of logs in a wood fire, but they also sounded wet.

'What do you think?' Seroff asked Schenk.

'I don't know.'

In her voice was the same concern he felt. And also the same curiosity. Seroff couldn't remember when he had last been curious about something.

They squeezed through a narrow pass between two slumped mounds of iron. On the other side, they found chaos. The impact site was half a mile away, and the fires here were raging. In the time it had taken to march from Seroff's tower, the conflagration had spread over the entire sector. A wall of flame blocked the way forward.

'This is not the result of a simple debris strike,' Seroff said. 'These are deliberate fires.' There must have been a cache of promethium somewhere nearby. Seroff smelled its harsh burn, and the fires had clearly been set with purpose. They billowed from doorways and windows, and blazed in an unbroken line on the rooftops. Pools of flammable effluent had been spread in the gaps between the patchwork habs and ignited.

Seroff squinted against the glare of the fire. He thought he saw figures pushing others into the flames.

'There is madness here,' said Schenk. 'I will need to interrogate one of the affected.'

'There!' Seroff shouted.

A man ran from a doorway and through a momentary gap in the flames. He stumbled towards the group, clothes and hair smouldering, eyes wide with pain and fear. Violent coughs wracked his frame. When they stopped, his vision seemed to clear and he saw the uniforms of Seroff and Schenk. He halted a few feet from them, wavering in uncertainty.

'Take him,' said Schenk.

Seroff nodded. Two soldiers moved forward. The man turned around as if he was actually contemplating running back into the fire. Then he stopped, his shoulders slumped, and he let himself be seized.

Schenk had the citizen brought to a low, squat bunker of a building less than a mile east of Seroff's tower. It was Schenk's quarters, her laboratorium, and her Inquisitorial prison. She led the way through ferrocrete corridors that stank of old blood and stale fear. The floors and walls were discoloured with dark splashes. The place had always been a prison. Schenk had simply diversified the pain it inflicted.

The troopers tossed the man into a bare cell. He curled up in a corner, trembling. His skin was patchy and red with burns and weeping blisters. His teeth chattered as if he were cold. His terrified, animal gaze was fixed on something outside the cell. He was barely aware of his captors.

'Leave us,' said Schenk.

The soldiers obeyed. Seroff remained and slammed the iron door shut. Schenk crouched before the man while Seroff stood beside him, looming.

'What is your name?' said Schenk.

The man's lips moved silently. He was shaking his head in short, rapid jerks, his eyes fixed on a greater terror than the inquisitor.

Schenk snapped her fingers in front of his face and squeezed his burned forearm. The man jolted in shock. He blinked, and looked directly at Schenk.

'What is your name?' she repeated.

'Remmis,' he rasped. 'Arven Remmis.'

'Good,' said Schenk. 'Citizen Remmis, why is your district on fire?' She kept his left arm in her grip, and squeezed again to keep his fear focused on her.

'Burn the dream,' Remmis said. He shook his head more violently. The words came out in a rushing, desperate mutter. 'We have to burn the dream.' His eyes fastened onto Schenk, and he gripped her arm with his right hand. 'Promise me I won't dream. You won't let me dream. Promise me, promise me.' He sobbed. 'They were all dreaming... my children... such dreams...' He began to keen. 'I can't dream. Will you promise, will you promise, *will you promise*?'

The inquisitor shook his arm off and straightened, taking a step back. Remmis wrapped his arms around himself and rocked back and forth, muttering about dreams and fire.

'This is getting us nowhere,' said Schenk.

'Maybe not,' Seroff said. 'But it does confirm there was something in that object.'

Schenk tried another tack. 'What landed? Was something let loose?'

'Dreams,' Remmis whispered. 'No, not dreams. Dreams of the end of dreams. Dreams of decay. Catching.'

Seroff exchanged a worried look with Schenk. '*Catching*,' he repeated.

'A plague?' Schenk murmured.

'This is more your territory than mine,' Seroff pointed out.

Schenk nodded slowly, thinking. 'I will need to see,' she said. 'When the fires die down, I'll go back in.' She grimaced. 'He keeps talking about dreams. This does not sound like a plague.'

'*No!*' Remmis shouted. '*NO!*' He looked back and forth between Seroff and Schenk, his eyes staring wide, looking as though they might jump from his skull. 'Don't let me,' he said. 'You mustn't let me dream. Why won't you stop the dream? You mustn't let me dream.' He scrabbled forward, reaching for the hem of Seroff's coat. A second later, he shrank back. Eyes closed, he clawed at the walls, breaking his fingernails. '*Stop the dream!*'

Remmis shrieked. He reached for his eyes. Bloody fingers hooked. As Seroff recoiled, Remmis' cries turned into a single, unending scream. He sank his fingers into his eyes, and the eyes welcomed the fingers. Remmis' eyelids liquified, and his eyeballs sucked at the fingers. His eyeballs became soft jelly, and then his eyelashes became tendrils, and sliced through skin and muscle, and then bone. With a splintering, sucking sound, his fingers came off his hand and disappeared into the hungry substance of his eyes. His arms fell back, the flesh around the stumps of his fingers turning black and flaking away. Rot gnawed its way along his hands and up his arms, spreading onto his torso.

Remmis' eyes ground his fingers to pulp, and then blossomed. Black, furry petals unfolded, their edges sharp as blades, their surface wet as tongues. A heady, cloying perfume filled the cell, and Seroff felt as if his nose were packed thick with buzzing flies.

The unholy flowers kept unfolding, pulling themselves further and further out of Remmis' skull. Soon they were a yard long, trembling and flapping against the ground. His screams finally choked off when his tongue swelled and coiled into a thick rope coated with slime and mould. The bones of his skull turned brittle and they collapsed in on themselves. It looked as though his head were deflating. The black petals kept growing until there was nothing at the junction of their stems but a trembling grey sludge. The petals slapped against the floor, the sound sharp, hard and slick, wet palms clapping. Then they, too, fell still and succumbed to the decay that had taken the rest of the body.

After a few moments more, there was only ash. It drifted back and forth, caught in a nonexistent breeze. Seroff thought he heard something whisper.

Seroff had his back against the door. His breath came in short, hitching gasps. Schenk had turned pale. She met his gaze, and they rushed out of the cell. 'You'll need to have this sealed,' Seroff said as he slammed the door shut again. 'What kind of plague is *that*?'

'I don't know,' said Schenk. 'I've never encountered anything like that before.' Given what she *had* encountered, her ignorance alarmed Seroff almost as much as what he had just seen.

'Airborne?' Seroff asked. 'Are we infected?'

'I don't know. I feel nothing. Do you?'

'No. Not yet, at any rate.'

'The symptoms seem to develop quickly. A few hours at most.'

Grimly, they moved to another cell and sealed themselves in. They waited out the next few hours in silence, trapped in their expectation of monstrous change. Seroff braced himself with every breath to feel a fluttering in his lungs, a swelling of his tongue. Towards the end of the third hour, when no symptoms had developed, he began to relax.

'The dust,' Schenk said, half to herself. 'Airborne, but larger particulates? I don't know. I think we're fortunate we didn't breathe it in.'

'If what we saw are the effects of the contagion,' Seroff said, 'we're lucky the residents set their quarter on fire.'

'A needed step, but we don't know if that was enough. I'll have to go in.'

'And we don't know how much further it might have spread,' said Seroff.

'Do you have the means to quarantine the zone?'

'I hope so. Troop numbers aren't the problem. But quarantining any sector is not going to be easy or certain.' With no real roads, his perimeter would be a ragged zigzag around the mountains of wreckage, and the boundary might still be porous. To do this right, he would need, at the very least, the means to dig a clear ditch all around the infected area. That would require an army of excavators he did not have. In the immediate, he would have to make do with infantry, and hope that Schenk could do something effective against the plague. 'Do you think there is any chance of an immunisation?'

'No. Not quickly.'

'Amputation, then.'

'Yes,' said Schenk. 'Purge the infected and the region they are in.'

A thought occurred to Seroff. 'It is worth investigating further, though, yes? I could just order an immediate bombardment.'

'That step will be necessary. But you are correct. There will be something of value to learn first.'

'Valuable in more than one way.'

'Precisely,' said Schenk.

For the first time since Armageddon, Seroff felt the thrill of hope run through his old veins. 'A new plague catalogued, analysed and contained,' he said.

'A threat to the galaxy halted,' Schenk added.

With the hope came Seroff's first real smile in living memory. 'Well,' he said, 'it may be that what has fallen from the skies will make us rise again.'

'The Emperor protects,' said Schenk.

'And He avenges.'

Schenk's rebreather was a bulky piece of equipment, a thing of brass that turned her head into an avian skull with a blunted beak. It was a relic of her early days in the Inquisition. She would never have been able to acquire a tool like this on Eremus. It filtered out almost every known toxin. The tinted goggles cycled through a wide range of light wavelengths, letting her see shifts in temperature and radiation that might point to sites of infection and vectors of contagion. They were controlled thanks to an interior mechadendrite that plugged into a socket in the base of her skull. This was the first time she had had cause to use it in the field on Eremus, though she wore it often during her experiments in the laboratorium.

The rebreather felt heavy on her shoulders, and the weight of her greatcoat pulled at her too. The juvenat treatments available on Eremus were flawed, and she was old now. Everything was heavier, and she was slower. The same was true of Seroff. They were both bent figures now. They weren't shuffling, at least, but they could no longer run as they once had. If she had to sprint, she didn't think she would be able to.

She doubted that would be necessary. The fires in the infected zone were dying down. Seroff had established a perimeter of sorts a mile away from the nearest fire. His perimeter was wider than it had to be, expanding the region that needed to be bombarded. Still, Schenk approved of the precaution. A few thousand more casualties lost to artillery shells was barely worth mentioning. What mattered was to contain the threat, identify it, and then eliminate it.

Perhaps she could learn from it, too. The symptoms were pro-
foundly disturbing, and understanding what caused them would,
she thought, make them less fearsome. She was relieved that it
was not the Plague of Unbelief that had come to Eremus. The
nature of the impact still bothered her. It felt so purposeful. Had
the Plague of Unbelief appeared, it would have seemed like her
past reaching out to claim her.

Schenk advanced beyond the perimeter with a squad of troopers. They were using rebreathers. If the plague travelled on
airborne particulates, those masks would not offer much protection. Schenk was not convinced it did, though. It seemed
extremely lucky that she and Seroff had not inhaled anything
at all in that cell.

Schenk hadn't advanced more than a hundred yards from the
perimeter's edge when she heard the cries. The screams were too
close to be from the burned region. The heaps of metal wreckage
scattered the echoes, and the screams were scattered too. They
came from ahead and from the sides. They were rising moans
and falling gurgles. They were grief and terror and agony, and
they blended together in a tapestry that surprised Schenk by
having a clear identity. The precise nature of the pain she heard
was new to her, yet she knew it immediately for what it was.
She was hearing the violent decay of a city.

She signalled to her escort. 'We may have to fight,' she said.
She could hear panic too, in the blend of shrieks. And there
would be no question of letting anyone past. She might want a
few specimens, though she was doubtful about the utility of trying to capture one. Remmis had died within less than a minute
of the symptoms appearing. She would have to content herself
with observing the effects, and trying to gauge the extent of the
infection and the speed of its spread. She had hopes of collect-
ing samples of contaminated matter for later study, but for now,
knowing how to contain the plague was her priority.

Schenk headed for the nearest screams. As she and the troopers rounded the gutted shell of a hab-block, the shrieks blasted through the empty window frames of the structure. The sound grew louder, and also harder to identify. Schenk frowned. Some of those voices did not sound human.

Around the corner of the building, she found the source of the screams. There were twenty or thirty people here. Most were dragging themselves along the ground, gouging their flesh open on the sharp edges of refuse, trying to scrape away ponderous masses of tumours. The infected were moving away from the centre of the contagion, and they were changing as they went. There was no pattern to the metamorphoses. One man had lost his legs, and was leaving behind a thick trail of slime that boiled and bubbled, lashing back and forth like a thing alive. The body of the woman ahead of him was spreading and flattening out, her ribs pushing out of her flesh and turning into pale blind snakes. Schenk saw tentacles sprouting from necks, heads that had become nothing but gaping, snapping jaws, and flesh that sluiced away like melting candle wax. The only constant was transformation followed by immediate decay. The sticky, squirming stench of the plague forced its way through the rebreather filters and stung Schenk's eyes. Her breath hitched in anxiety, but she did not fall to the plague.

Some of the infected were still running, fleeing their more corrupted kin. They sped towards Schenk and the troopers, but did not see them. Their eyes, the ones that were still truly eyes and not sprouting vines or snapping insects, were blank with horror. Perhaps they saw the world around them enough to keep moving, but visions of a greater horror assailed them.

The troopers opened fire before Schenk could give the signal. She did not object. Las cut into the bodies of the fleeing people. They dropped, their wounds smouldering, and their bodies erupted into sudden, explosive change. The dust of their final disintegration whipped up into the air. It spread in every direction, and Schenk saw that it was not carried by any wind, but driven by some other, unnatural impulse. Where it landed, the plague spread. The dust *was* how the contagion spread. She and Seroff had escaped its taint, but now she saw the unmistakeable evidence of its power.

It was more than the infected that made her start to back away. It was more than the dust arcing up from the bodies in plumes. It was the other way the plague spread. It was the other kind of infection she saw taking hold.

Schenk believed in the possibility of returning the Emperor to life, in having him walk again among his children. She had never abandoned her faith as a Revivificator, even though the Inquisition in its totality, her faction included, had abandoned her. She had continued her work on Eremus, still looking for the way to bring life to the dead. She never stopped believing such a miracle was possible, but she had ceased to believe she might be the one to discover the secret. She had vented her frustration, her anger and her bitterness on her subjects, dispassionately observing atrocious suffering and death on her medicae tables. That sour, petty vengeance on the galaxy that had betrayed her was all that she had left.

And now she saw the miracle. Now she saw life spring out of dead matter. Only it was the wrong sort of miracle. This was not revival, for the matter that cried out in the pain of birth had never been alive before. It was stone and rockcrete and iron and glass that stirred and screamed. The flat surfaces of building façades, of the broken road and of sheets of debris wrinkled like flesh. With grinds and cracks, rigid materials bent, tore and parted, revealing the glistening of teeth and the staring horror of eyes. What had been inanimate came to life, and it screamed and writhed to feel itself diseased and dying. Wherever the dust of bodies fell, new life stirred, and the pangs rippled outward along the full length of the girders or the stone blocks, infecting whatever they touched. The disease was rushing over the industrial landscape of Eremus like a consuming tide.

Schenk turned her gaze from the abomination transpiring close to her. She looked back towards the impact site, and saw the rise of more and greater ash plumes. Entire hills were moving, sliding down as they decayed, and struggling to lurch forward as if they might escape their doom. There was movement everywhere she looked, and it was spreading quickly. Somehow, a critical mass had been reached, and the plague was reaching out to grasp all of Eremus. The futility of her mission and of Seroff's efforts at quarantine hit her so hard she staggered.

She and the troopers were still backing up, still holding on to a form of order. The soldiers had killed almost all the mutating civilians. The bodies no longer crawled. They were not the threat. The dust they were turning into was the danger, the dust rising and spreading and grasping at the world.

'Run,' Schenk said. There was no mission to accomplish here. Her revived ambition turned to ash in her chest. 'Back to the perimeter,' she said. That would be no protection, but that wasn't her concern. She could barely think past that point. She found that she could run. Terror gave her energy, and she could ignore the pain in her limbs. She had to outrun the spread of the plague.

Outrun it to where?

She suppressed the thought. If she despaired now, she would die before she had a chance to think of a way to make good a true escape.

'The dust is contagious,' she warned the troopers. 'Do not let it touch you.'

The troopers heard her, and they ran. They had held true to their training until now, but when she broke and fled, they revealed the limits of how far Seroff had been able to shape them. Schenk had been their one shield against panic. She was the Inquisition, the authority who had the ability to end the crisis.

If the Inquisition was helpless, there was no hope. They dropped their weapons and ran, quickly outpacing her. They glanced back in fear at the rotting transformations spreading over the land, and ran faster.

More and more dust rose up. As the larger buildings and mountains of refuse caught the infection, their decompositions hurled tons of dust into the air, like ash from a volcanic eruption. For the moment the dust was relatively contained, climbing up directly above the bodies and mounds that produced it, but spreading only a short distance outward. As unstoppable as the contagion was, its spread was advancing in incremental stages, as if it were gathering strength for a shattering blow.

The sense of volition lurking behind that hesitation chilled Schenk's blood even further. The expanse of her ignorance before this plague was staggering. After a lifetime of study, she understood nothing. She was helpless before this foulness. She was no better than the lowest, most ignorant serf. She was just another tiny figure fleeing in panic, as if running would somehow be enough to save her life.

The troopers pulled further ahead of Schenk, though the way the path twisted through the industrial dereliction slowed them down. They were still in her sight when the plague caught them. One fell, then another, and then the rest in quick succession, the contagion jumping faster between them as more became infected. Schenk slowed down, her lungs rasping like rusted metal in her chest, her breaths thunderous echoes inside the rebreather helm. The twisting bodies blocked her path.

She stopped, exhausted and puzzled. She glanced back and up at the dust cloud. Its leading edge was still a short distance to the rear. As far as she could tell, no dust had fallen here yet. And if it had, why wasn't she infected too? Perhaps her rebreather was keeping the dust away from her, but that would not matter if it turned into a dying, snarling monster around her skull.

She could see no reason for the soldiers to be convulsing before her, their bodies opening up, their organs snapping at each other with stingers and claws, their bones whiplashing into contortions of ecstatic pain.

She was missing something. Even her diagnosis of her helplessness was lacking. She was failing to grasp even the most basic elements of the plague's contagion.

Think later. Run now. Even if she was wrong about how humans contracted the plague, she had seen the dust infect stone and metal. If she was caught in dustfall, she would die in gibbering rockcrete jaws. She hesitated a moment longer. The route blocked by the dying troopers ran between two long hab-blocks. It would take her half an hour to try to detour around either building and find her way back onto a route towards the perimeter.

Go now, before they turn into dust.

The mad hope of an immunity danced through her mind and she ran. There was no choice. Irrationally, she held her breath as she passed between liquefying humans. Her skin prickled in the anticipation of being clutched by disease. Then she was past the dying soldiers and running between the stained, leaning walls of the hab-blocks. She ran for the other end of the passage between the buildings as if it were a meaningful goal.

As if Seroff's quarantine line represented actual refuge.

And yet, even though terror snapped at her heels and squeezed her heart, she still felt immune. At her innermost core, where the bitter stone of her being had been shaped and polished by year upon year of frustrations and disappointments, she could not really believe she would succumb to the plague. Such an end was not permissible. The Emperor and fate would not allow it.

So she struggled onward, clad in the armour of soured pride. Behind her, the clouds of monstrous transformation gathered and thickened.

* * *

'What have you done, inquisitor?' Seroff muttered. One plume of dust after another climbed into the sky. From this position, on the perimeter of the quarantine, it was impossible to see their origins, other than being in the infected zone. This section of the perimeter was somewhat elevated, though, and Seroff caught glimpses of large movements. He thought he saw a hill of detritus drop out of sight with a plunging motion, then more dust shot upwards. All of this had begun within minutes of Schenk entering the contaminated sector.

'Lord commissar,' the trooper on Seroff's right said, pointing. 'Inquisitor Schenk is returning.'

Returning was not the word Seroff would have used. He would have said *fleeing* or *retreating*. His heart sank as he watched Schenk stagger uphill the rest of the way. She pulled her rebreather off when she reached Seroff's position. 'We have to go,' she hissed. '*Now.* This cannot be contained.'

Seroff hesitated. Whatever his mistakes had been, he had never abandoned a post. To do so was contrary to everything that defined him. He was still a lord commissar. He still had the duty of that identity, and that was to hold the position, no matter what the cost.

'Remaining is futile,' Schenk said, and it struck home to Seroff that it was a member of the *Inquisition* urging him to flee. 'There is no duty here. There is nothing that can be fought. There is only death.'

'What happened?'

'The plague is spreading everywhere. I cannot fathom how it functions, but I know we cannot stop it.'

Seroff looked again at the thickening dust clouds overhead. The moaning from the quarantined zone was growing louder and more and more inhuman. Schenk looked terrified. His mouth went dry. Duty fell away from him, ambition crumbled, and he was merely an old man who didn't want to die. 'We're pulling back,' he announced. 'Regroup at barracks and prepare for new orders.' Those orders would never come. He wanted the troops to leave the way clear for his own retreat. Then a finger of shame made him add one more command. 'If I fall, then do as necessity requires.' Meaningless words, but he used them as a shield against his guilt as he and Schenk began to run.

The quarantine line broke apart. The growing cries from inside the infected zone and the sounds of strange, heavy movement made Seroff's orders the signal for all-out flight. The soldiers ran with the moaning of doom at their backs. They were young and fast, and in moments Seroff and Schenk were alone. Seroff felt that he was, at least, spared being seen fleeing by his own troops.

Schenk pointed north as they struggled past an abandoned Administratum complex.

'The spaceport?' said Seroff.

'There will be no refuge anywhere on Eremus,' said Schenk. 'The only refuge is off-planet.'

'How long do you think we have?' The spaceport was more than ten miles from their position. It would take hours to reach it.

'I don't know,' said Schenk. She was breathing very hard, and Seroff slowed to match her pace. She had not had the chance to catch her breath back at the line. 'All we can do is try,' she continued. The words were a desperate prayer. 'We have no choice. It is our only option.'

Seroff nodded. He did not look back. The dust storm would come before they were ready, or it would not. There was nothing he could do about it.

Yet he wanted to understand. 'How have we not been infected?' he asked. 'Are we immune?'

'I have wondered the same thing. That both of us should be so lucky, and for no apparent reason, seems unlikely.'

'Even so...'

'Even so,' she agreed. 'And immunity does us no good when the city itself is infected.'

They cut through the site of a manufactory that had been so completely stripped of usable material that it had become an empty quarter. It was quick to pass through. The ground sloped upward, and they came to a rise, from which they were able to see the next few miles. To the north-west, on their left, Seroff's tower was just visible over the jagged hills. The spaceport was still far out of sight, but dead ahead, directly in Seroff and Schenk's path, another plume of dust was rising to the clouds.

'The prison,' Schenk groaned.

'We sealed the cell,' said Seroff.

'That doesn't matter. The dust spreads the plague to inanimate matter.'

As if the dust, or the will it embodied, had been waiting for them to bear witness, and to know their way was closed, the storm struck. The cloud over Schenk's quarters fell upon the city with a dark embrace of change and death. Seroff did look back now, and the gritty clouds behind them billowed, expanded, and came down too. In seconds, the vistas of Eremus before and behind them erupted with screams. Downslope from the manufactory shell was a group of malnourished scavengers. They stopped what they were doing and looked around. From where they were, they could not see the dust, but they could hear the cries. They dropped the scrap metal they had been piling up and broke into blind, panicked flight.

Seroff and Schenk ran too. They made for the lord commissar's tower. There was no logic in this decision either. There would be no shelter there. The tower was not immune to change. When the dust came for it, it too would fall to monstrosity and decay. But there was nowhere to go, and the familiarity of the tower created the illusion of refuge. They moved as quickly as they could, though they were slowed by obstacles and age.

The cries of the transforming city drew closer. It seemed to Seroff that they were caught in a tightening noose of plague. Despair and exhaustion dragged at him, urging him to lie down and accept his end. Fear drove him on. So did resentment, and bitterness. Containing a new plague would have been the chance to rise again. Instead, a world would fall under his watch.

'What is this plague?' he demanded. 'How have we avoided contagion?' That was the last shred of hope he had, that their luck might continue.

'I don't know,' said Schenk. 'I can't make sense of the infection's form. There is no clear pattern to what it does. It is irrational. The only constant is horror, as if *that* could be the contagion. The plague behaves more like the dream of a disease than the reality of one.'

The nightmare closed in on them. The sky was thick with the terrible dust everywhere Seroff looked. As they drew close to the tower, they passed another manufactory complex, one of the few still working. Its chimneys screamed. Maws opened midway up their height. Fire burst from between the teeth, and then came a torrent of black and green liquid that burned and writhed in pain. Even the molten, reclaimed metal was infected, coming to life only to die.

They reached the tower just ahead of the dustfall. Seroff slammed the iron door behind them. There was no power in the city any longer. The only light in the dim entranceway came from the narrow slits of windows. Seroff stared at the inquisitor and saw his own terror and helplessness reflected back at him. His knees buckled. His legs felt like lead. He could barely draw breath. They had run, they were here, and there was nothing left to do.

Now what? Seroff wanted to say, crying out to Schenk to give him an answer different from the one he already knew.

Now what?

The tower answered. The walls began to glisten. They twisted and groaned. Mould sprouted from the rockcrete and along the iron framework of the staircase. It grew tendrils with claws that jabbed into the new flesh of the tower. Foul-smelling blood ran in rivulets from the wounds. The tower swayed back and forth, moaning and gurgling wetly. The floor became spongy. Seroff lost his footing. He fell to his knees, his hands sinking into matter that was soft, gelid. It split, and red-flecked yellow pus oozed between his fingers.

The tower trembled as if in an earthquake. The floor heaved, throwing Seroff and Schenk off their feet. Deep fissures opened in the bleeding walls. The entire building was about to collapse, and it also seemed to be trying to uproot itself from the ground, as if it might walk.

The upheavals became more violent. The tower was not trying to walk, Seroff thought. It was trying to leap.

Over the deafening shrieks of the tower, Seroff heard what sounded like the roar of heavy engines. The moment was a brief one, and the howl of the tower's legion of mouths overwhelmed him. His ears bled. He could hear nothing except the screams.

The tower fell, and it wrenched upward at the same time. Rockcrete masses plunged down on Seroff, but they did not crush him. They were too soft now. They were flesh, turning to slime and soon to dust. They smothered and they choked. He was trying to swim through something that was midway between avalanche and waterfall. The foulness slammed down on him, but he was also rising. The sensation was dizzying. Gravity crushed him, and he knew they were ascending, and his words came back to him. *What has fallen from the sky will make us rise again.*

Seroff choked on the slime of the tower. He struggled, squeezed by liquefying flesh, the screams tight around his skull like an iron band. The foulness forced its way into his nose and mouth and filled his lungs. Decay was drowning him, and his bones cracked under the pressure of the ascension. He tried to cry out, but only inhaled even more deeply of the slime, and he blacked out.

Seroff came to, retching and coughing up dust in thick, blackened wads of phlegm. His ears still rang with the screams. He was coated in dust, and lying deep in filth. Every bone ached. He felt as if he had been used as the clapper in a huge bell. He managed to get to his knees, then rubbed at his face, cracking the layers of dust. He began to breathe again, and he managed to pry his eyes open. The ringing in his ears faded to an insect buzz.

Schenk was a few feet away, also regaining consciousness. They helped each other up, then turned around slowly, taking in their new surroundings. They were no longer in the tower. It was dead and gone and dust. They were in a huge, dark space. There was a faint vibration beneath Seroff's feet. 'We're on a ship,' he said.

'Yes,' said Schenk, her voice cracking with despair. 'We are cargo.'

The details of the immense hold came into focus for Seroff. He was surrounded by disease. The buzzing in his ears *was* insects. Bloated, thick-bodied flies, overfed and sluggish, droned in clouds over the suffering in the chamber. The stench was rich and layered, and thick as honey. The suffocating moistness of vomit and rot and roses wrapped itself around Seroff and forced its way into his lungs. The floor was deep in the muck of ruined flesh. It gave off a dim, green phosphorescence, as did the mould growing on the walls and drooping in furred stalactites from the ceiling. There were bodies everywhere. Most were human, though there were xenos as well. They lay half-submerged, groaning with the fevers that changed them. Tumours as long as Seroff's arm grew from bodies, twitching like blind worms. Some of the sufferers were arranged in pairs. Cataracts of maggots fell from the wounds of one victim, and twisted over each other in their hunger to climb inside the body of the other. In the centre of the hold, the bodies, many of them still moving, were heaped into a mound. On the top, haloed by huge swarms of flies, a gigantic figure sat on a throne of squirming, oozing, rotting bodies. The silhouette was armoured, and a single curved horn rose from its helm. It carried a massive, serrated, pitted scythe.

When Schenk saw the figure, she stiffened in shock. To Seroff's horror, he saw her grow even more afraid. 'Typhus,' she whispered. 'We're on the *Terminus Est*.'

Typhus. Seroff knew the name the way children know the names of the monsters that haunt their nightmares. Typhus was a whisper, a myth that must be shunned, yet insisted upon being told. He was the shadow that lurked behind the plague-deaths of countless worlds, the herald of endless decay.

Schenk was sobbing.

'So you know me,' said Typhus, with a voice that was deep and humming, like a pipe organ filled with insect wings. 'I thought perhaps you didn't. That would have explained your presumption.'

Typhus descended the mound of bodies. He approached, holding his scythe like a staff of office. His armour bulged and split, spewing insects and crawling abominations. Schenk took a step back, though there was nowhere to go. Typhus loomed over her, a colossus of plague. 'Perhaps you thought you had escaped judgement. After the first century had passed, I expect you did. It took me a long time to find you. And longer to watch you, and to tailor your sentence.'

'Judgement?' Seroff croaked.

The red eyes of Typhus' helm looked down on the lord commissar. Seroff felt himself wither even further before the contempt he felt behind those lenses. Something vital, more important and deeper than bone, began to fracture inside his chest.

'Yes, judgement,' Typhus said. 'She used *my* plague on

Molossus. I will not allow such presumption to go unpunished.'
He turned back to Schenk. 'I did you the honour of creating a
plague specifically for you.'

'I don't understand. I wasn't infected.'

There was a sound like thunder heard under depths of slime.
Typhus was laughing. 'Your ignorance is the point. You seek to
understand and control, and you fail. I have killed Eremus with
a nightmare. Its transmission from human to human was through
fear. Once their terror was great enough, the people were consumed by nightmares, and they became nightmares. And then
the dust of horror gave life and death to the inanimate.

'But you, in your wounded pride, you already believed you
were living a nightmare. You, who were strangers to Eremus,
who had known heights no native citizen of this dying world
ever had, you believed you had fallen so far that only ascension
was possible. Your bitterness was always there, a shield against
your fear. Until now.'

Schenk dropped to her knees, the full weight of despair at last
bringing her down.

'That's right,' said Typhus. 'Now you see. Time to end your
immunity, then.' Insects with long, multi-jointed bodies streamed
out of a rent in his right pauldron. They surrounded Schenk's
head. They stung her, and when she cried out, they rushed into
her mouth. She fell into the muck, thrashing in pain. Her greatcoat tore as hard-edged fungi emerged from her shoulder blades.

Seroff clapped his hand over his mouth and stumbled away.
Typhus laughed again. 'You flatter yourself, lord commissar. This
is her punishment, not yours.'

'I am immune too,' Seroff said, the sting to his pride making
him speak in spite of himself.

'For the same reason, but your pride is misplaced. The fall of
Eremus is Ingrid Schenk's tragedy. Not yours. You do not matter.'

The thing in Seroff's chest broke. The last blow snapped his pride, and he saw himself for the vain insect that he was. His self-worth fled, and the nightmare came for him.

Seroff fell, snakes rising up his throat and coiling in his lungs. His last sight before his eyes turned to dust was of the agonised Schenk being dragged off by Typhus, leaving him alone to be consumed by the nightmare of his unimportance.

PAUL KANE

TRIGGERS

The dream always started the same way.

In it, he was surrounded by riches, being showered by them. Precious gems and metals; jewellery. All the finery he'd become accustomed to, that he increasingly felt he needed to accumulate. The things that gave him the most pleasure, the most comfort: tokens, trinkets, charms from all the planets he had ever visited.

And he, Tobias Grail, would revel in it. At first.

Just as it always began with the same scenario, it would inevitably twist and turn. He'd find himself growing uncomfortable – that tingling sensation which always seemed to warn him, that he always relied on. Was somebody coveting the wealth he'd amassed, and was continuing to accrue? Did they want to take it away from him? Steal the fortune he had been working so hard to compile? If so, he would not let them! Grail would grab handfuls of the coins, the gems, the bracelets that he'd had specially made, gathering everything up so it would not be wrenched from his grasp.

Then he would stop, peer into the blackness that surrounded him. He caught flashes of movement there, heard whispers and shuffling. Someone watching, marvelling at his wealth, almost definitely. The more he acquired, the more he felt the need to protect it. Often he would caution whoever it was to get back, threaten them, for they were getting closer and closer the longer the dream endured.

'Stay away! I'm warning you!' he snarled. But this would only be met by more of the whispering.

Then things would change again, and Grail fancied that he heard snatches of those words. If anything, they were apparently encouraging him to add to his collection. But why? So they could take even *more* of his riches from him?

More, you can have even more!

Grail always squinted, attempting to make out exactly who this figure was in the shadows; that apparently *was* the shadows. But just when he thought he had them in focus they would move again, becoming vague, indistinct, and the whispers began once more. He was, by turns, excited and terrified by all this. His mind would flit from the possibilities they were suggesting, the outrageousness of the plans and schemes which would enter his head, to the sheer terror of putting them into effect. Of getting caught or, even worse, losing all that he had managed to stockpile thus far. Of going back to being in the Guard. Or even before that, to the gutters of his homeworld, desperate to escape and knowing there was only one way to do so. To become the scavenger he still was at heart.

More, always more!

Look how far he'd come, at how he'd earned his place and position; paid for it with blood and tears. He was not about to lose all that to anyone. However, this wasn't what the figure wanted – he sensed that much at least. In fact, sometimes Grail wondered if it had even been his idea to begin all this. Was it his or someone else's? Didn't matter in the end, the result was the same. Now he craved more, needed to make more, to secure his position.

And the dream would always end the same, that rush of exhilaration and fear as the figure moved closer, whispering, yet still out of sight. Or was it? Could he see... something?

Finish your work!

The heady cocktail of emotions caused him to sit bolt upright in bed, panting for breath. Gasping, and reaching down to prop himself up, Grail felt the wetness of the bed sheets beneath him, already slick enough because of the shiny fabric they were made from. He wiped his forehead with the back of his other arm, staring out at the space in front of him.

Something moved out there. A carry-over from the dream, the nightmare? Something shifting about in the darkness, whispering. Coming closer and closer. In a panic, Grail called for light and because he hadn't been specific the bedside glow-globe came on. It illuminated the massive bed he was in, but didn't really stretch far enough out to reveal who else might be present. He had no family here; no wife or children. The many guards and servants that resided in his home did not have access to his most private chambers.

Another whisper, and a tall figure stepped into the circle of light. Grail let out the breath he hadn't realised he'd been holding, his body visibly relaxing, shrinking as it did so.

'Russart,' he said, voice catching. 'It's you!'

'Who were you expecting?' asked the man, striding forward, the material of his form-fitting bodyglove causing the whispering now as its folds rubbed together. Grail took in his features, the thick dark hair and eyebrows, which arched over a solid brow. The squareness of the rest of his face, especially his equally strong jaw. The intensity of the man's stare, those steel-grey eyes throwing back his own gaze. And finally, that well-muscled body stretching the bodyglove tight, a physique that Russart had maintained in the years since they'd served together while Grail had let his own grow fat and soft. Even as he thought about it now, Grail pulled the covers up more around himself, in spite of the fact this was the one person he trusted most in the world... in *any* world.

Russart's right hand was on the hilt of his sidearm, nestled in its holster: a laspistol that Grail had seen him use without hesitation or mercy in the past. He was taking his hand off it, removing his finger from the trigger, now that he could see they were alone in the bedroom. Grail thought about the question his second-in-command, his bodyguard, had asked: who *had* he been expecting? Russart was the only member of security he *allowed* access to his inner chambers, and he was always on duty, even at night-time. That was something Grail very much insisted upon, in case he should require the man at a moment's notice.

But Grail hadn't been expecting anyone *real*, had he? Just a shade from the dream, somehow here in his bedroom.

'No... no one,' he said, more than a little embarrassed. 'What are you doing here, anyway?'

Russart nodded towards the surveillance pict recorders in the room that must have alerted him. 'You were screaming for help.'

'I wasn't *screaming*,' Grail argued.

'I could hear it even as I entered the room. I thought you were in trouble.' Russart stepped a little closer, concern etched on that face. It wasn't beyond the realms of possibility; Grail did have his enemies after all, though how they would have reached him inside his fortress was anyone's guess. 'Dreams getting worse?'

'I'm fine,' Grail assured him, clicking his fingers for Russart to pass his robe over from a nearby chair. Quickly, he pulled this around him, swinging his legs out of bed at the same time. He hadn't gone into any kind of detail with Russart about the dreams, had let the man assume they were of the battlefield: of Fennan's Pass and the hulking green-skinned xenos.

'But you–'

'I said I was *fine*,' Grail snapped. 'You're dismissed.'

Russart looked like he was about to say something else, then thought better of it. Questioning Grail when he was in this mood was not the wisest thing to do. Instead he nodded, concern turning to... what, resentment? Just a fleeting glimpse of it, but there.

'I'll see you in the morning for the inspection,' Grail added, his tone lighter. Because he *was* thankful for all that Russart did. Furthermore, Grail did not know what he would do without the man who kept so many of his secrets. It was the reason why he was paid so handsomely, although Russart didn't get much of a chance to spend that money. Apart from when they periodically played games of chance in various backstreet establishments, that was. Even then, Grail's luck was invariably better than his companion's. Better than most people's.

Russart nodded again, withdrawing from the room. Grail waited for the click of the door before reaching for the glass of water on the bedside table, desperately parched and needing to rehydrate himself. His hand shook as he brought the liquid to his mouth and gulped it down. Then he set it aside, rose, and wandered over to the far side of the room, out of sight of the pict recorders. He passed a mirror on the way, catching his reflection; though neat and well-groomed in his appearance, he couldn't help noting that the face staring back was a lot rounder than it had been a few years ago. His hairline was rapidly receding as well, and once again his mind turned to Russart, the difference in their appearances, comparing himself to his friend. Grail shook his head and continued on to his destination.

There he pulled the covering off a box that had been made to look like a bench, but was in fact a chest coded to his handprint. Grail looked about him, then opened it, gazed at the contents old and new. Quickly, he closed the box again, covering it up.

He just needed to check it was all safe. Just needed to be sure.

* * *

As part of his duties as governor of the mining world of Aranium, Grail was obliged to conduct a monthly tour of the facilities and it was to one of the larger mines that he had been taken to that morning via shuttle, accompanied by a full complement of guards. He'd passed over the workers' habs that filled this sprawling portion of the planet, most in various states of disarray and decay, not important in the great scheme of things. Streets filthy and sordid, the perfect home for filthy and sordid deeds.

Now he was observing the operations – from afar, naturally, as he didn't want to get too close to the slaves who mined the vital ore which kept the neighbouring forge worlds well supplied – and receiving reports about production.

It was a stark contrast to the place he'd set out from a few hours ago. His fortress home, though old itself, was sturdy and had stood the test of time. It had also seen quite a lot of funds channelled into it, giving it a new lease of life and fortifying it still further. The void shield, for instance, which he would be able to use to keep himself and the building safe in the event of insurrection or invasion. Unusual, to be sure, but a precaution Grail had insisted upon; just another level of security in order for him to feel safe.

Or take the renovations to the ballroom there, which would be needed soon for the party Grail was throwing, having sent out invitations to noble families, high-ranking officials and dignitaries. A way, as he saw it, of celebrating the good work that had been done since he'd been placed in charge; output having tripled in the last six months alone.

There were losses, of course, as was to be expected. You couldn't push the workforce as hard as they did without casualties. But their sacrifices were for a higher purpose, for the Imperium. Without their contribution, and that of hundreds of other worlds just like it, the entire Imperial war machine could grind to a halt. Grail and Russart, who was only inches from his side, as always when they were outside the fortress, expected all of those under them to give everything to the cause. If they couldn't? Well, then they were no longer of use and would be 'disposed of'. An impetus for the rest to work that much harder. Similarly, those who tried to escape – and they did exist, believe it or not – would be executed as an example to anyone thinking about disobeying or abandoning their posts.

Grail had witnessed many such executions first-hand, some of which Russart had carried out personally and had appeared to quite enjoy. The governor viewed it as necessary, although he, too, did enjoy witnessing the bloodshed, to some extent. Unlike when they'd served together in the Guard, there was no risk involved to him; no danger. Grail, for his part, had always been rather fond of his own skin, and had more reasons than ever lately not to be parted from it.

Before they'd set off for the mine, walking through the hallways of the fortress – passing the multitude of guards and servants alike, Grail actually chastising a few of them for little or no reason – Russart had enquired if he was feeling up to the trip, given his broken sleep the night before. Grail told him again he was absolutely fine, that he should let the matter drop.

'Do not forget your place,' he'd said, 'or how you came by it.' The debt he owed Grail, not just because he'd brought Russart along with him when he was rewarded for his efforts; how he'd *requested* Russart as his aide, but also because of what he'd done that day on the line at Fennan's Pass.

'I never do, sir,' the bodyguard had replied. 'How could I?'

Grail wasn't sure whether he meant the constant reminders, or the events themselves, which were seared onto his own brain.

The noise of the lasguns and lascannons all around the regiment, dug in for weeks at the pass: a position of strategic importance in this particular campaign. Attempting to make the handful of

men they had left, who were holding off the enemy out there –
advancing through smoke and fire – look like an entire army.

Risking glances over the top of the trench they were in, Grail
and Russart briefly spotting the green skins of their targets, where
they weren't armoured, at the hands or the heads. The ivory tusks
as mouths opened to let out terrifying cries as a call to arms. Urging their comrades on with mighty shouts of 'Waaaagh!' Wave
upon wave, now that the constant bombardment of missiles had
done their worst.

Not one of their comrades was sure their request for assistance
had been heard, whether the signal had even reached its destination. Nobody had come yet, but they had to hold the line. Had
to prevent the orks from getting past them.

Russart, to Grail's left, was rising and moving, aiming as he
went: targeting and hitting each of his targets from different angles
to try to make it look like there were more men firing.

But of course some inevitably broke through. Like the pair who
jumped into the trench off to their right, carving up Guardsmen
with their cleavers, painting the walls bright red. Grail fired indis-
criminately, hitting the enemy and, in his panic, his own men
too. He would be doing them a favour by ending their suffering.
Doing himself and Russart a favour by ending the enemy's intru-
sion into their camp.

Then that tingling sensation, a sense… a feeling that something
was–

There, above them, the rocket falling fast. Falling towards their
exact location. Suddenly Grail was pushing Russart, shoving him
as far away from where the explosives were about to land as possible. But still not far enough, the world turning upside down as
they were flung even further.

And then… Then only blackness.

Blackness, and something moving beyond it that–

* * *

'Sir? *Sir*?'

Grail looked about him, remembered where he was: back in the present, in the mine. The thoughts, the memories had returned towards the end of the tour. Probably because of the sound of the machinery, the figures – slaves and penal workers – occupying every level, going about their work in what looked like trenches, the smoke and the fire...

He shook his head, regarded the smartly dressed man with pinched features and slicked-backed hair in front of him, Lychin, who was in charge of meeting quotas. He had been in the midst of giving his report when Grail's mind had begun to wander again. The man was frowning, as was Russart when Grail turned his head to the side.

Lychin was waiting for his superior to give the nod of approval, perhaps a word or two of praise for how they had performed in the last few weeks.

More, you can have more! You can do more!

That voice again, from the dream. Urging him on...

They were ahead of schedule though, according to Lychin, which would result in more production than ever this month. Metallic ore, rock and other minerals which formed the basis of the Imperium's forces: guns, tanks, aircraft and even starships – there would be none of it without the raw materials that they provided.

Grail simply said: 'Carry on.'

The man smiled weakly and nodded to himself, though it was more like a bow. He turned and walked away, boots clacking on the metallic balcony they were standing upon. Grail looked at the hour: the inspection had taken the better part of a day. There was just time enough to eat and then he and Russart needed to be somewhere else. A less formal meeting, but no less vital.

A meeting that was still work-related, yet it would not appear on any official schedules or agendas. A meeting that, if the previous ones were any indication, would prove quite lucrative indeed.

'I thought we agreed, governor, same price as last time?'

They were in the wilderness to the east of Aranium's capital, in a hostile terrain of mountains and rock. The figure standing in front of the governor was significantly less smartly dressed than Lychin. He wore a jacket and trousers that were faded, even torn in places, and sported a week's worth of stubble at least. But then what was to be expected of a pirate like Sachael Dhane? Not that he ever referred to himself as such; rather he liked to think of himself as an entrepreneur, trader and all-round facilitator. Often he was a go-between, connecting people who would not necessarily associate with each other, and would never in a million years meet in person.

His principal crew were no less ragged, some wearing furs, others flak armour from several different sources. A couple sported augmetics: men and women who had been out in space, had survived out there, for far too long. Their ship, a modified Imperial transport that had been fired upon recently as the fresh blast marks testified, appeared just as sturdy, in spite of its somewhat shaky landing and the precarious way it teetered close to the edge of the cliff where they'd all gathered.

'The agreement has been changed,' Grail told him. 'Twenty per cent extra; another two bags. Or you leave empty-handed.'

Dhane muttered something under his breath, looked around at his people, then said: 'And what if I refuse?'

Grail could see Dhane's crew tensing, as was Russart, the only member of his security team present for this exchange. The less people who knew about these sorts of affairs the better, and he trusted so very few with secrets like these. It was safer that way. He was confident that his bodyguard was the better shot, that he could pick off all of them before they could even raise their weapons, but he was hoping it wouldn't come to that.

'Well, then I suppose you had better begin looking for another supplier.' Grail also knew that was more trouble than it was worth; they had a mutually beneficial ongoing arrangement and neither Dhane nor his buyer would want to jeopardise it. Certainly not for twenty per cent. 'Do we have a deal?'

Dhane sighed, then nodded. 'We do,' he conceded.

'Good, then let's get on with our business.'

The pirate gestured for the payment to be brought forward and placed in front of Grail for inspection. At the same time, Dhane's own slaves – workers he kept on board for menial labour, all dressed the same in dark grey coveralls – busied themselves loading up the containers of ore which had been deposited here earlier by servitors. Enough ore for their purposes, but not too much. No amount that would take away from the war effort, Grail said to himself. Nothing that would really be noticed, especially with their rate of production.

As Grail looked up from the payment, admiring the indigo glow of the precious stones in the bag he was holding, he thought he saw something move near the cargo bay door of Dhane's ship; beyond, in the shadows, which had lengthened now the suns had fallen in the sky. Grail's skin was prickling as he stepped forward, looking past the workers.

Yes, there! Definite movement. A figure, *the* figure from his dream. The blackness given form. Larger now than ever, bigger than a man or woman surely. Rising, *writhing* even; something flowing through the dark, like water in a stream. Except it was curling up and around, glistening, joined by more of its kind. Grail's eyes narrowed and he thought he saw shapes there that looked worm-like in nature, coiling and arching, only their outlines visible. And all the while Dhane's slaves were just getting on with their task, loading up the ore, apparently seeing nothing out of the ordinary.

More of the... tentacles, that was the only way of describing them, were joining the first. Revealing themselves slowly, letting themselves be seen as whatever had been hiding in the darkness finally came forward, catching the edges of the ship's floodlights. Grail let out a murmur, a small cry of shock when he realised that the tentacles were emanating from the thing's face. That they actually *were* the face, slipping and sliding in and out of each other, snaking out of its head. Something *alien* Dhane must have inadvertently brought with him, which had been clinging to the outside of the ship!

He dropped the bag he was holding and pointed over at the creature, attempting to speak, but nothing emerging. Then he looked over at Russart, jabbing his finger in the direction of the worm-headed thing as he did so, finding his voice again: 'Don't you... Don't you see it?'

'See?' Russart looked, but as the governor himself saw when he followed the man's gaze, there was nothing but blackness out there now. Nothing but night. Dhane and his crew, not to mention the slaves, had stopped what they were doing and were watching the governor.

'I...' he said, blinking once, twice. Still there was nothing to see. No figure, no tentacles.

'What are you gawping at? Get your people back to work!' Russart shouted at Dhane, who scowled but passed on the command. *Finish your work!*

Grail felt something touch his arm and flinched, then realised it was only his aide's hand. 'Tobias?' Russart asked in hushed tones. 'What is it?'

Grail stared at his aide, open-mouthed. 'I-I thought I saw...'

'What?'

Grail shook his head, then composed himself. 'It was nothing. Absolutely nothing.'

'But you–'

'Russart,' Grail said, stooping to retrieve the bag of gems, 'I told you it was nothing. And how many times do I have to remind you to refer to me as Governor Grail?'

'I'm sorry, but...' It was the square-jawed man's turn to shake his head. 'Nobody heard me, and Dhane's bandits don't care.'

'That's not the point!' Grail retorted. 'It's about authority, about respect.'

'You think I don't respect you?'

Grail sighed. 'Let the matter be, Russart. Please.' He handed him the bag of gems. 'Take all of these to the shuttle and pre-pare for departure. I'll join you in a moment.'

Russart nodded reluctantly, turning to leave when Grail added: 'And be happy, my friend – we will have much to celebrate this coming weekend. Other business to attend to.' Another nod, and Russart left the governor alone, to watch the last of the con-tainers being loaded up onto Dhane's ship. To watch the vessel itself rise, just as awkwardly as it had landed, and sail off into the night sky.

Grail stared at the space where he'd seen... *imagined* he'd seen the monstrous thing for a few more moments, then he too turned and entered the shuttle, ready to return home.

Grail's usual celebrations, at least the ones he enjoyed most, were always of a more private nature.

Gambling, yes, but his tastes were wide-ranging. And nowhere was this more in evidence than at an establishment run by a woman by the name of Madame Ellada. Located up yet another of those run-down back alleys, her place guaranteed discretion. Ellada's skilled employees were most accommodating, especially if the price was right. A business transaction of a different kind.

Grail had left Russart to his own devices in a room not far away, while he indulged himself. Intoxicants were always readily available, as well. Stimulants, relaxants... They were all on hand to ensure maximum pleasure, washed down with wine or spirits.

Consequently, much of the evening's entertainment went by in a blur. Desires were sated – Grail's anyway, which was all that counted – and it was only towards the end of the allotted time he'd paid for that Grail began to get a sense that something was wrong. Very wrong indeed, actually. The stimms and alcohol had dulled it, but the tingling was still there. That warning sign he always felt before–

His first clue was some sort of flapping noise, as if a bird had found its way into the room and was unable to get out again. The lighting was subdued – not pitch black, but not particularly bright either – so when Grail attempted to trace the sound, clumsily climbing over pillows and flesh alike, he could see very little of what might be responsible for it.

'Where... where are you going?' asked one of the girls with him, and exchanged glances with her companions.

Grail did not reply, he just continued to search, the flapping growing louder and louder. He whirled when he heard something else behind him, a swishing this time, followed by a thrashing noise. As if someone was wielding a whip; the kind that were often used on his workforce if they were falling behind.

What's in here with us? he asked himself.

Grail had the distinct feeling he was being watched. No matter which way he crawled or where he tried to hide, he couldn't escape the scrutiny of whatever was out there in the shadows. He swallowed dryly, backing away up the bed; almost falling off before regaining his balance.

'No! Keep them... Keep them away!' he said, his gaze flitting from girl to girl as he pleaded for their help. They just looked confused, had no idea what he was talking about. Couldn't hear what he heard, didn't have that selfsame feeling of being observed. They just thought he was mad.

But he wasn't. Grail knew he wasn't. There was something else in this room with them, a presence.

Then he saw it, an eye opening in the darkness. It was normal-sized, but instead of white it was pink, and the iris was as blue as an ocean. He sucked in a breath, then gasped when another eye opened alongside it. Followed swiftly by another, then another, and still another.

'N-no, it can't be!'

Several eyes, all inspecting him, belonging to something huge, lumpen and misshapen that was emerging from that murk, its skin – the colour of a bruise – rippling and undulating.

'Keep b-back! *No!*'

Grail averted his eyes, and lunged away, knocking one of the girls out of his path. Only to come face-to-face with what had been making the flapping sound earlier. The wings belonged not to a bird, but something much larger. Much more deadly. They opened up like huge fans, spines running the length of them and downwards at equidistant points, which stretched the leathery material taut. The body of the thing was well-muscled, in a way that would have put even his second-in-command to shame, while its head sported a huge beak. Iridescent blue in colour, the closer this creature drew the more Grail could smell of its foetid breath, drool cascading from its massive maw. He pulled a face, then retched.

'Don't let it… Don't let it get me!' he managed.

Scrambling away in the opposite direction did him no good either, because Grail only narrowly avoided what he was still thinking of as a whip. Seeing it this closely, however, he soon realised his mistake. It was in fact a tail which, even as he watched, flew up wildly into the air and then came crashing back down to strike the floor with a *crack!* Grail jumped as it did so, startled by the sound, and he began gibbering. But he was more disturbed by the sight of what the tail was attached to, a sinuous beast with vestigial forearms and two pairs of legs, its arms ending in curved talons. This one was a sickly grey and purple in colour, but here and there were black lesions – some of them weeping – which it bore with pride as if they were medals.

'No… *No!*' screamed Grail, reaching out for help. 'Don't let them hurt me!'

But the girls were already fleeing from the room, throwing open the door and rushing down the hall. Seconds later Russart appeared in the doorway. He activated the main lights, and as he did so all the visions around Grail winked out of existence, leaving him kneeling and panting for breath on the mattress. The governor was mindful that he must have been staring at his bodyguard with wide eyes, and slowly blinked a few times. Before he could stop them, tears escaped and ran down his cheeks, dripping onto his bare chest.

'Tob… Governor?' asked Russart. 'What happened?'

Once again, Grail felt intimidated by that man's towering form. Pulling the sheets around him quickly, like a toga, he covered his own plump body. 'N-Nothing. It was nothing.' He waved his hand as if to prove his point, but Russart didn't look convinced.

'Those girls were terrified, screaming. What was–'

'I said it was nothing!' Grail raised an eyebrow. 'Why, don't you believe me?'

'I… of course, of course. But–'

'Then stop asking me such stupid questions!' the governor barked.

It wasn't long before Madame Ellada herself was in the room too, far from happy with the situation, and with a look on her painted face that said she wasn't in the mood for debate. 'I know you are who you are,' she said, 'but my establishment still has a reputation to maintain.' Grail laughed out loud at this, but she ignored it. 'Jumping at shadows, at things that aren't there.'

'You will be well compensated, as always,' Russart informed her.

'I'd better be!' she replied. 'Now I think you two "gentlemen" had better get dressed and leave.'

'With pleasure,' Grail said as Ellada retreated, but he almost tripped on the sheets as he was clambering off the bed. Russart rushed to his side, helping him to stand, then guiding him over to where his clothes were: a simple outfit, thankfully, as they were here in secret.

'Something did happen, didn't it?' said Russart, assisting him as he pulled on his trousers. 'You *can* trust me, you know.'

Grail regarded him, thought about telling him exactly what had occurred, then just sighed and shook his head. 'Overindulgence, Russart. Nothing more, I assure you. Too many stimms, too much to drink. They did not mix well together this evening.'

Russart gave him a sideways look, but Grail paid no attention. He did not want to discuss what had happened here tonight until he had been able to process it himself. And that really wasn't going to happen while he was in this state.

In fact, the more he thought about it, the more he became convinced that it *was* just the effects of the drugs and alcohol, feeding into his dreams; the shapes he'd been unable to discern in the darkness. A waking nightmare?

And what of the creature at the exchange? The thing just beyond Dhane's ship? he couldn't help asking. He had taken nothing then, had drunk nothing alcoholic. Yet Grail could still see that putrid face, those tentacles. Still see the monster they'd belonged to.

Just as he would see those from tonight for some time to come, he felt sure.

Grail's prediction was not an inaccurate one.

Over the course of the next week or more, he began to see more of the monstrosities not only in his dreams – when he was able to sleep, that was – but in the real world as well. They would crop up when he least expected it, sometimes as he walked down halls, and he would find himself grabbing servants and screaming into their faces; insisting that the guards do more to defend him.

And were those halls less crowded these days, the staff inside growing fewer and fewer in number – or simply avoiding him?

The visions would occur whether he drank or not, whether he took intoxicants or abstained. What remained unclear was whether his dreams were feeding this, or it was the other way around: manifestations of his anxiety becoming those shadows in his nightmares, or the creatures seeping out into his consciousness from the dreams.

He cancelled meetings, leaving the decision-making chiefly to others – Russart, he assumed – and eventually eschewed the company of *anyone*, for fear they might see him getting worse and worse; jumping at those shadows, as Madame Ellada had put it. Indeed, he barely left his chambers now, making the excuse that a sickness had taken hold of him (it wasn't technically a lie) and when he looked in the mirror now Grail saw someone who was exhausted and unkempt. Who sported more stubble than Sachael Dhane, his hair wild and sticking out as if electrified, and with thick, dark rings around his eyes.

During one particular acute episode Grail became unsure whether he was even awake or asleep, the lines between his world and the one when he closed his eyes blurring into each other, that tingling taking over his entire body. The shadows were no longer as subtle as they'd once been, the creatures he'd seen with the tentacles, eyes, and now horns and spikes, were not hiding anymore. His whole body shivered with terror. They'd surrounded him, as he stood there in the middle with all his wealth. Bony things with swollen bellies, horns on their heads, who wore their ribs on the outside of their bodies, mucus dripping from them, making droning noises as they approached. Others, creatures of multi-coloured flame, bounded along dribbling fire and sparks behind them. Alluring women with the legs of birds, arms ending in snapping claws, slavering and licking, veins throbbing underneath their grey skin. The whispering was there again too, more demands. Grail almost got the sense that his desire and greed were somehow attracting them, feeding them.

More, you can do more! Finish your work!

At any moment, though, he expected to see Russart burst in, to ask if he was all right. Only this time he didn't.

So, instead, Grail steeled himself and burst through the circle enveloping him. He escaped out into the corridor and rushed to his bodyguard's quarters. Gaining access, he slammed the door behind him and pressed himself up against it.

'Gov... Governor?' said a shocked Russart, who was at his table poring over documents. 'I wasn't expecting–'

'R-Russart, what are you doing? You're supposed to... supposed to be protecting me!' Grail spluttered.

'I am busy doing just that. I'm going over the final security arrangements for the ball tomorrow,' he stated. 'Why?'

'Tomorrow?' Grail had lost all track of the time and the days.

'You look...' Russart pulled a face, but didn't finish. 'Are you not feeling any better?'

'I'm... I'm all right,' said Grail but he couldn't convince himself, let alone Russart. 'Just tired.'

'The dreams?' said Russart, rising. 'Or something more?' When Grail didn't answer, he continued. 'You know, I often think about that time on the frontline, at Fennan's Pass. I often dream about it as well. Especially those final few moments, the waiting.'

And now, having heard that, Grail couldn't help remembering lying there in the mud and dirt, in the aftermath of the explosion.

His body had shielded Russart's, protecting it as if he knew he would get that protection back in return one day. Feeling the pain in his shoulder, seeing the redness there. But neither of them moving. Moments stretching out into eternity, losing track of time. Grail silently calling out for help with all his mind and soul to anyone that would listen. For them to be saved.

Then the sounds of warfare still raging up above, but something else: the distinctive sound of Thunderhawks descending, of bolter fire. The sound that meant help had finally arrived.

And now flashes of blue and white amongst the green, of giants in armour taking up the battle.

'Down here, two Guardsmen!' Grail heard someone shouting. Then people in the trenches with them, moving them, lifting them. Congratulating them for holding the line, for holding off the orks as long as they had; the enemies of the Imperium had lost one battle here today.

The helmeted figures in front of them. Helmets turning into horned and bony faces with lots of teeth.

Encouraging him to–

He was being shaken and Grail started, realised he was back in Russart's quarters.

'Governor?' asked Russart. 'I lost you there for a moment. What is it? Please tell me.'

Could he? Could he really confide in him? 'I-I feel like something has finally awoken inside me. Does that make any sense?'

Russart shook his head.

'Perhaps even something that's always... That was set in motion long ago, a connection, that is, at last... And it wants something from me. Something important, to do with this place. You've heard rumours about what's out there, as well as I. And...' Grail put his head in his hands.

'You're scaring me, Tob... Governor, sir.' Russart led him to his chair and sat him down.

'I-I'm scaring *myself!*' he admitted. Grail suddenly grabbed hold of Russart's sleeve, clutching it, pulling him in closer. 'My enemies, Russart, they cannot be allowed to...'

'You're safe, sir. You're quite safe.'

Grail's eyes dropped to the plans on the table Russart was

examining. They were, as he'd come to expect, incredibly detailed. He would be kept safe, no one would be able to get to him.

'If you need to postpone tomorrow...' Russart said. 'Or perhaps I might act in your stead?'

Grail rose again sharply, knocking over the chair. 'Is *that* it?' he cried out. 'Is that what you want?'

'No, it's just–'

'You would seek to ingratiate yourself with the dignitaries attending? I see now, I see... I thought you were happy with our arrangement, Russart?'

'I am,' said the man, but couldn't look Grail in the eye. 'That is, I mean... I work hard for you, sir. A little more acknowledgement might be–'

'More acknowledgement!'

More, you can have more!

Grail backed away. 'You want to broker some of the deals I have initiated myself, is that it? Take advantage of some of the contacts who are arriving?'

'I simply meant–'

Grail held up his hand, continued to back out of his bodyguard's room. 'I shall be there to greet them myself, Russart! Do not worry about that!' He would make sure of it, he'd decided; wouldn't allow Russart or anyone else to take credit for his accomplishments.

No matter what it took, he would be there.

It had been worth it, simply to see the look on Russart's face.

Shaved, bathed and in full dress uniform, Governor Tobias Grail had arrived at the ball in his fortress with plenty of time to spare before the first of the guests arrived: one Baron Kinnsel from the neighbouring mine-city of Forndosa, who brought with him his wife and two daughters. As the event dictated, as well as dressing in their very best finery – he in a frock-coat and breeches, the ladies in cream and white silks, satins and frills – each person was wearing a mask. The baron's was a gold affair, which covered his eyes, while his companions had chosen delicately patterned silver façades that they held up on the end of sticks, and which constantly seemed to be getting in the way of the curly wigs they'd donned.

'And are you not wearing a mask yourself, Governor Grail?' asked the baron, once the introductions to his family had concluded.

It was the one thing missing from his own 'costume', and he explained that he preferred people to see him as he was. 'I have nothing to hide,' he said with a small chuckle.

'Oh, where is the fun in that?' tittered Lady Kinnsel.

'Indeed!' said the baron, then lowered his voice, leaning in. 'In fact, I'm hoping we can have a talk later about a few... matters of business?'

Grail nodded. 'Yes, of course. But for now, please do enjoy the hospitality on offer.'

Russart, for his part, was wearing a charcoal-coloured mask that fitted over his entire forehead, matching the colour of his own attire. He was flitting about, making sure his security teams had entrances and exits covered, not to mention everything in between, as more and more guests arrived.

'You really have transformed this place,' the Duchess Sillerby said to him, craning her neck to take in the pillars of the enormous room, the paintings adorning the walls of various battles from the Imperium's history. Her puffed-up, mustard-coloured dress and mask made her look even more washed out than usual. 'I haven't visited in... oh, it must be four years now. You've done wonders, as indeed I hear you have with ore production everywhere on Aranium.'

'You must be very proud,' said her husband, who looked more

like her father; white-grey beard flowing down from his own mask and cushioning his neck.

'We… I am,' said Grail, accepting the compliment gratefully.

Very proud. You've done well. And your work is not yet finished!

Over the course of the evening, the ballroom steadily filled up with bodies, dresses and masks in rainbow colours; some of the guests eating the food that had been provided, which ran down the sides of the room on never-ending tables; others dancing now that the full orchestra had started up. Grail had finished eating a large serving of cake, washing it down with some of the finest wine available in the province, when someone tapped him on the shoulder.

'Excuse me, but would you care to…' asked a woman in an electric-blue dress, her auburn hair cascading over her shoulders, a mask that was of a much darker blue covering the top half of her face. She nodded towards the dancers in the hall. Grail recognised her from somewhere, but wasn't sure where. Madame Ellada's perhaps? He knew Russart had arranged for a few of her employees, male and female, to be on hand, in case any of the guests might want entertainment of a more exotic nature later on.

'Charmed, I'm sure,' said Grail, holding out his hand to take hers, which was gloved, up to her elbow. He led and they began to dance, mixing in with the other people in the crowd. The lady with the auburn hair laughed and he couldn't help doing the same. Maybe he would enjoy her company himself, he thought; it had been some time since his last visit to the backstreets, after all. Once business had been concluded, perhaps. Yes, then.

The music swelled, the pace quickened, and the pair began to spin. Grail smiled, then laughed again. The woman laughed too, hair flying around madly as she danced. Flying around her head with a life of its own, almost like–

Like tentacles attached to her head, coming out of her face.

Grail squeezed his eyes closed, then opened them again. The scene had reverted back to normal. Just a flash of–

He felt that tingling sensation, a warning.

Grail banged into a dancer on his right, turning to apologise but seeing, instead of a man or woman, a thing with beaked features. Some of the masks were indeed of this variety, he reminded himself, but the one gazing at him now was so intricate it had to be real. The sound accompanying it: that of flapping, leathery wings.

He let go of the woman he was dancing with, veering off to the right and away from both her and the bird-man. Falling instead into someone whose face was all scales and jagged teeth, eyes jet-black and reflecting his own sweating, fleshy countenance.

'No, this can't be! Not here. Please, *not now!*' he was crying out. Grail stepped on someone's toes, and looked down – only to see a fine line of coloured scales curling around that dancer's bare calves. He felt the bile rising in him at the sight of such corruption.

He couldn't hear the music for the sound of the whispering.

Finish your work! More!

Grail pushed one body aside, then another, just as he had when he'd been trying to escape from his chambers. Except that seemed like the only secure place for him now, in his room.

'Russart!' he bellowed, though he couldn't see his aide. 'Russart, get all of these... Get them *out of here!*'

Grail looked from face to face. He saw the bewilderment of regals and the high-born, then the green-skinned ugliness of orks, tusks protruding from their mouths, before finally monsters of a different kind. Those he had only encountered of late. Things low-born from the shadows but now so varied in their palettes: pinks, blues, greens and reds. Approaching him, waking something inside him.

It felt like it went on forever, losing track of time.

There were cries and screams as the guests assumed they were in danger, which actually helped clear the room. The music had ceased, the musicians being ushered to the exits. Grail staggered on, tumbling away from them all, attempting to escape up the corridor. Leaving the panicked noise of over a hundred people–

The explosions, the sound of las-fire.

–leaving it all behind him, eager to be back in his chambers. To be safe, to protect what was his. Grail virtually fell through the door, shutting it again and barricading it after him; shoving a chair and table against it.

He rushed into the bedroom, grabbing the box that looked like a bench, dragging it onto his bed and opening it with his hand-print. Checking to make sure they were all still there, his most precious items.

Then, a sound. Out in the shadows. Grail called for the light, but just as before it only turned on the smaller bedside one; didn't extend far enough to identify who was present. Someone who'd snuck in, who wanted what was his.

You can have more!

'W-who is it? Identify yourself!' More monsters, more of the creatures he'd seen in his dreams and in the real world? That had truly awoken him?

No. As the figure stepped out into the light, Grail saw his old friend Russart once more, his mask discarded. He sighed with relief. The man had got here before him. Had been waiting for him, to protect him.

'Governor, sir.'

'Oh, thank goodness! I thought–'

'Enough of all that. Let's get on with our business, shall we? You know what it is that I want,' said his bodyguard. 'You've known all along. Suspected anyway.'

'What?' spluttered Grail.

'Your power, your wealth. All of it. I'm tired of being in the shadows. We both survived that day at Fennan's Pass, but only one of us became governor of this world.'

Grail pointed accusingly: 'You? You did this to me? Poisoned me? What? Was it taking too long?'

Russart didn't reply, he just drew his laspistol, finger on the trigger.

'Russart, *no!*'

'Yes,' said the man, and fired.

Grail didn't hear the shot, but he felt the searing pain in his chest. Realised he was tumbling backwards onto the bed; knocking the box over with him, releasing the precious gems and metals, jewellery. The things that gave him the most pleasure, the most comfort: tokens, trinkets, souvenirs and charms; being showered in them.

But something else. The thing that fell to the ground with him, the last item he saw before everything went totally black. Before the shadows surrounded him a final time.

The medal he'd received for his actions that day on Fennan's Pass, now dark and tarnished, covered with intricate, repellant designs like nothing he'd ever seen before. It – and he – now belonged, he realised in his final moments, to those very same monsters that had been haunting him.

Reminders of promises he needed to keep, a transaction when the time came. Getting him away safely, from his old home-world, from the warzone at Fennan's Pass. More than simply luck, building up his career, his station. But with a debt to be paid; a mutual understanding.

To create a point of weakness on Aranium, which was not only of strategic importance – a planet from which to launch a whole new wave of attacks – but whose natural resources would support their own mortal armies.

The forces of Chaos. The masters he had been serving without fully understanding it, and who he had failed.

Just as they had failed to keep him alive this time.

To keep him safe.

Laspistol still raised and out in front, the figure stepped closer to Governor Tobias Grail.

They knew the pict recorders were recording everything, that evidence of what had happened here would be found by the right people; they would make sure of it. That when he woke up, the real Russart would be charged with murder, and a new governor would be appointed to the mining world of Aranium.

The figure sorted through the items Grail had kept hidden away; but took only one, an old military medal.

The figure looked up and made sure the recorder above got a decent image of that borrowed face, then withdrew again. It was a face that had been altered using the drug polymorphine, made to look like Grail's second, while the man himself slept in his own quarters. It had been easy enough to get to him, incapacitate him; easy as well to get to the governor's chambers ahead of its owner.

Easy enough for *her*, thought Vess, a member of the Officio Assassinorum's Callidus Temple. A highly trained killer. She'd been here, observing, for some time. One of the slaves during the exchange with Dhane; one of the girls at Madame Ellada's; a nameless woman at the ball. Making sure the psykers' predictions would never come to pass. That the Dark Gods and their forces, who had been using greed and paranoia to manipulate Grail, would never gain control of this planet.

Vess left quietly now, the same way she'd entered; faded into the shadows, barely seen, her task finally completed. It always started off the same way, but would end up different every time: would twist and turn, getting on with business until the job was done. Until her work was finished. There was no satisfaction, no feelings either way.

Because it wasn't about pride or principle. It was about the Emperor. It was about the Imperium and those who opposed it. All about holding the line.

And its enemies had lost another battle here today.

JOSH REYNOLDS

A DARKSOME
PLACE

'This is a kindness.'

His eyes opened, as her voice rustled above him and around him, like leaves on the wind. Panicked, he flailed, searching. But she wasn't there.

For an instant, he thought it was over. That he'd made it. Then, like the splash of something far away, but drawing steadily closer, her voice echoed through the tunnel again.

'This is a kindness.'

Her words reverberated through him and he knew that it would never be over. Could never be over until she had what she wanted.

So Padmar Tooms rose, gasping. As he had every time before, and would, until she was satisfied. He could feel her touch all over him. All around him, and in him. He felt it deep in the meat of him, like a hook in his belly, pulling him up when he just wanted to fall and sink. The water lashed up against him, colder than cold, and hard. Stones made rough messes of his palms and face as he swayed from one side of the passage to the other, and the dark and the light went around and around until he couldn't tell which side was up and which was down.

Every time he fell, there she was.

'This is a kindness.' That was what she'd said. That was what she always said, in a voice like falling rain and cracking ice.

Tooms fell again, heavy and full. Her kindness moved in him, readying itself. His stomach clenched, his bowels knotting up, and he rolled onto his back in the water, hands pressed to his mouth. Trying to keep it all in. His head jerked back, struck the stones.

Jostling the past loose from the present.

Tooms stopped, and lifted a fist.

In the darkness somewhere ahead, something heavy moved through the water. The sound grew louder. As if whatever it was, was coming closer.

Behind him, the other underjacks came to a halt. Five of them in all, counting him, the stories of their lives etched on scarred faces and darting glances. Not long stories, by any stretch. But familiar ones, to a man like Tooms.

They traversed the narrow tunnel single file, walking carefully through the knee-deep water. There were paths to either side of the stream, but only a fool trusted those, unless he had no other choice. The soup was slippery and smelly, but it wouldn't crumble unexpectedly beneath your feet. Tooms glanced at the man behind him. 'Cover the lantern, Skam.'

Skam, a narrow-faced Aqshian with hair the colour of damp ashes, quickly hooded the lantern he held, casting the sewer tunnel into darkness. The Aqshian hefted the fyresteel hand-axe he held, his dark eyes narrowed above the handkerchief he wore about his mouth and nose. 'Want me to look?' he whispered, his voice muffled and hoarse.

Tooms waved him to silence. No reason to cause a fuss, if they didn't have to. That was rule number one for an underjack. Or it had been, in Tooms' day. Things had changed, of late. Greywater Fastness wasn't what it had been, but then, neither was Tooms.

He was old now. Maybe the oldest underjack left in the city, if Agert were dead. He'd never been a soldier, but he'd fought in wars aplenty, down in the deep dark. He wore battered leathers, and waterproof boots. His knives hung within easy reach, and a heavy, iron-headed truncheon slapped reassuringly against his thigh. Swords were almost useless down here. No room to draw one, let alone swing it, in most passages. Only a fool carried a sword.

Proper underjacks knew that. Had known that. They'd known what it meant, to work down below. That it was an honour, not a punishment. Times had changed and not for the better. Once, men had fought for the right to patrol the soup. Now, that duty went to the last chancers and the no-hopers. Once, only the best had gone down into the depths, and people had cheered when they'd returned. But now, no one cared if they came back at all.

Except this time. This time, Agert was gone. And if Agert was gone, something truly bad had happened. Even them above, who never set foot down here, knew that. Too many had disappeared of late. Too many had gone into the dark, never to be seen again.

The splashing continued, as whatever it was slid on by, on its way to wherever it wanted to go. In the dark, every sound was magnified. Every intake of breath, a roar. Every splash, a tidal wave. And beneath it all, the steady murmur of the water.

When the sound of splashing faded, Tooms said, 'The lantern.' The lantern was duardin-made, and the oil would burn forever, if properly tended. Even the deepest shadows were no match for its glare.

Light flared. Around Tooms, stone walls stretched into the dark, their lines broken by ornate archways and alcoves that shaped the water's flow. The stones had been worn smooth by a century of water, and soft, green things grew across the walls – the only green in the city that he knew of. Buttresses held up the ceilings, their surfaces carved to resemble the stern face of what he assumed was some god or spirit of the duardin. As the light of the lantern swelled, they seemed to scowl.

Above, the streets were narrow trickles of stone and metal, winding their way through the city. But down here, the streets were rivers, and Tooms knew them all. Maybe he was the last man who did. That was why he was here. 'Come on,' he said.

'What was that?' one of the others – Huxyl, the Chamonian – whispered, his fingers tight about the haft of his own truncheon. Huxyl was short and dark, and wore a bit of obsidian, carved to look like a serpent, about his neck. He whispered to it, sometimes, when he thought no one was watching.

'Doesn't matter.' Tooms didn't look back.

'I can still hear it,' Huxyl said, clutching his amulet.

'Just echoes,' Tooms said.

'Sounds big,' Huxyl insisted.

'Troggoth, maybe.' That was Guld. Big Guld, with hands like spades and a face that had been broken so many times that it no longer hung quite right. Guld had been born in Ghyran, but claimed to be from Azyr. He even tried to put on the accent. Tooms, who had been born in Azyr, found it irritating, but said nothing. Just like he said nothing about the sword Guld carried, even though the big man ought to have known better. Then, Guld wasn't a proper underjack. None of them were. Not like Agert. Not like Tooms.

'I heard there were whole packs of them, down this deep,' Huxyl added, nervously. 'Think that's what Agert was looking for?'

Guld spat. 'Maybe. Not like troggoths to leave no sign though.'

'Doesn't matter,' Tooms said, again. More firmly, this time. Curiosity got you dead in the deep dark. You started to wonder, and then you started to fear, and then the dark took you, because you were too busy searching the shadows instead of paying attention. 'We keep moving. Cathedral Hill is a day's walk from here. Let's go.'

'Never been this deep before,' Huxyl muttered, as they started forward again, still walking in a loose single file. Tooms glanced back every so often, keeping them all in sight. You had to look in every direction at once, down here. 'Smells strange.'

'Clean, you mean,' Guld said. 'Ever known a troggoth to leave things smelling clean?'

Tooms sniffed the air. They were right. Where was the slightly acrid odour of human waste and ash, the hot tang of a city's effluvia? It smelled like a forest. But Greywater Fastness was far from any forest. The blasted mire that surrounded the city was barren and flat, thanks to the cannons of the Ironweld, and the pyre-gangs who burned back the vegetation. And oh, the trees didn't like that, did they? Nor what lived in them.

A chill ran through him, at the thought. He wondered if *they* had anything to do with Agert's disappearance. He shook his head. It didn't matter.

Underjacks had a job, and they did it. At least they had. These days, they didn't seem to do much at all. They hid in the substations – the outposts that hugged the city's great sluice-gates – and pretended to patrol, before tramping aboveground to waste their pay in brothels and dreamweed dens.

And now Agert was dead. No. Not dead. Missing. And not just him. Poor folk from the rookeries, and canal-men. Hundreds, even. A drop in the bucket, in a city of teeming millions. Agert had seen that something was wrong, and now Tooms saw it too. Someone had to deal with the problem. That was what underjacks did. They dealt with problems no one else could deal with.

'We should have found some sign of them by now,' Guld said, as if reading his mind. 'It's been almost three days. Are you sure we're going in the right direction?'

'I'm sure,' Tooms said. Agert would have walked against the current, from the Old Fen Gate to Cathedral Hill. That had been his weekly route since before Tooms had first come down into the soup, and only a fool deviated from his route down here.

'How do you know?' Guld pressed. Guld liked to push. Liked to argue and bully. Tooms knew his type. Knew, too, that he'd eventually crack, in the dark. 'How do you know we're going in the right direction?'

In reply, Tooms gestured to the water. Moving south, away from Cathedral Hill and the great cistern there, down towards the canals. 'Because that's where the water circulates from.' Tooms turned and pointed upwards. 'It pours down from the sluice-gates and fills the deep cisterns, before being circulated back through these tunnels and into the canals.' He paused. 'You'd know that if you were a proper underjack.'

Guld shook his head. 'Water doesn't always flow the right way, down here, these days.'

'It'd be flowing right if you'd done your jobs,' Tooms said, not looking at him. Underjacks were meant to maintain the tunnels, as well as keep them clear of vermin. That was why they patrolled, looking for signs of weakness in the city's roots. 'Instead of hiding in your substations, and pretending the rest of it didn't exist.'

'We guarded the Old Fen Gate, that's our job. Agert had no right, taking Samon and the others out into the dark. That's not procedure...'

Before Tooms could reply, someone changed the subject. 'Have you noticed there's no rats?' A young voice. Thin. Dayla, another Ghyranite. 'Usually, there's rats.'

'What?' Tooms asked, looking at her. Vine-like tattoos marked her skin, and one of her eyes was the colour of milk. She wore a frayed uniform of ochre and grey, and carried a short-barrelled handgun, the stock cut down. Tooms had laughed, the first time he saw it. The only thing more useless than a sword down here was a handgun.

'No rats,' she repeated. 'No little grey squeakers, no big black creepers. Agert said...' She trailed off, uncertainly.

Tooms frowned. There were always rats, down deep. Wherever men went, there were rats. When the rats left, it meant something was wrong. 'What did he say?'

'That he'd been seeing fewer of them. Like something was eating them. Like maybe whatever was taking people took the rats first.'

Tooms grinned mirthlessly. Guld and the others traded glances. They were scared. They were right to be. But when in doubt, it was best to keep moving. 'Come on.'

'Keep moving.'

'Round and round, up and down. Whatever you do, keep moving.'

Agert's voice, echoing in his head.

'Agert,' Tooms moaned, dragging himself – being dragged – along the passage. Where was Agert? Had he found him? He couldn't remember. Couldn't remember anything. Hadn't he been in the water? When had he gotten to his feet?

'This is a kindness.'

Her voice echoed in the spaces between the silences, drowning out Agert's. Or maybe just in his head. His head hurt. Like it was full of broken stones, all pressing against one another. What was she talking about? What kindness? There was no kindness, here. Just the dark, and the water.

He clutched his stomach, feeling as if he were about to split open. Soft things moved beneath his skin and he tried to laugh, only it came out as a high-pitched whine. He'd heard a dog whine like that once, just before the rats had got it.

But there were no rats. No noise. It was quiet, but for the murmur of the water, leading him on. Leading him up and down, round and round.

'This is a kindness. Do you see? It will be better, this way.'

Tooms slipped. Fell. Water surged up to draw him down, like

*the arms of a lover. He forced himself back up – no, was drawn
up, ripped up, torn loose and set adrift. Momentum carried him
against the wall, and he felt softness under his battered hands.*

*The walls around him were slick with it, climbing and creep-
ing, floating on the water. Soft, soft. A vibrant patina of mould.
Puffballs that had once been rats burst quietly at his touch, and
hazy spores danced on the wet air, riding the currents upwards
and downwards through the city's depths. He felt them alight on
him, and he shoved away from the wall, keening. Feeling the
things inside him respond to their touch.*

*Something wet on his face. Not water. His vision blurred, and
bled. The air and the water were one, tied together by a storm
of spores, circling him.*

Round and round.

Anemone-like filaments waved lazily in the wet air.

Glistening undulations the colour of sunset clumped and
hugged the walls, spreading upwards and outwards. An extravagance of toadstools encrusted the dour faces of the duardin gods
who stood sentry over the nearest archway. In the lantern light,
it almost looked as if the toadstools were twitching.

Tooms shook his head. It had never been this bad, in his day.
You always got some mould down here, of course. That was only
to be expected. A bit of black, creeping on the dampest stones,
but nothing like this. Nothing like sour patches of mould, floating on the surface of the water, riding the currents until they
bumped against something solid.

'Things shouldn't be growing down here,' Dayla said. 'Not
like this.'

'It wasn't here last time,' Guld muttered, as he lifted one of
the fungal caps with the blade of his sword. A rat's carcass,
half-gummed up in the mould, flopped down into the water,
startling him, and he cursed.

'How do you know?' Tooms said. He watched the rat sink. Its body was heavy with a thick encrustation, and from within its black hair, vibrant yellow filaments extended. His skin crawled at the thought. Had the rat been alive when the mould had taken root?

Guld looked at him. 'Agert would have reported it.'

'Agert's gone.' Tooms' words hung on the air for a moment. The fungus on the walls, soft and fleshy, seemed to pulse in time to the echo. He and Agert were two of the last. Two of the oldest, who'd seen the city grow past the Old Fen Gate. Seen troggoths crawl out of the canals, and worse things burrow up through the dark.

He looked down at the water. It pulled at his legs, flowing past him, just like it always had. That meant they were going in the right direction. There were waterfalls in the deep places, spilling thunderously down into the great duardin-crafted cisterns. The cisterns were artificial lakes, filling high-vaulted chambers larger and more magnificent than any cathedral. There was a world down here, unseen by most and forgotten by the rest. Only underjacks like Tooms knew it. Or they had, once.

Things were different now. Things had changed. Things were always changing.

'It goes on forever,' Skam said, then, lifting the lantern. 'Like the jungles of home.' In the light, the fungus seemed to quiver and twist, as if trying to reach out. For a moment, Tooms had the impression that there was a face there, amid the sagging, flabby folds. Then it was gone, and he was left wondering why it had seemed so familiar.

Huxyl yelped. Tooms spun, reaching for his truncheon. The Chamonian splashed back from the wall, cursing. Shouting. 'Look. Look!'

In the lantern light, something grinned. Skam stepped closer to the wall, and Tooms brushed aside a lump of mould with his truncheon. The skull of a man stared at them, with sockets full of feathery strands of yellowish mould. Crumbling bones, wrapped in rags that might once have been clothing, sank into the mould beneath it. The rest of the skeleton was missing, carried away by the current.

'Like they sat down and died,' Dayla said, her voice hoarse. She muttered something, in the heathen Ghyranite tongue. It sounded almost like a prayer. 'We shouldn't be here,' she said, softly. 'It's not our place.'

'She's right, we should go back,' Huxyl said. 'Right now. We should report this.'

'We don't go back until we find them,' Tooms said. 'We press on.'

Guld shook his head. 'This is stupid.' He glanced at Dayla, and Tooms thought there was an understanding between them. As if they knew something he and the others didn't. 'We shouldn't even be down here. Nothing good comes out of going this deep.'

Tooms looked at him. 'Why are you complaining, boy? You volunteered.' He swept his gaze from one to the other. The oldest was still a decade younger than him. Too young to remember how it had worked, or to know the secret knowledge – the routes through the darkness. Too young to know the things Tooms and Agert knew. 'You *all* volunteered.'

'I didn't,' Huxyl protested.

'You got volunteered, same thing,' Tooms said. 'While we're down here, you follow my lead. You do as I say, or I'll let the rats have you.'

'Only there's no rats,' Dayla said, her voice almost a whisper.

'There's something,' Skam said, quietly. He held the lantern up, washing the shadows from the nearest archway. 'I can hear it. Listen.'

Tooms heard nothing. But Skam did. There was a look on his face Tooms didn't like. As if he were half-asleep, and dreaming. 'What does it sound like?' Dayla asked, and there was something in her voice that caught Tooms' attention. She glanced around, nervously, and Tooms wondered what she was thinking. Whatever it was, Guld seemed to share her misgivings. He gripped the hilt of his sword tight, his face pale.

'Singing.' Skam took a step, and Tooms interposed his truncheon, stopping him from going any further.

'Best not to listen.'

Skam shook his head, as if suddenly awake. He nodded blearily, and Tooms gestured to Dayla. 'What are you thinking?' he asked, in a low voice. Dayla frowned.

'Nothing. Maybe.'

'Maybe?'

'Maybe something,' she said, glancing at Guld, who shook his head.

'Don't look at him,' Tooms said. 'Look at me. What is it?'

'Just… stories. Tales my gran used to tell.' Dayla swallowed, and looked at the mould, as if expecting something to look back. She gestured, and Tooms leaned close. 'I think it's listening,' she said, in a hushed voice. 'We need to leave. We shouldn't be here. This isn't our place, not anymore.'

Tooms blinked and looked at the sagging folds of fungus, considering. Finally, he shook his head. They had a job to do.

'We keep going.'

'This is a kindness.'

Whose voice was it? Hers, or Agert's? Tooms couldn't tell anymore. He knew only that he was up again. But he didn't remember standing.

He lurched forward on wooden legs, numbed by cold and pain. There was no light, but he wasn't looking where he was going anyway. He was just following the water. His head hurt, and he felt loose at the ends, as if he were coming unravelled.

Unravelled, just like the others.

A kindness, Agert had said, but not in his own voice. In her voice, like the creak of branches in a strong wind, and the rush of water over smooth rocks. Had it even been Agert, or had it been her from the beginning? This place had been hers, once, and it would be again. Life was change, a cycle, a wheel turning forever – birth, death, decay, and new life in the ruins. Why should here – why should he – be any different?

He slumped against the wall and looked at his hands. Even in the dark, he could see that they were the colour of sunset, and that the flesh sagged. He had torn his palms on the walls, but there was no blood. His skin felt pliable, and rubbery. He itched all over, and had to fight the urge to scratch.

Tooms coughed, and the air filled with dust. He watched as it danced above the water, briefly consolidating into what might have been a face, smiling sadly, before dispersing on the air. The cloud of dust stretched away, like a beckoning hand, and he lurched forward again, though he couldn't feel his legs.

He couldn't feel anything.

'This is a kindness.'

Her voice beat at the air like sweet rain, singing a gentle song. He wanted to scream, but his voice was gone. Just like Agert was gone. Just like Skam and Guld and all the rest.

Gone.

Tooms awoke.

He did not otherwise stir, but instead scanned his surroundings. Just in case something had crept up. Skam was supposed to have woken him, but the Aqshian was nowhere in sight. Tooms rose slowly to his feet, drawing a knife.

The lantern still burned, casting flickering shadows on the walls. They'd made camp in a wide alcove, set back from the water. They were close to the Cathedral Hill cistern, and the water was deep here, and the current was fast, running north.

But he could hear distant splashing – and something else. Almost like – singing?

Quietly, he woke the others. Questions followed, but he ignored them, instead, searching for any sign of what might have happened. But the only thing he found was Skam's axe, lying beside the lantern. As if he'd forgotten it.

'I knew it.' Guld frowned and flexed his big hands. 'I knew it.' He looked at Dayla, who sat hunched and silent, cradling her handgun as if it were a talisman. Tooms watched them both for a moment. Then he turned away, straining to catch the sounds he'd heard earlier. But it was gone, lost to the water's murmur. He let his hand trail through the water and ran it through his thinning hair, cooling him. The tunnels were humid at the best of times, and sweat had soaked through his clothes.

It was quiet. Tooms had always preferred the quiet. That was why he'd taken a job down in the deep dark in the first place, despite the smell. Down under the streets, where the sky was stone, a man could think. Up there, with the smoke and noise, you were lucky if you could hear anything other than the city, humming its tune.

Down here, all there was to hear was the water. The water flowed everywhere beneath the city, from one side to the other, round and round it went. And if you followed the water, it always led you right where you wanted to go. That was what Agert always said.

He heard it then, a snatch of sound, soft, high and sweet. Like a woman, singing to a sleeping child. He strained to listen, despite himself. If he could hear it, he might know what had happened to Skam. Or Agert.

Why had Agert come all this way? Had he heard the singing, and decided to investigate? Or had he found the mould? Or maybe both. The singing rose and fell, and he wondered that none of the others seemed to hear it.

Maybe they did, and they were just pretending not to.

'What do we do now?' Huxyl asked. 'Should we go back?'

Tooms looked at him, water dripping from his face. Huxyl looked away. Tooms grunted and stared at the water. A scattering of gold and orange spores floated on its surface, riding the current. He saw patches on the walls that hadn't been there when they'd made camp. Whatever it was, it was spreading. 'Time to break camp.'

'You mean to go after him?' Dayla asked. She sounded frightened.

'I mean to go after them all. You don't leave a man in the dark.' Underjacks couldn't count on anyone but other underjacks, down in the dark. You'd brawl with each other, even steal from each other – but you never left someone in the dark. Never that.

Not unless there was no choice.

He stepped down into the water. The current shoved against him, and tiny islands made of spores swirled about him. They formed strange shapes as he swept them from his path. Almost like faces.

Out in the dark, the singing swelled and stretched into silence. The others fell silent. Tooms frowned and looked at them.

'On your feet.'

'On your feet, friend.'

Tooms surfaced, water streaming from him. He'd fallen again, though he couldn't remember when or how. Agert's voice – or maybe Skam's, or Guld's – echoed through his head. Beneath the words, someone was singing.

'Up and down, round and round.'

'No,' he croaked, gripping the wall, trying to hold himself in place. 'No, no farther.' He could see his surroundings, though there was no light. Everything had a damp sheen to it, as if he were peering through wet glass. His throat felt raw and full, and there was a taste on his tongue that he could not name.

He wanted to scream, but he couldn't find the air to do so. He felt hollowed out and full all at the same time, and wondered if Agert and Dayla and the others had felt the same. As if he were coming apart at the seams.

'Not yet, just a bit farther,' she said. 'It is a kindness, really.'

'No.' He bent his head and leaned against the stones, feeling the rhythm of the city. The heartbeat of the beast. Life, but not as most knew it. A life of stone and steel, of pulsing smoke-stacks and clanging hammers. Greywater Fastness lived.

'It doesn't,' Agert said, only it didn't sound like Agert. Her words, his voice. 'But it will, in time.'

Tooms closed his eyes, trying to ignore the feather-light touch of spores as they choked the air of the passage. Great clouds rose from the water and drifted along, following him – or maybe leading him on. He couldn't tell anymore. He didn't know what he was doing or where he was, only that he had to get back. Back to the light. Back above.

They had to be told. They had to be warned.

He stumbled on, shoulder dragging against the wall, leaving a smear of something that glistened in his wake. But he kept moving, following the current, hoping it would take him where he needed to go. Just like Agert always said.

'Follow the current.'

Huxyl was the next to disappear. Dayla followed soon after.

The Chamonian had followed a sound around a corner, and vanished. Dayla had slipped and fallen. By the time they reached the spot, she'd gone. There one moment, gone the next. But her voice was still there, and Huxyl's, calling to them from far away. Skam, too. All three of them singing, somewhere in the dark.

Guld said he couldn't hear it, but Tooms knew he was lying. He could see it, in the way Guld jumped at every sound, and muttered under his breath. He was saying prayers, but not to

Sigmar, like a proper Azyrite. To another god, one whose name was all but forbidden in the city, and for good reason.

Tooms said nothing, though. He was having a hard time focusing on anything but putting one foot in front of the other. Sweat stung his eyes. It was hot, down here. Hotter than it should have been, and the air was thick with gossamer spores, dancing on humid currents.

The stones felt strangely soft beneath his feet, and the lantern flickered like it was struggling to stay lit. Overhead, the city went on about its business. There was a rhythm to it. Noises slipped one into the next, until it sounded as if all of the realm were in uproar. Greywater Fastness clanged and groaned throughout the day and into the night. It was a beast of iron and smoke, always hungry, always growling. And the deep dark was its belly.

Only now there was something in its belly – an infection. A tumour. It needed cutting out. Tooms knew that. Every underjack knew that. You found infection, and you cut it out. That was their duty. That was their honour. He glanced back at Guld. At least it had been, once. Tooms felt old and worn down, and wondered if Agert had felt the same. Things had changed, and the city wasn't what it had been. Nothing was what it had been.

'What do we do?' Guld whispered. 'What do we do now? We can't keep going.'

'Follow the water,' Tooms croaked. 'Just keep following it.' He held Skam's lantern in one hand, illuminating floating spores and hummocks of fungus, rolling in the current. The walls were shaggy with the stuff, and the light caught on gleaming lengths of bone, picked clean by the mould that cocooned them. Not just one skeleton, but dozens – more, even, than that. Not just rats and men, but other things as well. Hundreds, perhaps, attached to the walls and rolling underfoot. As if they'd died, one after the next, all in a line.

He could not say how long they had been walking through the

forests of the dead – days? Hours? Only minutes, perhaps. He was tired, and the song made it hard to concentrate.

'They're gone,' Guld said, hoarsely, from behind him. 'You understand? We're alone, old man. Just you and me. We can't keep going. We can't.'

'We will, or I'll gut you here and now.' Tooms turned and shoved the bigger man back against the wall. Puffballs burst around them, and Guld gasped as bones clattered down around him, freed from their mouldy prison. Tooms drew a knife and pressed the tip to Guld's face, just below his eye. 'We find them. We find Agert. That's what underjacks do. You understand?'

'Yes,' Guld muttered.

Tooms let him slump, and turned. The water was still flowing, leading them on. Dayla and Huxyl couldn't have gone far. Something told him that they were closer than he thought. 'We're close. The Cathedral Hill cistern is through the next archway. If Agert is down here, that's where he'll be.'

'And the others?'

Tooms glanced at him. 'We find Agert first. Then the others. Come on.'

The aperture that led to the viaduct wasn't far. Two grim-faced duardin statues crouched to either side of the opening, their stout forms shrouded in mould. Clouds of water vapour emerged from the aperture, warm and damp. Tooms passed between the statues, without waiting to see if Guld followed him.

The cistern-chamber was like some great cathedral, rising up and spreading out before him. Great sheets of water hammered down, pouring through culverts and grates, filling the air with condensation. The thunder of its fall blocked out Guld's voice, as he shouted something. Tooms shook his head.

Waters poured down, running to either side of a set of wide, semi-circular steps. The steps led up onto the stone causeway that crossed over the lake-like cistern and passed to the other side. Broken statues lined the causeway. Whether they had been duardin or human, Tooms couldn't say and didn't care. His attentions were elsewhere.

Shimmering fungal orbs of monstrous size floated in the waters of the cistern, or hung pendulous from the chamber ceiling. They spread across the walls and floor. A forest of human-like shapes stood silent around the cistern and along the causeway, their features hidden by the clouds of heat and vapour.

Guld leaned close, shouting. 'What are they?'

Tooms lifted his truncheon. 'Let's find out.' He started forward, ignoring Guld's shout of dismay. As he drew close to one of the shapes, he saw that it was rooted to the stone of the causeway, its form covered in a thick, fungous shag. The others were the same. They swayed in the damp air, and he felt something – a pulse, a current travelling between them. As if they were speaking.

'Can you hear them?'

The voice was hoarse and raw. But familiar.

'Agert,' Tooms said, as he turned.

Agert smiled, and mould burst and tore as his face moved. He was only barely recognisable, his body hidden beneath a tabard of mould and his head half eaten away. But it was him, the same Agert who'd taught Tooms about the currents and the dark.

'What happened to you, Agert? What is all of this?'

Agert nodded slowly, and made a hoarse, gasping sound, as if trying to speak again. But the only sound Tooms could hear was the soft pop of puffballs, and the roar of the water as it carried the spores away. Agert uprooted himself, and took an unsteady step. Then another, growing more sure with each. Behind him, Tooms saw others – shuffling, shambling fungal shapes, creeping towards him out of the clouds of water vapour.

He hefted his truncheon, but they stumbled past him, heading away, into the dark of the tunnels. They crumbled as they walked, and he could see bone, in places. The fungus was eating them alive, devouring them bit by bit. But they sang as they stumbled, the same strange, sad song he'd heard in the tunnels. Sickened, he looked at Agert.

'They... feel... nothing,' Agert said, in a voice like breaking glass. 'Kind. She's... kind.'

'Who?' Tooms asked, not wanting to know the answer, but unable to stop himself.

Agert pointed. And Tooms saw her, then, and wondered how he'd missed her. His stomach lurched at the sight, and Guld made a strangled, animal moan. The... woman crouched over them all, a giantess made of spores and water and sound, filling the cathedral-like chamber with her presence.

She cupped her hands and thrust them into the cistern. Shambling, fungal petitioners knelt in her palms, in their hundreds, as she lifted them from the mould-shrouded waters. She lifted them up with gentle, hideous strength and blew on them gently. The petitioners came apart in clouds of spores that swirled away, filling the upper reaches of the chamber. The mould clung to every stone and duct, growing, creeping, spreading.

Vaguely, he thought he heard Guld screaming something that might have been a name, but he couldn't look away from her. She loomed mountainous and impossible, filling his vision and his senses. She smiled at the shuffling things in her hands, and he felt his heart stutter in primal terror.

He knew her name, but could not bring himself to say it. He tore his eyes away, unable to bear such awful majesty, and found himself face-to-face with Agert. Over his shoulder, Tooms saw Skam, and Huxyl and Dayla. They surrounded Guld, moving with awful slowness, their voices raised in that sad, strange song. As he watched, Guld's blade dipped, and they closed in.

'It's a kindness,' Agert said, only it wasn't Agert's voice, now. It was a woman's voice, issuing from Agert's mossy lips. The words sliced into Tooms like knives. He shook his head, trying not to listen. Not to see. He backed away, but Agert followed. 'You do not deserve pain, though you have caused much. It was not malice, but ignorance.'

'Who are you?' Tooms whispered.

'You know who I am. This place was mine, before it was his, and it will be mine again. In time. I am patient. Eventually, my song will be heard by all, and all will know me and join their voices to mine.' Agert's face sloughed away, and something new peered out of his skull, a new face – one of golden spores and water vapour. Her eyes caught him, held him, and she began to sing, and Tooms felt as if he were burning under his skin.

For a moment, he saw things as Agert and the others must. The song folded him into itself, and he saw great shapes dancing in the light of phosphorescent mould. The fungal spheres were not simply spheres but shapes that were all things and none, silvery and bright. There were faces there, and he could hear them crying out, impatient and eager to be born. To see the light and taste the air.

He knew what they were. Every underjack did. They were the reason men kept to the roads and never went into the forests. The reason that the pyre-gangs had been formed, to clean the land around the city walls. They were worse than any orruk or troggoth. Older than any city, they had ruled this realm once, and some thought they would again, though it was a fool who spoke of such heresies where the witch-takers might hear.

And even as he recognised them, he knew at last what Guld had been trying to say. What Dayla had been afraid of. He knew her name now, though he could not say it.

They are beautiful, aren't they, she whispered, in a voice like rustling leaves. *And strong. So strong. Stronger than flesh, stronger than stone and steel. And they are kind, my children. So kind. They let you hear the song. They let you join it.* Her voice became harsh. Sharp, like branches cracking in the cold. *It is a kindness that you do not deserve.*

He felt a different sort of heat now, and crushing, grinding pain. Smoke filled his lungs, and his flesh blistered. *You burned them. Chopped them and beat them. For what? A grove of stone and iron? Is this what he teaches you, your God-King?*

Tooms wanted to scream, but had no tongue. He wanted to beg forgiveness, to flee, but could do neither. Her eyes filled his vision, burning like the green suns of Ghyran, boiling into him, searing away all his courage and hope. Leaving him hollow and withered.

Stone does not live. Iron does not live. It is cruel.

He saw Greywater Fastness, a jumble of hard angles, and choking smog. Narrow streets, filled with huddled forms, and clattering machinery. Home, but distorted to grotesque proportions that he barely recognised. A darksome blotch – a tumour of stone. Was this how they saw it?

But we are kind... so kind. And you will thank us, when the rains fall, and the streets sprout, and you all, at last, hear the song he has denied you.

The city changed. It twisted and thrashed and was no longer a beast of stone and iron, but a great, heaving mound of fleshy, fungal growth. And within its runnels, hundreds of thousands of shaggy, unmoving shapes the colour of the dawn.

We will sing the song together–

'No!' Tooms' truncheon sank into what was left of Agert's head, ripping the top away with a sound like tearing paper. The body sagged, deflating like a puffball, filling the air with spores. He tried to hold his breath as he turned.

Panic seized him, as mould-covered shapes closed in on all sides. Soft, flabby hands reached for him, and he drove the truncheon down, splitting Dayla's skull. It came apart in swirling clouds and he staggered past her crumpling shape, blind.

He heard Huxyl and Skam as they clawed at him, but he ignored their voices – no, not their voices. *Her* voice. Her voice, issuing from a hundred mouths. Singing now, as the soft fungal bulges along the walls and floor sang, and he reached up to clutch his head.

He'd dropped his truncheon somewhere, but he still held the lantern. And it still burned. Maybe–

Tooms stopped. Turned. She was looking down at him now, her face vast, her expression strange and sad. A hand, massive, shaped from a cloud of spores, reached for him, as if to scoop him up. Her eyes burned like a summer wildfire, and her words were like the crash of distant waves. He could hear, but could not understand now. He had torn himself from the song, and her words were not meant for him, or any mortal. Yet she spoke nonetheless, like a mother attempting to reassure a frightened child.

'Don't you see, it is a kindness we do you,' a hundred mouths murmured, in her voice. 'We only want to help you – we only wish you to hear what we hear...'

Tooms slammed the lantern down, splattering burning oil across the patches of fungus. Even in the damp air, it couldn't help but catch. Duardin oil could burn, even on water. And it spread greedily, leaping and prowling through the forest of swaying bodies. The singing became shrill – a keening wail. Not of pain, but of disappointment.

As the fires roared up, Tooms ran into the dark, leaving the others behind.

He fled from the goddess and her terrible garden.

But the sound of her voice followed him.

Her voice took root in Tooms, as he stumbled.

'A single seed was all it took. A single spore. Just a tiny thing. And look. See. Is this not better? Is this not preferable to the noise and the smoke and the noose?'

Not far now. That was what the water said. *A good thing, because his legs weren't working at all. He fell against the wall, and tried to pull himself along, but his fingers broke off one by one, leaving yellowish smears on the stones.*

'Don't look back,' Agert's voice said. 'Just follow the current.'

He tried to draw in the breath to speak, but nothing happened. Not even a whisper of a groan escaped him. His leg gave way, cracking like a rotten log, spilling him down into the water. There was no pain, only a sense of vertigo as he fell.

He was unravelling. Coming apart, but still following the water. Not towards Cathedral Hill now, he knew, but back towards the Old Fen Gate. He wasn't going to make it. He'd go missing, just like Agert. Just like the others. And then someone would come looking. He wondered what they would find.

'A single seed. A single spore,' she crooned as she lowered him gently into the water. He had not heard her come, but here she was, smaller now, and beautiful, rather than monstrous. 'One tiny thing. That is all it takes. Fire is nothing. Stone is nothing. Life persists.' She leaned forward and kissed him upon the brow.

Something in his skull gave. All of his fears and worries, all of his pain, were caught in the current and carried away. The water closed over him and the song rose, drowning out everything else.

Tooms closed his eyes and let it.

J C Stearns

THE MARAUDER LIVES

'What a clever animal you are.' The drukhari commander stretched out one hand to caress Monika's face. The interrogator grimaced but said nothing.

The drukhari forces spread out across the rooftop landing pad, their sleek, chain-studded raiders circling overhead. Only a fraction of the craft had managed to disgorge their occupants; the rest of the fleet circled the towering Munitorum building like predatory jungle cats just waiting for an opening.

The two wyches who had been holding Monika aloft dropped her to her knees on the rockcrete surface, abandoning her to slice trophies from the fallen. Monika wasn't certain which was worse: that so many of her friends and colleagues in the service of the Inquisition were dead, or that she had been captured alive. She struggled, trying to get her hands free of the barbed net that restrained her, but her attempts at escape only drove the hooks deeper into her flesh. Each time she tried to work herself lose, the agony from the many-tined barbs drove her to the verge of unconsciousness.

The wyches disappeared into the building, presumably to look for the human captives they'd come in search of. Their kabalite companions took up lines at the edges of the landing pad and braced for a counter-attack. Several of the warriors bore banner poles on their backs, displaying the same symbol emblazoned on the side of the raiders: a twining knot of barbed wire crowned by a blue flame. Like the raiders themselves, the warriors' armour was painted an oily black, trimmed at the edges with a bright, cold blue.

A horned incubus emerged from the flight control room. His bone-white armour gleamed in the lights of the open landing pad. He held up a rigged bundle of wires and circuits, and shook his head with the slightest of movements.

The drukhari commander looked down at Monika, placed a boot on the human's shoulder, and pushed her over to lay on her side. Monika stared up at the archon, wishing she could wrench even a single hand free. The drukhari had a repulsive beauty. Her movements, even in her cruel, segmented armour, betrayed a grace that the pure human form could never emulate.

Her features were delicate and cold, devoid of any spark of empathy or compassion. The drukhari's hair, dyed brilliant pink, was styled into a stiff, sharp mohawk. Tattoos of entwined serpents coiled across the left half of her face.

'The beacon. It was a decoy?' the archon asked. Her diction was flawless, but her sing-song accent betrayed her. The alien tongue refused to speak Low Gothic with the flat, dull cadence of a human being.

'What? The mighty aeldari can't tell the difference between a real beacon and a fake one?' Monika felt no need to clarify things for the drukhari, especially when the truth was painfully obvious. There were no evacuees at the landing pad, and there never had been.

Monika's friend and mentor, Inquisitor Deidara, had discovered the impending drukhari raid, even uncovering the traitors in the governor's household, but there was no way for a single inquisitor *to change the currents of the warp. The world of Telesto would receive no military assets in time to repel the drukhari, save for those already there. Half of Deidara's retinue had organised an evacuation to Telesto's moon. The other half had set up the false beacon, broadcasting where the primary 'evacuation point' for the city would be for all the drukhari forces to hear. Monika only regretted that they hadn't been able to flee the rooftop before the drukhari assault had begun.*

The drukhari looked at the device her incubus held, and Monika readied herself for death. Before the incubus' blade could fall, a series of explosions drew the attention of those assembled on the rooftop. Several of the raiders began weaving defensively. The archon's head snapped down to stare Monika in the eyes, the alien's mouth drawn into a predatory grin.

'Is this your doing as well, mon-keigh?'

Monika just laughed. Bait was no good without a trap to accompany it, a role the Telestonian 87th had been only too happy to play. An autocannon found its mark, blasting a hole through one of the raiders overhead, which plummeted out of view. The drukhari commander appeared calm, but the other xenos were scrambling back to their craft. Monika winced, but knew her torment was nearly at an end. With any luck, one of the Telestonian artillery rounds would put her out of her misery before the drukhari got the pleasure of it themselves.

To her surprise, the drukhari archon laughed, her voice a cawing, grating sound, like a murder of crows.

'You lured me here with the promise of ten thousand defence-less refugees,' she said, 'and it is no small thing to deceive the Marauder, Archon Kelaene Abrahak, Ilarch of the Lords of Iron Thorn.' At a gesture from her, the wyches grabbed the shard-net and hauled Monika up for Kelaene to take. 'As a prize for your accomplishment, I shall keep you alive until you've been given each and every gift that those ten thousand slaves would

have received at our hands.' The Ilarch began dragging Monika
towards a waiting raider, pulling her over the rough landing pad
by the hooks embedded in her body. Monika closed her eyes and
screamed.

Monika awoke in total darkness. Waking from the visceral, all
too real dreams of the past was always disorienting. Her heart
was hammering, her teeth locked onto her own lips. A low crack
of thunder brought her attention to the fading sound of rain on
stone. That was good. There was no stone on a drukhari raider.
There never had been. Stone meant the monastery. It meant the
relative safety of St. Solangia. She lay in the darkness, breathing
slowly, and allowed the tension to drain away from her limbs.

Carefully, Monika took stock of her whereabouts. The hard,
cold stones of the monastery floor beneath her were a comfort,
giving her something solid and ancient to focus on while she ori-
ented herself to the present. The thick steel bed frame, centimetres
from her face, meant she was still safely hidden. She flexed her
lips, feeling the familiar pain. Stifling her screams had become a
survival strategy, so much a part of her that even in her sleep she
would bite clean through her lips before she opened her mouth to
shriek. Shifting first her shoulders, then her hips, she worked her
way out from underneath the bed. She took a moment to stretch,
working the soreness out of her neck and back. She slid the bed
from beneath the window, across the floor, and back to the corner where the Sisters wanted it, working slowly and carefully in
order to keep the heavy bed frame from making enough noise
to alert the hospitallers. She moved the small bookshelf that was
allowed to her away from the door, and placed the empty water
glass back on her night stand. She made sure to rumple the lin-
ens on the bed to make them look slept in.

Monika went to the polished metal mirror set into the wall.
Although her status as a servant of the Inquisition afforded her

many freedoms at St. Solangia's, the privilege of a real mirror had been revoked after a violent misunderstanding with another patient whose schizophrenic patois had borne an unfortunate resemblance to the aeldari tongue. She checked beneath her eyelids, behind her ears, and at the base of her neck, searching for marks of chem-injection. Monika paused for a moment to assure herself that the face in the mirror was her real one. When she had first been recovered from Kelaene's forces, Monika's visage had looked quite different: fishbelly pale from years spent in near-total darkness; scars and brands spiralling and crisscrossing, decades' worth of torturer's graffiti; her teeth filed to wicked points. Through Inquisitor Deidara's beneficence, the hospitallers had restored much of her body, including rad-scrubbing her tattoos and replacing her unnatural dentition with a more human set of ceramite implants. Satisfied that she hadn't been drugged during the night, Monika turned back to her cell.

'Cell' was an apt word, but only because St. Solangia's had been an abbey before it had ever been a medicae facility. In truth the room had been furnished comfortably, if sparsely. Anything more lavish would have set Monika's teeth on edge, long experience having taught her that good things were usually a trap.

Monika went and stood beneath her window. A thick iron bar crossed in front of the arched alcove. Once it would have hung a tapestry, but Monika preferred the sunlight: a warm, tangible reminder that she was far from the realm of the drukhari. She stood there for a moment, letting the still-emerging morning sun warm her shoulders, savouring the feeling while it lasted. The spring storms were coming more frequently, and soon they would have days where the sun never shone at all through the black thunderheads. After a moment, she stretched her hands up and took hold of the tapestry bar and began her pull-ups. She used to use gymnastics to train, but her confinement made that prohibitive. Sister Rozia had taught her a combination of military calisthenics and intense bodyweight exercises, and Monika found the strength training and combat readiness more valuable than the manoeuvrability of a gymnast.

The Sisters brought her breakfast to her. One of them watched Monika carefully while the other set her tray down on the stool in front of Monika's bookshelf. They nodded to Monika, who nodded politely back and waited until they'd left the cell to approach the tray. Common sanatoria might cut costs by feeding their patients on ration packs, but St. Solangia's catered to the psychoses of the powerful and the wealthy. The patients there received actual food, if simply prepared. Monika examined the meal critically: protein-rich porridge with two slices of bread, a link of canid-meat, and various pulses in a dark orange sauce. Monika sniffed the tray, then carefully dipped her finger in the porridge and dabbed it on her wrist. She did the same with each offering on the tray, rubbing it on a spot further up her arm. Then she began counting softly, and resumed her exercise.

After counting out fifteen minutes to herself, she went to the window and examined her arm in the sunlight. Satisfied there was no rash on any of the applied food-spots, she returned to the tray and took a small bite of each food, chewed them briefly, spat them into her chamber pot, then waited another twenty minutes. After not becoming ill, she returned to the plate and swallowed a small bite apiece, then returned to her calisthenics. Half an hour later, finally satisfied the meal was safe, Monika knelt in front of the stool and wolfed her breakfast down. The pulses had grown cold and the gruel clumpy, but these were trivial concerns. She finished her meal with a swallow of water from the jug on her nightstand. The water in her jug wasn't provided by the Sisters; she was allowed to draw it herself each night, so it did not require her counts to ensure its safety. One piece of bread she saved, and added to a small emergency cache of food she kept hidden behind a stone she'd loosened in the wall beneath her bed. It would go stale quickly, but in the dry air of the monastery it would take some time to go mouldy.

Sister Superior Amalia normally visited her in the mid-morning to escort her to the gardens, so Monika was surprised when the opening door revealed not the pinched face and stocky frame of Amalia, but that of Inquisitor Deidara. Sister Amalia liked to use their journeys to the gardens as an excuse to try to coax Monika to speak about her memories, ostensibly to help her recovery. She resented Amalia's unflappable calm, which too often felt like condescension, but suffered her counselling in the hope of serving the Inquisition again. On the occasions that Deidara was able to visit, however, laying bare the torments she had suffered at the hands of the drukhari *was* a service to the Inquisition, and Monika opened her psychic wounds readily for her old friend.

Monika chewed the edge of her thumbnail as they walked. She didn't look Deidara in the eye. The inquisitor could be trusted; if there was a threat it would come from any angle *but* her old friend.

'Do you remember what we talked about last month?' Deidara asked. Monika gave a nod that would have been imperceptible to the average person.

'I found the butts from six lho-sticks in the west garden,' Monika said. She worried at a hangnail. She had always hated nail-biting, but faking the habit gave her an excuse to keep a hand in front of her mouth. 'Eight sticks, if distilled for their pure components, can provide a lethal dose of niqatrate.' Monika glanced around quickly. She trusted Deidara to keep a faithful eye out for danger, but she still needed to verify that there was no one behind her. 'I thought someone might be brewing a poison in their cell, but Sister Rozia says that Hembra the orderly is just a lho-addict.'

'Very good,' said Deidara. The two of them walked slowly. To all appearances, Deidara's gait was the slow, deliberate shuffle of an old woman. Her weakness was as feigned as Monika's nail-biting, but the leisurely pace helped keep Monika calm and centred. 'However, I was referring to the story you were telling me about trying to escape to an aeldari corsair fleet by posing as a hellion.'

Monika nodded again. She fell silent, considering her words carefully as they passed out of the monastery and into the south garden. Sister Amalia believed the fresh air helped calm her patients, but the garden always made Monika a little uneasy. She knew the island was isolated, but the garden itself still felt perilously vulnerable to attack. Save for a single gardener tending the twin rows of vitiberry vines, no one else was present. Rather than sit on one of the ornamental stone benches and enjoy the view of the sun over the Cressidian Sea, Deidara guided her former protégé through the low acicularis hedges surrounding the vine trellises. Monika respected her old mentor's wisdom. Amalia always encouraged her to sit during interviews, but staying in motion helped Monika stay focused on the present.

'I knew the flagship wouldn't be much safer,' she said, 'but I reasoned it would at least be larger, with more places to hide and more opportunities to escape.' Her ceramite teeth neatly clipped through the nail she was working on. Rather than spit the clipping into the shrubbery, she wiped it away and gazed absently into the distance.

'Can you describe the colours you saw on the aeldari corsairs?'

Monika blinked and shook her head, focusing her mind on the present.

Inquisitor Deidara stared at her. Her countenance held only a quiet patience, waiting for an answer that would come eventually.

'I... I can't be sure. They bore orange, I think. Orange tabards, with white face masks.'

Inquisitor Deidara jotted a note with her stylus. Monika hated these meetings as much as she loved them. Seeing her friend and mentor again thrilled her in a way nothing else could, just as it crushed her again to see Deidara leave, knowing she would probably never be allowed outside these walls. Monika hated her own ignorance every time Deidara asked for an answer she couldn't immediately provide. She knew that her mind was like a spoil pool: broken, tainted and ruined, but still dotted with useful nuggets of ore for a searcher with the patience to sift through it.

'Is that helpful?' she asked.

Inquisitor Deidara hailed originally from Baal, and her face was customarily as expressive and emotive as the graven masks of the Blood Angels that protected it. Monika had spent years travelling with her master, and had learned to read the tiniest traces in the inquisitor's visage, the barest hints of what she truly felt. The inquisitor favoured her with the tiniest upturn of her mouth, an expression Monika knew to be a warm smile. The inquisitor had changed in the years of Monika's captivity, and incrementally more so in the months of her convalescence, but beneath the strands of hair gone steel-grey, behind the eyes now framed by a few wrinkles more, Deidara remained the same woman that Monika had sworn to follow to the end of her days.

'It is,' said the inquisitor. She tapped her data-slate and considered for a moment. 'Your sojourn to the corsair flagship: how many escape attempts had you made before this? How long into your captivity was it?'

Monika shook her head. 'It's hard to recall, precisely. They all blur together. Each time the Ilarch played this game, where she allowed me to believe I'd escaped, she let me go for longer and longer before revealing herself. I wandered the corsair ship for a few hours, so I would have already been a prisoner for over a year. But it would have been before the capture of the *Maw*; that time lasted days.' Then, drukhari had fought agents of the Inquisition on the space hulk known as the *Maw of Famine*, so hopefully the inquisitor would be able to establish an approximate time range. The Ilarch had allowed Monika to escape into the space hulk in the forlorn hope of finding Inquisition forces, although of course Kelaene had recaptured her before she ever got close to rescue. As she had wandered the pitch-black labyrinth of the space hulk, where one wrecked starship melded jarringly into another, amid the damning, oppressive silence of the void, odd auditory hallucinations eating away at her sanity, time itself had begun to bleed away...

'Sister Amalia tells me you've been having trouble eating.'

Monika shook her head, forcing herself back from the siren call of her memories to the safety of the present. She bit down on the inside of her lip, the sharp pain and slight tinge of blood reminding her to say here, here, *here*; at least long enough to do her duty and be of use to the inquisitor.

'I eat. Just very carefully.'

Deidara nodded and continued making notes on her data-slate. The water of the Cressidian Sea was clear and blue, but the horizon was marred by a line of thick, black clouds. The storms would be coming, soon. Monika sometimes wondered why they used St. Solangia's as a sanatorium, given its annual weather and the terror it caused among the patients, but she supposed a few days of disruptive weather was worth a year of peace and tranquillity otherwise.

'There's something else we need to discuss,' said the inquisitor.

'Which is?'

'Sister Rozia.'

Monika nodded, her attention fully on the present again. Although St. Solangia's was officially a medicae facility, the abbey was still a holy shrine to the Emperor, and warranted His protection. The Adepta Sororitas assigned only a single Battle Sister to it, but her value was immense, certainly to Monika. When her mind began to spin and connect events with no apparent link save her own paranoid imagination, Sister Rozia alone gave her

words credence. Where Sister Amalia dismissed her every statement as the twisting creation of a damaged mind, Sister Rozia
treated Monika as a fellow warrior. She gave Monika's words
due consideration, and weighed the evidence that Monika presented without bias.

'She's off-world,' said Monika. 'The Order of the Sacred Rose
requires her to attend live-fire combat exercises once per solar
cycle. She's currently on Summanus Primaris, set to return by
the end of the week.' She sounded rote when saying it, which
she was. Sister Amalia had reminded Monika of Sister Rozia's
absence several times a day for weeks before it came. Sometimes,
when Monika's psychoses grew particularly pronounced, Rozia
was the only person in the abbey that could talk Monika down,
and Sister Amalia wanted to be sure that Monika didn't have an
episode of paranoia compounded by being unable to remember
where the person she trusted most had gone. When the storms
reached their peak, plunging the abbey into darkness for a day or
more, the hospitallers would have their hands full with patients
unable to cope with the stress. During the nights, parts of the
abbey would become a screaming madhouse.

'Sister Rozia is dead,' said the inquisitor.

Monika's face went cold. She heard the inquisitor speak on,
but she was only half-engaged. Killed during the live-fire exercise. True servant of the Golden Throne. Accidental discharge
of a krak grenade.

She half-listened to Deidara. The inquisitor asked her perfunctory questions, which she gave perfunctory answers to, but
Deidara had to realise that her former interrogator had slipped
back into the refuge of her own mind. The last thing Monika wanted was to lose herself to paranoia right in front of her
old mentor, but she needed time to *think*. The yearly storms
were always the most dangerous time. The typhoons that blew
in across the sea would block out communications for a day,

sometimes as long as a week. For the last three years, Rozia had always listened to her and been especially alert, but without her, who would keep the abbey safe?

She couldn't control the currents of an uncaring universe. Sometimes, Monika knew, you couldn't even control what happened to your own person. The only thing you could control was your own reactions. She admonished herself over and over to stay calm and controlled. The garden faded away, leaving Deidara's presence as her only connection to the world. Eventually, even that faded away.

Monika opened her eyes. This was no time to get lost in delusions. The halls of the corsair vessel were large and arched, echoing every sound within them. The smooth white surface of the floor seemed determined to betray her, and it took every ounce of effort just to take a single step without her boots sending up an echoing warning of her presence.

She'd come too far to fail now. She had starved herself for weeks to ensure her features were gaunt enough to pass as one of the drukhari. She'd spent several agonising hours with a pilfered blade sharpener, filing her own teeth down to the wicked points that marked the aerial gang members. She kept herself clothed head-to-toe in one of their body-hugging flight suits, which she'd stolen from a dead hellion. She had armed herself with his weapons, and even then kept herself as far back as she could from the other skyboard-riding maniacs that the Ilarch seemed to attract so readily. She was as prepared as she could make herself.

The Marauder was set to meet a corsair baron to trade supplies for the Imperial captives the corsairs had recently acquired. If they had taken as large a force as the rumours claimed, then Monika knew there had to be a shuttle or small landing craft among the prizes. The drukhari would have no interest in such primitive technology, but the corsairs would keep such 'treasures' to trade with other xenos, or with renegades from the Imperium of Man.

From behind her, she heard squabbling: the hellions she'd accompanied aboard, arguing vehemently with the corsair reavers they were fraternising with. Each minute Monika had spent among the hellions had been both elation and torment in one. If the squabbling killers realised her deception, they would torture her to death before even considering the consequences of destroying the Ilarch's favourite pet. Monika didn't care; an agonising death was preferable to the ceaseless anguish of being Kelaene's plaything. Her captor had allowed her to attempt an escape several times before, but each time had revealed the opportunity to be nothing more than a trap to taunt her. Never before had she gotten so far, however, nor dared so much. This deep in the bowels of a corsair ship, she was beyond Kelaene's power. If she was discovered now, at least her death at the hands of the corsairs would be swift.

Monika heard the corsairs before she saw them. The hallway made a sharp curve, and there they were: two reavers clad in the bright orange armour of the corsair forces. They stood guard before a door that, by Monika's guess, had to be their secondary cargo bay. If there were captured enemy ships, that's where they would be. Fortunately for her, it seemed that aeldari troops were lacking in any sort of discipline outside of the craftworlds. The two guards were bickering with themselves over a small cache of intoxicants they'd purchased, won or stolen from their drukhari guests.

Monika didn't give them time to formulate an opinion of her. As she passed the guards, she shot the closest one in the back. The hissing splinter pistol discharged a cluster of needles into her victim, who arched his back and collapsed, the poison flooding his system so quickly that it paralysed his lungs before he could even scream. Before he had hit the ground, shaking and foaming at the mouth, she lunged over his collapsing body to stab the *other guard with her wychblade. He started to yell, but her blood was up. Two years of drukhari captivity had honed her reflexes to their peak, and her arm moved like lightning, slamming the slim blade into the reaver's throat, cutting his cry of alarm short. He tried to grab for a weapon, but she bore him to the ground, stabbing him over and over.*

If anyone had heard the noise, she would be discovered in moments. She emptied the small satchel of drugs into her pockets. She tucked the splinter pistol into the combat webbing of her stolen gear, but left the wychblade protruding from the dead reaver. If anyone found the corpses, let them assume they'd died in a fight with a visiting hellion over stolen drugs.

Monika spun and hit the rune on the bay door. It hissed open, revealing a cargo bay stacked with materiel. Her intuition had been correct: half a dozen escape pods littered the spoils, along with an Aquila lander. Only a single obstacle remained between her and salvation: a mob of aeldari, mixed between the drukhari and corsair crew. At the head stood the twin forms of the Ilarch and the corsair baron. As Monika reeled, the assembled crews burst into laughter.

'You may remove your ludicrous disguise whenever you wish, mon-keigh,' Kelaene said. 'Your stolen apparel will need to be burned, I think. My hellions have been complaining of your stench since our wager began, so I doubt anyone will wear it again.' The Ilarch smiled suddenly, as if cruel inspiration had struck her. 'However, as reward for your success, I'll permit you to keep those wicked teeth you've fashioned for yourself.'

The aeldari laughed all the harder. Monika stumbled away, their laughter echoing behind her. She ran, looking for a place to hide, but knew it was futile. The Ilarch would always find her.

A low metallic squeal woke her. Monika opened her eyes, her heart pounding. The crisscrossed springs of her bed stared back at her. Something was wrong. She listened intently, and a moment later was rewarded with the sound of the window above her bed slowly being opened.

Monika moved her arm slowly and silently, over to the loose spring. It had taken her days to work it loose with no tools, and still more time to straighten a third of its length and grind the tip of the straight portion to a crude point. The bed groaned as a weight pushed on it from above. Monika smiled. No matter how horrible the prediction, there was, at least, small comfort in knowing that you were right. The agents of the Ilarch had finally come for her. Monika pulled her arm tight to her chest, and waited for her moment as the intruder shifted their weight again, making the springs above her shift and pop.

When a pale face finally peered beneath the bed, Monika struck, driving her shiv into the enemy's eye socket. She wrenched her body to the side, hurling herself out into the cell as the would-be assassin howled. Monika leaped to her feet and ran to the door. Before she could throw it open, a pair of pale hands grabbed her shoulders and yanked her back.

Monika threw her head backwards, and the wet crack of a breaking nose told her that the pain blossoming on the back of her skull was nothing compared to her attacker's. She stamped on their instep and turned, wrenching her arms loose.

The intruder was slight, his one remaining eye the fathomless black of the drukhari. He wore no uniform or insignia, but his feet and arms were bare, a sure sign of either a wych or a hellion. His features were delicate but drawn, in the feral manner of a drukhari gone too long without inflicting suffering. He reached for her, her shiv still protruding from his face. Monika hissed and yanked the weapon from her assailant's ruined eye. With a ragged scream, she buried it in his abdomen over and over, in a flurry of vicious strikes. The drukhari grasped his bleeding gut and staggered away and the moment he disengaged, Monika bolted.

Stone halls were much quieter than corsair ships. Monika fled through the halls of the abbey as silent as a shadow, running on the balls of her feet to reduce her noise nearly entirely. She crouched as she scurried, keeping to the corners and the darkness; she couldn't be certain how many of the Ilarch's servants were after her, or, more worryingly, how many of the abbey's staff were secretly working for the drukhari. The wing of the old abbey that had been given over to guest quarters was close, though. That's where she would find Deidara.

'Do you think you've learned everything she knows?'

Sister Amalia's voice brought Monika up short. She pressed herself against the wall outside the inquisitor's quarters. That an agent of the Imperium as exalted as Amalia could betray her Order for the drukhari was almost unthinkable, but Monika's paranoia was just deep enough to encompass the notion, and so she listened intently to Amalia's conversation rather than burst in.

'Not by half.' Inquisitor Deidara's voice was tinged with scorn. 'She spent a decade in the clutches of the drukhari. The intelligence she's gathered has already proven valuable, and likely will continue to do so.'

'But you worry it takes too long?'

'No,' said Deidara. 'Monika withstood her trials with more resilience than most would have, and I'm willing to leave her to her well-earned rest, taking anything she might provide for me as a service beyond what was required of her. Some within the Ordo Xenos disagree, however. The raids in the sector grow bolder each year, and there are some who would leave no stone unturned in their quest to find a weakness among the drukhari, even if it meant putting Monika to the question with the harshest of measures.'

Satisfied that neither of the women were conspiring against her, Monika rolled around the corner. Deidara and Amalia, sitting on the bed and a stool respectively, leaped to their feet.

Monika held her hands up, the blood on them dragging sharp focus from their shock.

'Drukhari,' she said. 'Trying to abduct me. The Ilarch wants her pet back.'

'The Ilarch is dead,' said Sister Amalia. 'You slew her yourself.'

'The Marauder lives,' said Monika. She held her hands aloft. 'Do you need further proof?'

Amalia started to respond, but Deidara cut her off. 'Let us see this intruder,' she said. The inquisitor put up a hand to stave off Amalia's protests. 'Blood doesn't come from nowhere, Sister Amalia.'

The three of them returned to the cell.

It was empty.

'He was here!' Monika protested. She gestured to the bed. 'He came in through the window, and tried to attack me!'

There was no trace of the attacker. Not only was there no corpse, there was no blood either. Only Monika's sharpened bed spring, its metallic point coated with nothing more than a faint patina of rust. The window was closed; securely locked from the outside.

The world spun rapidly out of control. Monika argued, insistently. Amalia denied, forcefully. Deidara tried to calm her friend, to ask reasonable questions, but Monika knew the truth: Rozia's death was no accident, and this proved it. The Marauder was coming for her. The worst part was seeing the dwindling trust in Deidara's face. The less she was believed, the angrier she grew. The orderlies had to be called. It took three of them, plus Amalia and Deidara, to hold her down and administer the injection. She bucked and twisted as Deidara whispered in her ear, swearing to get to the bottom of whatever was happening to her, but it was too late for Monika to respond: darkness rushed up to pull her down.

* * *

The darkness of toxic clouds parted to reveal the sprawling urban hellscape beneath them. The Ilarch's raiders knifed through the twisting streets below them, gleefully gunning down the panicking civilians. Lines of Astra Militarum troops blocked the thoroughfares only to see wyches vault over their heads, carving their ranks into sprays of blood and gobbets of quivering meat. Many of the manufactoria were in flames, their safety mechanisms disabled and running amok. Roiling chem-smoke turned the sky black, punctuated by the explosions of missiles being traded between Razorwing jets and the scattered remnants of the planet's aerial defenders.

The lead raider rushed towards the ground. Monika knelt beside her master, a slender chain running from her neck to the hook on the Marauder's belt. The archon's oily black armour glistened with fresh oils that Monika had applied herself at spearpoint. Her hair had been shaved to the scalp on the left side, and hung long and straight to the right, dyed a pale, ethereal blue.

'Is it not glorious, my pet?' The Ilarch smiled as she gazed out over the devastation. She no longer bothered to speak Gothic to her slave. Years of exposure had taught Monika to understand the buzzing drukhari tongue. 'Like good little rodents, your people scurry for the densest brush they can find, heedless of the fact that their cowering retreat only draws them together so they can all be taken in a single stroke.'

Monika scowled. Amid the wreckage of the shanty-town they approached, once home to thousands of the workers that toiled daily in the vast manufactoria, her experienced eye picked out the hidden aerials and gun emplacements of a concealed command position. So did Kelaene's.

'Shall we play the game, mon-keigh?'

Monika rose to her bare, filthy feet. Her clothes had long since been reduced to rags, and her flesh was marked by uncountable scars. Every indignity that could be imagined had been heaped

upon her, but behind her eyes boiled enough rage to play the
Marauder's game still one more time. Always one more time.
Before each final attack, the Ilarch's bravado compelled her to
wager her entire empire on a fool's gamble. The drukhari would
hand a lethal weapon over to her slave, giving her a chance to
strike her master down and be free.

If she failed, she would be beaten severely. After the raid her
flesh would be carved to ribbons and her body suspended from
razored hooks. Monika had lost count of the number of times she'd
lost. She saw the arrogance in the Ilarch's eyes, and felt again
the temptation to refuse. If she stayed down, proved that she had
finally and truly been broken, she knew the Ilarch would tire of
her and, finally, let her die. Still, she rose, meeting the drukhari's
contemptuous gaze with all the fury she could muster.

The Marauder smiled, unbuckled the holster at her side, and
tossed her pistol to the slave in a graceful arc. Monika grasped
the weapon, staring down at the gun in her trembling hands.
She'd been handed a live pistol before only to discover it wouldn't
fire when she tried to turn it on her mistress. Drukhari weapons didn't feature a safety, but Monika checked that the power
core was active before turning her gaze back to the Marauder,
who unhooked Monika's thin chain from her belt and let it fall
to the deck.

'Well?' her mistress taunted. Behind her, the flags of the command centre were whipping by. The raider crew were leaning
over the barbed rails of the raider, yelling in glee as their splinter rifles tore through its defenders. Monika didn't know what
form her humiliation would take, but she had played the game
long enough to know its general shape: her shot deflected by some
kind of force-field, or intercepted by an underling shoved into her
line of fire by a chuckling bodyguard. Kelaene never played games
that weren't rigged in her favour. She won not because she was
inherently superior, but because she only picked foes who couldn't

defeat her. It might have taken her years, but Monika had finally learned the truth of that lesson.

Monika turned, aimed at the pilot of the raider, and pulled the trigger. The pilot's face was a mask of shock as the darklight beam slashed through both his chest and the command strut he stood behind. Its only method of steering destroyed, the raider lurched starboard with a sharp, whining cry. Monika just had time to turn, to see the Marauder howling with laughter, before the raider slammed to the ground.

Along with the kabalites, Monika was hurled from the deck by the impact. She tried to tuck and roll as she hit the ground, but she heard a dry snap, and felt her arm go numb to the fingers. Her left hip was in agony, the leg twisted in an unnatural way from the knee down. The broken form of the raider tumbled through the lines of infantry and exploded, sending a rain of thin, twisted metal down on her and anyone fortunate enough to have escaped the blast zone.

The Guardsmen were already rallying, veterans lunging forward to bayonet the drukhari survivors lying on the battlefield. Monika let her head sink to the ground. One of the Guardsmen was trying to speak to her, but she could barely understand him. It had been so long since she'd heard Gothic spoken aloud. Compared to the drukhari she'd been surrounded by, he sounded like a man speaking through a mouthful of potatoes.

'Find the Marauder's body,' she whispered, 'or she'll live. Find her corpse, or the Marauder lives.'

Monika's eyes snapped open. Ephemeral suspicion had crystallised into grim certainty.

'The Marauder lives.'

She lurched from her bed, the lingering after-effects of the chemical restraints weighing her limbs down and filling her joints with putty. Monika pumped her arms and breathed heavily, desperate to burn the traces of the drugs from her system. The little window over her bed was completely dark, but the meal sitting on her stool was breakfast, albeit a cold one. If it was this dark at midmorning, then the leading edge of the storms had arrived.

She exercised her body, did her counts, and ate her meal. No one came to lead her out to the gardens: the weather was too foul to allow the patients outside. One of the hospitallers came to the cell to read her scripture, which Monika listened to in numb silence. For once, her retreat into her own mind didn't plunge her into the abyss of her past; the dangers of the present focused her attention to a hard, bright point.

She knew she couldn't have been out for more than a day. The chem-restraints the hospitallers used were good for a few hours, although her own habitual lack of sleep had probably kept her down longer. Still, the storms would have just hit the island. By nightfall, communications would be blacked out for at least a day, maybe longer. Long enough for the Marauder to sweep through and carry every soul in the abbey screaming to the Dark City. By the time anyone realised something was wrong and sent someone to investigate, St. Solangia's would be filled with nothing but echoes and mystery.

Her first count for her midday meal produced no rashes, but during her second count she noticed a tingling numbness on her tongue where she'd chewed the kenthia pasta. A tiny, distant voice, that sounded distinctly like the interrogator who had been lost and presumed dead eleven years ago, whispered that the hospitallers were probably just slipping a mild sedative into everyone's food to minimise patient agitation during the storm, but the Monika who had survived over a decade of hell knew poison when she tasted it. She left the rest of her lunch untouched.

Monika's bed spring shiv was gone. So was the shard of glass she'd carefully wrapped halfway up with a strip of sheet and hidden behind her bookshelf. Even the dentabrush she'd filed to a point and tucked under the lip of her chamberpot was missing. She comforted herself by spending the afternoon working the leg of the wooden stool back and forth. Initially there was no give, but by the time the hospitallers came with her dinner, she'd made significant headway. Like a loose tooth, it would need only a single sharp tug to pull free.

Dinner went untouched; having avoided the laced food earlier, she couldn't chance a more sophisticated poison. She pulled up her loose stone and ate from the food she had hoarded from previous meals, being careful to do her counts anyway in case the searchers had found her cache while she was unconscious and dosed it as well.

Throughout the day, black storm clouds raged beyond her cell. The winds howled like fanatical priests, leading their engines of war on a crusade of destruction against the fortress that resisted their assaults year after year. Monika sat in her cell, alone with her thoughts, and realised she was at peace for the first time since she had freed herself from the drukhari. The tranquil gardens and sheltering walls of the abbey had created an anxiety in her, a paranoid anticipation of an attack that never came. The mounting chaos calmed her in a way that the abbey's manufactured serenity never could.

They came for her in the night, as she knew they would. When the door to her cell creaked open and a single silhouette crept into her room, Monika felt no surprise whatsoever. Crouched behind her stool, pressed against the wall behind the opening door, she stared at her would-be abductor for a moment, reassuring her senses that they were correct, that they had always been correct. Wyches in Kelaene's service were unmistakeable. The right side of the kidnapper's head sported thin, tight braids. Monika couldn't make out hues in the darkness, but she knew the hair was the same electric blue that tinged the edge of the

Marauder's armour. The left side would be covered in spiralling tattoos across the face and neck. The wych stared at the bed, clearly deciding whether the clump of blankets was her target's sleeping form, or the lure for an ambush.

The wrenching squeal of Monika tearing the leg from her stool was enough to give the answer away. The wych turned and raised one arm to block Monika's strike with reflexes honed over decades in the arenas of Commorragh. The thin armoured plates of the wychsuit absorbed the blow easily, the nail of the improvised club squealing against the armour. The wych swept her own weapon, a grey-green dagger, under her upraised arm, nearly disembowelling Monika with her opening stroke. The wych pulled her blow, clearly trying to subdue her quarry rather than kill.

Monika jerked her weapon up again, then feinted a knee towards the wych's gut. The key to fighting the drukhari gladiators was to play on the weakness of their drug-fuelled skills. The wyches' reactions were superhuman, but they made them prone to overreaction. When the wych bent low to get her abdomen clear of Monika's knee, Monika brought her stool-leg club down hard on the drukhari's head.

A pale, clammy hand clamped itself over Monika's mouth, and she felt the hard point of a knife dig into her back. This was no lone agent, then. Suddenly the fight was about more than survival. With no telling how many drukhari were moving through the monastery, she knew she had to alert the inquisitor while there was still time. Monika tried to raise her stool-leg, but the nail was imbedded in the skull of the first wych, who was thrashing like a fish on the line. With a mighty dying heave, she managed to wrench the weapon from Monika's grasp.

The second kidnapper dug its hand into her face and started to pull Monika into the hallway. Monika grabbed at the hand on her face, at the arm pulling her backwards, but the drukhari's grip was like iron, its drug-enhanced physique lending her attacker strength. The drukhari's chest heaved in a sharp rhythm, and Monika had a brief hope that the wych's drugs were having an adverse reaction, before she recognised the chuffing whisper as soft laughter. She stretched her mouth wide and bit down on the wych's hand.

The ceramite teeth bit through ligaments, tendons and metacarpals as easily as a mouthful of soft boiled pulses. The drukhari's grip on her face vanished, and the murderous silence of Monika's attackers was finally broken by a sharp, pained wail. Spitting the bloody meat and ruined finger of her assailant aside, Monika lunged forward out of the alien's grip and lashed backwards with a mule kick. She was rewarded with a soft, yielding impact and an abrupt end to the drukhari's scream.

Monika snatched the first wych's fallen knife and turned on her second attacker. He was young, but covered in scars from the arena. His head was entirely bare, save for his coiling tattoos. The gladiator rocked on the stone floor, struggling to regain his breath and his footing. Monika charged in a flurry of stomping feet and frenzied stabs with the stolen wychblade. When the blood stopped spraying in great fans, she darted away into the darkness.

Monika didn't need the abbey's power to make her way through the halls; she might not have the perfect night vision of the drukhari, but she'd spent over a decade abandoned in the blackness they thrived in. She'd never recovered, not fully, and carried a piece of that darkness away with her. She might have been the least of the night's children, but a portion of their birthright was now hers, and she moved through the pitch-black halls with the grace and assurance of a jungle cat.

She had to find Deidara. Monika had a wychblade in hand; the inquisitor would have to believe her now. The drukhari were coming. Keeping to the corners, she raced ahead, twisting and turning her way to the inquisitor's guest cell.

Once again, a voice from within stopped her cold. With reflexes born from years of anxious preparation, Monika threw herself against the wall and listened. What she heard made her blood run cold. A single voice, speaking the rolling, buzzing tongue of the drukhari, but in the unmistakeable cadence of a human unfamiliar with the language.

'If she's not in her cell, then she's apt to be heading this way. Someone better get here and back me up on the double. I'm not paid enough to fight maniacs in the darkness.'

Monika crouched low and slipped her head around the doorframe. A human, one of the orderlies employed by the hospitallers, stood in the inquisitor's room, staring around with the aid of a hand-lumen. The room was in disarray, with books lying on the floor amid a scattering of discarded clothes. The orderly tossed his handheld vox-unit onto the unmade bed and pulled an autopistol from his pocket, tapping it anxiously against his thigh.

The traitor never heard her approach. She wrapped her right arm around his shoulder and drove her wychblade home just under the apple of his throat. With her left hand she clamped down on his autopistol; the hammer fell painfully on the web between her thumb and forefinger, drawing blood but preventing the gun from firing and sounding the alarm.

Monika searched the room. There was no sign of the inquisitor. Neither was there any sign of her weapons, her equipment, or any of her sensitive documents. Monika crept back into the hall, still hopeful that her friend was fighting through the abbey on her own. If she could rendezvous with her former mentor, there was every chance they could somehow summon reinforcements, coordinate some kind of defence, or even effect an escape. She angled her direction towards the abbey's landing pad. The grav-cars and landing vessels there offered little chance of escape. Such light craft would be unable to survive a journey through the storm, even if a pilot were suicidal enough to attempt it.

Deidara's personal ship would be the inquisitor's most natural fallback point, though. With luck, her more robust vessel might even be able to survive a hop through the storm.

The arched door to the landing pad was locked down, but the ability to bypass a maglock was one of the first skills Deidara had ever taught her. Lock disengaged, it was a simple matter of throwing her weight against the sliding door, forcing it to recede into its wall slot with a strained push. The wind immediately howled in, driving a sheet of rain that soaked Monika to the bone the instant she was exposed to it. Heedless of the typhoon's fury, Monika slipped through the gap to the promise of freedom.

The sight of Deidara's lander, cockpit empty and running lights dark, stole the breath from her. Monika stopped, trying to convince herself that her traumatised mind was playing tricks on her, but for once reality refused to let her go. The inquisitor's ship stood silent and alone, a mute testament to Monika's lost hope. The spacecraft might as well have been graven from stone: a black, lifeless monolith; a memorial to Rozia, Deidara and all the other lives that the Ilarch had claimed.

'Monika! We have to go back inside!'

Monika whipped around. Sister Amalia had slipped out of the half-open door. The sister was as soaked as Monika was, the rain drenching her, and she had to shout to be heard over the gale of the storm. The wind threatened to tear her mantilla from her head, and Amalia was forced to clutch it tight to her scalp.

'No! The Marauder is coming!'

Amalia shook her head. 'The Marauder is dead!'

'No!' screamed Monika. She pointed with her knife back at the abbey, at her cell and the dead abductors. 'The Marauder lives!'

Sister Amalia stared at the knife, then to the autopistol, as if seeing them for the first time.

'Where did you get those?'

Monika glowered. She was tired of being treated as a danger

just because she was the only one who seemed aware of the threats around her.

'The Ilarch has sent her servants for me,' she yelled.

'Monika, listen to me: there are no drukhari here!' Amalia took a step closer, holding her hand out, pleading with Monika. 'Look at the weapons in your hands. Are those xenos weapons?'

Monika glanced down, not missing that Amalia took another step closer. She held the wychknife out, pointing it directly at the hospitaller.

'You think I don't recognise a wychknife when I see one?'

'That's not a drukhari knife,' Amalia yelled. 'Look at it! It's a gardener's vitiberry knife!'

Monika stared at the blade, the tiny voice that lurked in the back of her mind growing stronger. Sister Amalia had a point: the tapering point and backswept hook did bear a strong resemblance to the gardening implements she'd seen the servants using.

'The stresses of the storm and Sister Rozia's death are wearing on your mind!' Amalia yelled. She took another step closer towards Monika, close enough to be heard without yelling. 'You're frightened, and you're hurting people, but I know you: you're stronger than this. You're strong enough to put your weapons down, to come inside where it's safe. You're strong enough to trust me.'

Monika looked at her hands, at the rain-streaked bloodstains.

'Where's the inquisitor?'

Sister Amalia shook her head. 'She was called away on urgent business; a xenos raid in a neighbouring system. She swore she would come back to resolve your situation as soon as she was able.'

Monika frowned. The voice of compliance died.

'No,' she said, taking a step back. 'Why would she leave without her lander?'

Amalia took another step forward, imploring Monika with her outstretched hand.

'The Ordo Xenos sent a ship to pick her up,' the sister said. 'She left on that vessel. Please, Monika. Let's go back inside. Take my hand.'

The final piece of the puzzle clicked into place for Monika as she remembered the white-clad arm stabbing her with a syringe, injecting the chem-restraint into her while she was trying to convince the inquisitor of the imminent attack.

'Let me see your other hand, Amalia.'

The Sister's eyes widened, which was all the proof Monika needed. She fired, the sound of the autopistol drowned out by the roar of the typhoon. Sister Amalia's head snapped back and her body collapsed on the landing pad. A small chem-restraint syringe bounced from her dead hand to roll away across the rain-drenched rockcrete.

Monika punched her old code into the lander's keypad, smiling when the ship unlocked for her. She could hear a chorus of screams from deep within the abbey announcing the arrival of the full force of the drukhari, but the door soon closed behind her, sealing her away from the wind, rain and noise. She slid into the cockpit, firing the lander into its pre-flight sequence. If the Ilarch wanted to waste her time searching a hospital full of maniacs and traitors, she was welcome. By the time the drukhari pirate realised her quarry wasn't there, Monika would be gone. It was only a short jump to a port city, to a black market identity and to freedom. Let the Inquisition think her dead, let the drukhari think her vanished. It no longer mattered what other people thought about her.

Lifting off from the landing pad, Monika banked in a wide loop and flew into the storm.

THE NOTHINGS

Cade peered out from between the mountain crags and gazed across the forbidden lands beyond the Cradle. He was always struck by how those rolling prairies below seemed limitless, unbounded by the sheer cliffs that enclosed his own domain. He tried to pick out roads or villages, or perhaps one of those great walled cities of which Abi had spoken. He had been born somewhere out there in that ocean of green. In a farmhouse, perhaps. Or some lofty palace tower. Who knew? His parents had known, their graves lost too beneath these darkening skies.

Cade squinted at the storm clouds mounting a barricade across the horizon, seemingly in defiance of the prevailing wind.

A voice bellowed up at him from behind and he jumped in fright, almost losing his grip on the rocks.

'Get down from there, boy!'

He looked back to see Barrion frowning up at him from below, a tusked hog slung across his huge shoulders and a brace of purple gillybirds strangled at his belt.

'I got tired of waiting for you,' said Cade, feigning annoyance as he clambered down the rock face as casually as he could manage.

The master hunter continued barking at his apprentice as he

descended. 'What's gotten into you, lad? You know the Lands Beyond are not for your eyes. Nor for anyone's.' His icy blue stare was livid above the black beard that consumed the lower half of his face. 'Unless you want the Nothings to come after you.'

Cade could not help but shiver at Barrion's words and hoped his companion hadn't noticed.

'I'm too old to be scared by fairy tales, Barrion.'

'Disobey the Horned Throne and you'll soon see what's a fairy tale and what's not, lad.'

Cade jumped down beside him and threw him a look of defiance.

Barrion chuckled. 'Oh, so he's a big man now at seventeen harvests old? Big enough to carry that all the way back to the village, is he?'

Barrion indicated the enormous dead stag that Cade had somehow managed to roll onto a makeshift sled. It must have been some ten harvests old, its antlers grown to a sprawl. The thing weighed as heavy as sin, heavier still after being hauled from the woods in which Cade had killed it, those antlers catching on every root and branch on its way out.

Barrion shook his head. 'Did I not explain that we were coming up here for small game? Sweetmeats, Cade. Easy to carry. The harvest feast is tonight. Do you think the women will have time to prepare a beast that size? 'Tis a mortal waste.'

Cade spoke excitedly. 'I was in the trees gathering eggs when he plodded out the woods beneath me. The wind was before me for an hour. He had no notion I was there. It would have been a mortal waste *not* to take him.'

'And how many herds did you scare away in taking him down?'

Cade grinned. 'One shot, straight in the eye.' He patted the slender throwing axes at his belt.

'Like hell, you did,' said Barrion, taking a sudden interest in the corpse. Cade waited, and Barrion concluded his inspection with a snort. 'And why did you feel the need to perform such a feat, lad? Who were you looking to impress by dragging this monster through the village?'

Cade swallowed. 'No one.'

Barrion eyed him doubtfully and spat over the trail's ledge.

'A man should choose his burdens wisely,' he said and trudged away, muttering under his breath. Cade grabbed the rungs of the sled and dragged it behind him, the stag's weight already unbearable. He clattered down the narrow mountain trail after Barrion, careful to avoid the sheer drop beside them as they descended towards their village buried deep in the foothills below.

They walked in silence until evening threatened the sky, casting an orange gloom over the horseshoe of mountains that encompassed the Cradle, shielding it from the Lands Beyond. Cloud-shadows crawled down those grey slopes, down acres of purple heather, over the bristling green woods and across the lake, a gleaming grey sheet spread across the valley's basin.

The Cradle was said to be accessible by a single secret road known only to the Matriarchs. But Cade knew the truth. The mountains were not completely impassable. His exploits as a hunter had taken him into every corner of the valley and he knew where in the lower ranges a man might pass into the Lands Beyond. Yet he also knew ancient measures had been put in place to prevent such excursions.

The trail followed a bend and the Tor came into view. It had been carved out of the shoulders of the northern mountains aeons ago, a huge monarch reclining upon His throne. Even from this distance, Cade could see His cloven hooves awash with bright tributes of summer flowers and wicker poppets. The Horned King bowed His great goat's head, forever contemplating His kingdom.

Cade mumbled a prayer. 'I am an orphan of the Cradle. I give thanks to the Horned Throne. He is sky and soil, root and branch.'

A cooling breeze blessed him with the scent of wildflowers. The smell reminded him of his boyhood, exhausted in bed after a day of mad games in the fields with his friends, cool sheets wrapped tight and safe around him. How empty of such excitement and comfort the Cradle seemed to him now. For all its majesty, the valley seemed devoid of allure and mystery these days. The Horned Father could give him no answers and all Cade had was questions he wished he could ignore. Why were they forbidden from leaving the Cradle? What was out there in the Lands Beyond?

Barrion was trying to break the ice.

'A fine harvest this year, lad. Enough to brew twice the mead we had last year. I doubt we'll wake 'til long past sunrise two days hence.'

Cade grunted, preoccupied, his arms in torment, though he was determined not to show it as he dragged the clattering sled behind him.

'You know Estrilda?' tried Barrion. 'That dark-haired one from the stables? She was asking after you. Wanted to know where you'd be seated at the feast tonight. That Sara from the smithy asked the same, and so did her sister.' He laughed.

Cade scowled. Barrion clearly thought him a fool, a child, easily patronised.

'Fish from the rivers, fruit from the soil, girls from the village.' Barrion winked. 'The Cradle provides, lad. Don't let anyone tell you otherwise.'

'You're wrong about Abi,' Cade said.

Barrion stopped dead and turned with a look of concern.

'The rest of us call her "Abigael", lad. When we have to. Sounds like you two have become close. For how long?'

'Long enough to know that what everyone says about her is not true.'

''Tis true she's trouble, lad.'

'So you keep telling me.'

'So does everyone in the blasted village, but still you won't listen.' Barrion managed to staunch his frustration and laid gentle hands on Cade's shoulders. 'Understand. She's not...' Barrion struggled to find the words. 'She's not right! She doesn't fit. You know even the Matriarchs couldn't divine a use for her.'

Cade snorted. 'Abi shamed them all, that's why. She could interpret the old scrolls better than any in the cloisters.'

'And questioned those scrolls too often, which is why she's shovelling dung in the goat pens these days. Not only that, she's got your nose turned places it shouldn't be. What are you thinking? I can see she's got pretty eyes and a full figure. Come on, lad. Tell me that's all you're after...'

Cade calmly set down the sled.

'Speak of her that way again, Barrion,' he said, 'and see if I don't raise my hand to you.'

Barrion stepped back, muttering in astonishment.

'It's as they say, then,' he said. 'First she has you peering over the walls into the Lands Beyond. Then she has you threaten your master without a glint of fear in your eye. She has a hex upon you, lad, whether you know it or not. I knew she was wrong. She's a mistake. She doesn't belong here.'

'Of course she belongs here, Barrion. She's an orphan like us. Like all of us. She was sent to the Cradle from the Lands Beyond to be cared for after her parents died.'

Cade jabbed his finger at the Tor. 'Is that not His custom? The creed of the Horned Throne welcomed her. If there's a mistake, Barrion, then is it not of His making?'

The blow landed hard across Cade's cheek, knocking him onto the sled. The stag shifted beneath him, the sled slipping down a shelf of rock onto the ledge beside the trail. He went to stop it, but Barrion grabbed him by his tunic, lifting him off his feet and bellowing in his face.

'No orphan leaves the Cradle! That is His law. He provides

and so we obey. *That* is His custom. For even one of us to cross
the boundary would bring ruin to us all.'

Cade struggled but Barrion's arms were like branches of oak,
his teeth bared behind his spit-flecked whiskers.

'The Matriarchs cannot protect her forever, boy. Not when she
persists with her blasphemies, and poisons others with them.'

Cade looked down. The sled's escape had been stopped by a
sapling, perilously close to the brink. Realising his own feet hovered near the ledge, he grabbed Barrion's arms for fear of being
dropped. The man glared back at his apprentice, eyes cold.

'Folk won't stand for it,' Barrion said. 'And nor will I.'

'She's not what you think she is,' Cade said. 'She's not a witch.'

Before Barrion could answer, their attention was stolen by a
soft but insistent chime, carried upon the wind. The village bell.
Someone far below was hammering that bronze shell in a panic.
Barrion flung Cade to the ground, shrugged the dead hog from
his shoulders and bolted down the slope like a hound. Cade's
own heart rang as he gathered himself to sprint after him. The
great stag shifted on the slope beside him, then vanished over
the ledge. Cade peered after it. He watched the animal tumble
through the air for a second before it cast a sheet of blood and
spinning splinters over the rocks below.

The goats had got loose. They were everywhere – braying, hump-
ing, clashing in the streets. They nibbled at the white cloths laid
upon the feasting tables, spilling empty plates and cups onto a
ground now strewn with dung. They gobbled fruit from the over-
turned horn-baskets woven by the children in annual thanks for
the Horned Father's protection. The animals munched and gazed
stupidly as their human keepers raced about them.

Cade stumbled and kicked his way through the whinnying
throng, close behind Barrion as he entered the village. The alarm
bell had ceased long before they arrived, but the place remained

in a state of panic. Cade saw frightened nursemaids dragging children behind doors, infants bawling. Men rifled through sheds, barns and cellars, frantically searching. Cade froze as he heard one of them call out.

'Abigael?'

Barrion grabbed one of the field workers and demanded to know what was going on.

'The queer one,' the man said. 'She's gone missing, slipped away. Some say she's already fled the Cradle!'

Cade's legs were reeds in a gale, his belly an empty pit. Abi was gone? She had been so distant these last few weeks, fearful. The awful logic of her disappearance knocked him dizzy. Perhaps she was only hiding in the woods. Perhaps she had stumbled upon a bear or a pack of sabre-wolves.

Perhaps she was even more reckless than he thought. She may have crossed the boundary into the Lands Beyond, and she had done so without him.

'Where is she?' Barrion had Cade by his jacket once again, shaking him, flecking Cade's face with spit.

'I don't know,' Cade spluttered.

Cade had never seen Barrion so wild, his lips curled, snarling like a cornered bear.

'You two are wedded in this mischief, I know it. Now tell me!'

'Upon the Father,' Cade said. 'I know not.'

Barrion swore and dragged Cade beside him as he lurched on, towards the heart of the village. He called others to his side, a captain rousing men to war.

Cade did not struggle; his mind was too addled. Had she crossed the boundary already? Was he and every other orphan in the village already doomed? How could she be so callous? Again, that awful logic reminded him. She had terrified him in the past with talk of the Lands Beyond, yet intrigued him with her theories that nothing at all would happen should anyone leave the Cradle. The warnings of the Matriarchs were but an empty custom, she insisted.

She had told Cade of things that she had read in the ancient scriptures, things that men like Barrion would call blasphemy, grounds for murder, even. She had been vague in detail, but seemed to suggest that the cult of the Horned Father was but a fragment of a truth greater and more glorious than any of their people might realise. Cade knew her certainty had been absolute; as absolute as her fear of those who hated her.

But what if she was wrong? No one knew what punishment the Horned Father might visit upon His children for their disobedience. Tavern scholars spoke of harvests crumbling to ash or a winter that would freeze them to death in their homes. Others spoke of ghost stories heard as children, of spirits known as the Nothings. Then men would discreetly make the sign of the Horn-Star and talk would progress to other matters.

Barrion hauled him into the village square amid a throng of other villagers, dragging him up to the huge table erected upon the steps of the Cloven Altar. Here the Matriarchs, honoured brides of the Horned Father, should have been sat feasting. Instead, Mother Alder stood alone, already addressing a fearful crowd. She wore only her green shift, still looking tall and proud, though shockingly plain and vulnerable without her veil of leaves and horned crown. The crowd had gathered bows and muskets. Torches had been lit, fogging the evening air with the angry stink of smoke and hot resin.

Barrion thrust Cade into the arms of another man with orders to hold him tight. Cade felt strong hands gripping his jacket as he watched Barrion shoulder through the crowd, unsling his hunting bow and kneel as he presented it to Mother Alder. Ice wriggled down Cade's spine as he heard Barrion speak.

'In the name of the Horned Father, for the safety of the Cradle and its orphans,' he said. 'Mother, bless this, my humble weapon, for a witch may only be killed by an instrument thus sanctified.'

Cade cried out, jostled by the crowd. 'She's not a witch!'

'Whatever she is,' said Barrion, still staring up at Mother Alder. 'She means to cross the boundary and bring the Horned Father's wrath upon us all.'

Mother Alder looked weary. 'You don't know that, Barrion. None of you know that.'

'She has stolen food and water from the stores,' someone cried.

'And clothes from our porch,' yelled another.

Another was angrier still. 'She flirts with blasphemy before our children, and she has done so for too long.'

The men roared their approval, but Mother Alder did not wilt before the blast, though her handsome face darkened with a private sorrow.

'Mother, quickly,' Barrion said. 'She may have passed the stones already.'

Cade cried out as Mother Alder raised her hand.

'Make it swift,' she told Barrion, then made the sign of the Horn-Star over his bow, then over the lowered heads of the assembled. The men received her grim sanction with admirable humility. For they were to murder one of their own, an orphan of the Cradle.

'But where are we to start looking?' one of them hissed.

'Fear not,' another replied. 'Cade here is the finest tracker in the Cradle.'

The man's words trailed off. Cade had already sidled from the crowd and he imagined his captor's astonishment at the sight of the vacant jacket in his hand. He felt a glint of satisfaction and shivered as he scurried away down a darkened lane.

Cade found her trail heading upstream. Blades of grass were broken, torn by the passage of stiff shoes, the kind worn by one who meant to travel far. He wet his parched mouth with a scoop of chill water then stooped to examine the ground. The emerald moon blazed green, full ripe tonight. Cade felt comforted by the presence of that great shining apple still dangling above his benighted world.

The grass had not been pressed beneath any great weight. The shorter, stiffer reeds had already sprung back in place. Abi had passed through here less than an hour ago, ploughing this subtle furrow through the pasture as she hurried uphill. The stream wriggled for a quarter-league up the mountainside, a green snake glittering in the moonlight as it passed a dense line of trees that Cade knew all too well. A good long run lay ahead of him – longer still for Abi, a scribe from the cloisters unused to traversing the wild. But Cade could see no figure moving along the glimmering waters ahead, no tell-tale shadow creeping about the distant banks.

Glowing green faun lights swarmed in bunches along the stream. As a boy, Cade had believed the old stories that told how these insects were actually spirits, servants of the Father, sent to guide wanderers to a safe destination. But he knew he would receive no such guidance tonight. Cold fear soaked him at the thought of Abi reaching the boundary before him.

He sprang up the trail, settling into a bounding run, his hunting axes clacking at his hip. This was all his fault. Abi could be in danger, as could every orphan in the village. His sheltered world faced an apocalypse of his making. May oak and earth forgive him. Fool that he was for showing her this route. Madman that he was for allowing her to approach the boundary and giving Abi her first glimpse of the Lands Beyond. That forbidden vista was the preserve of no one in the Cradle but the Matriarchs and master rangers such as Barrion.

His pace slowed as he reached the foothills, his breath laboured as he fought his way up their steep banks. His last visit to these pastures had been during a happier time, when the goldlace and bloodthistles bloomed. Cade had been helping re-thatch the sheds when Mother Alder had condemned Abi to the goat pens for the rest of the season. Cade had helped her carry dung barrows to the fields, a favour that quickly became habit.

She appreciated his assistance and he was fascinated by her seemingly endless capacity for talk. She spoke at first of her duties under the Matriarchs, who dwelt in stony chambers in the high reaches of the village. She had been taught to understand the ancient runes, then progressed to tedious copywork, salvaging with her quill the history of the Horned Throne from countless crumbling scrolls. But oh, how she devoured those endless lines of information. It was for her like opening a door into a new world, a world beyond her dungeon cloisters. She asked much about Cade's exploits as a hunter and he obliged her with casually audacious tales of stalking dangerous beasts among the treacherous margins of the Cradle. How he relished the look of fascination in those inquisitive brown eyes.

They had discussed philosophy in the privacy of the empty fields, shovelling pellets of dung along the furrows as they debated what might lie beyond the stars. She had been punished with her current duties for her ceaseless questioning of Mother Alder, whose every answer, whose every angry demand for silence, served only to inspire more questions.

'We orphans are told our parents are dead, but did we not have other family to care for us in the Lands Beyond? Who dictated such a tradition? Who are the founders of our custom? The Horned Father? Or someone else? If we are never to leave the Cradle, then is this all our lives are to be?' Abi's questions troubled Cade, though her curiosity was infectious. Her passion enthralled him as much as it terrified him.

'The truth is bliss,' she once told him. 'Not ignorance.' Those words had struck him hard, made him ashamed of his comforts, of his fears. He was no sheep in thrall to the shepherd, but a man. And he became determined to prove that. He yearned to inspire her.

Cade paused for breath atop a steep rock and looked back at the village. How quickly might Barrion follow his trail? What might he and his followers do to Cade when he eventually caught up with him? Cade skipped on, from rock to rock, bounding like a billy goat, away from the gushing stream until he reached the shelf of trees. He hauled himself onto the ledge and a wall of pines stood before him.

He pounded sparks from his flint to set ablaze a stout torch from his belt. Was she waiting for him by the stones on the other side of the trees, too afraid to cross the boundary? Could he reach her in time? If so, what would he do? Talk sense into her? If she refused to listen, would he have to stop her? The thought of harming her, even for her own good, set his belly churning.

He entered the trees, his crackling torchlight washing over the ground, revealing a shifted pebble, tufts of moss smeared underfoot. The smell of pine smothered him, a carpet of dead needles flesh-soft beneath his feet. He pinched a tassel of hair from a splintered branch. The strands were long and milky-yellow, plucked from the roots. Abi had battled her way through these branches, determined. Perhaps she lay injured nearby. If he was lucky. Perhaps she was dead, her carcass sprawled and wolf-ravaged, awaiting his discovery. He felt a sickening glimmer of hope.

The pines eventually released him onto a grassy mountain ledge dominated by a single towering stone. It was coffin-narrow, flat as a headstone. Beyond lay a sea of hills and fields, ghostly green beneath the moon.

Cade stood alone, his torch whooshing in his hand as he spun around in search of Abi. He sobbed her name.

Nothing.

The air here seemed to tremble with a gravelly hum that haunted the edge of Cade's hearing. He felt a slight but dizzying pressure in his head, like palms pressed hard upon his ears. Two more stones stood glowering a short distance away, either side of the stone before him. Countless more stood beyond those, Cade knew, erected centuries ago along the mountains of the Cradle, forming a ring that surrounded the sacred valley.

The boundary stones watched as Cade probed the grass. Abi's trail passed between the standing rocks, continued down the grassy slope and vanished into the Lands Beyond. Those black clouds Cade had seen to the north that afternoon were now advancing, a sarcophagus lid moving to shut out the moonlight.

Cade felt weightless with panic as he comprehended the unavoidable truth that lay pressed into the grass before him. The boundary had been crossed. An orphan had left the Cradle. Catastrophe would follow. His torch fell dead to the ground and he dropped before the stone, pressing his hands in entreaty upon the lichen-splattered rock.

'Forgive her, Father! This is my sin, not hers. Punish me and spare the others, I beg you. It was I who caused this. It was I who inspired this blasphemy.'

He ground his forehead against the stone.

'I should never have brought her here.'

Cade looked out across the Lands Beyond, remembering the eternity of blue skies and green pastures it had been months ago. But he had been more enchanted by the sight of Abi, standing beside this very stone. She had stripped off her dairymaid's cap, pale hair shamelessly aflutter, shielding her eyes as she fell in love with the horizon. He knew then that he had lost her. In bringing her here, in attempting to draw her closer to him, he had succeeded only in casting her away, striking in her a longing for that which neither he nor the Horned Father nor anything in the Cradle could ever hope to satisfy.

The Horned Father gave no answer. There was only that dead-ening murmur in the air as the boundary stones considered Cade's entreaty. His hands fell away, his palms tingling. He had seen something move in the Lands Beyond.

Cade instinctively flattened himself upon the grass, thankful his torch was extinguished. He was unsure what he had just seen, but something about it caused his heart to beat hard against the earth. Not daring to raise his head, he stared into darkness, cold grass nuzzling his face. Had he seen only a scarecrow? He recalled something with outstretched arms, its ragged garments licking the air. Yet he knew full well that scarecrows stood staked in their fields; they did not shamble silently about the earth of their own volition.

He must be mistaken. Horned Throne preserve him, he had to be mistaken.

He slowly raised his head, struggling to steady his hastening breath as he peered out from behind the stone, and over the bushes that covered the steep slope.

Ice drenched his scalp at the sight of a shred of darkness bob-bing on the spot some distance below, far too big to be a rabbit. It vanished beneath the brow of a hill before he could identify it.

A fox, then. It must be a fox, he thought.

As he struggled to convince himself, the shape rose again, nearer this time. It was steadily mounting the hill. He could see a figure, perfectly visible in the moonlight, cloaked it seemed, its long vestments flapping in the wind, arms thrashing as it clawed its way up the slope towards him.

Cade heard himself whimper, feeling his limbs shake with a sudden energy as he went to bolt back through the pines. The figure stumbled and fell. He heard a distant yelp of pain. Long pale hair flashed in the moonlight.

'Abi!'

Cade sprang, eyes fixed on the exhausted figure struggling up the hill below. He took several strides past the boundary stone before he realised what he'd done.

As he passed between the boundary stones and down the hillside, Cade's skull rang like a bell, its shimmering echoes ceaseless, entrancing. He shook his head to clear it and stumbled onto his rump, suddenly fascinated by the feel of the grass caressing his palms, cold and damp. He could smell foxglove and heather, richer and sweeter than anything that grew in the Cradle. The sky shone black, bedewed with diamond stars. Cade felt as though some cataract had been lifted from his eyes, enabling him to behold the world with a new and hypnotic clarity. The pale green moon gazed down at him and he could see every ring and grain on its radiant surface as clearly as if he were holding it in his hand. He reached out, half-expecting to touch it, when the moon opened its eyes and screamed at him.

Cade recoiled in terror, flailing as he realised someone was shaking him, trying to drag him upright.

'Get up!' Abi screamed at him, her hair wild, her face streaked with dirt. 'Move, Cade! Run!'

Cade gazed up at her, struggling to comprehend, to sober himself from the haze of newfound sensations.

A shock of pain lashed his cheek as Abi slapped him. She dragged him to his feet, clawing at him, urging him back up the hill towards the boundary stones. Cade could feel his new alertness settling into focus and he found himself absorbed by the sight of his legs steadying into a run beneath him. Whatever was happening to him could wait for an explanation. Abi gasped at his side, her skirts clawed to rags, her baggage lost. The crags tumbled into the empty foothills far below. Nothing but the wind stirred the cascading grass that swept away into the Lands Beyond.

'It's gone,' Cade said. 'Whatever you're running from, Abi, it's gone.'

She cried out as he pulled her back, pointing into the empty chasm below.

'Look,' he said. 'I see nothing.'

She seized him by the shirt, her breath hot in his face, eyes white rings of terror in the dark.

'That doesn't mean it's not there.'

She wrenched him back up towards the boundary stones, but Cade shrugged her off. Something else had moved down there. A thicket of tall grass some sixty paces below had shifted against the wind. Cade was already crouched, weighing a slender throwing axe in his hand. A grabbler perhaps, lumbering through the weeds in search of worms?

He tried to pinpoint the spot, but the space at which he was trying to stare seemed to keep pushing his eyes away. Try as he might, they simply would not focus on the spot where he had seen the grass move. Yet every time he looked away, he thought he could see something moving steadily towards him. He looked again, trying to catch himself out, but his eyes just slipped across that benighted patch of ground, as if whatever stood there was too abhorrent to behold. Cade could see nothing.

Abi shrieked as she tugged at his arm, begging him to move. But Cade refused to stir. He knew Abi to be as fearless as any hunter. To hear her voice ring with such terror felt to him somehow indecent, and he craved to obliterate the cause of it. Spurred by anger, he pounced, gauging the distance between them and that shuffling patch of grass as he flung the axe high in the air. Its thin steel head dulled with charcoal, the axe was almost invisible in the moonlight, silent as an owl as it dived for its target. Cade tried to glare at that ruffling grass, impatient for the death-squeal of whatever lurked there. But the harder he tried to look the more readily his vision bounced aside. His head throbbed.

The axe rang as it shattered in mid-air, just short of its mark. Cade froze. There came no threats, no snarls of rage. The wind carried no musk. There was nothing there, and yet on it came. When Cade looked aside he could perceive the grass continuing its bristling path up the hill towards him, the sward flattening as if beneath a heavy and implacable tread, slowly closing the distance between them.

'Why?' he said, his voice sounding slow and stupid. 'Why isn't it dead? What is it?'

He felt another splash of pain across his cheek as Abi released him from his stupor.

'Now's not the time to ask, Cade. Run!'

Suddenly he was scrambling back up the hill with Abi, neither daring to look back. The boundary stone rose before them, imperious as it watched the two young sinners struggling below. He and Abi had put themselves beyond the Horned Father's reach, beyond salvation. How could He welcome them back into His blessed sanctuary? How could He possibly protect them, when the very thing that pursued them could have been sent by Him to deliver punishment?

Cade clawed his way uphill. The long grass snagged the toes of his shoes; sharp stones slit his hands and shins. The boundary stone loomed black, its silhouette melting into the night sky as if fading from reach. His movements felt dream-slow and he sensed a presence gathering behind him, hungering for him. He imagined it reaching for him, tearing through the caul of reality, about to clamp an immovable hand upon his shoulder.

Cade whimpered as Abi dragged him after her, pulling him past the stone, back into the Cradle.

Cade saw Abi sink to the ground, limp and breathless. He hauled her onto his shoulders as though she were a hunter's kill, his legs threatening to buckle under her dead weight as he carried her into the pines. She was too exhausted to protest as he dumped her in a hollow at the foot of a tree. He peered back through the ramrod trunks at the boundary stone that guarded their retreat. The air was still. Nothing yet stirred near the stone. As his own breath returned, he felt giddy with relief. He rested his head against the bark and thanked the Horned Throne for His forgiveness of two foolish children.

'Are you hurt, Abi?'

She shook her head, a thicket of hair masking her face as she panted.

'That thing out there,' said Cade. 'What manner of abomination was it?'

She brushed her hair aside and looked up at him, her face ghostly and imploring. She spoke in gasps.

'I know not, Cade. And it matters not. All that matters is that we are safe. Thank you. And thank the Throne.'

Relief engulfed them both and they threw their arms around each other. Cade enjoyed a moment of wondrous surrender before rage erupted and he snarled at the girl.

'What madness possessed you? Crossing the boundary. Your mischief risked us all.'

'They would have killed me if I'd stayed. You know that, Cade. You too, had they thought us partners in witchcraft.' She shook her head, wincing in regret. 'I was so sure nothing was there.' She laughed as if realising a poor joke. 'Throne forgive me.'

'They mean to hang you still, Abi. They believe you to be a witch.'

'A fine word for a woman who questions their thinking.'

'Do you think I jest?' Cade said, irritated by her remark. 'We cannot return until we have planned what to tell them.'

'I know exactly what to tell them, Cade,' she said with a hopeful smile. 'I'll need to speak to Mother Alder. She'll understand.' Now it was her turn to shake him. 'We know the truth, Cade. No orphan must ever leave the Cradle and now we know why.'

'What do you speak of, Abi?'

'The boundary stones, Cade. They stand for our protection. I've read about them in the ancient texts. I think they divert spirit matter, the energies of the earth, in such a way as to hide us from what's out there.'

Cade shivered. 'From the Nothings?'

She steadied him with a zealous grip. 'I fled because of doubt. Now I return to the Cradle with a faith stronger than ever, with proof of the Horned Throne's power.'

The earth shuddered.

Cade looked about him, searching for the source of the tremor. The great boundary stone shifted beyond the pines. It lurched like an enormous tooth loose in its socket. Then it cracked, bursting into rubble as it collapsed in a cloud of dust.

Before he could comprehend the impossibility of what he had just seen, Cade felt a familiar chime in his head. It passed through him like a seismic wave, leaving him feeling somehow cleansed, liberated. He felt he could pinpoint every cricket chittering in every thicket about him.

Abi was screaming.

The boundary stone adjacent to the one that had just fallen was itself crumbling from view. Its death howl resounded with a tenor too substantial to have been a mere echo. Cade knew the ring of stones that surrounded the valley was collapsing, one stone after the other. He stumbled under the weight of his realisation and toppled into Abi who knelt now beside him, sobbing and pleading.

'What have I done? Oh, Horned Throne, forgive me.'

Cade felt weightless, dizzy with loss. The Cradle was no more. His home since infancy had been invaded by the Lands Beyond, and whatever vengeful energies dwelt there. The dust that lingered where the boundary stone once stood blew apart as if at a sudden breeze. Abi saw it too, though she looked away, wincing in pain.

Something stood there, he knew, the dust disappearing around it, as if the stone and whatever sacred energies it possessed were repelled, shattered by the very presence of its conqueror.

Cold fear squirmed in Cade's belly, wriggling through his guts like an eel, as a half-glimpsed silhouette moved through the dust towards him.

And several more followed.

Cade fled with Abi back through the pines, numbly aware of the branches slashing his cheeks, tearing at his hair. They eventually broke from the line of trees, welcomed by the gushing stream that would lead them all the way back to the village. They paused for a moment, hands on trembling legs as they caught their breath. The Horned Father watched them from atop the darkened Tor, His curled horns bowed as if in mourning.

'We have to warn them,' gasped Cade. 'The village. They need to know what's coming. What we've done. Even if they kill us for it.'

Abi lowered her head and nodded, sobs punctuating each gasping breath.

He took her hand and they slid together down a high bank of dirt and roots. Cade relished the reckless speed of their descent, thankful for the distance it put between him and whatever drifted after them through the pines above. They rolled onto a grassy bank in a cloud of dirt.

The meadow lay empty before them, the stream a glittering path, merry with faun lights. They had a clear run, but men carrying torches and muskets were already lumbering up the rocks to their left. Cade went to hide Abi in the plunging stream, but Barrion had already seen them. By the time the others were aware of their quarry, the master hunter had an arrow aimed at the chest of his former apprentice.

Cade froze, covering Abi, though he knew the shaft would go straight through him at such close range. The arrow's tip did not tremble and Cade caught himself marvelling at the unfamiliar clarity with which he could see Barrion's blue eyes piercing the darkness, stark and merciless.

'Did she cross the boundary?' asked Barrion, his voice cold.

Cade knew the truth would earn him instant death. 'Hear me, all of you,' he said. 'Something's coming.'

'Did an orphan leave the Cradle?' Barrion said.

Haylan the smith growled beside him, his face wolfish with rage. 'Why else would the boundary stones have fallen, Barrion? The Father's wrath is upon us. Killing that witch now might at least curb our sorrows.'

Abi snarled back at him. 'Don't think I wouldn't meet death in glad payment for the ruin I've caused, Haylan. But you need to listen. Something followed us through those trees. Something that means to kill us all.'

Another man cried out. 'The village!'

Everyone turned to look. Smoke was streaming from the distant thatched roofs. Cade staggered back at the sound of ghostly screams carried on the breeze. Abi seized him and thrust her head into his chest.

'I'm sorry,' she sobbed, repeating the words until they choked her. He hadn't the strength to catch her as she dropped to her knees and vomited at his feet. The men ignored them, bellowing in outrage, most of them now fleeing back across the meadow. Cade reeled at the thought that there might be yet more pursuing spirits, that the destruction of the boundary stones may have permitted some kind of invasion. Abi caught his shoulder as she hauled herself upright, her eyes dazed, jaw slack and dripping.

'I know a place,' she croaked, then raised her voice to shout after the fleeing mob. 'Upstream,' she cried. 'Come with us! There's a fissure in the rock beneath the Tor. Within there are tunnels through which we could escape.'

But the men had already fled. Only Barrion remained,

staggering on the spot, staring at the ground as if it might disclose a solution to this madness.

Cade caught her. 'What tunnels?'

'The Iron Caves,' said Abi. 'The scrolls say they were explored by our forebears.' She called to Barrion, imploring. 'There are passages within, passages that could lead us to the Lands Beyond.'

Barrion looked up at her. Cade knew that ravenous glare. It was the last thing seen by countless beasts the instant before an arrow entered their eye.

Barrion's arrow whispered past Cade's ear as he threw Abi into the tumbling stream. She disappeared into the rushing waters and Cade leaped after her. A vortex of freezing water enveloped him, seconds before disgorging them both a short distance below.

Abi went to climb onto the bank, but Cade pulled her back into the bubbling waters, behind a cloud of faun lights. They were in a brook at the foot of the Tor with no hard cover between them and the master bowman positioned high above. Abi shivered beside him as he waited for the arrow that would kill one of them. Seconds passed. Barrion was clever. He knew how to tempt his prey out of hiding.

Cade pictured his mentor's piercing blue eyes awash with tears as he scoured the dark for a sign of his former apprentice. This was a good man driven to murderous madness by fear, by betrayal. For a moment Cade welcomed the thought of that arrow piercing his treacherous heart.

The thatched roofs of the village were now ablaze, weaving a veil of smoke over the moon that carried to where they crouched in the water. The rest of the mob had disappeared to join the conflagration. The cold of the water was intense, stiffening Cade's muscles. His head ached. He thought he heard something above the rattle of water. Shouts nearby, a scream, a clash of blades.

Cade led Abi in a sprint from the stream, directing her towards a sheltered goat track that he knew wound up the side of the Tor.

Again, he almost yearned for Barrion's arrow to find his back; its absence would mean the master hunter had been claimed by the Nothings.

When he and Abi reached the trail, the two of them battled their way up the foot of the Tor for several minutes without looking back. Urging Abi ahead of him, Cade risked a single glance over his shoulder, though he already knew they were being followed. He knew from the pain burrowing into his temples, and from the way his vision wavered upon several figures making their way up the foot of the track behind him.

Cade ran his hand along the cavern wall. Beneath a crust of lichen, it was unnaturally flat. He kicked it.

'It's metal,' he said.

'The Iron Caves,' said Abi, dreamy with exhaustion.

Cade swept his crackling torch about the narrow walls of the passage ahead, revealing lines of rivets, a vaulted ceiling, a floor black with dirt, arrow-straight into the waiting darkness.

Abi's memory had served them well. With his help, she had found the trail she was looking for. It wound like a fading scar up the east face of the Tor, ending behind a waterfall. A ledge had once existed behind that sheet of water, but it had long been destroyed, no doubt to thwart the curious. But the intervening centuries had grafted a network of vines in its place, strong enough to allow him and Abi to climb across and through a gaping fissure in the rock beyond. Casting nervous glances into the night behind them, they lit the last two of Cade's torches and scrambled into the darkness.

'This is no cave,' said Cade. 'Yet we're inside the Tor. How can this be?'

He began brushing aside a curtain of moss, gradually revealing a corroded frieze. It depicted a human monarch seated atop a mountainous throne. Cade inspected it fearfully and saw the figure wore a wreath of laurel that curled upon his head like a crown of horns.

'What blasphemy is this?' he said.

Abi had wandered ahead. 'It was a heretic who discovered this place,' she said. 'She was an orphan, sent to the Cradle as a babe, just like us. She believed a race of demigods from beyond the stars had built this place beneath the mountains, but abandoned it aeons before she was born.'

'But the Horned Throne is real,' said Cade, shaking his head. 'He is soil and sky, root and branch.'

'That He is,' said Abi. 'Throne forgive me, but I see that now. Yet what we know of Him may be an echo of something else, something greater, a truth that exists still among the stars.'

She ran her fingers over a fearsome crest stamped upon one wall: a bird of prey, double-headed, wings flared in defiance.

'We must hurry,' said Cade, trying not to look at it. 'This passage heads north, towards the other side of the mountain. Following it gives us our best chance of escape, does it not?'

Abi shrugged. 'If such a chance even exists.'

Cade took her arm as they hurried down the seemingly endless passageway, slowing only to scramble over mounds of earth that had spilled through the walls long ago. They ignored the empty corridors branching left and right, past doors and stairs so immense that this place must surely have been populated by a race of giants. They scurried through halls so vast their torchlight couldn't find the walls and ceiling, and it felt like they were running on the spot.

Cade murmured to himself. 'Uncanny, this place. Is it not exactly what you spoke of, Abi? Is this not the truth you sought?'

She didn't answer.

Cade let his thoughts gather pace, eager to distract from his fears as they hurried down another dark and level passage.

'You're right. You must be, Abi. The Father, the Cradle, the

Nothings. They must all be part of it. We ourselves could have a place in some wider world we've yet to discover. 'Tis a marvellous thought.'

'Aye,' said Abi, grimly. 'Though others have paid dearly for this revelation.'

Her pace was sluggish. Cade had to hurry her again. He hadn't had time to cover their tracks, so the Nothings would likely have found the fissure. If so, they must have entered the tunnels by now. He glanced behind him but saw nothing. The smell of stale earth sickened him, reminding him that the rain and sky could not reach him through the immensity of dirt piled above. The only moisture in the air down here stank of rot and rust. Dead roots sprawled through fissures in the iron walls, clutching at his arms as he hastened past.

Even down here, in the insistent darkness, Cade was aware that he could feel his surroundings more acutely somehow. He was familiar with the excitement of the hunt, how it invigorated his senses until the world around him sang. But this was something more. When he had crossed the boundary in pursuit of Abi, when the stones surrounding the valley had collapsed, he had heard that strange chime inside his skull. More than that, he had felt it, comprehended it with something beyond his physical senses. And he felt it still, an echo that sank quivering needles into his brain.

The passage eventually hit a wall of earth, the ceiling ahead of them having long ago surrendered under its titanic burden. Cade's sharp eyes picked out a column of iron rungs fixed to one wall. He quickly led Abi up through a twisted hatch in the ceiling, beyond which lay another corridor. Trusting to instinct, he headed left. Abi followed, almost reluctantly.

The metal walls now cramped his shoulders. The flames of his torch tickled the ceiling, stinging his eyes with smoke as he squinted down the tunnel ahead.

'Do you know where you're going?' said Abi. 'Because I don't.'

'I have a sense,' said Cade, knowing he had none. With no sun or stars by which to maintain his bearings, he knew he could be leading them away from the other side of the mountain and instead deeper into this unfathomable maze. He fancied no faun lights would find him down here and guide his way to safety.

'We need to keep going,' he said, expecting each step to bring him within sight of another unyielding wall. If they had to double back, he knew they would become lost. He thought of the Horned Father brooding in His seat somewhere above him. What better way for a heretic to perish than buried alive beneath the shrine of his former deity?

He and Abi both turned with a gasp as something hissed in the passage behind them. It sounded like the rattle of dirt, or perhaps the crunch of an approaching footstep. They stared into the darkness, paralysed. Cade could feel Abi shuddering beside him as the heat of the flames neared his thumb. Soon the warmth and light of his rapidly shrinking torch would abandon them, releasing them into that waiting blackness. They would be left clawing blindly at the walls for an escape they would never find, and that which hunted them would then find them.

Cade heard no advancing footsteps, but then considered whether the Nothings even trod upon solid ground. Perhaps walls of earth could not impede them. Perhaps reality was to them like water to a fish. Even now, he thought, they could be swimming through iron and bedrock towards them. He imagined a thin hand reaching up through the dirt to grasp his ankle.

The thought was too much. It spurred him to a panting run, dragging Abi behind him. She had fallen unnervingly quiet, her pace slowing until she shambled after him like a dead thing.

Cade dashed past another passageway and felt a chill wash over one side of his sweating face. He drew back, probing the darkness with his torch. The flames brightened momentarily, engorged by a nearby breeze. Abi stumbled behind him, dropping to her knees, gasping as her torch rolled away from her.

She was struggling to breathe, eyes wild and imploring in the torchlight, strangled by her own terror.

'Look at me,' Cade said, gripping Abi's shoulder as he drew a long slow breath. She stared back at him, every intake of air a convulsion. 'We are almost free of this place. Just a little further. I promise.'

She gulped for air.

'Dead.' She strained the word through gritted teeth. 'All dead. Mother Alder. Mother Malin. Ilda. Girtrid. All they did for me. All they gave me, taught me. All their love. All gone. All dead.' Tears glimmered down her cheeks.

'You don't know that,' said Cade, unsure what he was even saying. 'Just breathe, Abi. Like this.'

She ignored him and her torch expired in the dirt beside them, the darkness now barely held at bay by Cade's own sputtering light.

'All this,' she snarled. 'This is all because of me. This is my fault. Mine. Mine!' She repeated the word over and over, pounding at her skull. He went to stop her, but she shoved him away. 'They can have me,' she moaned. 'They deserve me. For what I've done.'

'You don't mean that, Abi.'

'I'm nothing, Cade,' she said. 'Nothing worth saving.'

'They would have hanged you if you stayed, Abi. What choice did they give you? Kick a bear up the arse and you can't blame it for biting you.'

'I should have listened. Should have done as I was told.'

'How can you do as you're told when you were born with a brain the size of yours? Wanting the truth is not a crime, Abi. It's who you are.'

He winced. The pain in his skull was returning, drowning that strange echo in his brain. Perhaps the Nothings could hear that echo too. Perhaps it was leading them straight to him, like wolves tracking the scent of wounded prey. He tried to shut out the discomfort, push it back, and as he did so, felt the passageway throb like a living thing. The pulse tightened his skull until he cried out.

'Cade?'

'Abi,' he whispered, fighting back a mounting nausea. 'When I crossed the boundary, I felt something. I felt it again when the stones collapsed. It was like a bell ringing inside my head. It left me feeling like I was seeing things clearly for the first time in my life.'

Abi's look of fear was melting into one of astonishment.

'You felt it too?' she said.

Cade strained to see into the gloom behind her. The pain in his skull narrowed to an audible whine. No distant footsteps echoed towards them. Nothing breathed. And yet it seemed to Cade as though that very absence was itself a kind of presence, a blackness that seethed with vitality. He remembered how his eyes had refused to behold those terrible figures as they crossed the ruined boundary. Now he wondered if his ears might similarly refuse to detect their approach. If the Nothings could not be seen, perhaps they could not be heard.

The very thought of it made his brain boil, as if something were mauling it, trying to wrest the organ from his skull.

'I can feel them coming, Abi,' he groaned.

'No,' she said, her voice thick, slurred with dread and pain. 'They're already here.'

She snatched Cade's torch and bolted down the passage, pulling Cade after her.

They tumbled into a huge antechamber where a pair of immense iron gates confronted them. The torch cast its dwindling glow upon a monstrous lock clamped above their heads. Cade could see a sliver of familiar green luminescence at the apex of the door-frame.

Abi thrust the torch into his hands as she reached to examine the lock. The velvet gloom seemed to tighten around him, absorbing everything in the room but the locked gates standing before them. Cade could sense it again, the emptiness a living thing closing in on him, trapping his heart until he could feel it fidget like a rabbit in his chest. There was nothing there, nothing visible, nothing tangible. But it was there, a wound in reality, bleeding darkness into the world. Abi cursed and snatched Cade's knife from his belt, though the lock appeared devoid of any keyhole.

He was being hunted by servants of a god. Things of the night, of fairy tale. Nightmares come to life. He was but human, as helpless as the deer he had once hunted in the Cradle, preyed upon by beings of a cunning unfathomable to his primitive instincts. The Nothings' victory was inevitable. What hope had he? His eyes darted about him. Darkness everywhere. Distance was no obstacle to such as the Nothings, Cade now felt sure. They could be watching from a mile away. Or perhaps they waited in this very room. He imagined faces fishbelly-pale, blackened grins lined with a thousand crooked teeth, eyes smiling as they savoured the thunder of his heart, waiting for the darkness to drown him.

He yelped, dropping the torch as its dying flame nipped his hand.

His world went black and blindness sent him mad. Goaded by fearful imaginings, he became a caged animal battering at the iron gates. Terror strengthened his onslaught, but the barrier barely trembled.

He felt Abi pulling him back, trying to calm him. His elbow struck her face, but he was beyond caring. Nothing mattered but tearing his way through this metal wall and escaping that which hunted him in the dark. He scrabbled at the rough metal, tearing fingernails, wetting his hands with blood. The knot in his belly tightened to breaking point as the darkness deepened.

A flash of white suddenly drove it all away, blinding him again. He stumbled back, a flickering light now illuminating the chamber from its rubble-strewn floor to its high, vaulted ceiling. Abi stood nearby, blood streaming from her nose, shielding her eyes as she stared at him. It took two more heartbeats before he realised.

Each of his hands was enveloped in a dazzling bouquet of lightning.

Cade yelled in alarm, casting his arms about him, trying to fling away the crackling light that swarmed about his fingers.

Abi's face flashed in the dark, eyes wide with anguish. 'Cade, calm down!'

Her voice steadied him a moment, and he held his shaking hands before him, long enough to realise the lightning didn't burn. It merely prickled his hands, fizzing like blood returning to a numbed limb. *Impossible.*

'Steady, Cade,' said Abi. 'I think I know what's happening.'

She was laughing. Why was she laughing? Cade didn't want to know. He wanted no more of this terrible new world. He wanted it gone. He wanted blue skies and familiar green. The maelstrom in his hands intensified, seeming to feed upon his distress. He couldn't breathe. He wanted to be gone from this place. He brought his hands together, gathering the coruscation, then hurled it away with a cry of rage.

The blast of lightning struck the gates, shattering the ancient lock as it shoved the doors aside with a groan that shook the chamber. Behind them stood a crumbling wall of roots wallowing in blessed emerald moonlight.

Cade fell whimpering into Abi's arms, his hands smoking and shaking as the archway's lintel sagged high above, dribbling dust. She pulled him through the rain of crumbling dirt. The debris rattled on the floor behind them as they clambered up the screen of roots. Cade heard the lintel come free with a momentous gasp. A torrent of earth and stone followed after it. The deluge thundered to the ground, shaking the wall of roots to which he clung, deafening him. Choked by the uproar of dirt and blinding dust, he climbed on, spurred by the sight of the pale green moon peering through an aperture in the earthen ceiling.

Cade clawed his way up through the soil, pulling clods of turf down upon Abi as he fought his way through the hole, hungry for the air of the outside world. She struggled up after him, tearing the rags of her skirts as she hauled herself through the gap. Cade glanced back through the hole at the mounting wall of collapsed rock and earth.

Nothing could get through that, he told himself. Nothing.

An enormous oak whispered above him. He pulled himself out from between its roots and fell onto a grassy slope, gasping in the fresh night air. The mountains of the Cradle rose behind him. Before him lay the Lands Beyond.

Cade knelt on a grassy shore before an ocean of corn, deep enough to drown in. The shaggy stalks stood taller than any crop that grew in the Cradle, their stiff leaves clacking in the night breeze. The rows combed the land all the way to distant hills patched with farmland. And beyond them one would find cottages, towns, even cities, all populated by strangers who knew nothing of life within the Cradle. He was no longer looking down upon this world as if studying a map. He was now part of it, thrillingly vulnerable to all it might contain. Yet his wonder soured as his reason returned. He shuddered to think of Abi seeing him so unmanned before those awful gates. He felt suddenly naked, piteous in his terror. Throne forgive him, he had even struck her. He clutched the ground with his wounded fingers, welcoming the pain.

Abi stood in silence nearby. As he struggled for words, Cade felt subtle currents shift in the air. Light flickered nearby. He turned to see threads of lightning squirming over Abi's knuckles. As she watched the little bolts play about her fingers, Cade recognised her look of awe. He had seen it before when she had stood by the boundary stone and surveyed the Lands Beyond for the first time. The lightning vanished obediently as she closed her hand.

She looked up at him, grinning despite her bloody nose.

'I was right,' she said, delighted. 'This is what they were keeping from us for all these years. The boundary stones, Cade. They cast a pall to hide us from those that would hunt us, as I said. But they did so by cloaking our abilities, by cutting us off from whatever sphere we derive these powers. But now that spell is broken. The veil has been lifted from our eyes. Now those energies could be ours to command.'

Cade did not want to think about 'energies', about how he had destroyed those unbreakable gates. All he wanted was as much distance as he could muster between himself and that which had hunted them through the metal catacombs beneath the Tor.

From the north, those storm clouds had now conquered the sky, blotting out the stars and reaching for the pale green moon. He hungered for dawn to arrive and chase them away, give him time to think, to make sense of his shattered world. The destruction of the Cradle, the Nothings, lightning conjured out of the air. The cornfield began to whirl sickeningly, forcing him to look away.

Abi paced about, oblivious to his disquiet as she jabbered on. 'Our folks brought us to the Cradle as babes, brought us there for our protection. They must have known what we are.'

'Our parents are dead, Abi. We were brought to the Cradle because tradition demands every foundling be raised there.'

'Perhaps our parents still live,' she said. 'Perhaps we were told they were dead to keep us from leaving. We cannot trust anything we've been told, Cade. The world is bigger than we knew. This morning, did you think the Tor could have been anything other than what you have been told it was?'

Cade recalled those iron halls wrought by some unimaginable race, the ancient frieze of that laurel-horned monarch, a mocking echo of the world he once knew. The thought that his parents may still live felt yet more fantastical. His mother and father had been so complete an absence in his life, they may as well have never existed.

Cade groaned, his fists bunching the grass.

'Don't hide from this, Cade. Don't hide from what you know you are.'

'No, Abi.'

'We're witches.'

The words seemed to vibrate as Cade heard them, blurring the world and its few remaining certainties.

'And not just us,' said Abi, relentless. 'Everyone in the village, every orphan in the Cradle. Mother Alder. Even Barrion. Everyone!'

'How could that be, Abi? They would have known. Wouldn't they?'

'How could they have known when none of them ever set foot outside the boundary? Not even the Matriarchs.' Her eyes flashed with mounting excitement as she hounded her thoughts, chasing a grand revelation. 'It's why we were told never to leave, never to think. It's why I was forbidden from questioning the scriptures. Everything we did, everything we were taught, everything we worshipped was to keep us hidden from those that might harm us, from superstitious folk, from creatures like the Nothings. All was done to preserve the lie.'

Cade wished he could fault her logic.

'If it was done as you say, Abi, then it was done to keep us safe. The Father, the Matriarchs, they sought to protect us.'

Abi smiled darkly. 'Well, I no longer need protection.'

The certainty in her voice unnerved him. 'Even if you're right, Abi. We still must be cautious.'

Cade's head throbbed. The Nothings were near. He imagined them scrabbling below ground, perhaps even burrowing like worms through the barricade of rubble that had descended beneath the tree. Abi muttered to herself, absorbed in her own epiphanies. Cade stared at the hole between the roots of that great tree, half-expecting pale faces to emerge. They were definitely near. He could feel them like a precipice at the rim of his senses, an absence waiting to engulf him.

'I'll be a slave to guilt no longer,' said Abi. 'Not for the crime of knowing the truth.'

Cade stared at the hole, realising that his eyes could linger there without pain. There was nothing there. Nothing. Surely nothing, though he could feel something's gaze upon him from somewhere. Stubble bristled on the back of his neck.

He turned to look out across the corn.

The rumbling storm clouds obscured the moon. Gloom was descending.

Abi was nodding to herself. 'And if that power be bought in blood, then I swear to honour its cost.'

'Abi?' Cade pointed into the distance.

Things were moving through the corn, steadily ruffling the leafy avenues. Though it burned his eyes to do so, Cade counted at least six of them, still far away but steadily advancing. Cade felt the icy cloak of terror settle upon his shoulders once again. Those that had pursued them through the Tor had been left buried to the south, while the ones that attacked the village must still be within the Cradle. These were approaching from the north, shadowed by the storm. Were the Lands Beyond infested with Nothings?

'The scrolls,' said Cade, his mouth dry. 'Did they tell you where next we might run?'

'Why would we run now?' she said.

Cade felt a fresh ripple of terror, thinking she may have gone mad.

'Remember what you did to those gates?' she said, eager and excited. 'Think what destruction we could summon together. We could blast these things back to the realm that spawned them.'

'We don't know that,' said Cade, his voice quivering.

'There is nowhere we can run that the Nothings cannot follow,' she said. 'We need to stand and fight them.'

The thought of facing such darkness again stole his voice away. He tugged at her arms, whimpering like an impatient child. She shook him steady.

'I may not be able to destroy them alone,' she said. Her voice was firm, though bubbled with fear. Her eyes were bright in the darkness, expectant. 'Don't be afraid,' she said.

Those words steadied him like magic, recalling his shame before the gates of the Tor, a memory he longed to obliterate. He stiffened, making ardent promises in his head to stand by her, protect her, tear apart with bare hands any horror that threatened her if it would but prove himself a man in her eyes.

His hand found hers and something shivered in the air between them. The clouds devoured the last of the moon, obscuring the cornfield and all that lurked there as they ran down the hill and plunged into crackling blackness.

Cade dashed as stealthily as he could between the ragged walls of corn, shielding his eyes from the deluge of leaves. He gripped Abi's hand as she followed, as sightless as he. The soil underfoot felt soft and treacherous, keen to twist an ankle as they ran.

Cade halted. Abi bumped into him, breathing hard. He heard a steady crackle nearby, leaves disturbed by the passage of something other than the wind. He tugged Abi and they moved on. His hand was numb from squeezing hers. Something throbbed between them like a heartbeat. Together they would banish the thing back to the netherworld with a rush of lightning, perhaps set the corn ablaze in doing so, then flee as the conflagration consumed the others. He blundered through another wall of stalks, pain beginning to knuckle at his temples, announcing the presence of the Nothings.

What was he doing? This was folly, glorious insanity. Cade welcomed the waves of fear he felt crashing through him. Abi groaned beside him, their grip now squirming with sweat. He hurried on, the blackness settling into a jungle of dark shapes as his eyes adjusted to the gloom. The pain in his temples burrowed into the backs of his eyes.

He paused again to listen. Something crunched nearby. The sound was blurred somehow, as if his ears fought to reject it, though the creature's tread was unmistakably heavy. Cade did not welcome the sudden conjecture that these things might once have been spirits, but by now had passed fully into this world as things of muscle and fang. Perhaps they had been nourished by his fear, gorging themselves until their forms congealed into some kind of unholy flesh.

The leaves rattled like talons. The sound sliced through him, a blade of fear that threatened to slit loose his bowels. The thought of fouling himself before Abi only encouraged his rising panic.

'Ready?' whispered Abi.

Cade shook aside his dread long enough to concentrate, to reach into that well of energy beyond the world and draw lightning into his hands, summon light and power enough to drive the horrors away.

Agony was all he found there, a spike of it transfixing his brain.

His eyes bled dancing lights. Abi shrieked too as they collapsed in the dirt. Their powers had abandoned them. Why?

The corn was crackling, louder and louder, rushing towards them.

Abi reeled, moaning in pain as Cade pulled her away and they broke into a run. Pelting through the corn, he continued in his flight for at least a minute before realising that she had slipped from his grasp.

He swayed on the spot. The realisation that he had lost her sent his insides spinning. He wheezed her name, hands groping for her in the dark. He could hear her calling him, though her voice seemed distant.

Something else was crunching steadily through the corn towards him.

His spit turned to dust. His heartbeat choked him. His head screamed. Pain and darkness wove a delirium of childhood nightmares: spidery fingers picking at his window; voices giggling dark promises under his bed; his young hands lifting the sheets beneath which he lay and revealing a pair of famished yellow eyes peering up at him. Impossible things, childish delusions banished by maturity. And yet, just such an aberration was moving towards him with a hunter's tread, its existence an affront to everything he knew of the world. Fear sucked strength from his legs, slowing his pace until the field felt like a swamp. The universe was broken, fractured into madness and chaos. Cade clutched his head as if it might burst with pain.

He staggered through several banks of corn, dazed as he paused to stare into each darkened alley for any sign of Abi. He fumbled for an axe from his belt and lurched into the next row of corn.

Something stood there.

Cade froze, tormented by the sound of his own whimpering sobs, as the shape turned to face him.

Its outline was obscure, Cade's senses resisting the sight of it. But he glimpsed its eyes, gleaming and merciless. The sight of them choked the scream mounting in his throat just as it sent a fresh wave of agony exploring his brain. He dropped his axe before he could hurl it, dazzled by pain as the monster came at him. Reduced to instinct, Cade bolted off through the corn like a startled hare, only to see another oily silhouette emerging from the stalks to receive him. Gleaming hands flowered in the dark, reaching for him.

The thing flinched back as something glittered past its face – the slender blade of Cade's own hunting knife. It had been flung without finesse, well wide of its target, but it granted Cade the second he needed to pivot and spring in the direction of the girl who had thrown it. Buoyed by relief, Cade caught Abi with such force that he almost lifted her off her feet. They stumbled into a run, Abi leading the way, their hands locked in the darkness.

The Nothings rushed after them as they blundered through the corn. The pain in Cade's skull seemed to shepherd him left and right like a buffeting tide. But Abi held him tight on course as she crashed through wall after wall of corn ahead of him, never slowing. They gained ground and the pain in his head began to evaporate. He felt like he could run forever. His palm began to tingle in Abi's grip.

They smashed through leaves, tripping on stalks, deaf to any sound of pursuit. Cade felt the pain start gnawing at the back of his skull every time he slowed his pace. This cornfield was another maze, nothing but dark lanes of dirt and leaves to left and right, endless and identical, a relentless monotony. It was as if the earth itself had succumbed to the night's madness and was replicating the walls of their prison as they ran, hoping to lead them on until they collapsed from exhaustion. His hand throbbed.

Abi pulled him to her every time he stumbled or slackened his pace. His lungs felt like bloody rags, struggling to feed his tortured limbs. There was no way out of here. Even Abi was slowing, stumbling, her breath reduced to drowning gasps. The Nothings would soon be upon them. He closed his eyes.

Horned Throne, hear my prayer.

He thought of the earth beneath their pounding feet, the fertile loam beneath its crust. His fingers tingled, aching to feel that crumbling soil, moist and cool.

I beg not Your forgiveness, only that You receive Abigael, orphan of the Cradle, into Your keeping. She was just. She was kind. She was loved.

Cade reached deeper into his vision until he felt himself electrified by roiling whispers, the secret energies of the soil.

Lead Your foundling into pastures green, for she has served You well.

His hand stiffened as if in seizure, though Cade barely felt it.

Deliver her from darkness, Father.

Abi's cry startled him. A blinding thicket of lightning was writhing in the air between their parted hands, the fulmination apple-green, ripe as the moon. They both fell aside as they pulled their hands away and the lightning snapped into nothing, releasing a luminous green vapour into the air. Abi lay gasping in the dirt beside Cade as they watched the smoke thicken. Its tendrils thrashed like wounded snakes, knitting into a pair of unreadable yellow eyes either side of a narrow head crowned with curling horns.

For an instant, Cade thought he might still be in the Cradle, perhaps in bed, stricken with fever as the imaginings of his childhood frolicked before his eyes.

The Faun Light shook itself into existence, its body twice the size of any goat herded in the Cradle, its shaggy black fur steaming green, casting a lantern-glow about the swaying corn. Another miracle sprung from a fairy tale, an envoy of the Horned Throne, an angel of soil and sky sent to lead benighted wanderers from the dark.

He could feel it drawing vigour from him, using him to channel energy from beyond the veil. The Horned Throne was reaching out beyond the sundered boundary of the Cradle to help them, despite all they had done. If evil sorcery dwelt in the world, then so too did mercy and goodness. The Faun Light skipped as its cloven hooves materialised, each leg thudding in the dirt.

Abi wheezed with exhaustion as she touched its muzzle, confirming its miraculous reality, then bowed her head as if she couldn't bear to meet its gaze.

Cade felt pain cramping the back of his skull once again, heralding the approach of the Nothings. The Faun Light pawed the ground, eager to lead them to safety, but they were both too drained to move. Spurred by pain and fear, Cade managed to lift himself. He hauled Abi onto the Faun Light's bony back. Its thick fur smelled like soft summer apples. Abi suddenly struggled, realising what he was doing. She clasped his hand as fiercely as ever, but the sweet green vapour steaming from the creature's fur seemed to send her into a daze. Cade could hear the approaching rustle of corn through the pain shrieking in his ears as he gently transferred Abi's grip onto a fistful of the goat's fur.

The Faun Light fled through the corn before Cade could slap its rump. Within seconds they had vanished, leaving Cade in darkness. He burbled prayers of thanks as his killers drew near. Exhaustion numbed him, though his brain buzzed unbearably. Cade heard the first of the Nothings approach from behind, its presence heightening that buzz to a razor whine. He fought through it. Without turning to look at it, he gauged its height, its position, waiting for it to move again. He closed his eyes and gripped the last of his axes.

The Nothing shifted behind him and Cade sprang from the ground, eyes still closed, twisting as he lashed out with the axe, intent on burying it in the creature's skull. He felt the blade connect, shear through flesh. The Nothing recoiled, though it issued not even a whisper of pain. Cade enjoyed a bewildered instant of triumph before something hit him deep in the belly, robbing him of breath and dropping him to the dirt.

As he gasped on the ground, he saw the moon briefly unsheathed from the clouds, casting its pale green light upon the scene of his death. He was surrounded. As he rolled onto his belly, something struck his back, electrifying him. His limbs spasmed in the dirt and he spiralled into unconsciousness, dreaming of the last thing he had seen lying in the dirt beside him: his throwing axe, smeared with blood, pasted with a slice of human ear.

Cade felt a pinprick in his throat. A soothing warmth restored him to his body, culminating in a rush of strength that threw him shrieking and thrashing onto windswept hills. His heart thundered. Beside him knelt a bald young woman in glorious bronze armour. The filigree plates on her shoulders gleamed in the glowing dawn that was gathering to confront the sullen storm clouds.

'You're safe.' She spoke in a voice lilting and sweet. 'Take a moment to steady yourself. I've given you something for the pain.'

She had a foreign accent as grand as her armour. Her pale skin was flawlessly smooth, untouched by the sun, miraculously unblemished by scars or pockmarks. Cade felt he should have been mesmerised by this angel but there was something oddly repulsive about her placid green gaze. It was like staring at needles inching towards his eyes. He had to look away.

The cornfield had gone and he was alive, resting against a soft bank of moss. Bushes of pale grass hissed before him, whispering all the way to the distant glimmering sea.

'The girl,' she said. 'We need you to find her.'

Cade felt drunk, struggling to wrangle his thoughts through a migraine fog. The Horned Throne had sent help. Abi had escaped. Now he himself had been saved from the Nothings by this strange young maiden.

His voice slurred as he spoke. 'The Nothings. They had me. They were here. Where did they go?'

Someone grabbed him from behind and hauled him to his feet. He was wrenched around to face another armoured figure. She seemed to have appeared out of nowhere. The woman glared at him over a grille that covered her mouth and neck, her copper-eyed stare unbearable. On the right-hand side of her stubbled skull was a patch of bloody gauze where her ear had once been.

He squirmed in her grip, overwhelmed by an inexplicable repulsion, and she slapped him curtly across each cheek. Startled, he watched as she jabbed an accusatory finger at his face, then lifted her nose in a silent gesture of sniffing the air. She then pointed at the grass and traced an imaginary trail somewhere off into the distance. Her stare was like a blazing summer sun. He struggled to look away. The pain of it seared through whatever narcotic addled his senses. Before he could cry out in protest, she slapped him twice again then dropped him to the ground, kicking him up the backside with an armoured boot to hurry him along.

Cade scrambled out of reach, his body prickling with gooseflesh, shivering with disgust, as if he had just escaped the embrace of a flyblown corpse. Several more women stood behind her, spires of bronze, muzzled and cloaked, their shaven heads crested with a proud ponytail. They carried strange blocks of iron which Cade realised must be some form of rifle. These muskets were absurdly bulky, though the women hefted them as easily as if they were toys. Though their ponytails stirred in the mortal wind, the women did not seem part of this world. Their presence seemed to elude Cade's senses, evading his comprehension. He thought himself deaf when their heavy armour betrayed no creak or clamour as they moved. He could not hear them breathing. They were like silent spectres projected from some netherworld, statues of living bronze, whose icy sheen repelled his eyes every time he tried to study it. All he could feel was their absence, holes in reality. Nothings.

'What I've given you for the pain should also help you see a little clearer now,' said the girl. 'Should make our presence a little more tolerable.'

Realisation dawned, and with it came anger. He snarled at them all.

'It was you all along. I thought ghosts had murdered my people, but it was you.'

He recalled the suffocating maze beneath the Tor, the deadly avalanche, the terror of the cornfield. Through it all, he had borne a delusion. The thought of such stupidity – of his peasant ignorance – pained him, stoked in him a fearless fury.

He closed his eyes and reached deep, deep into the earth. He sought lightning, a horned angel, anything to drive these women away. The girl tried to stop him, but it was too late. The resulting pain hit him like a chunk of rock and he almost blacked out. He shrugged her aside as she went to steady him.

'I am Novice Maia,' said the girl. 'And these are Null Maidens of the Sisters of Silence. We are anathema to your kind. Just as the standing stones of your valley nullified your powers, so do we.'

Cade snorted. 'You don't sound very silent to me.'

'Unlike my sisters, I have yet to take the sacred Vow of Tranquillity. For now, I act as their interpreter.'

Cade struggled to his feet. 'You want me to find Abi for you? Well, interpret this.'

He hawked and spat on the ground at her feet.

The woman with one ear glowered at Cade. He recoiled as she advanced on him, soundless as a phantom, but the younger woman intervened. She did not speak, but instead made a series of gestures, her hands dancing, fingers fluttering as she spelled out her entreaty. One-Ear gestured back, harsh and abrupt. The younger woman signalled her reply, insistent and beseeching. The older woman turned away, exasperated.

'We are not murderers,' said Maia, turning to him, her voice tender. 'We gathered your people for their own safety. Our comrades are tending them in the valley as we speak. They are all in our care. Safe from harm.'

Cade looked about him. Nothing but grassland. Nowhere to run.

'Are you witchfinders? Sent from the city?'

Maia smiled. 'Not from any city you could comprehend,' she said. 'And we have been sent to do nothing more than protect you.'

'The Horned Throne protects us,' he said. 'He is soil and sky, root and branch.' He half-hoped his words might conjure another Faun Light to spirit him away.

'Then we serve the same master,' said Maia. 'What you know only as the Horned Throne is in fact part of a greater truth, a truth that spans the galaxy.'

'What's the galaxy?'

Maia's look of sympathy rankled him.

'A kingdom of worlds that you know only as glimmering stars,' she said. 'Each ruled by the Emperor of Mankind, on the Throne of Terra.'

The greater truth. Emperors of Mankind. How Abi would have been fascinated by all this.

'His light shines upon pastures just like these,' said Maia. 'And you would have been hidden forever from that light if we hadn't found you.'

Once again, he pictured the laurel-crowned figure on that ancient frieze beneath the Tor. Was that the god of which she spoke?

'Enough,' said Cade, dazed by thoughts of worlds, people, even gods beyond his own. He felt nauseous, sick with perplexity. The eerie presence of these women was pouring agony into his brain.

'You are already connected to a world wider than we will ever know,' said Maia. 'You are a witch, blessed with a connection to energies beyond anyone's understanding. But with that gift comes great danger, which is why we must find your companion.'

One-Ear gestured impatiently. The novice stalled her.

'I don't know how she got away,' said Cade. 'We got separated. She just disappeared.'

One-Ear clenched her fists.

'Things dwell in the immaterial realm from which your kind draw power,' said Maia. 'Things that would mean you harm.'

Cade swallowed at the thought of him helping Abi onto the Faun Light's back, sending her off into the gloom atop that spectral beast.

Maia read his face and her expression hardened. 'Have you seen such a thing?'

'I have not.'

'Hear me, boy.' Her voice suddenly rang like steel. 'They know your thoughts. They will assume the shape of that which you trust. If you have seen any such thing, you will tell us this instant. You cannot conceive the dangers involved.'

She was right. He could not. To him, all she said was just a morass of fear and bafflement. He thought of Abi, how she had stood by him, dragged him from danger time and again. It was the only thing that still seemed real.

'If I help you find her,' he said, 'what will you do with her?'

One-Ear exchanged amused looks with her Sisters. She made a curt gesture.

Maia looked grim. 'She says perhaps you should ask what will happen to her if you *don't* find her.'

The Faun Light had been moving as fast as a stallion. Its prints were grouped tightly, its forked hooves tearing up sprays of dirt in its wake. It had galloped through this lonely wood perhaps an hour or so ago, hammering out a trail that wove through the gnarled trees. In the dawn sunlight sprinkled through the murk of leaves above, Cade could see the creature's bulk had pressed its hooves deep into the ground, its weight squeezing moisture from the soil. The beast seemed much larger than he remembered.

He jumped, startled yet again to find one of the Sisters lurking behind him as he waded through the waist-high ferns. These armoured women seemed to vanish from sight every time he looked away. They were holding back, giving him room to interpret the trail, though Maia was never far from his side and he could feel One-Ear keeping a baleful watch upon him.

Cade still could not comprehend these women, let alone trust them. What they were, where they came from. Their appearance had kicked the world out from under him. The Horned Throne had been an indisputable presence in his life, as real as the earth upon which he walked. Now it seemed He was merely a primal echo of some greater cosmic truth, just as Abi had said. The concept defeated him, and he was glad of it. The possibility that Abi was in danger was all that mattered now, the only truth Cade cared to understand.

One-Ear gestured angrily.

'You need to move faster,' Maia told him.

'Tell her ladyship, I'm moving as fast as I can.'

'She can hear you perfectly well,' said Maia. 'So please be aware that you are addressing an honoured Oblivion Knight of the Silent Sisterhood.'

Not so high and bloody mighty that she could stop me from shaving an ear off her, thought Cade with a smirk, then paused to wonder fearfully whether One-Ear and her Sisters could read minds as well as cloud them. He quickly resumed brushing aside the ferns, picking out hoofprints, moving as swiftly as he could without losing the trail. He considered the sprawl of woods ahead. A thousand hiding places beckoned. Dense trees, dark hollows, green hillocks, everything drowning in thick ferns.

The path to Abi was known only to him. Without his guidance, these imperious gargoyles stalking behind him would be lost. Though he didn't like to think what one of those enormous guns might do to him if they caught him trying to slip away.

Damn these bald hags, he thought, sizzling with resentment. He and his fellow orphans had been happy in the Cradle. They never wanted for protection. Why were these wretched Sisters of Silence even here?

One of them was carrying some kind of small metal utensil. It clicked and whirred in her hand as she scanned their surroundings, probing the undergrowth like she was dowsing for running water. The woman gestured at Maia, frustrated, her mysterious tool ineffectual.

'We need human eyes out here, a hunter's eyes,' Maia told him. 'If you see anything unusual, you must tell us immediately.'

Cade ignored her, absorbed in the trail, which now was staggering sideways and back, the hoofprints seeming to balloon in size with every step.

'What is it?' said Maia.

He motioned she be silent and immediately heard the jostle of guns made ready.

He could find no trace of Abi, no threads of hair or fabric, no streaks of blood, though judging by these tracks his quarry was now large enough to have swallowed her whole. He brushed aside another fern and trembled at the sight of what he found there. Hoofprints now bigger than those of a carthorse had resumed their progress north-east. But that was not all that had sent a shimmer of fear down his back.

Whatever beast he and Abi had summoned into that cornfield, it walked now upon two legs.

The bracken ahead of him was undisturbed, though the thing that had moved through it must have stood twice the height of a bear. It had moved with stealth, aware of its pursuers.

Again, Cade thought the Sisters had vanished, but there they were, aiming their guns into the trees. Maia had drawn a bulbous pistol. The surrounding leaves chuckled in the breeze, boughs creaking like rope. Cade could sense an unnatural stillness that spoke of something watching them from afar. He could sense it, the way a deer can sense the drawing of a bowstring. He scanned the distant undergrowth for an outline hunkered among the trees, some tell-tale movement that would betray the position of an adversary. But his vision throbbed with pain, disturbed by the Sisters' unearthly presence. Cade felt panic brimming in his chest, then realised his mistake.

The trees were empty. Something had scared the birds from even the highest branches. Something was already here.

The attack erupted from behind before he could yell a warning.

He turned to see a black wave, like a hill tearing itself loose from behind the trees and crashing into the Sisters' midst. He saw the woman with the dowsing device scooped off her feet by huge ribbed horns that smashed her through a tree, showering Cade in blood and tumbling leaves. He screamed in fright at what he thought at first to be a volley of thunderbolts. The Sisters' guns were more like cannons, booming beasts that spat flashes of lightning, turning the woods into a flickering hell of noise and violence. They blasted bloody splashes across an immense muscled back before the giant disappeared into the trees.

The Sisters of Silence ceased fire, the air now a blizzard of tumbling leaves and wood dust. Cade felt a long arm enclose him. It was One-Ear, pulling him behind a tree. Cade squirmed in her grip; he felt like a mouse being dragged into a spider's burrow. The others had cleaved to the larger trees, melting from his sight. One-Ear remained motionless, breathless as a dead thing. The stiffness of her embrace sent waves of maddening revulsion through his body. She was thumbing a large rivet built into her gauntlet, silently tapping out an order to the rest of the squad.

Minutes passed. The snow of leaves dwindled. Silence resumed. One-Ear finally stirred from cover.

'Wait,' said Cade. One-Ear hesitated and clicked the rivet in her gauntlet several times more.

By now the smaller predatory mammals – the bristlers and branch rats – should have emerged from their burrows. Yet Cade could hear no telltale rustling among the bracken. Even the ever-present moss midges had been dispelled from the air. The beast was still here, manoeuvring among the dense trees that cloaked its bulk, calculating its next devastating charge.

The limb of a tree lunged out from the swamp of ferns to his right, crashing aside a Sister who had been protecting One-Ear's flank. The branch was gripped in a huge dark fist. The air suddenly ripened with a steamy perfume of sweat and honey as a familiar figure tottered into view on cloven hooves.

Half-drunk on its musk, Cade felt his knees buckle, though whether out of terror or adoration he did not know. Though it looked like the Horned Father risen in outrage from his throne upon the Tor, Cade knew it was not He. It was something else, something that wore His image. He knew from its malicious smirk, long brown teeth leering from behind human lips. Yet some instinct of self-preservation screamed at him to believe it was indeed the Horned Father.

It is Him. It must be Him.

He lied to himself over and over, for to believe anything other than the lie was to suggest a universe gone mad, a reality that harboured horrors beyond his imagining. Merely to contemplate such a concept was to invite madness.

Cade stared helplessly as the beast thrust its club at him like a spear. His head jerked as a powerful hand shoved him away. He heard an explosion of splintering wood. The earth trembled as he scrambled behind cover. Peering out from behind a fallen log, he beheld a scene out of legend, a primordial monster locked in mortal combat with a champion of humanity.

One-Ear had drawn a fabulous silver sword from her back, carving the air in silent flashing swirls. Her long legs needled the ground as she swirled about the beast's flanks, her blade guiding away every crash of its immense club, threading herself into a series of counter-strikes.

The other Sisters surrounded the monster, their guns at the ready, giving their leader room to express her artistry. Slashes of luminous sap drooled over the black fur that covered the beast's crooked legs, its bulging loins. Its naked torso was nut-brown and slabbed with muscle, its huge arms veined with green. A gnarled star of horns stood erect at its brow, tearing at the branches of the trees as it fought. Its eyes were pinpricks of gold.

It had hoped to strike and run, but its prey had proven tantalisingly elusive, an affront to its bestial majesty. It snorted as it stabbed at her again, trying to nail the bronze spider scuttling about its legs. But One-Ear turned the blow with an expert glance of her silvery fang, webbing the air with patterns that made Cade's eyes burn to look at them.

He could see rows of scars cratered across the creature's straining back where the guns of the Sisters had struck it. The thing had somehow healed. Cade recalled how it had drawn psychic sustenance from both he and Abi, rendering their arcane energy into solid flesh. Was it using Abi to regenerate its wounds? Charging into the Sisters' ranks to deliver as much damage as it could, then retreating out of range to restore itself and charge again?

The creature struck a ringing blow upon One-Ear's armoured shoulder then swung its club in a wide arc to deter her allies. The weapon descended, about to slam One-Ear to paste as she staggered back. But she spun her blade in a glimmering parry and the club fell in half, sheared in two. One-Ear had already moved aside, letting the creature stumble under its own momentum.

Cade ducked, clutching his ears as the Sisters' cannons roared once again, blasting divots of flesh from the creature's body. It ran at them, trampling two of them as it barged through the trees to escape the deadly fusillade, vanishing into the woods, too swift to follow.

One-Ear paused. Something was amiss. Her hand went to her waist, seeking Cade's axe. But he had already slid the weapon from her belt with nimble hands when she had pulled him behind cover. He gripped the wooden shaft between his teeth, invisible beneath the bed of ferns as he elbowed along the ground towards freedom.

Cade knew the beast would eventually wear the Sisters down and kill them all. He could feel the creature restoring its wounded body, drinking from the same boundless reservoir of energy from which he had summoned it. He could feel the weight of that energy lapping like water at the edge of his consciousness as he crawled further away from the Sisters.

He broke into a stealthy run, letting the pulse in the air guide him to its source. He could feel his head clearing, his arcane senses returning, filling him with power once again. But with that power came other things, voices that whispered at the edge of his hearing, icy things that writhed like smoke, seeking human warmth. As he paused to comprehend these vagaries, he could sense them reaching for him and quickly shut them out with a shiver.

Whatever power he had inherited, Cade knew it was polluted. This was how he and Abi had summoned that horned monster into their world, believing it to be their salvation. He cursed himself for the peasant fool he was, knowing it would take more than bare hands and courage to save them now.

Distant gunfire thundered at his back and braying laughter rolled about the trees.

If he was to save Abi, as she had saved him, he would need to do it alone. The Sisters of Silence would not hesitate to kill her should they realise she was the source of the beast's vigour. She was just beyond those trees, closer than he had realised.

He banged his shin on solid stone and tumbled over, cursing in pain. He sprawled across rubble carpeted with dead leaves. Walls of stacked rock stood nearby, furred with grass. The ruins of stone cottages, roofless and ancient were visible too, impaled by generations of sprouting trees.

'Abi?'

There came no reply. He limped on, passing yet more crumbling walls sinking into greenery. She was here, he could feel her somewhere among these stones. Things moved nearby. Animals, he thought, though he could see none. The derelict village was empty, populated only by trees. The clouds brooded over the gauzy light of dawn. Something rolled beneath his foot. A torch, reduced to a nub of charcoal, discarded less than a season ago. He found more nearby, lots more, along with footprints and tracks from a heavy wagon. Folk had gathered here on more than one occasion, but for what purpose? He thought he felt someone glaring down at him from above. He turned to look and saw nothing up there but a length of frayed rope.

He could see a well up ahead, its roof and pail long disappeared. Its stones had been cleared of vegetation, as if the thing were still in use, though it must surely have run dry centuries ago.

Cade called for Abi again, reaching out with his consciousness into the ruins, surprised at the ease with which he could do so. He turned to see an empty doorway. He was sure he had seen someone standing there, gazing at him askance as if their head lolled unnaturally to one side.

His senses bristled. He could feel something ringing in the air, echoes of a grim drama that had played upon this remote stage season after season. Men had gathered here from miles around. He felt their excitement, a thrilling fear that tickled his innards, bitter with a hatred that could be quenched only with violence.

Figures watched him from empty windows, from behind trees. Though he dared not turn to look at them, he could tell their hair was long, their dresses tattered, each standing somehow on legs horribly crooked. They gazed at him, resigned to his late arrival, every one of their heads resting oddly on one shoulder, those that had heads at all.

They were directing him towards the well, from which arose the miserable stench of rot upon rot that spoke of heaps of discarded meat and bones. Despair, thick as tar, boiled up from that throat of stone, soaking everything around it, softening reality until Cade felt the ground might fall away beneath him.

'Don't be afraid,' said Abi.

She stood beside him, alone and with a dreamy smile.

'This day's reckoning shall be beautiful.' She sounded wistful. 'Such wonders shall be born here. The truth. Finally. The answers we've been looking for.'

Cade was so relieved by the sight of her that he couldn't help but hug her before trying to shake her from her stupor. He could feel her body pulsating with energy, writhing about her like an invisible fire.

'The Horned King,' she said. 'He shall save us from the Nothings.'

'That is not the Horned King.' Cade steadied himself against the insanity of what he was suggesting. 'And the Nothings are not monsters. They're not spirits. They're women. Flesh and blood. Warriors. I know not from where, but they're our protectors, Abi. And they will die, as will we, unless you wake up. Now. And that's the truth. Whatever that monster has told you, it's a lie.'

Abi stiffened and Cade shrank back, his hands stung by the

livid energy now pouring from her. She drifted up off her feet, her toes lifting from the ground. The beast crouched in the ruins nearby, its body a wreck of dripping wounds, its broken arm outstretched as it channelled restorative energy through Abi.

Abi was sobbing. 'I'm sorry, my Lord. I should never have doubted you.'

Cade shivered when he heard a growl invade his head, promising Abi that absolution would soon be hers. Its words felt like spiders scurrying in his skull.

'My thanks, my king,' Abi wailed. 'Oh, my thanks.'

The voice promised to forgive her sins, excuse her of the sorrows she had visited upon her fellow orphans.

Tears streamed down Abi's face. 'Forgive, forgive.'

Cade stared in horror as the beast's wounds slowly contracted. He caught her hands, trying to pull her back to earth, driving his consciousness through his grip, trying to intersect the nourishing flow of energy.

'It's feeding on your guilt, Abi. But none of this is your fault. You said yourself.'

The beast brayed in frustration as it took a halting step towards them, another of its wounds sealing to a puckered scar.

The voice assured Abi that she was a witch, that power untold was who she was. If she would but aid him, love him beyond all others, it would help her achieve that power, power to protect those weaker than herself, to learn answers to questions beyond imagining.

'You know a lie when you hear one, Abi.' Cade's voice trembled, knowing he spoke in defiance of something like a god. 'You swore you would be a slave to guilt no longer, remember? Your only crime is knowing the truth.'

'Cade?' Abi's eyes fluttered as if awakening from a dream and she dropped to the ground. Cade felt his mind seized by invisible claws as the beast rose with a growl and swaggered towards

him. Freezing terror held him in its grip as he felt something
open inside him. A freezing flood of roiling, whispering energy
coursed through him and into the creature that held him. He
watched helplessly as the last of its wounds disappeared, its
body whole and beautiful once more. He listened, transfixed,
his panic melting as it spoke inside his head. Its voice was silvery, hypnotic. It made him think of wildflowers nodding in the
glades of the Cradle, the smell of mead and sun-warmed hay-
fields, rich and drowsy.

*I am no monster, Cade. I am everything you ever wanted.
I am mother. I am father. I am happiness, contentment. The
truth? The truth is myriad, merely paths waiting to be chosen.
So choose yours wisely, Cade. You are blessed with a strength
most will never know, but you must be taught to wield that
strength. Or else others shall wield it for you. Why do you
think they are here? Those armoured harpies? They seek to
harness your power, my son.*

Cade knew it was a lie, though the question haunted him:
Why were the Sisters of Silence here? Why had they come to
the Cradle?

The beast laughed.

Indeed. And they would deign to call me *'monster'.*

Cade's gift was his speed. He was thin and wiry, supple as a
cat. The beast reached for him, poised to drain the last of his
will, as Cade hurled his axe. The weapon lodged deep in the
beast's left eye.

There was no bellow of pain, merely a flinch of displeasure.
Then the ground shook as the beast charged through the ruins
towards him, snatching Cade off his feet, squeezing him like fruit.
He thrashed in the beast's grip, arms pinned awkwardly at his
sides, struggling for breath as his ribs constricted and cracked.
He saw the well several feet below, a dead black eye staring up
at his flailing legs. He could sense the dead things heaped at the

bottom of that pit, bones enriched with rage and sorrow. This is why the beast had chosen these ruins, this arena of misery – its psychic pollution would ease the ingress of its brethren. Cade could feel them, other monsters waiting beyond the veil, allied spirits eager to be drawn hither and clothed in flesh, hungry for the ruin of man.

The beast peered at him, as if curious to see the gradations of terror cross Cade's face as he slowly crushed the boy's body in his fist. Abi lay sprawled nearby. Cade's frustration boiled inside him. He had endured a lifetime of horror in a single night, only to die like this, mashed like dung in a monster's paw. His fury swelled as he glared deep into the beast's gleaming eye.

He saw flashes and thought for a second that he was dying. But then he realised branches of lightning were springing about him, churning up from his insides. Free of the Sisters' malignant presence, he was drawing power from the world beyond, channelling it into lances of destruction and hurling them into the beast. He felt rather than heard the creature roar in pain as it released him. He tumbled to the ground, feeling his leg strike something hard, tendons cracking in his knee. He felt his body's anguish as a distant thing, anesthetised as he was by the cascade of lightning flowing from him. But this twitch in his concentration was enough; it had opened the floodgates to that vast sea of energy from which he drew. It filled him in an instant, flooding his being.

He tried to contain it, channel it like a river, but already it was a deluge, and he was but a leaf, shrinking, somersaulting as he plunged into its depths. But still he could feel the beast, and still he refused to let go. Cade let the creature's agonies anchor him as he continued to reach out, lashing it with lightning, flails of white-hot fire tearing its body, restoring it to ruin.

But it was not enough. He kept losing focus. His attacks grew weaker. His attention kept branching here and there. He had become a storm, striking everything around him, each flash blinding him with images of another world, another time, another horror. He gripped his head, too stunned to breathe, deafened by a tidal roar fit to crack his skull. His eyes bulged and saw nothing but a frenzy of lightning streaking around him, sketching predatory faces, hands that reached, clawed, caressed, bodies that coiled and spasmed in the chaos. He was melting, drowning in the maelstrom of energy overwhelming his body, prickling his every pore, crushing him, strangling him to admit a drowning breath.

Yet still he refused to let go.

His consciousness was everywhere. He knew everything. He was being consumed by a realm known as the immaterium. The other names by which it was known flashed through his mind before turning to smoke in his memory. The warp, the ether, the empyrean, a sea of souls composed of pure psychic chaos. A realm traversed by a race of gods in floating iron ships, navigated by a terrible beacon of pure thought projected by a being upon a mountain throne. Yet more truths swarmed him, complexities and contradictions, and the impossibilities that made a mockery of it all. The beast was right. The truth was myriad.

Yet still he refused to let go.

Cade's consciousness alighted on a shard of truth. In its prism he saw Abi. He saw himself. Splinters of their past, their present and future. He also saw the reason why their world had tonight become a nightmare. The horror of that truth froze what little was left of him.

He let go.

But something else would not let go of him.

Something was channelling his energy for him, focusing it.

He flinched at the brilliance of the dawning sun. He was on his back, his body steaming as he convulsed in the dirt, grinding his teeth as he strained to lift himself. He managed to turn his head and saw the beast raging nearby, its body shredded with wounds.

Abi clung to its horns, her hair and tattered skirts flung to and fro, like a sailor clinging to the mast of a squall-tossed ship. She had saved him, pulled him back from the warp before his mind could be consumed entirely, sustaining the energy he had summoned, holding it in place like a cork in a bottle. The beast staggered and thrashed, too weak to claw his tormentor from her perch.

Cade felt a familiar dullness creeping over his senses. The Sisters of Silence were coming, cutting him off from the energies of the warp. Abi slid from the beast's crown, exhausted. The creature was now barely a skeleton clothed in rags of smoking meat, though it rose in dignity to meet its executioner. It went to swing a claw at One-Ear, but the woman had already cleaved a leg out from under it. Its great horned head followed, bursting to ash as it spun through the air.

Cade screamed at his limbs to move, but they remained frozen, buckled like the legs of a dead spider. That part of his brain which motivated his body had been scoured by his exposure to the warp. Yet it mattered not. What dominated his mind was the last thing he had seen in that realm of Chaos, those glimpses of the future, of the present. They had shown him the reason why the Sisters of Silence had come for them.

Abi was beside him, gasping as she tried to comfort him. She tried to calm him as he puffed spittle from his teeth, struggling to scream a warning.

Run, Abi! Run while you can!

She smiled down at him, brushing hair from his eyes, deaf to his pleas.

As the Sisters of Silence fanned out to secure the ruins, One-Ear gestured something to Maia. The armoured novice nodded and approached Abi with caution. Cade watched, horrified as Abi's expression flickered between fear and fascination.

'As your valiant friend may have already told you, I am Sister Maia,' she said. 'And you have led us a merry dance.'

'You need to help him,' said Abi.

Cade wriggled, gagging as he fought to release a scream from his throat.

'That's why we are here,' said Maia. 'If you'll just come with us, all shall be explained.' She inched towards Abi.

'Who are you? Where do you come from? I'm not leaving here until you tell me.'

Maia paused, gazing at Abi in mutual curiosity. 'You are not afraid of us at all, are you?'

'Being afraid never does anyone much good,' said Abi.

'A fine philosophy,' said Maia. 'You're her, aren't you? The one who we spotted crossing the boundary. If not for you, we would never have found the others.'

Abi frowned.

'You misunderstand,' said Maia. 'Your people are unharmed, I promise you. You're the strongest of them all, did you know that?'

Abi glanced about her. She looked as though she was calculating her options, though clearly she had none.

'If you say so,' she said.

'We can show you how to harness those talents, that formidable intelligence of yours. We can teach you to wield your strength.' She smiled like a serpent. 'Lest others wield it for you.'

'You make it sound like I have a choice,' said Abi.

'No one has a choice,' said Maia. 'But I sense your destiny is the one you've always wanted.'

Abi looked down at Cade.

'All I've ever wanted is the truth,' she told him.

Those words made something crack like an egg deep in Cade's

chest, slipping a terrible bitterness into his belly until he felt he might die.

Abi's hair rose to veil her face as a sudden wind stirred the air and a strange pressure stiffened the atmosphere. Cade watched in terror, helpless to prevent the vision he had beheld in the warp from coming to pass before his eyes.

He had always thought it to be nothing more than a thundercloud. When he had first seen it in the distance from the cliffs yesterday afternoon he had been too innocent to think it anything but an approaching storm. The world had been so much smaller back then. Cade had seen it in the sky again when they emerged from the Tor, a tide of black blotting out the moon above the cornfields. Now, as it obscured the dawning sun, the thing was unmistakable.

Wreathed in cloud, the great black ship resembled some fossilised behemoth, another monster out of legend come to threaten his world. It grumbled overhead, a landmass of iron machinery. Countless dwelt within. Cade had seen them in his vision. Witches, millions upon millions of them, soul crops yielded by innumerable worlds just like this one. They languished in chains, their powers sedated. Like the boundary stones that surrounded the Cradle, the ship cast a protective aura that hid it from the warp. Like him, these innumerable wretches were gifted, but their powers were limited, unfocused, distracted by primal emotion. Their destiny would be to lend their screams to that great psychic beacon Cade had felt blazing through the immaterium. That was their function within the awful machinery of the universe. Their souls would be added to the pyre, to blaze for an instant and then become nothing.

This was the fate from which his parents had sought to protect him. The Cradle was a sanctuary for witchkind, erected to save gifted innocents from the grim farmers of the Imperium, who would one day arrive to gather their harvest.

'Wondrous,' Abi murmured. 'What is it?'

'The truth,' said Maia. 'Yet this is just the beginning. You have so much yet to learn. We have so much yet to teach you.'

The warp had already shown Cade the fruit of Maia's promise. He had seen Abi, recognisable though her face was lined with age and scars. She remained wild and strong, bolstered by decades of training, her full potential unleashed. He had seen her driving bolts of lightning into the ranks of some unearthly foe, again and again, careless that her comrades had fallen, that she was alone. Eventually the enemy swarmed her, pulled her to the ground and tore her down to her bones. All Cade had known of her – of her potential, the future he had imagined she could achieve – had come to nothing, ruined in an instant.

Abi was watching a smaller vessel descend to collect them, the craft even uglier than the vast ship that had spawned it. She had the same look on her face as when Cade had first shown her the Lands Beyond, as when she played with lightning in her hand, enthralled by glorious potential.

'What about Cade?' she said.

'Fear not.' Maia smiled. 'He too shall be welcomed into the Emperor's light.'

Abi tried to soothe Cade as he bucked and jerked in her arms. She insisted on carrying him herself, her face bright with thoughts of the wonders that awaited them aboard the great ship.

One-Ear and the Sisters ushered them towards their destiny as Cade screamed in silence.

ABOUT THE AUTHORS

Cassandra Khaw is an award-winning games writer,
an award-nominated author, and a scriptwriter
at Ubisoft Montreal. She is best known for her
Lovecraftian Noir series 'Persons Non Grata' and, as
of the time of writing, is based in Malmo, Sweden.
'Nepenthe' is her first story for Black Library.

Peter McLean has written the short stories
'Baphomet by Night' and 'No Hero' for Warhammer
40,000. He grew up in Norwich, where he began
story-writing, practising martial arts and practical
magic, and lives there still with his wife.

Lora Gray lives and works in Northeast Ohio. Their fiction has appeared in various publications including *Shimmer*, *The Dark* and *Flash Fiction Online*. When they aren't writing, Lora works as an illustrator, dance instructor and wrangler of a very smart cat named Cecil. 'Crimson Snow' is Lora's first story for Black Library.

David Annandale is the author of the novella *The Faith and the Flesh*, which features in the Warhammer Horror portmanteau *The Wicked and the Damned*. His work for the Horus Heresy range includes the novels *Ruinstorm* and *The Damnation of Pythos*, and the Primarchs novels *Roboute Guilliman: Lord of Ultramar* and *Vulkan: Lord of Drakes*. For Warhammer 40,000 he has written *Warlord: Fury of the God-Machine*, the Yarrick series, several stories involving the Grey Knights, including *Warden of the Blade* and *Castellan*, as well as titles for The Beast Arises and the Space Marine Battles series. For Warhammer Age of Sigmar he has written *Neferata: Mortarch of Blood*. David lectures at a Canadian university, on subjects ranging from English literature to horror films and video games.

Paul Kane is an award-winning, bestselling author and editor of over eighty books. His non-fiction works include *The Hellraiser Films and Their Legacy* and *Voices in the Dark*, and he is currently co-chair of the UK chapter of The Horror Writers Association. His work has been adapted for the big and small screen, including for US network primetime television. 'Triggers' is his first story for Black Library.

Josh Reynolds is the author of the Warhammer Horror novella *The Beast in the Trenches*, featured in the portmanteau novel *The Wicked and the Damned*. He has also written the Horus Heresy Primarchs novel *Fulgrim: The Palatine Phoenix*, and two audio dramas featuring the *Blackshields: The False War* and *The Red Fief*. His Warhammer 40,000 work includes *Lukas the Trickster* and the Fabius Bile novels *Primogenitor* and *Clonelord*. He has written many stories set in the Age of Sigmar, including the novels *Shadespire: The Mirrored City*, *Soul Wars*, *Eight Lamentations: Spear of Shadows*, the Hallowed Knights novels *Plague Garden* and *Black Pyramid*, and *Nagash: The Undying King*. His tales of the Warhammer old world include *The Return of Nagash* and *The Lord of the End Times*, and two Gotrek & Felix novels. He lives and works in Sheffield.

J C Stearns is a writer who lives in a swamp in Illinois with his wife and son, as well as more animals than is reasonable. He started writing for Black Library in 2016 and is the author of the short story 'Wraithbound', as well as 'Turn of the Adder', included in the anthology *Inferno! Volume 2* and 'The Marauder Lives', in the Warhammer Horror anthology *Maledictions*. He plays Salamanders, Dark Eldar, Sylvaneth, and as soon as he figures out how to paint lightning bolts, Night Lords.

Graham McNeill has written many Horus Heresy novels, including *The Crimson King, Vengeful Spirit* and his *New York Times* bestsellers *A Thousand Sons* and the novella *The Reflection Crack'd*, which featured in *The Primarchs* anthology. Graham's Ultramarines series, featuring Captain Uriel Ventris, is now six novels long, and has close links to his Iron Warriors stories, the novel *Storm of Iron* being a perennial favourite with Black Library fans. He has also written the Forges of Mars trilogy, featuring the Adeptus Mechanicus. For Warhammer, he has written the Warhammer Chronicles trilogy *The Legend of Sigmar*, the second volume of which won the 2010 David Gemmell Legend Award.

Alec Worley is a well-known comics and science fiction and fantasy author, with numerous publications to his name. He is an avid fan of Warhammer 40,000 and has written many short stories for Black Library including 'Stormseeker', 'Whispers' and 'Repentia'. He has recently forayed into Warhammer Horror with the audio drama *Perdition's Flame* and his novella *The Nothings*, featured in the anthology *Maledictions*. He lives and works in London.

Richard Strachan is a writer and editor who lives with his partner and two children in Edinburgh, UK. Despite his best efforts, both children stubbornly refuse to be interested in tabletop wargaming. 'The Widow Tide' is his first story for Black Library.

C L Werner's Black Library credits include the Age of Sigmar novels *Overlords of the Iron Dragon* and *The Tainted Heart*, the novella 'Scion of the Storm' in Hammers of Sigmar, the Warhammer novels *Deathblade*, *Mathias Thulmann: Witch Hunter*, *Runefang* and *Brunner the Bounty Hunter*, the Thanquol and Boneripper series and Time of Legends: The Black Plague series. For Warhammer 40,000 he has written the Space Marine Battles novel *The Siege of Castellax*. Currently living in the American south-west, he continues to write stories of mayhem and madness set in the Warhammer worlds.